The KING of KAZOO

by NORM FEUTI

graphix

AN IMPRINT OF

■SCHOLASTIC

For Charlotte and Ben.

Library of Congress Control Number: 2015957762

ISBN 978-0-545-77088-0 (hardcover)
ISBN 978-0-545-77089-7 (paperback)

10 9 8 7 6 5 4 3 2 1   16 17 18 19 20

Printed in China 62
First edition, August 2016
Edited by Adam Rau
Book design by Phil Falco
Creative Director: David Saylor

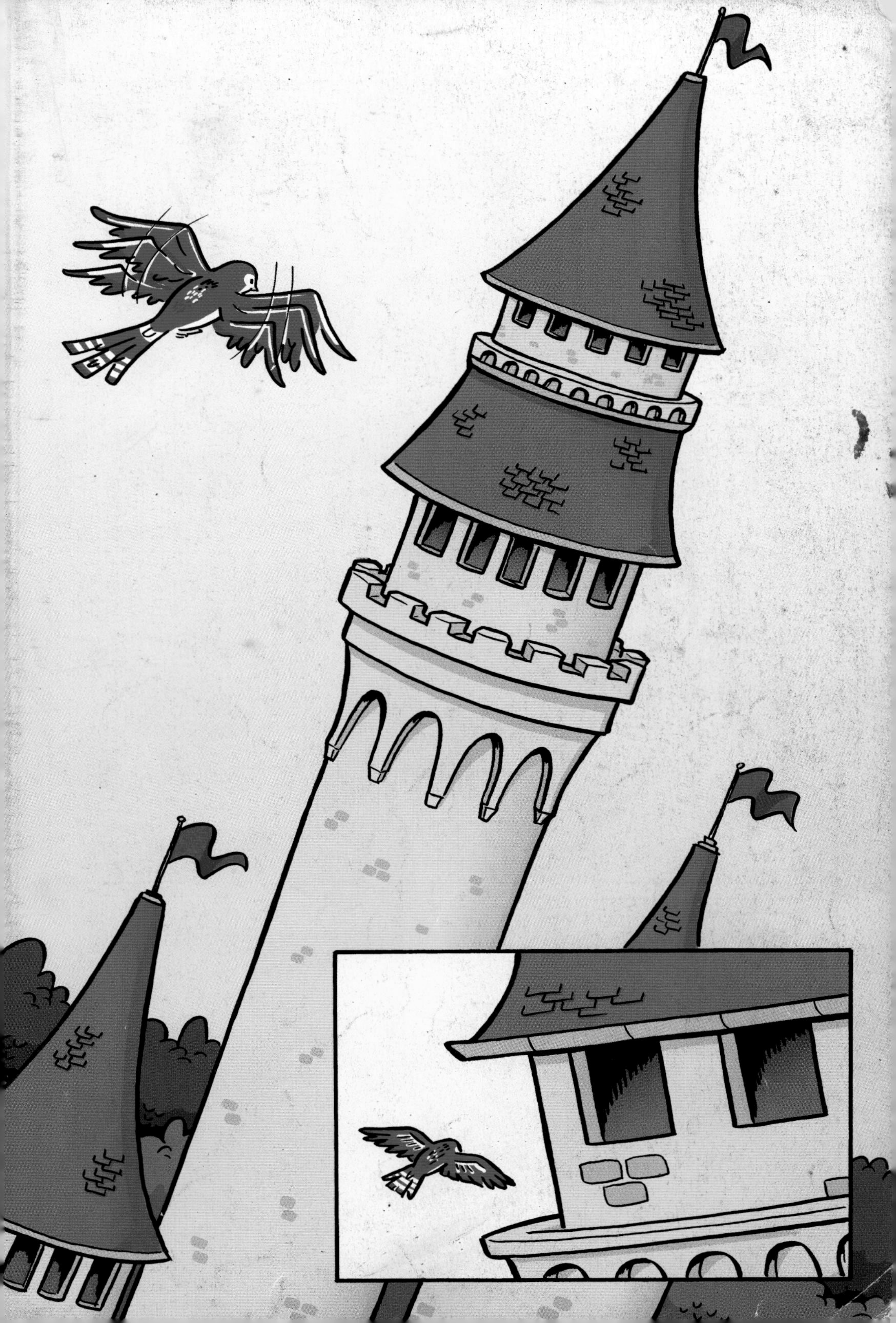

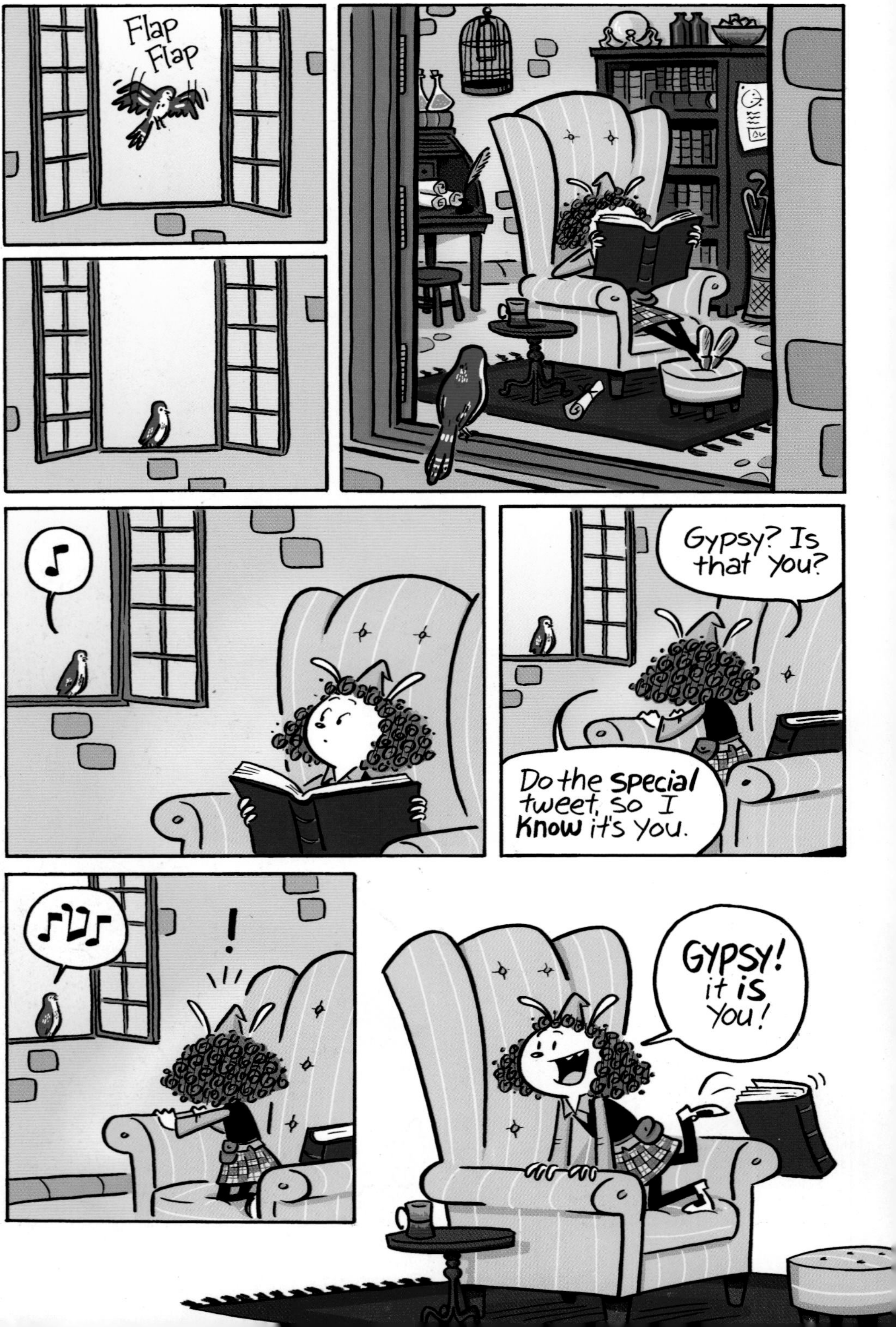

Flap
Flap
♪
Gypsy? Is that you?
Do the special tweet, so I know it's you.
♪♫♪
!
GYPSY! it is You!

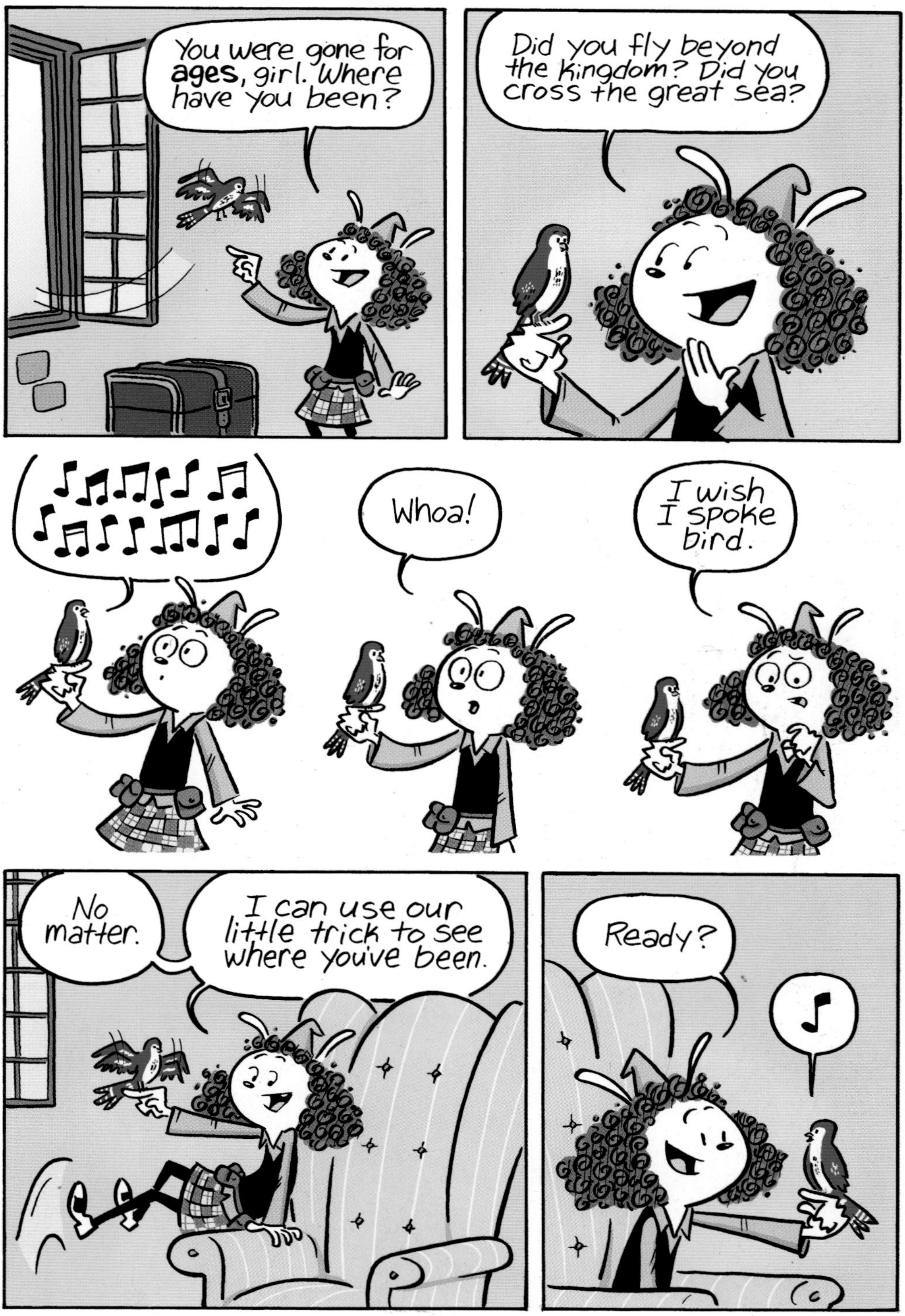
You were gone for **ages**, girl. Where have you been?
Did you fly beyond the Kingdom? Did you cross the great sea?
Whoa!
I wish I spoke bird.
No matter.
I can use our little trick to see where you've been.
Ready?

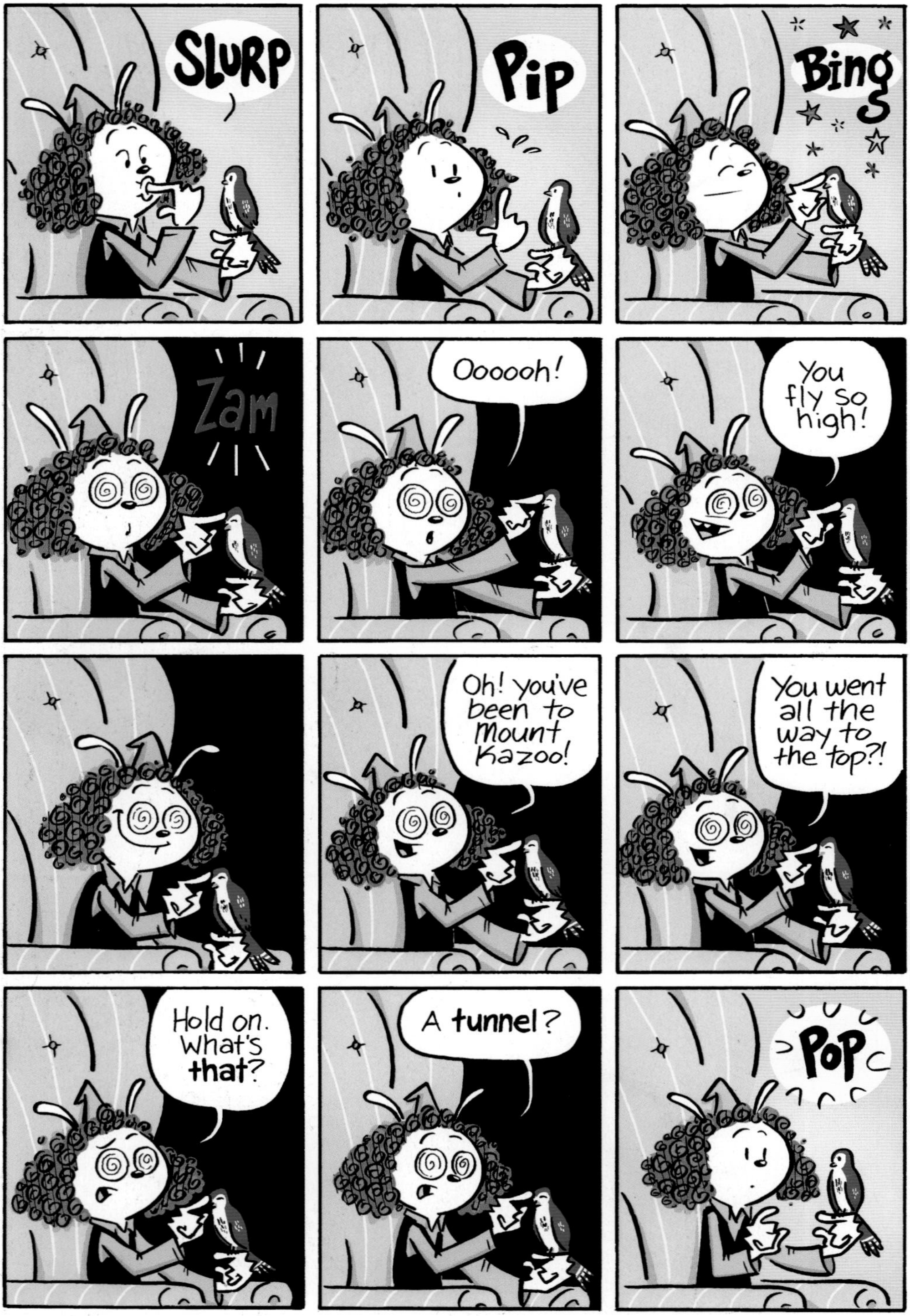
SLURP
Pip
Bing
Zam
Oooooh!
You fly so high!
Oh! you've been to Mount Kazoo!
You went all the way to the top?!
Hold on. What's **that**?
A **tunnel**?
POP

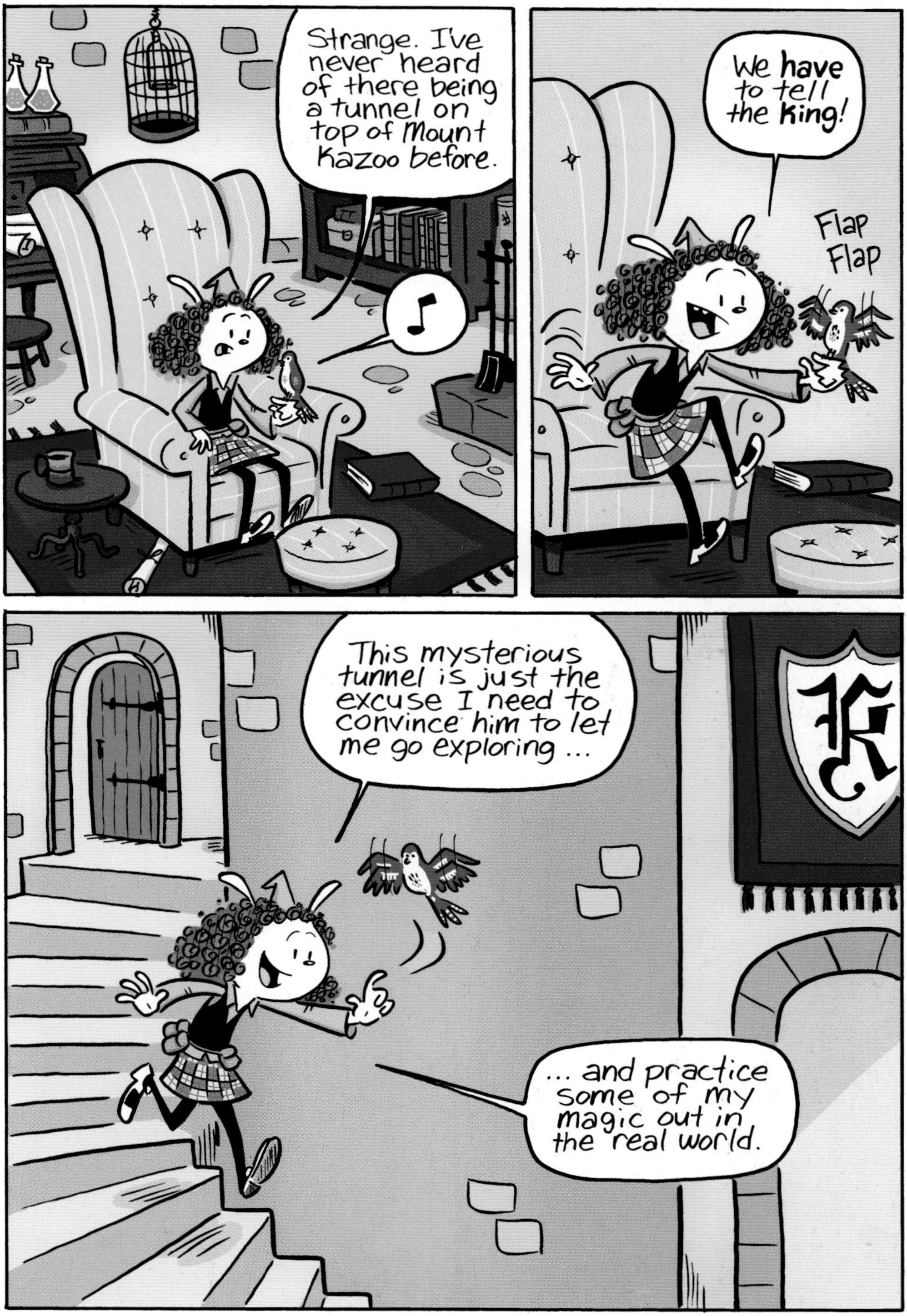
Strange. I've never heard of there being a tunnel on top of Mount Kazoo before.
We **have** to tell the **King**!
Flap Flap
This mysterious tunnel is just the excuse I need to convince him to let me go exploring ...
... and practice some of my magic out in the real world.

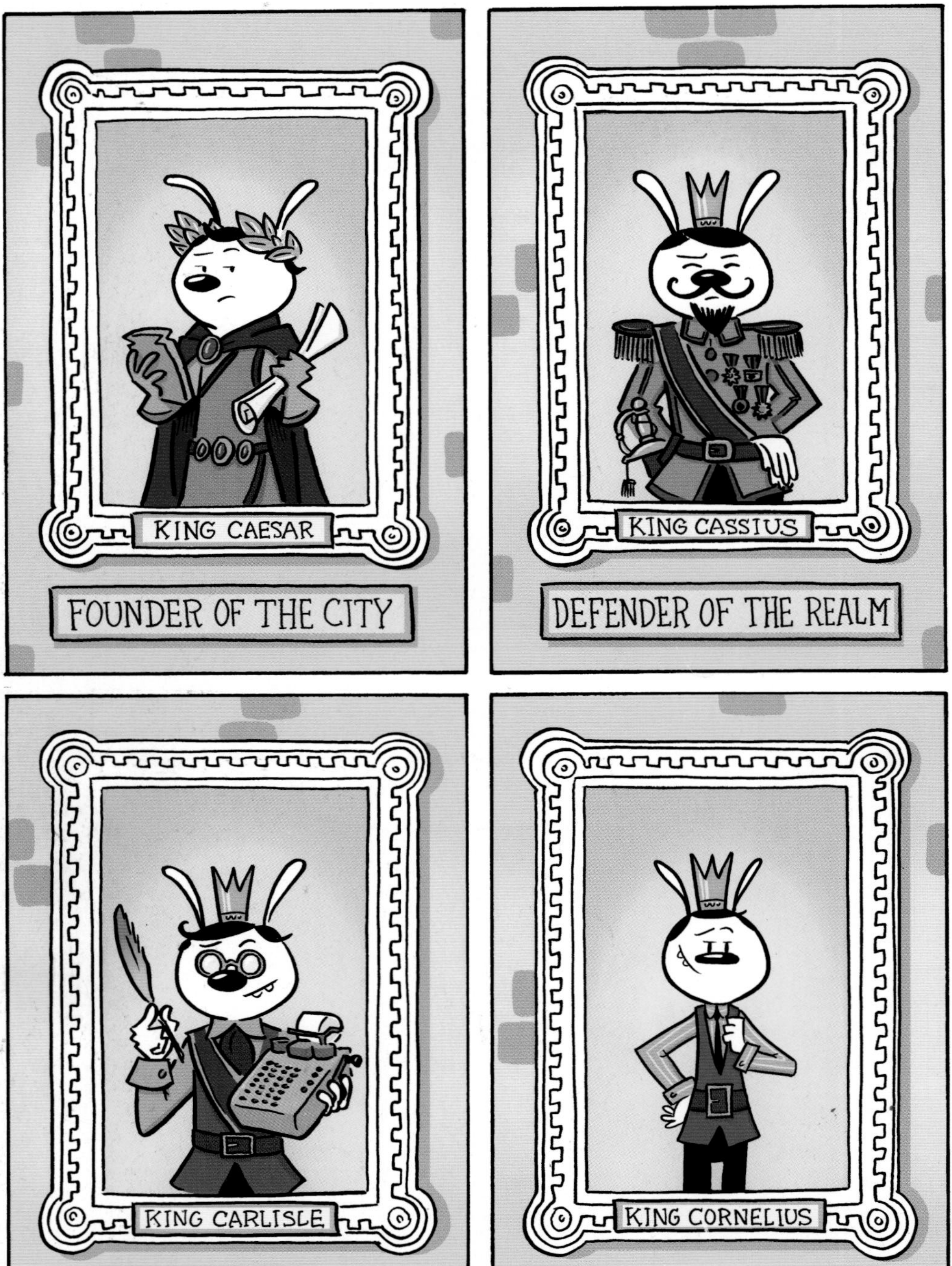
KING CAESAR
FOUNDER OF THE CITY
KING CASSIUS
DEFENDER OF THE REALM
KING CARLISLE
SIMPLIFIER OF THE TAXES
KING CORNELIUS

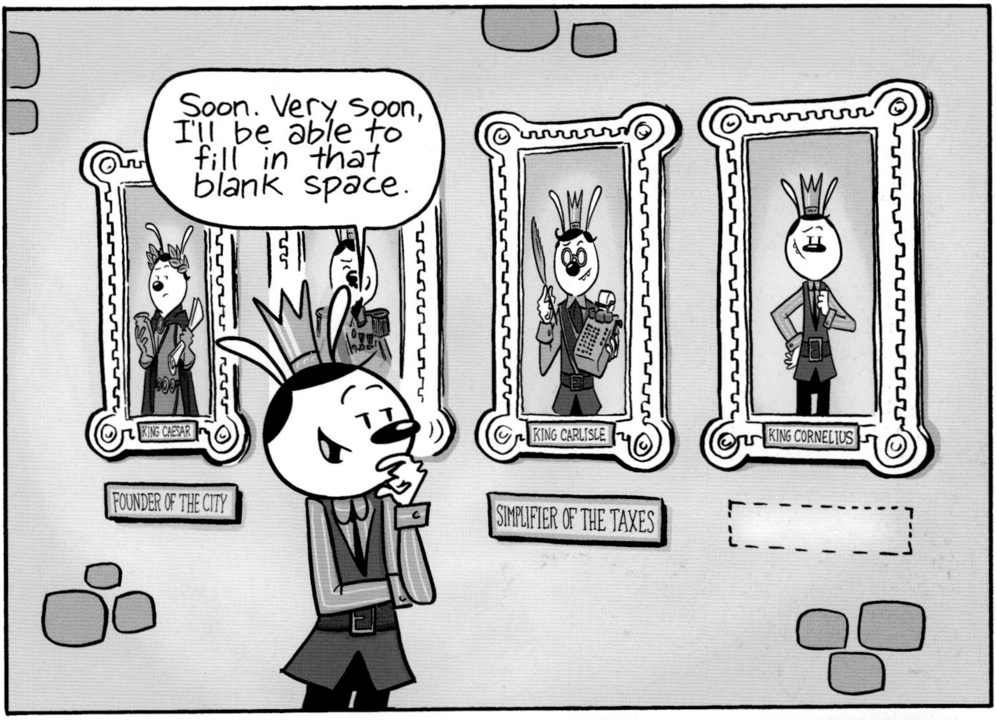
Soon. Very soon, I'll be able to fill in that blank space.
KING CAESAR
FOUNDER OF THE CITY
KING CARLISLE
SIMPLIFIER OF THE TAXES
KING CORNELIUS

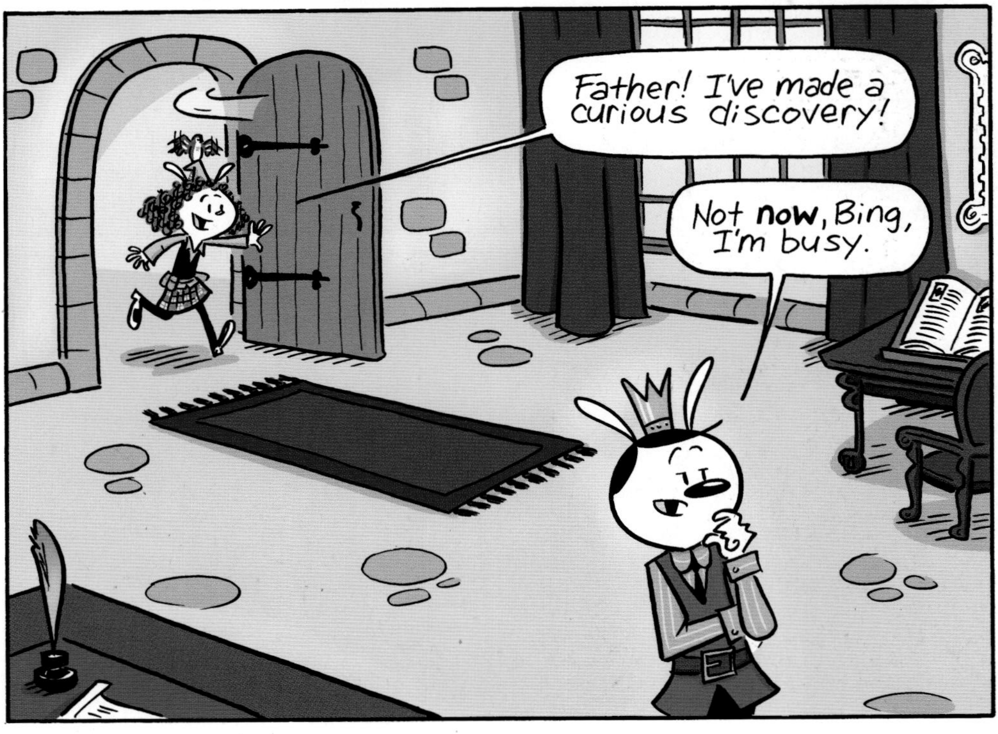
Father! I've made a curious discovery!
Not **now**, Bing, I'm busy.

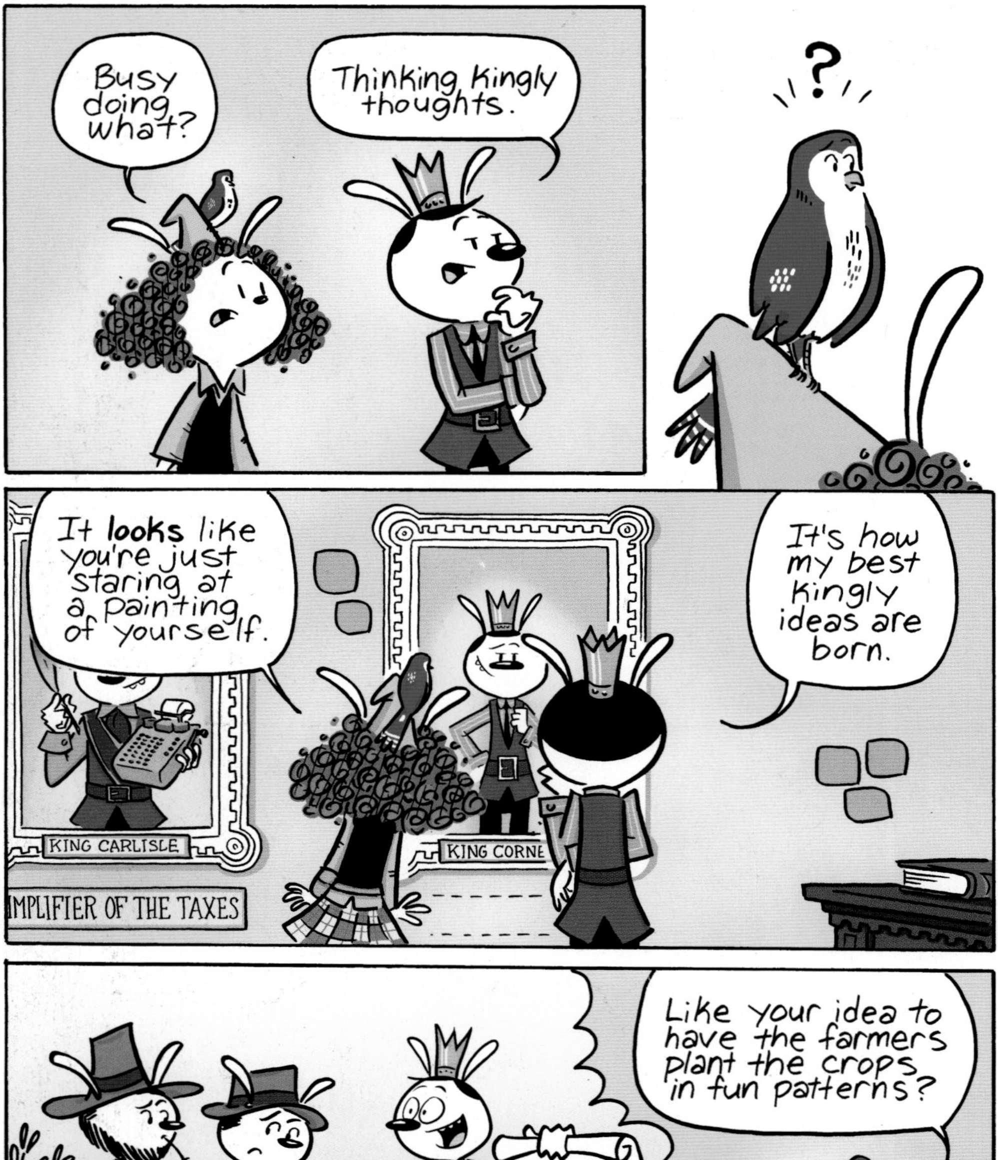
Busy doing what?
Thinking kingly thoughts.
?
It looks like you're just staring at a painting of yourself.
KING CARLISLE
IMPLIFIER OF THE TAXES
KING CORNE
It's how my best kingly ideas are born.
Like your idea to have the farmers plant the crops in fun patterns?
Oo

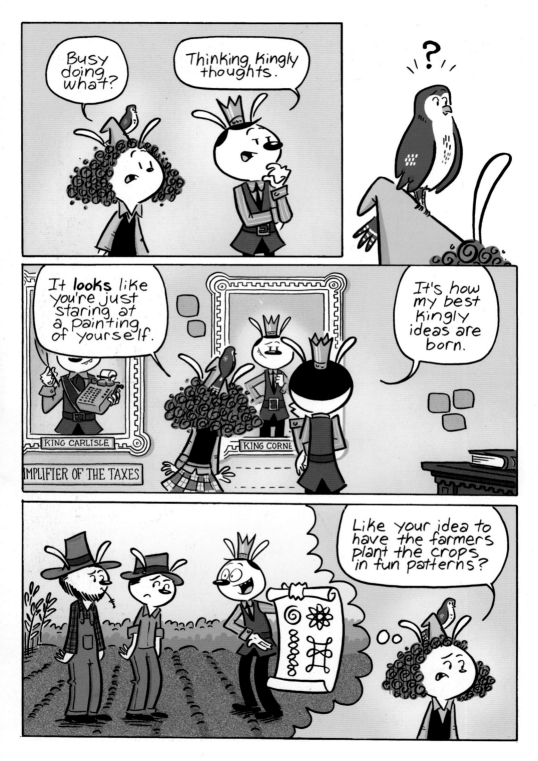

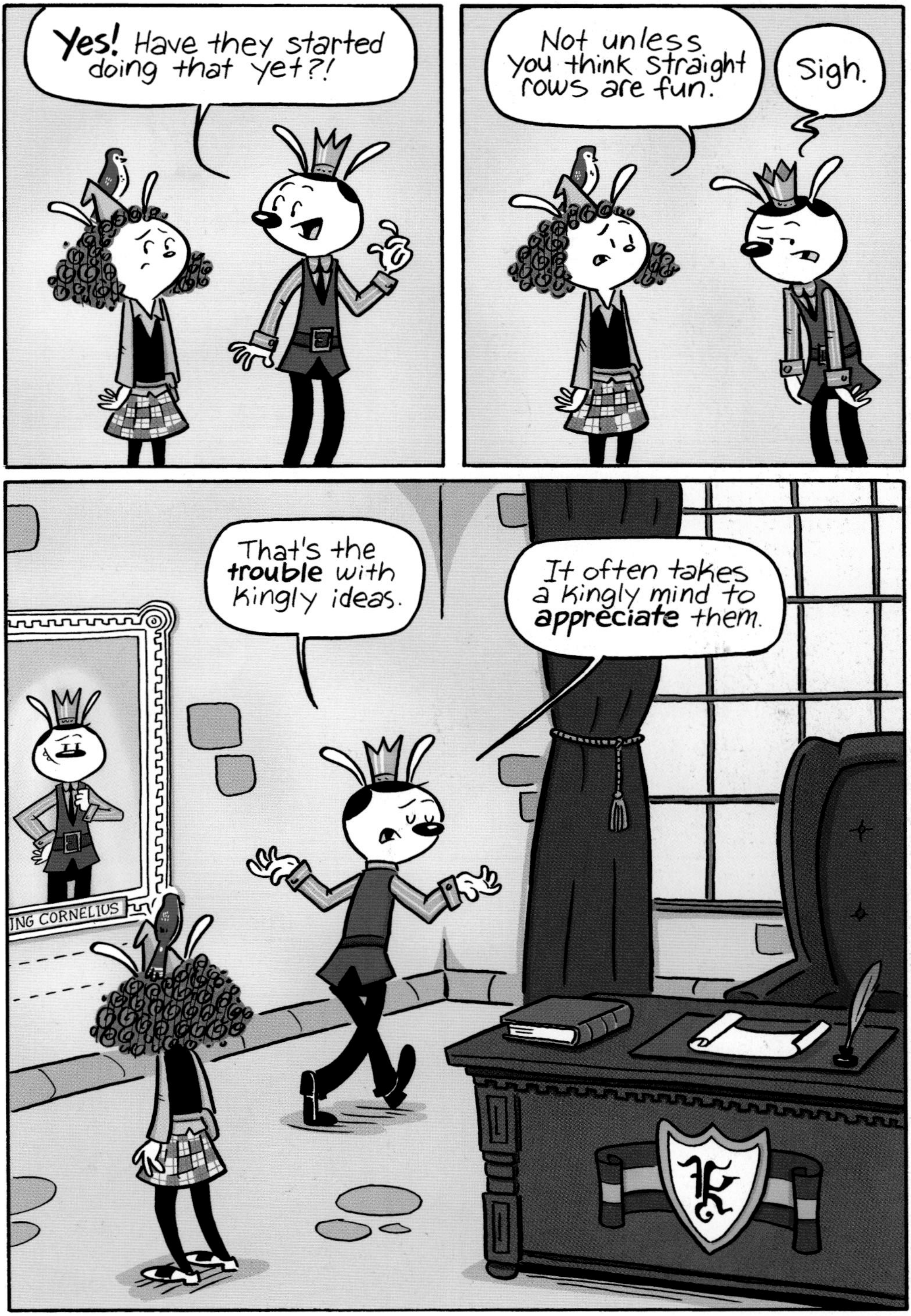
Yes! Have they started doing that yet?!
Not unless you think straight rows are fun.
Sigh.
That's the trouble with kingly ideas.
It often takes a kingly mind to appreciate them.
ING CORNELIUS

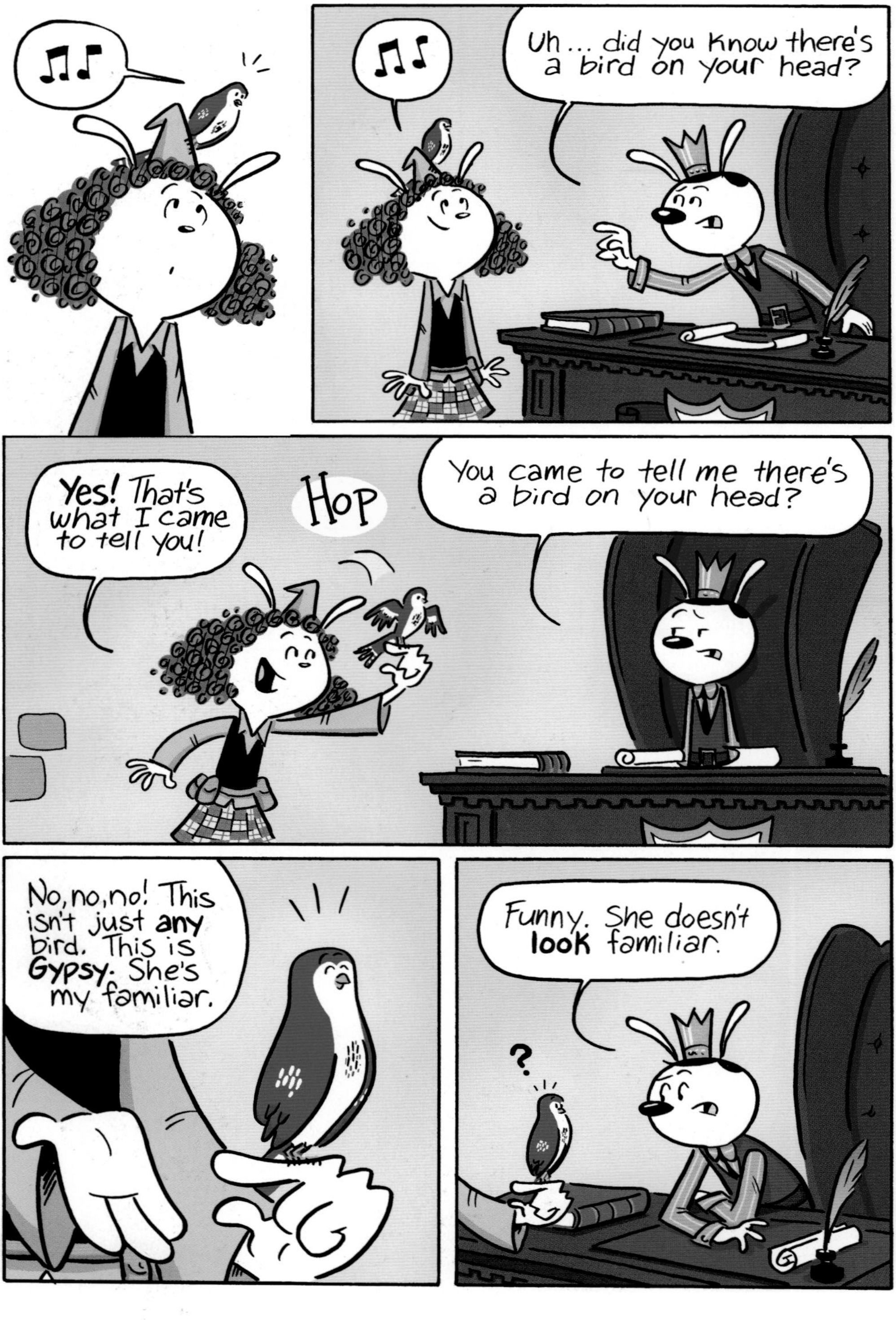
♫♩
♫♩
Uh... did you know there's a bird on your head?
Yes! That's what I came to tell you!
HOP
You came to tell me there's a bird on your head?
No, no, no! This isn't just **any** bird. This is **Gypsy**. She's my familiar.
Funny. She doesn't **look** familiar.
?

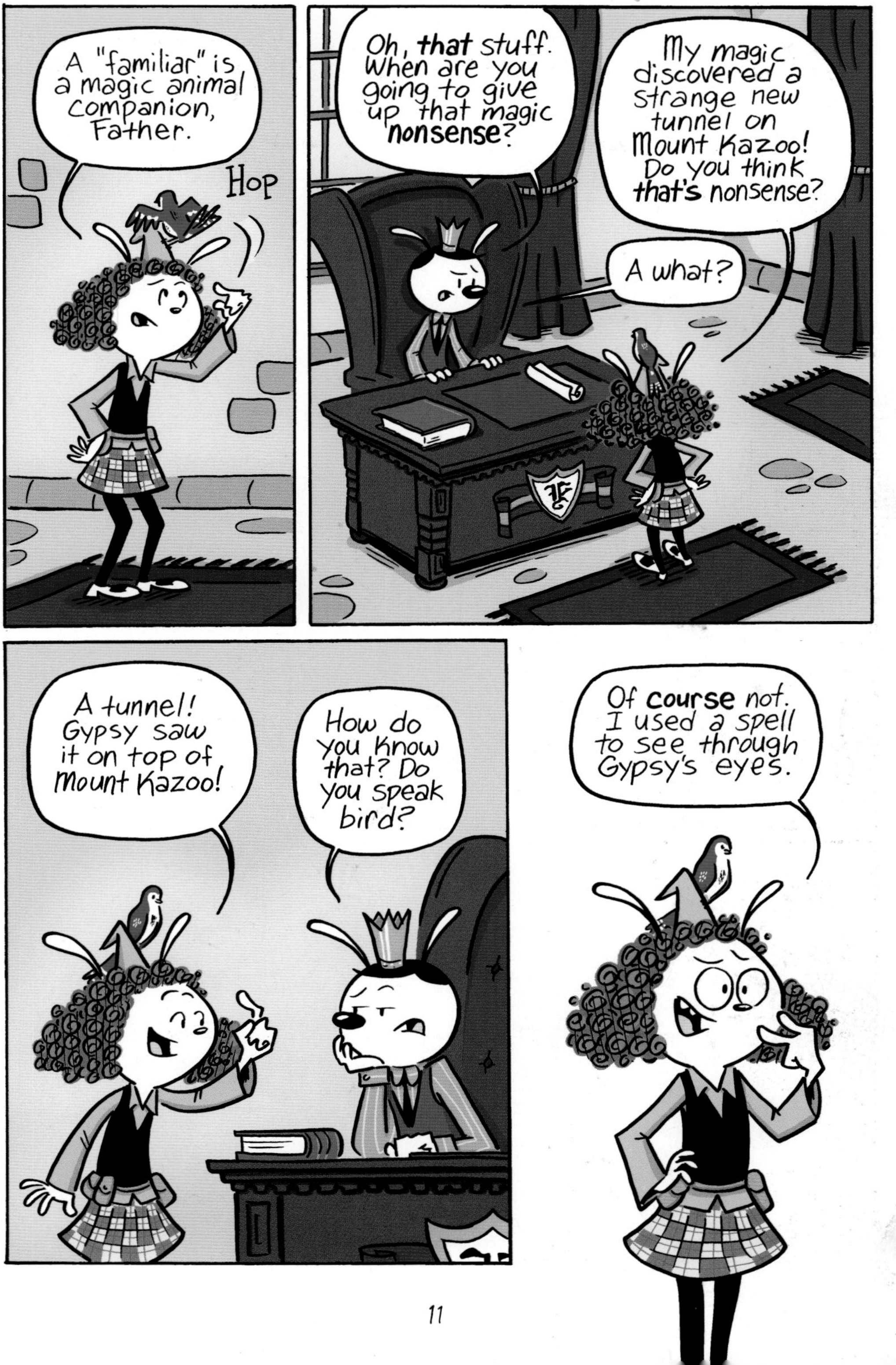
A "familiar" is a magic animal companion, Father.
Hop
Oh, **that** stuff. When are you going to give up that magic **nonsense**?
My magic discovered a strange new tunnel on Mount Kazoo! Do you think **that's** nonsense?
A what?
A tunnel! Gypsy saw it on top of Mount Kazoo!
How do you know that? Do you speak bird?
Of **course** not. I used a spell to see through Gypsy's eyes.

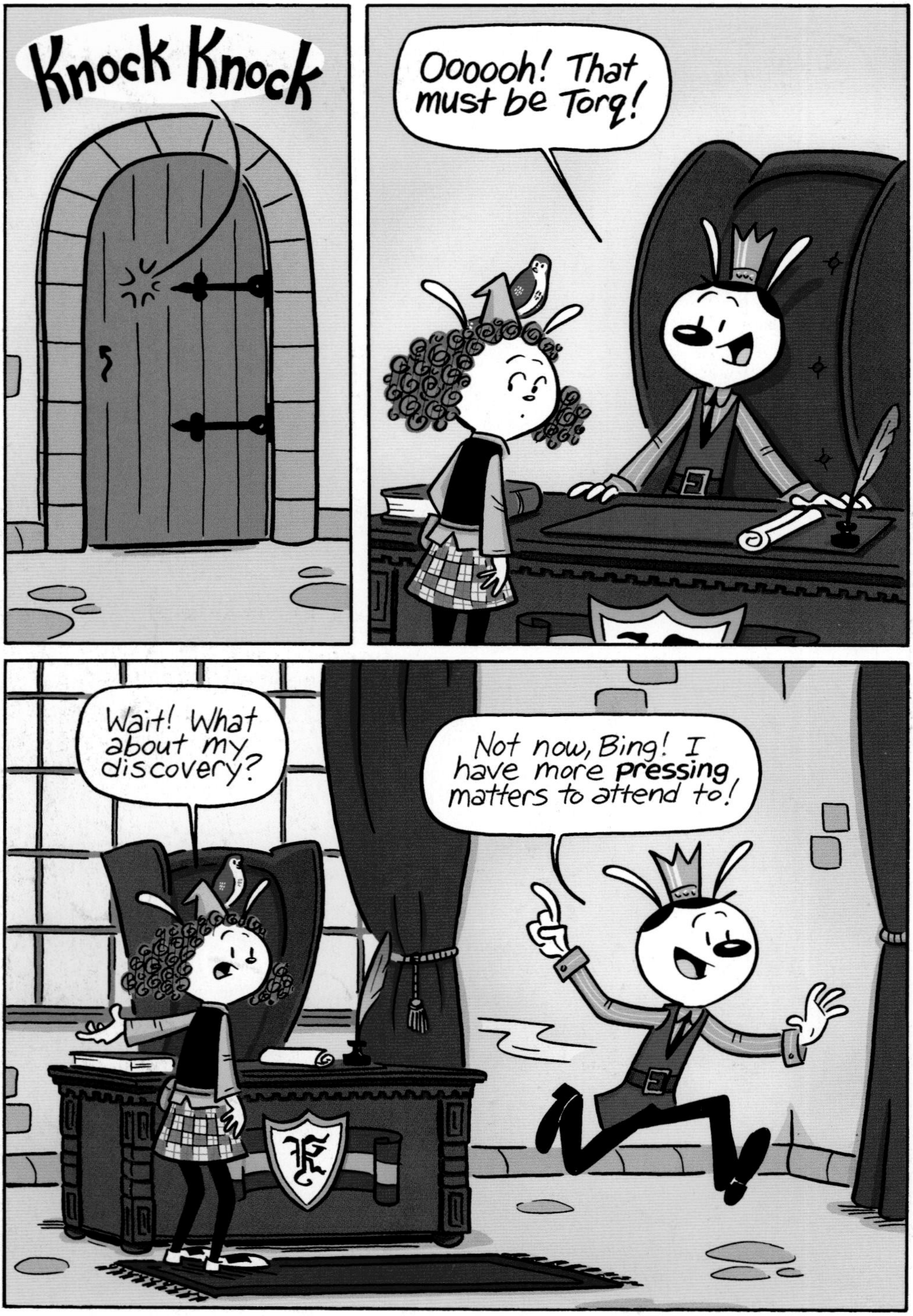
Knock Knock
Oooooh! That must be Torq!
Wait! What about my discovery?
Not now, Bing! I have more **pressing** matters to attend to!

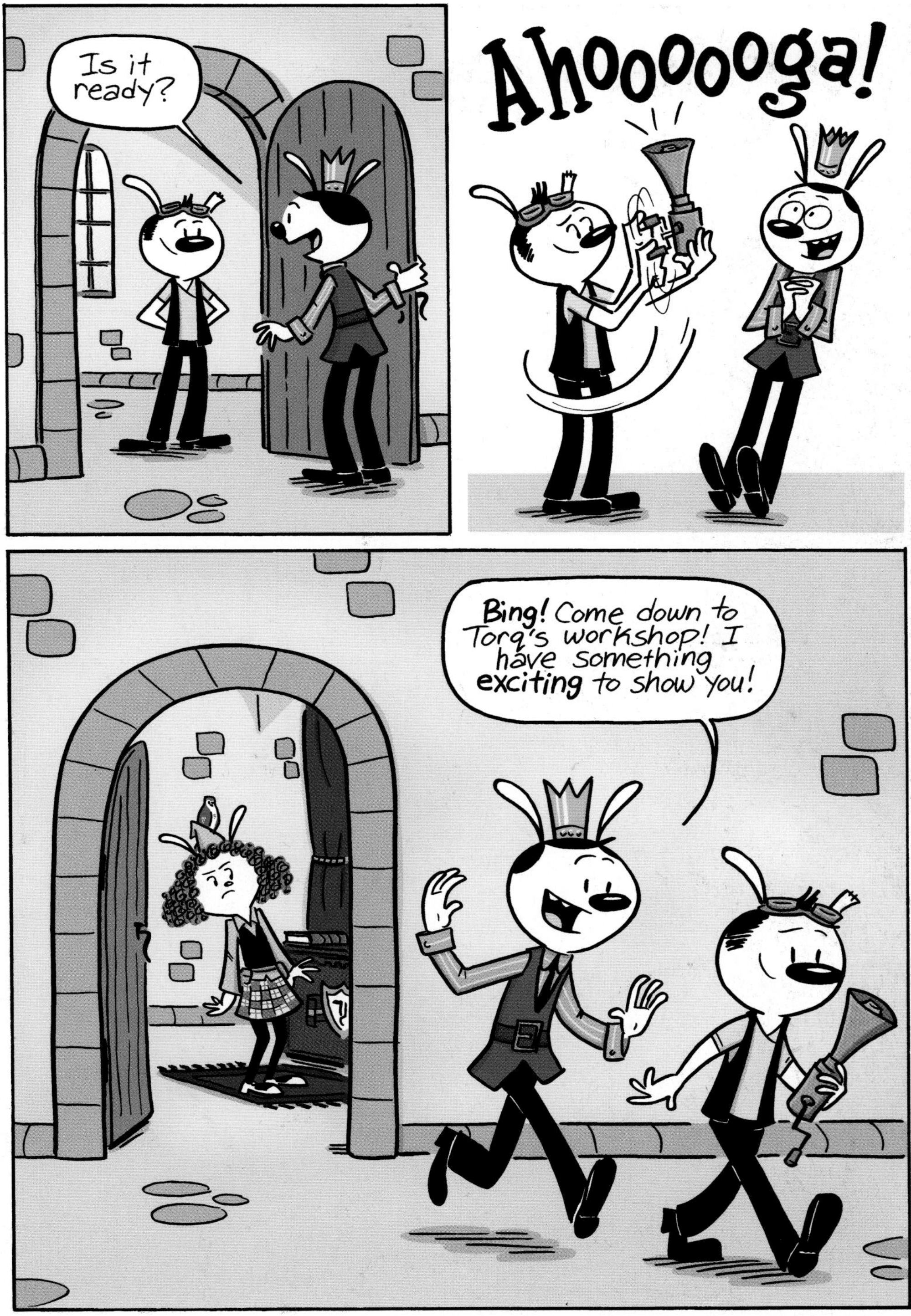
Is it ready?
Ahoooooga!
Bing! Come down to Torq's workshop! I have something exciting to show you!

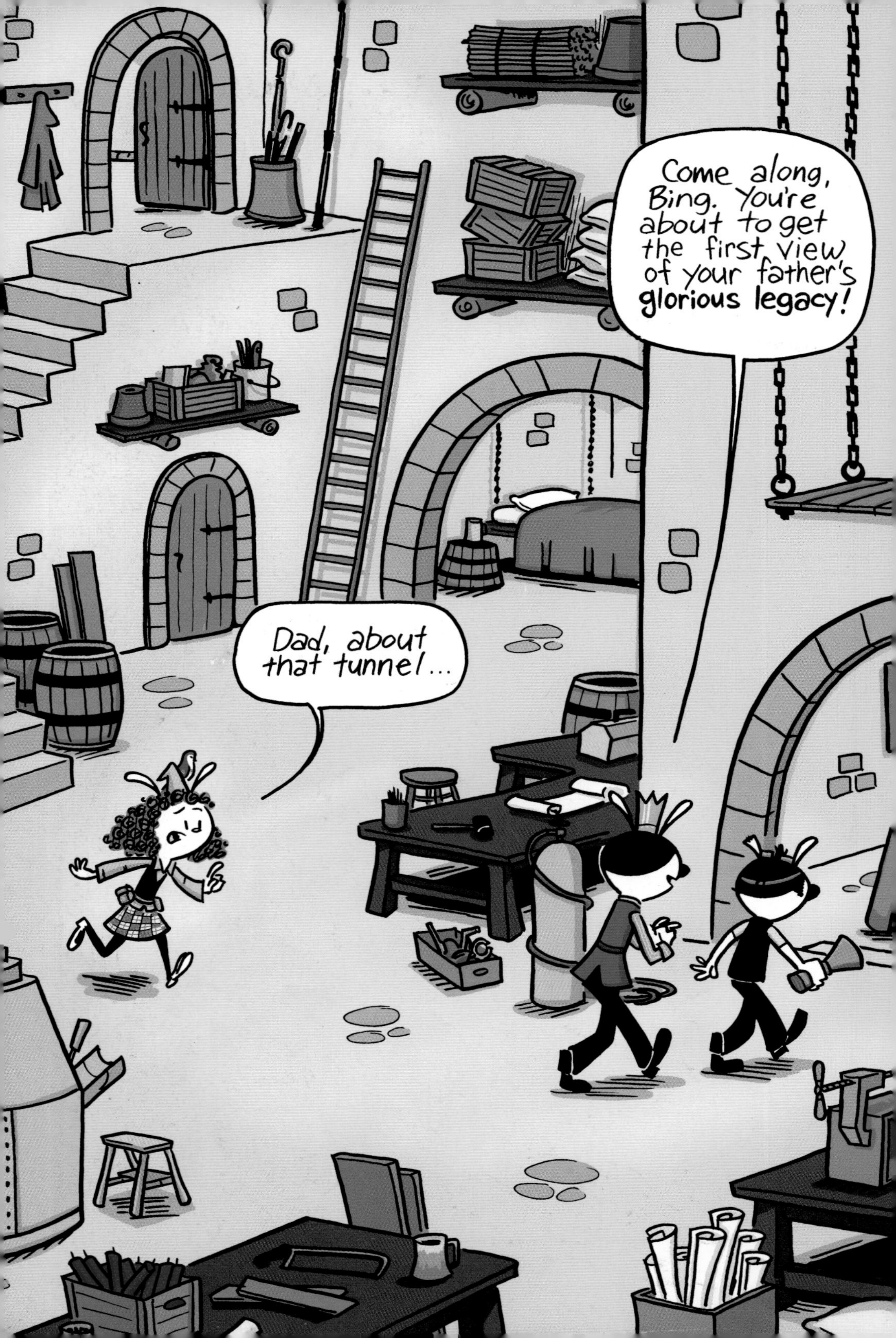
Come along, Bing. You're about to get the first view of your father's **glorious legacy**!
Dad, about that tunnel...

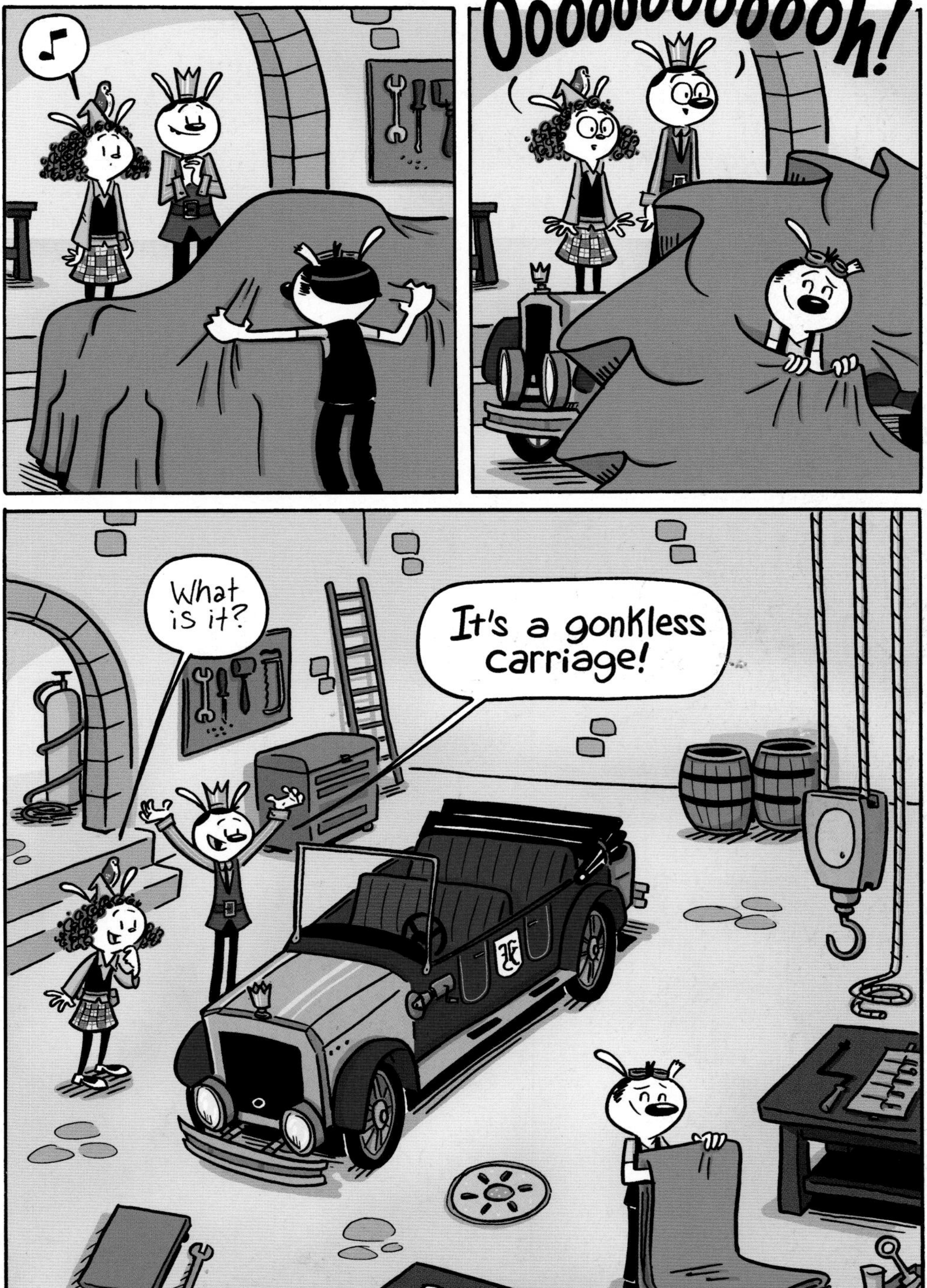
Ooooooooooooh!
What is it?
It's a gonkless carriage!

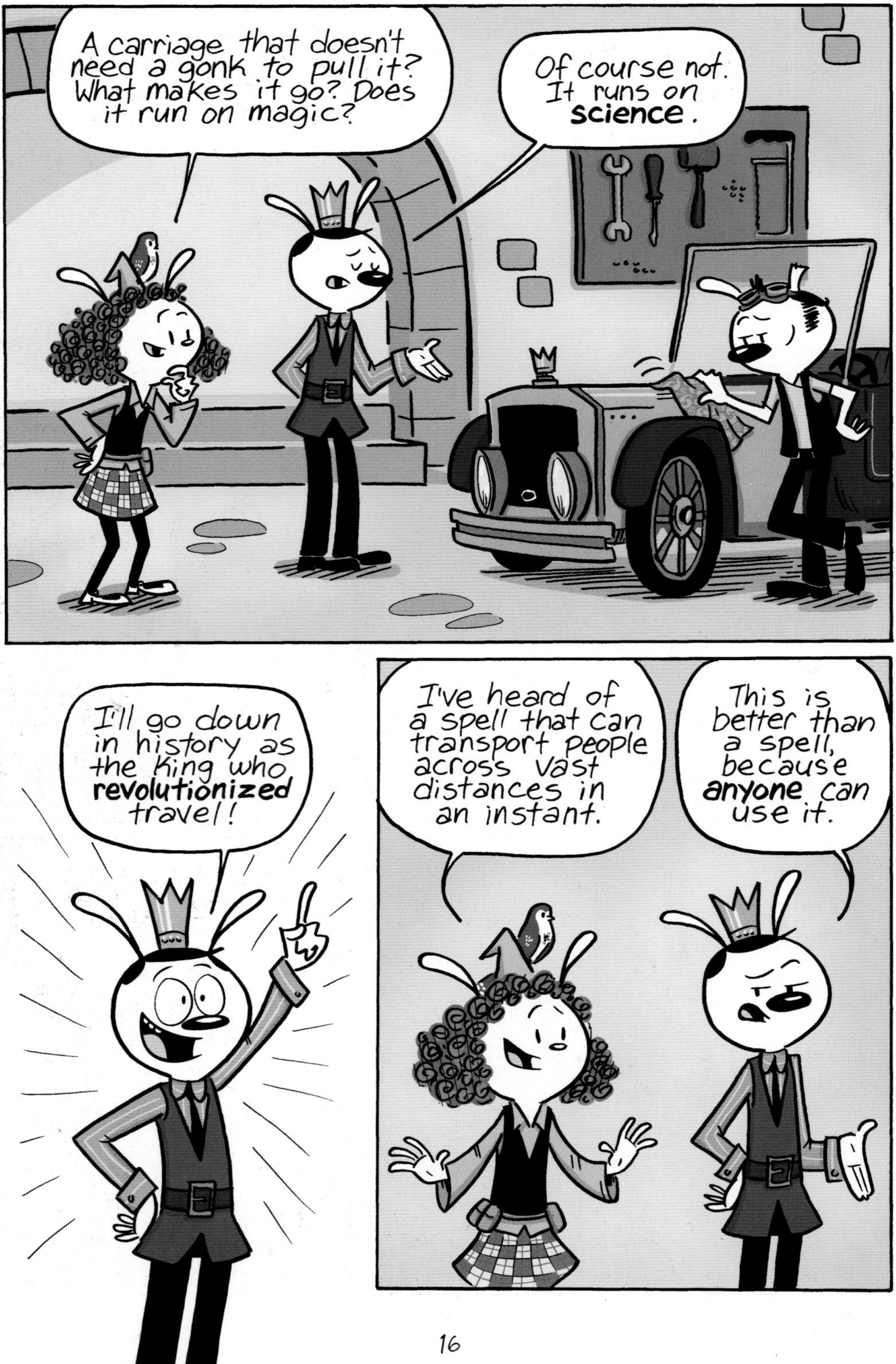
A carriage that doesn't need a gonk to pull it? What makes it go? Does it run on magic?
Of course not. It runs on **science**.
I'll go down in history as the King who **revolutionized** travel!
I've heard of a spell that can transport people across vast distances in an instant.
This is better than a spell, because **anyone** can use it.

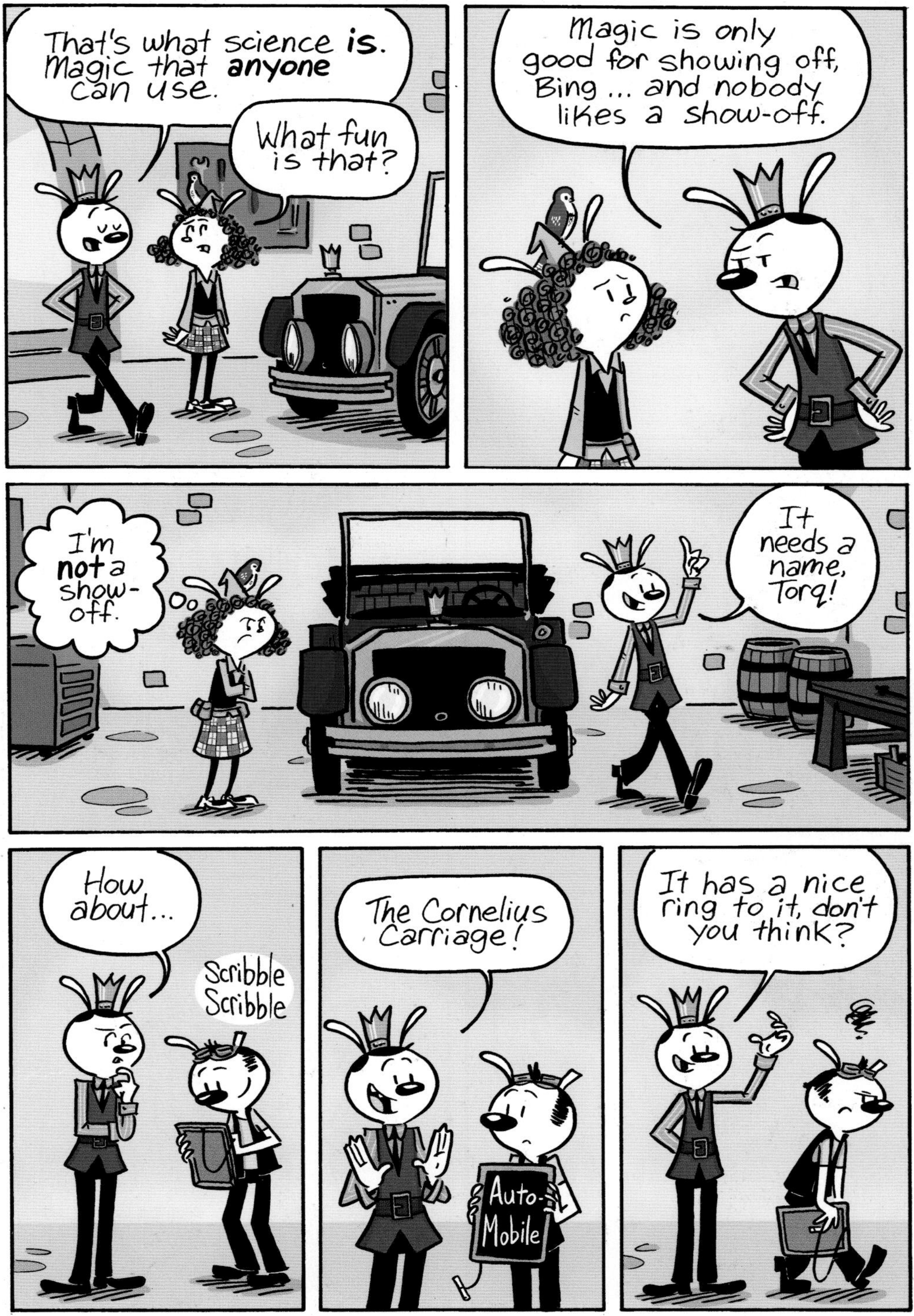
That's what science **is**. Magic that **anyone** can use.
What fun is that?
Magic is only good for showing off, Bing ... and nobody likes a show-off.
I'm **not** a show-off.
It needs a name, Torq!
How about...
Scribble Scribble
The Cornelius Carriage!
Auto-Mobile
It has a nice ring to it, don't you think?

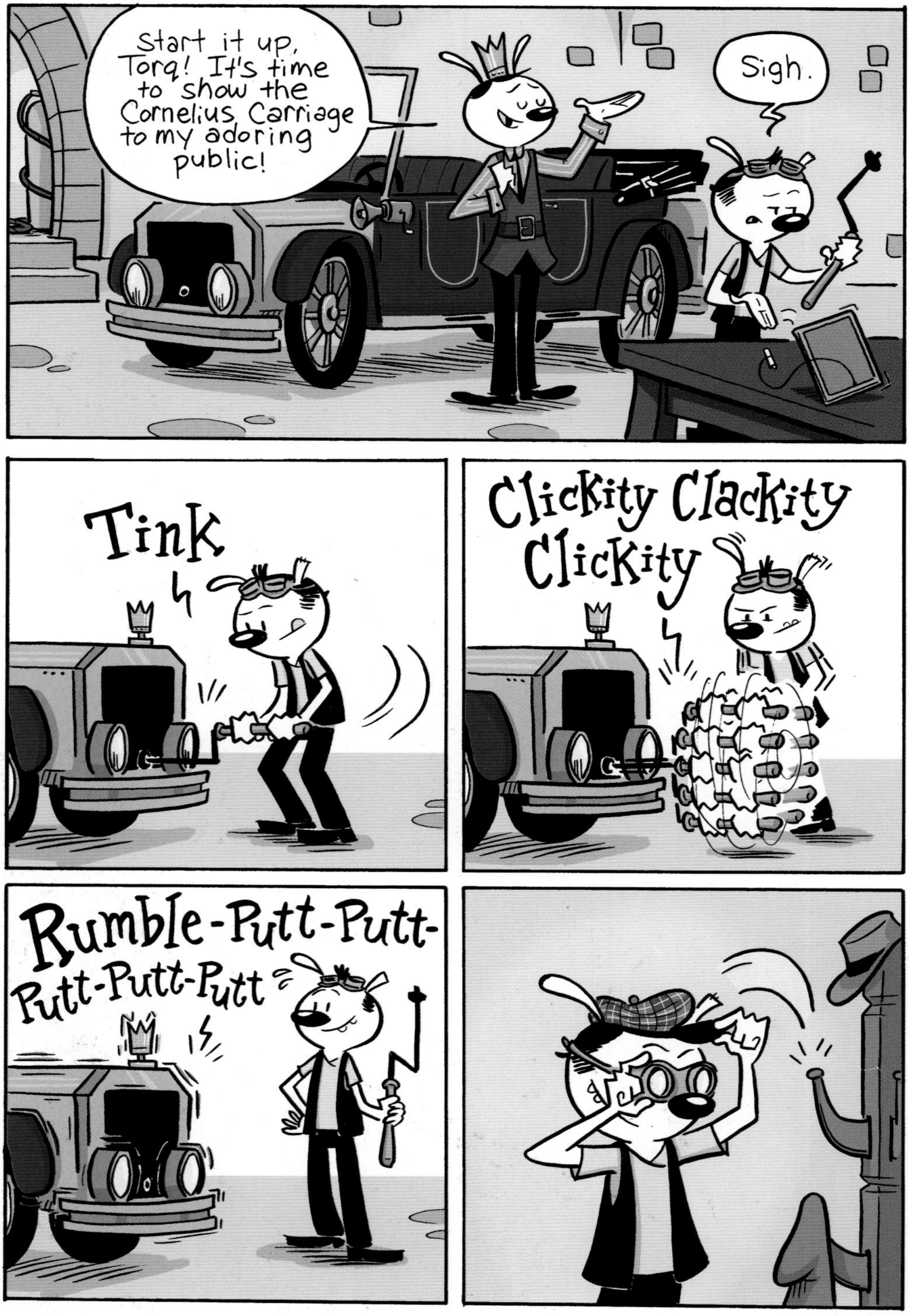
Start it up, Torq! It's time to show the Cornelius Carriage to my adoring public!
Sigh.
Tink
Clickity Clackity Clickity
Rumble-Putt-Putt-Putt-Putt-Putt

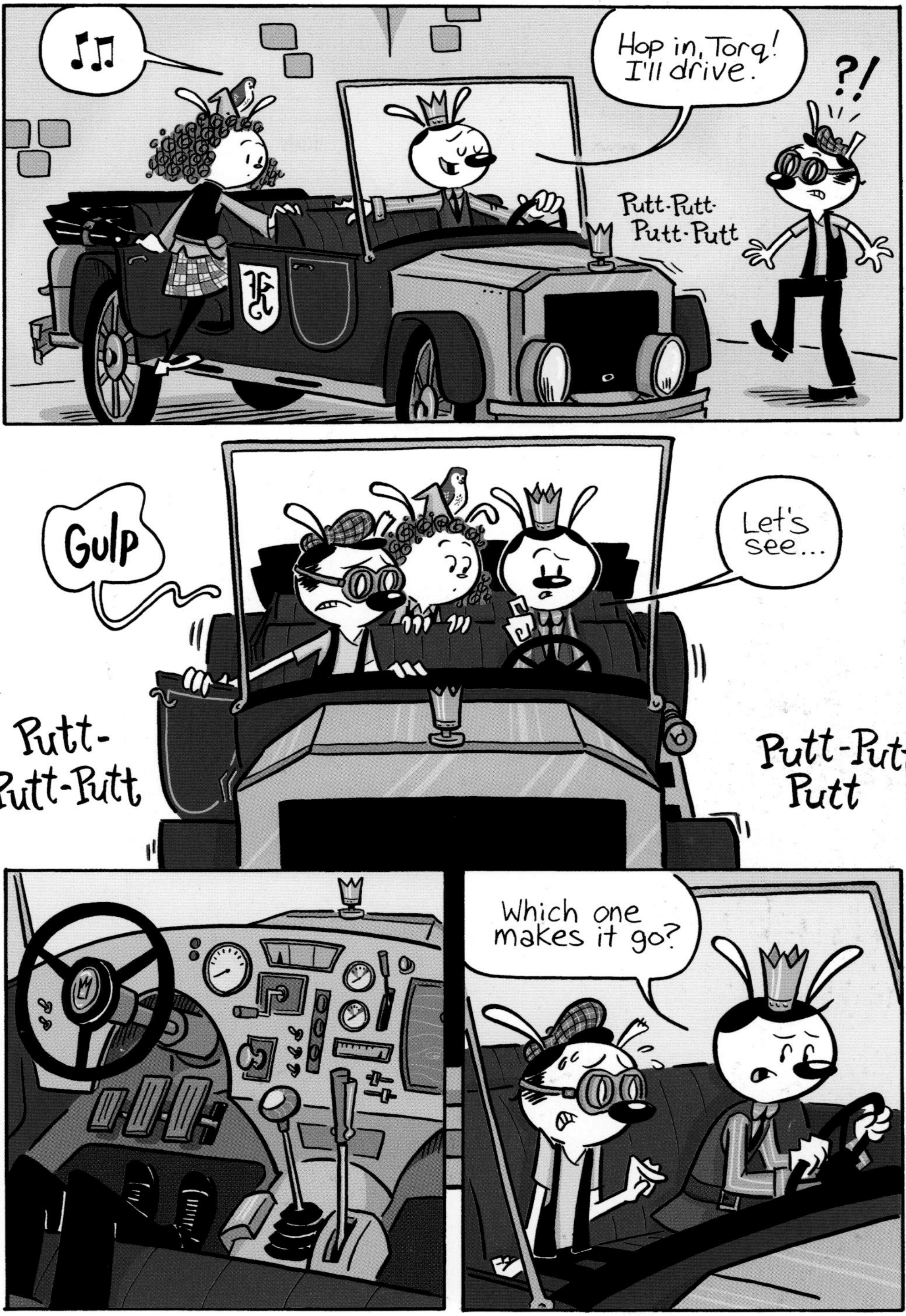
♪♫
Hop in, Torq! I'll drive.
?!
Putt-Putt-Putt-Putt
Gulp
Let's see...
Putt-Putt-Putt
Putt-Putt-Putt
Which one makes it go?

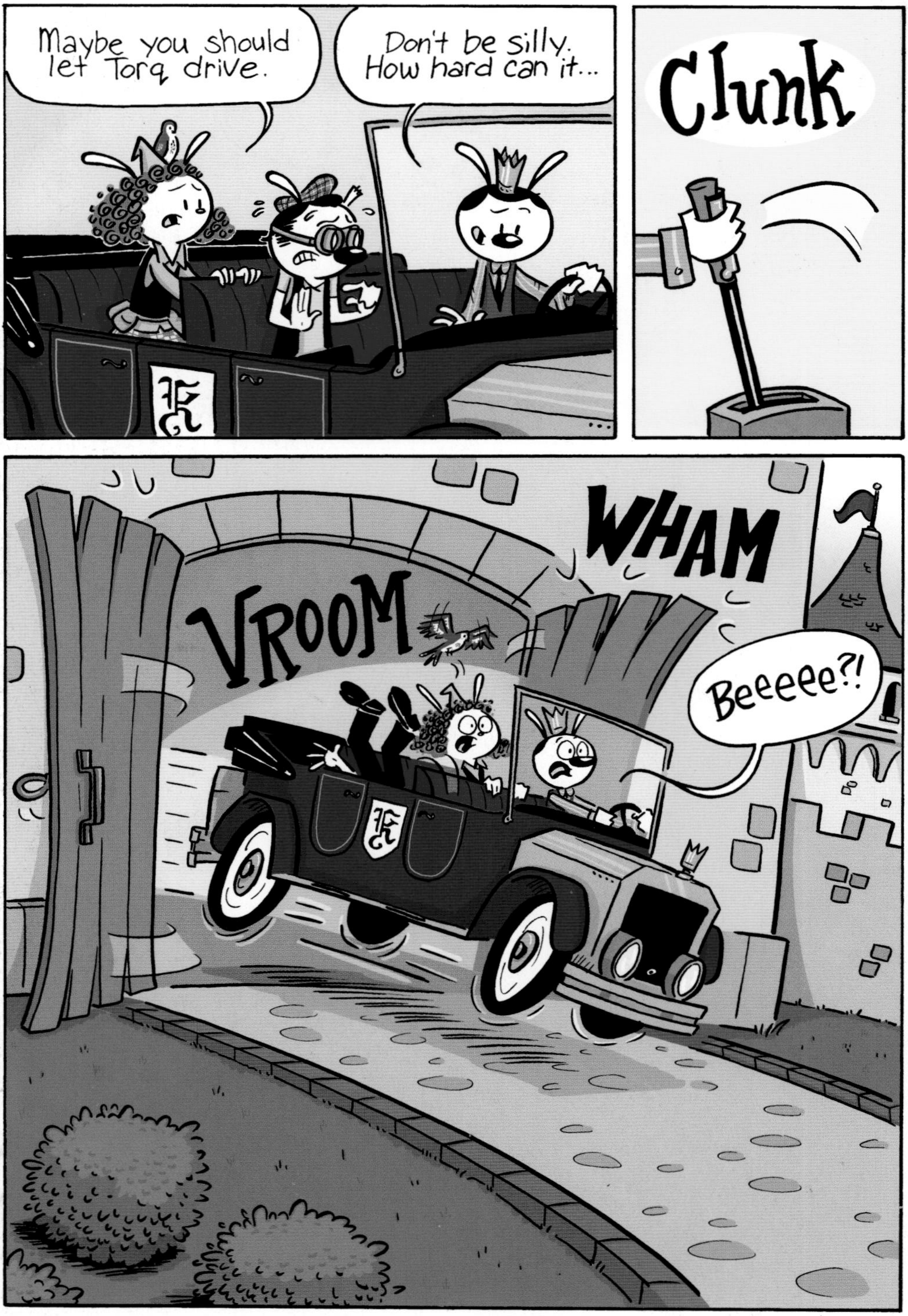
Maybe you should let Torq drive.
Don't be silly. How hard can it...
Clunk
WHAM
VROOM
Beeeee?!

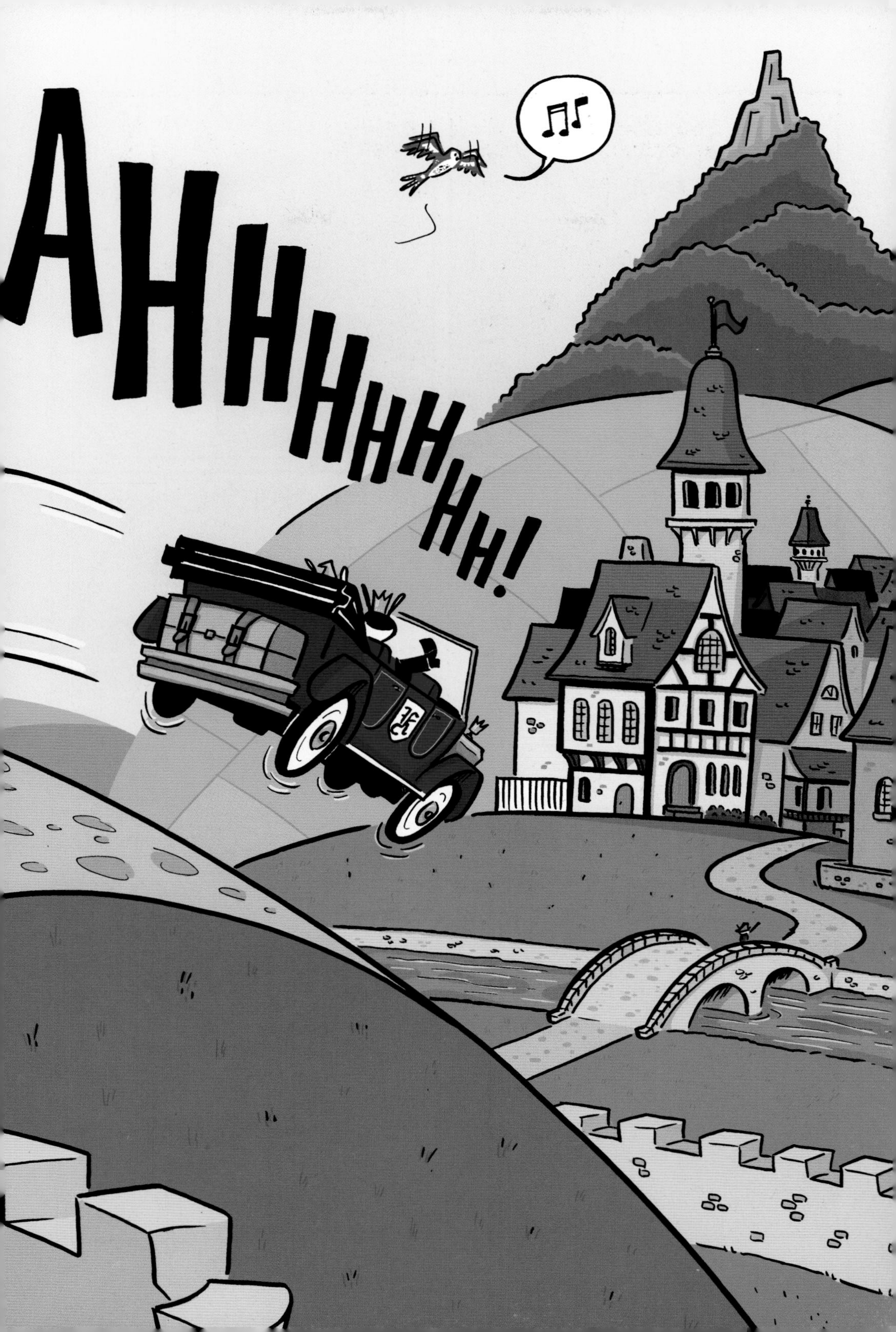
AHHHHHHHHHH!

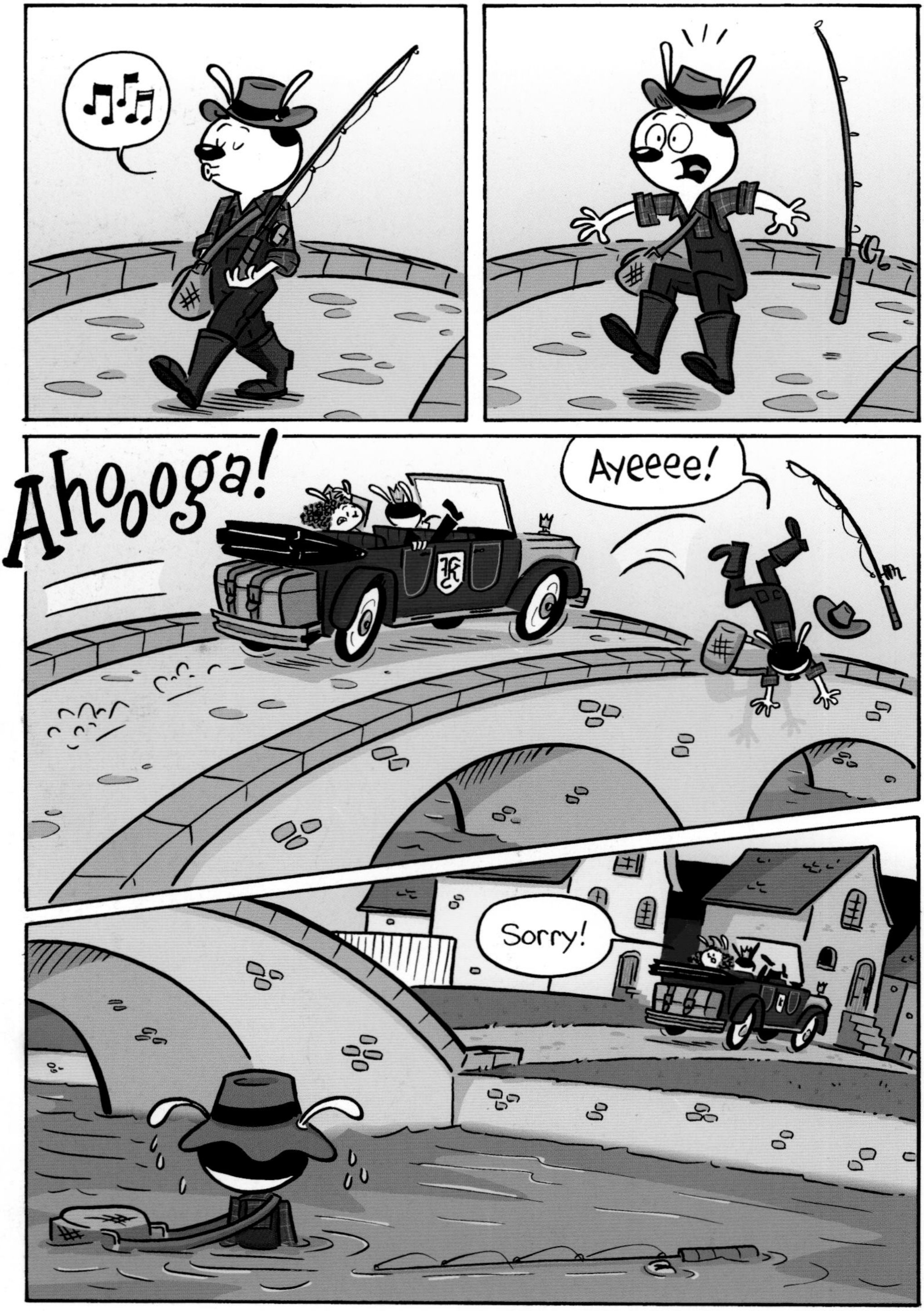
Ahoooga!
Ayeeee!
Sorry!

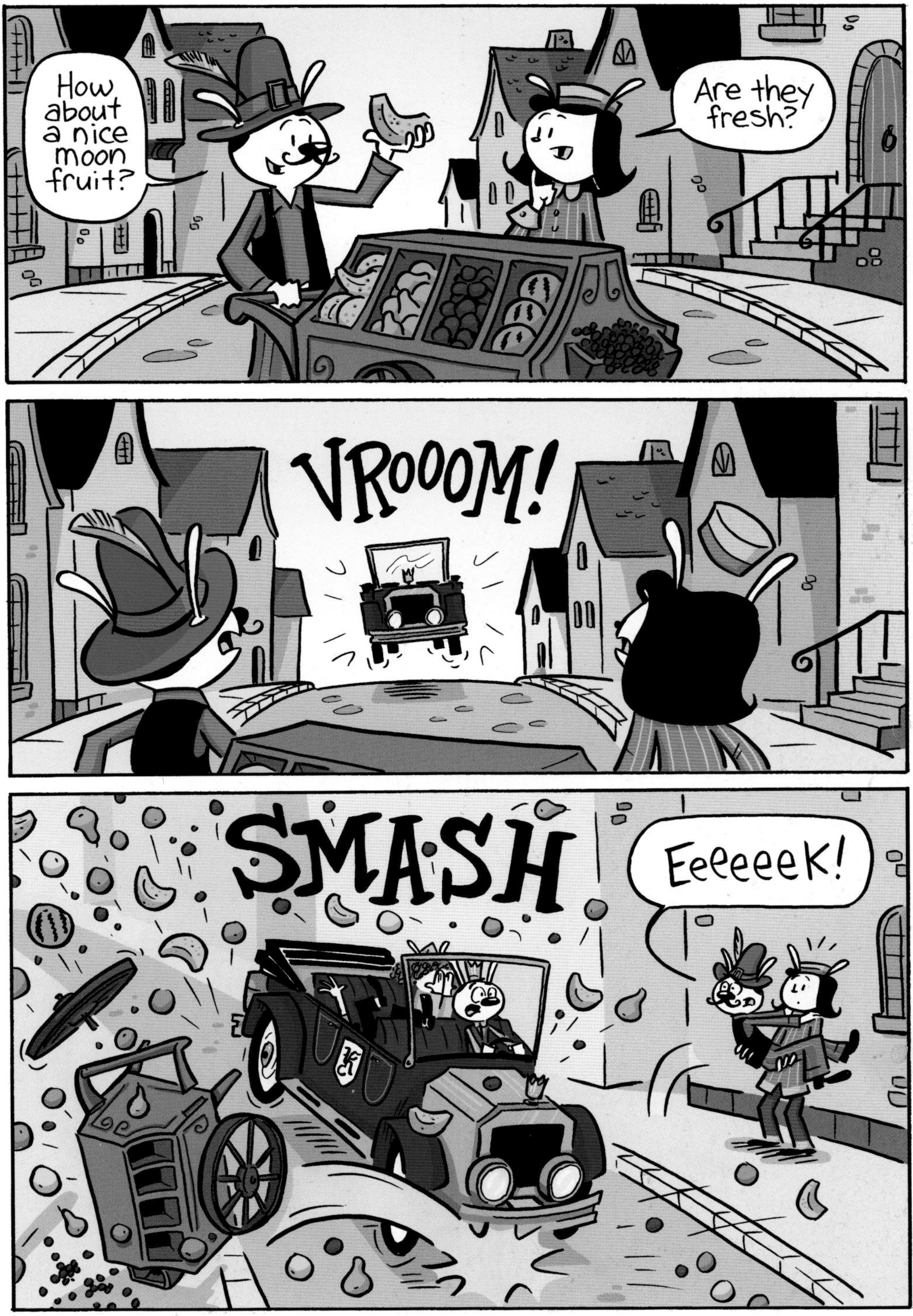
How about a nice moon fruit?
Are they fresh?
VROOOM!
SMASH
Eeeeeek!

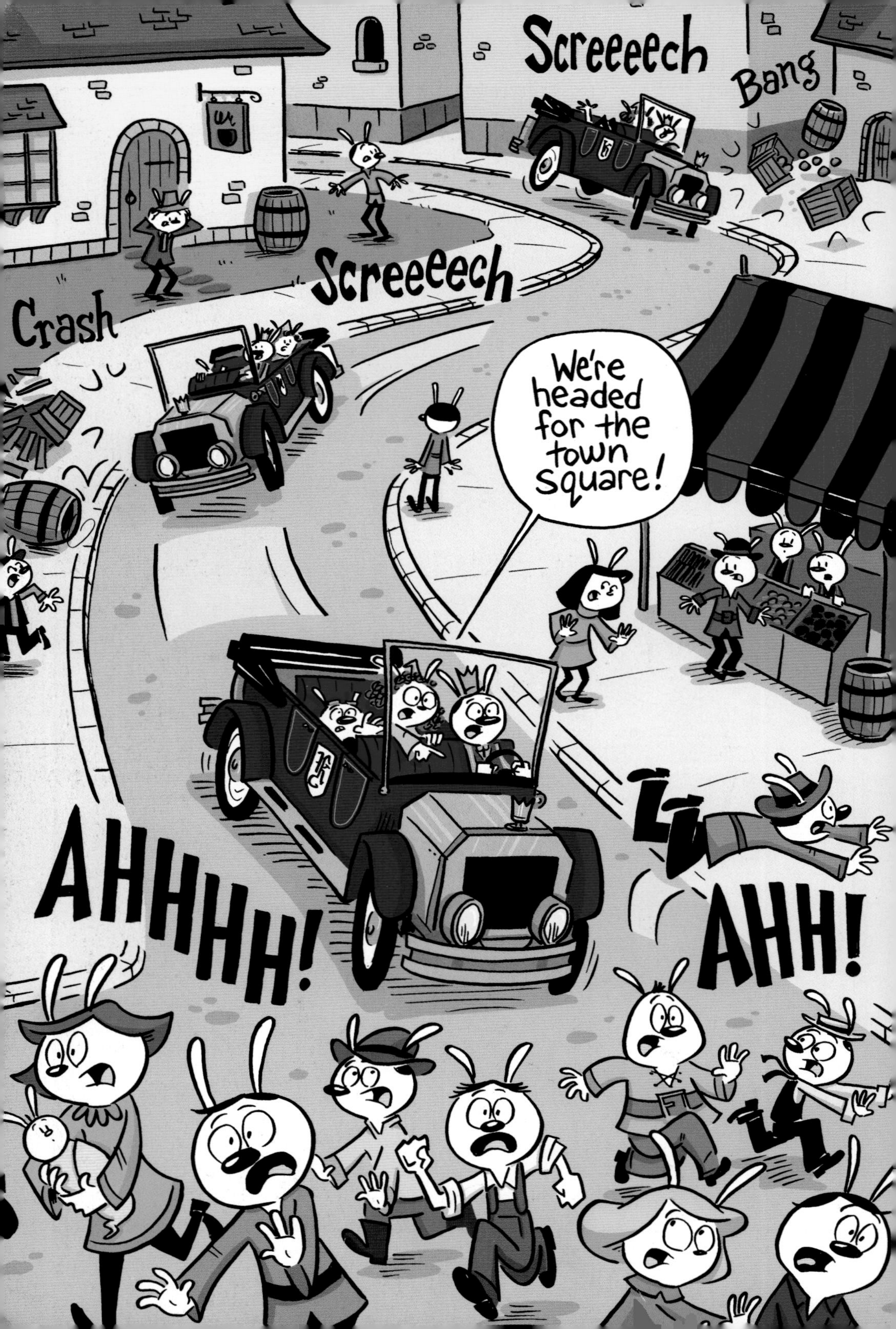
Screeeech
Bang
Crash
Screeeech
We're headed for the town square!
AHHHH!
AHH!

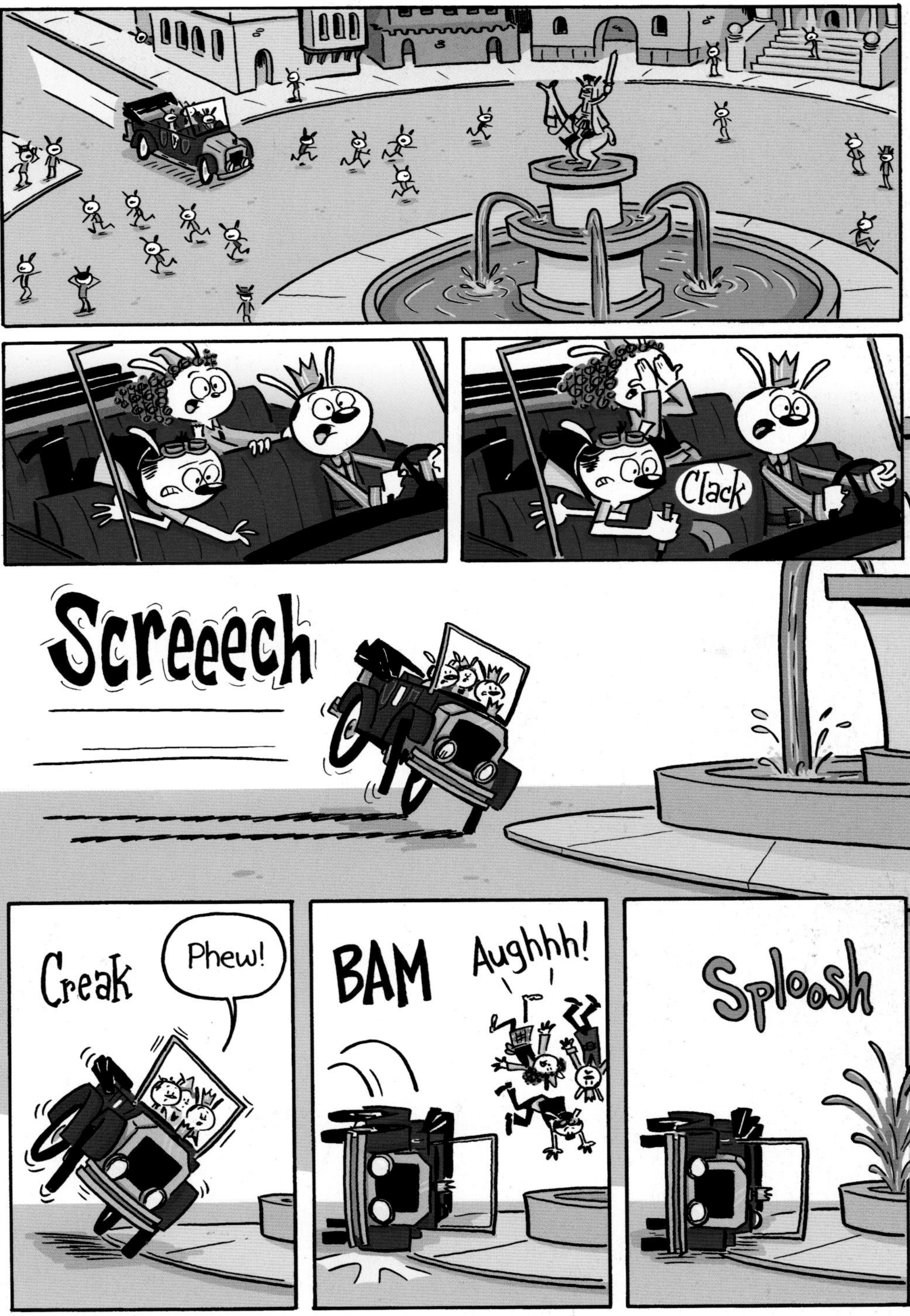
Clack
Screeech
Creak
Phew!
BAM
Aughhh!
Sploosh

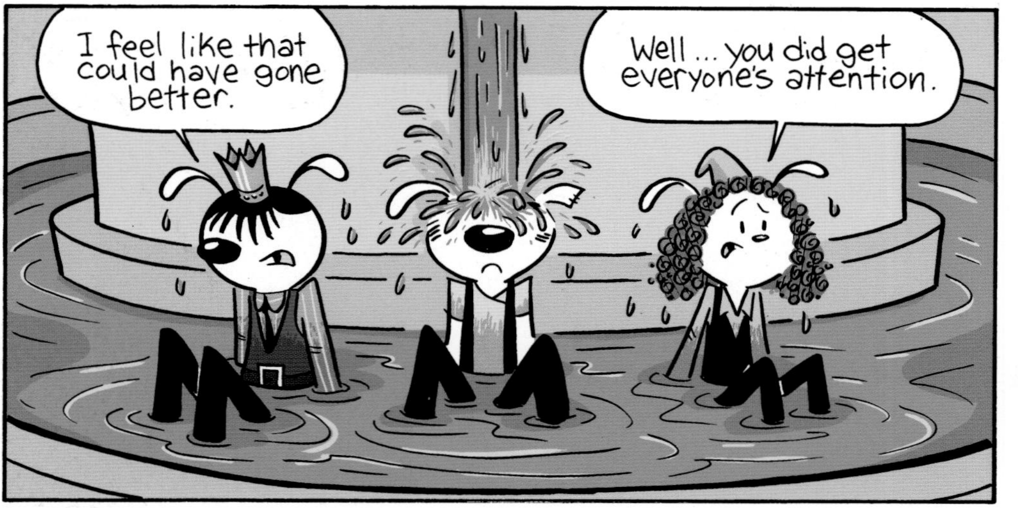
I feel like that could have gone better.
Well ... you did get everyone's attention.

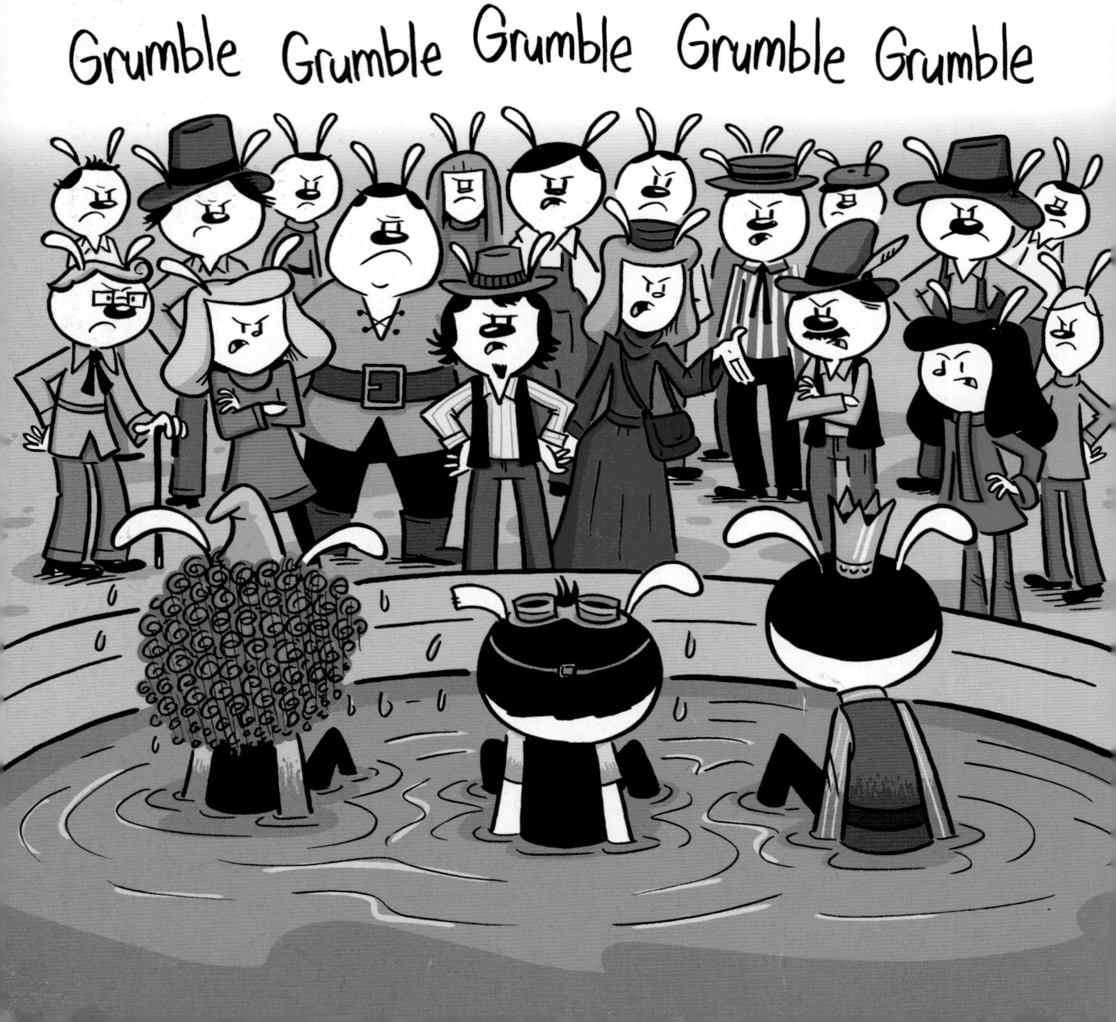
Grumble Grumble Grumble Grumble Grumble

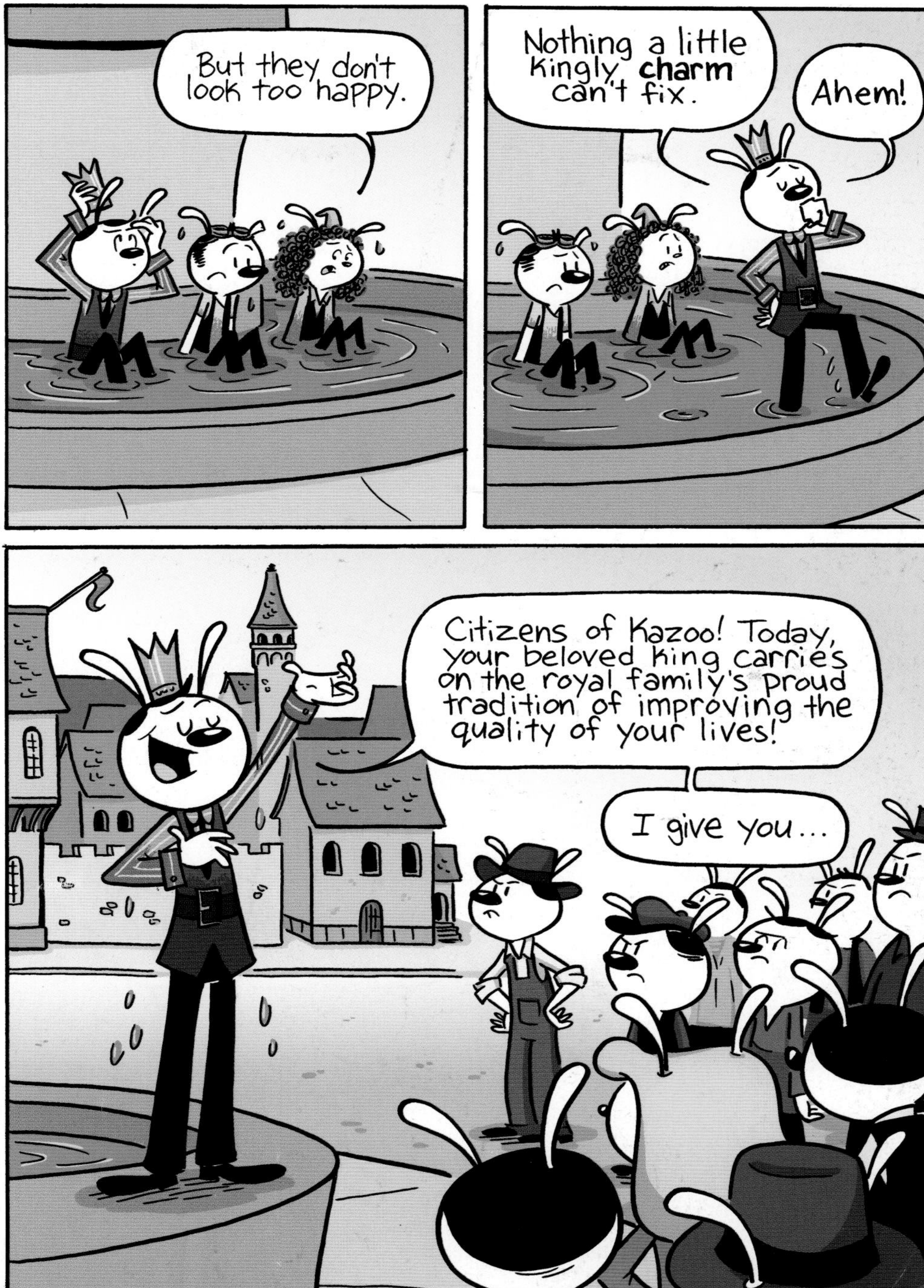
But they don't look too happy.
Nothing a little kingly **charm** can't fix.
Ahem!
Citizens of Kazoo! Today, your beloved king carries on the royal family's proud tradition of improving the quality of your lives!
I give you...

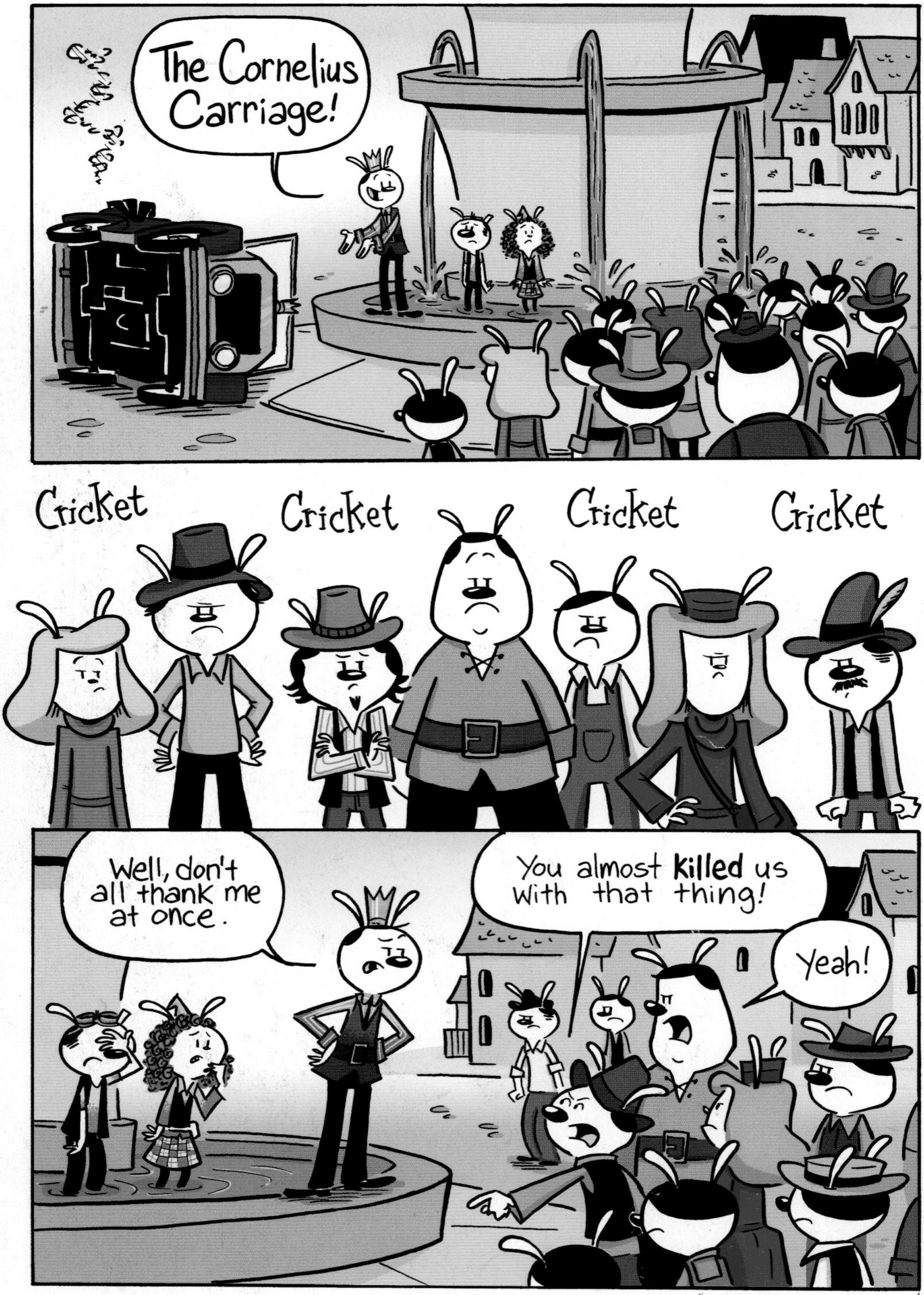
The Cornelius Carriage!
Cricket
Cricket
Cricket
Cricket
Well, don't all thank me at once.
You almost **killed** us with that thing!
Yeah!

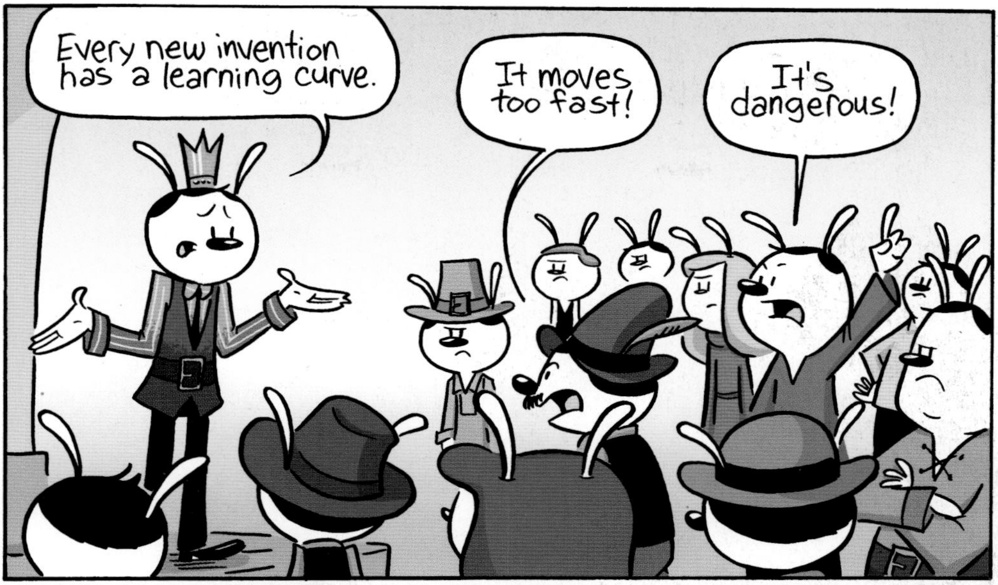
Every new invention has a learning curve.
It moves too fast!
It's dangerous!

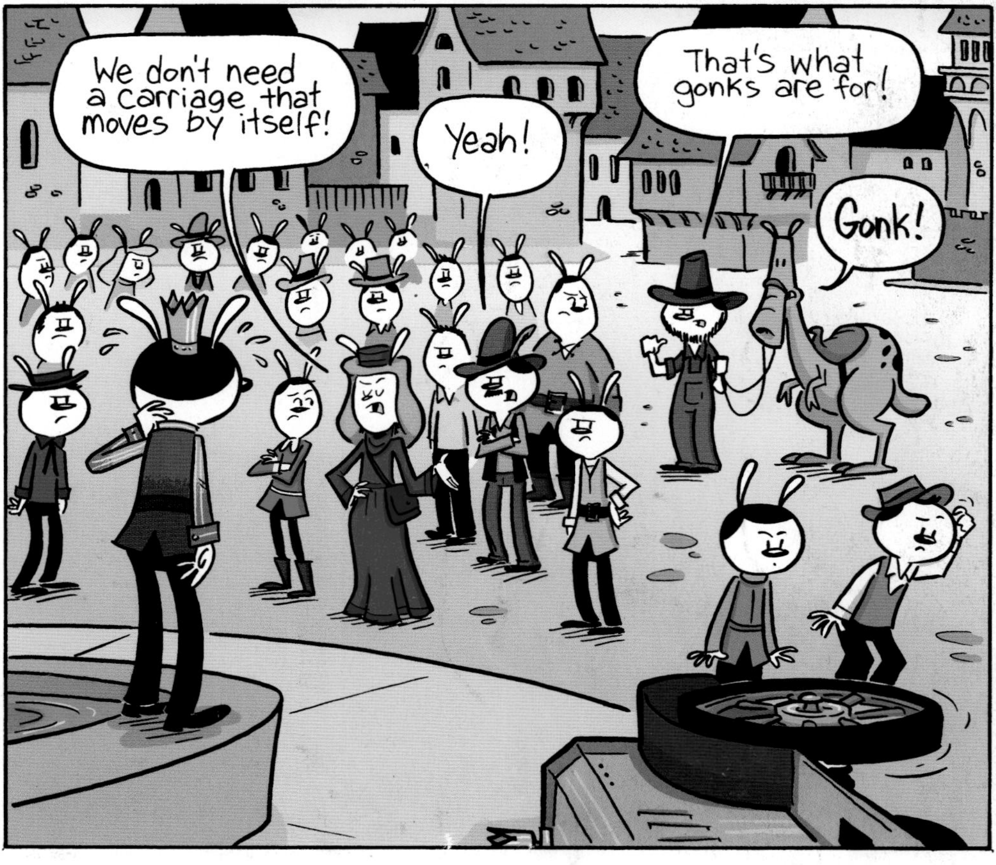
We don't need a carriage that moves by itself!
Yeah!
That's what gonks are for!
Gonk!

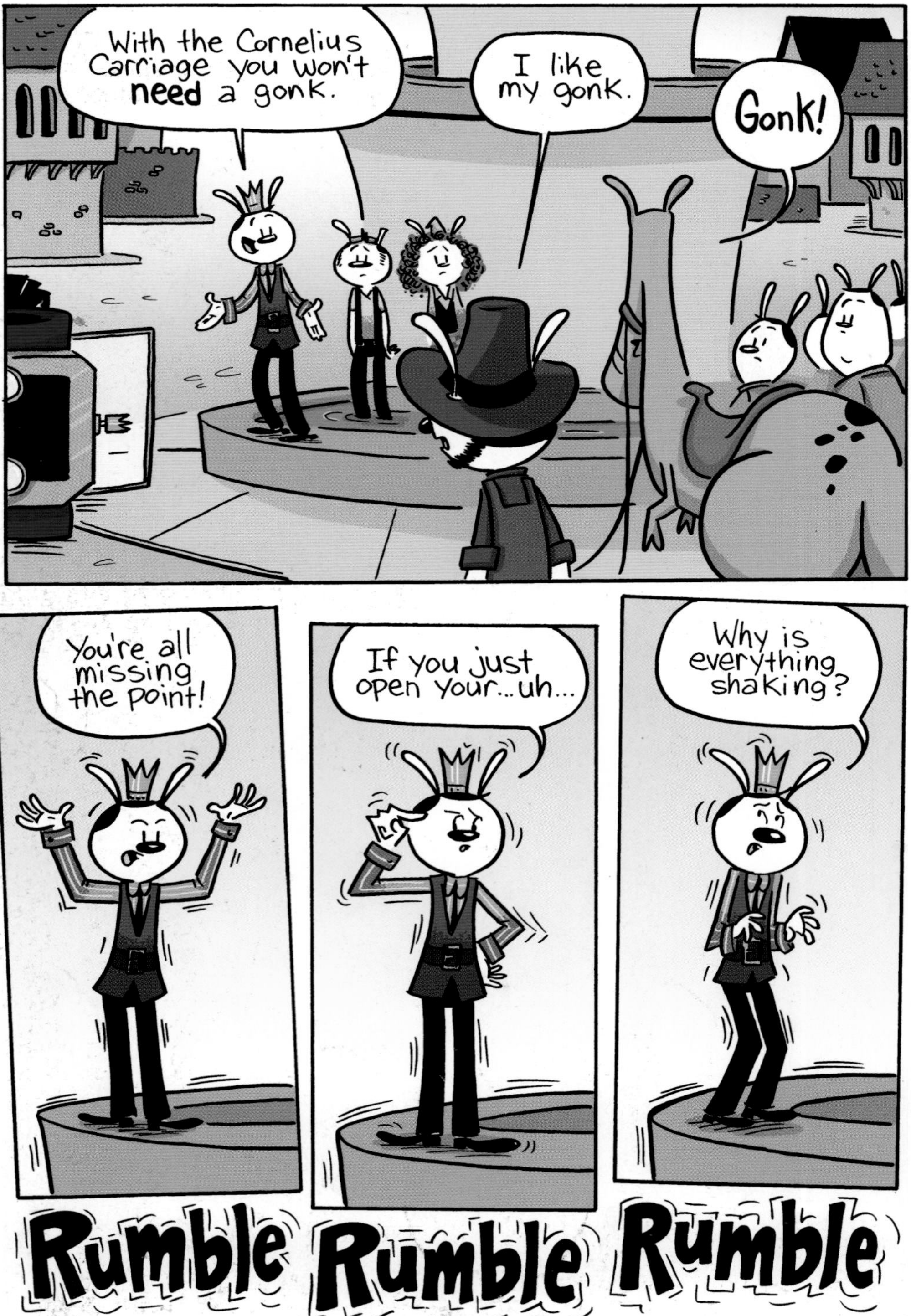
With the Cornelius Carriage you won't **need** a gonk.
I like my gonk.
Gonk!
You're all missing the point!
If you just open your...uh...
Why is everything shaking?
Rumble Rumble Rumble

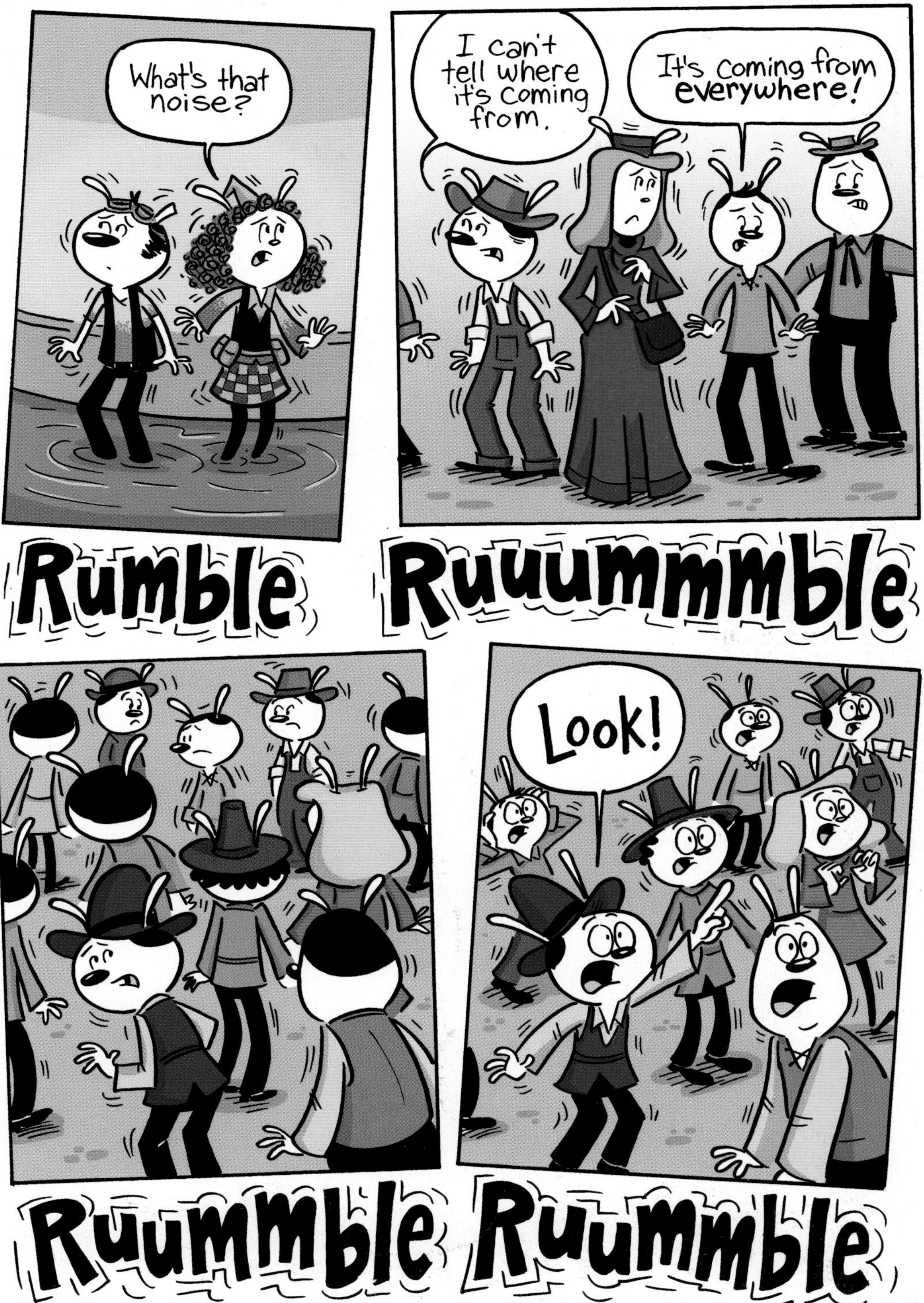
What's that noise?
I can't tell where it's coming from.
It's coming from everywhere!
Rumble
Ruuummmble
Look!
Ruummble
Ruummble

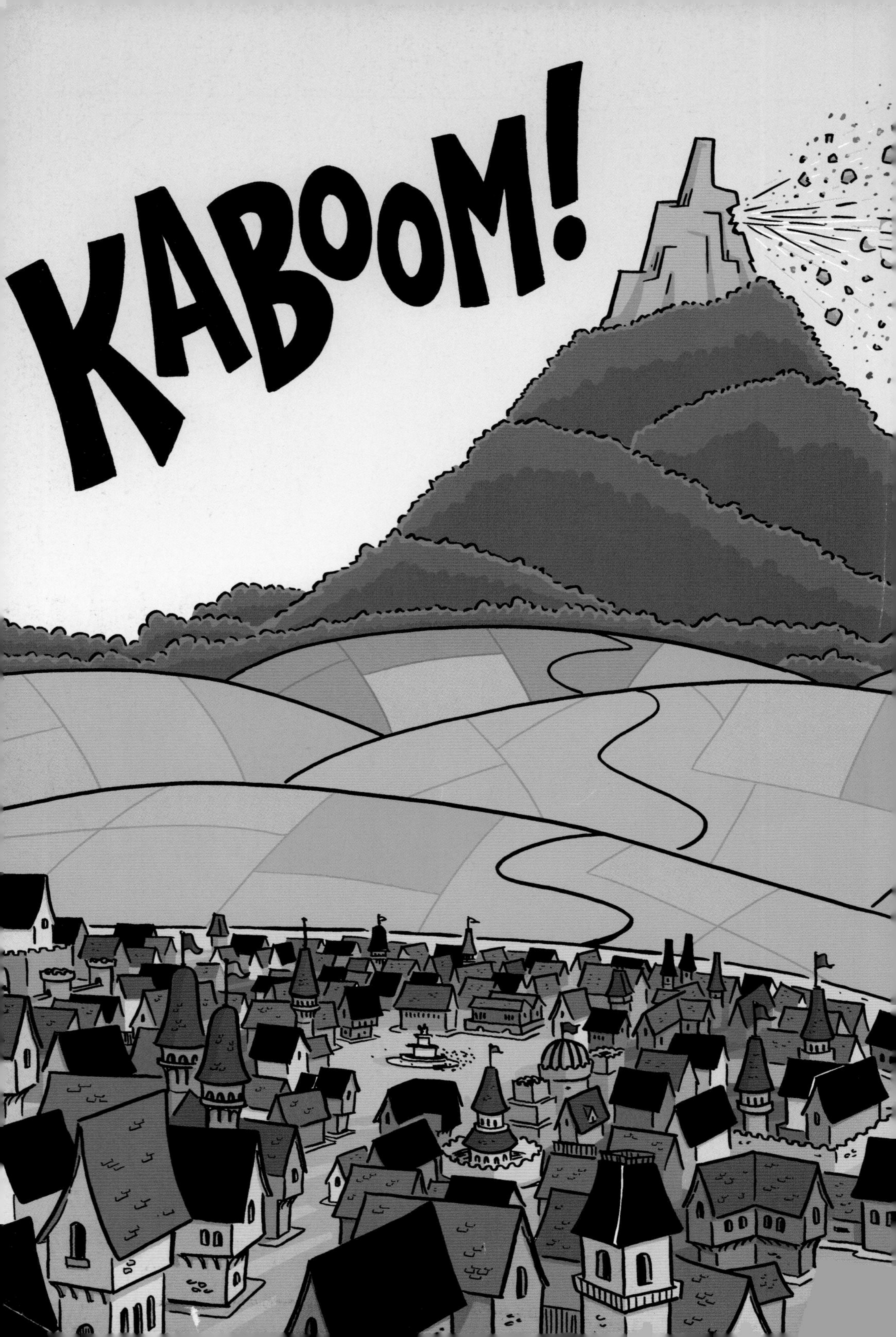
KABOOM!

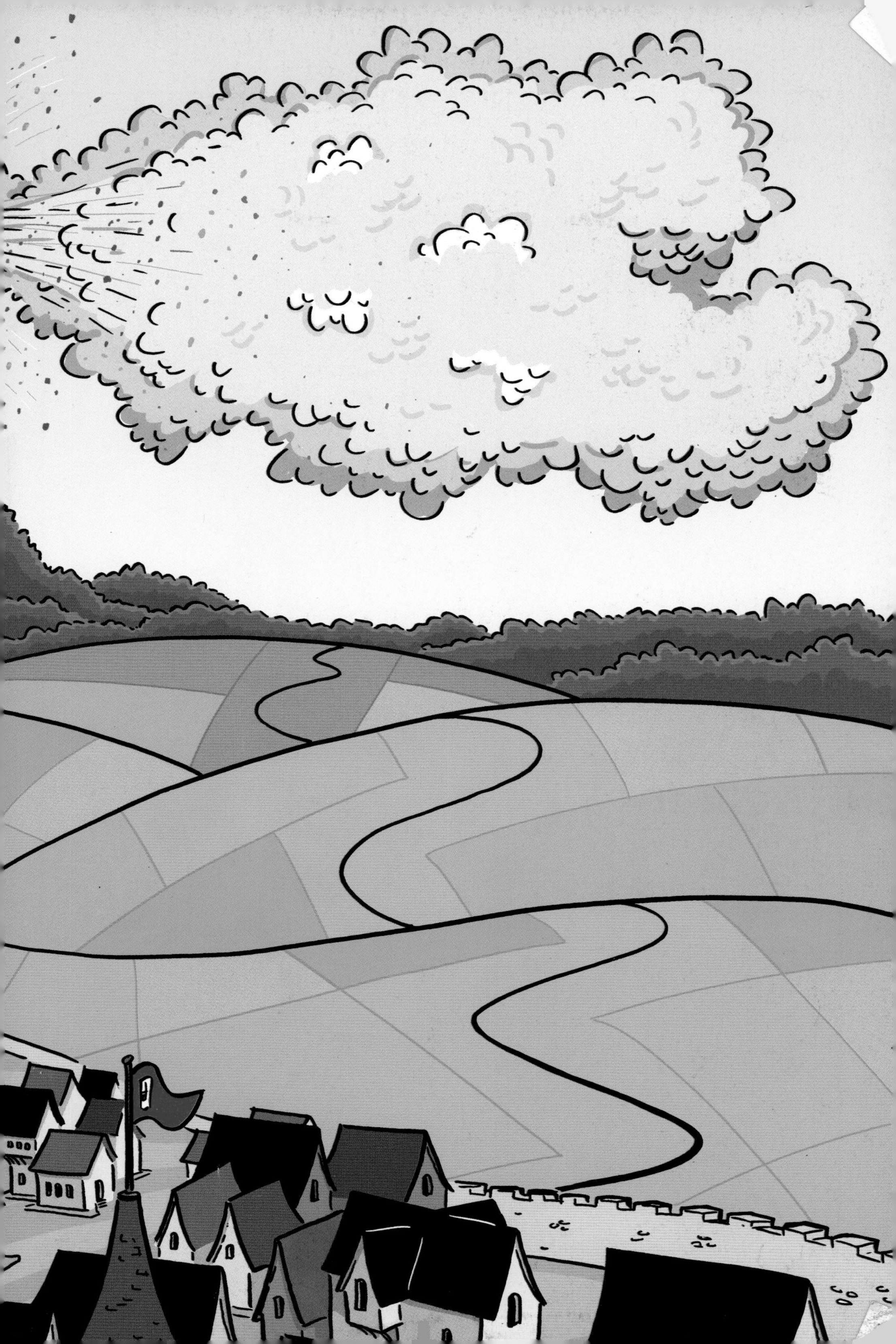

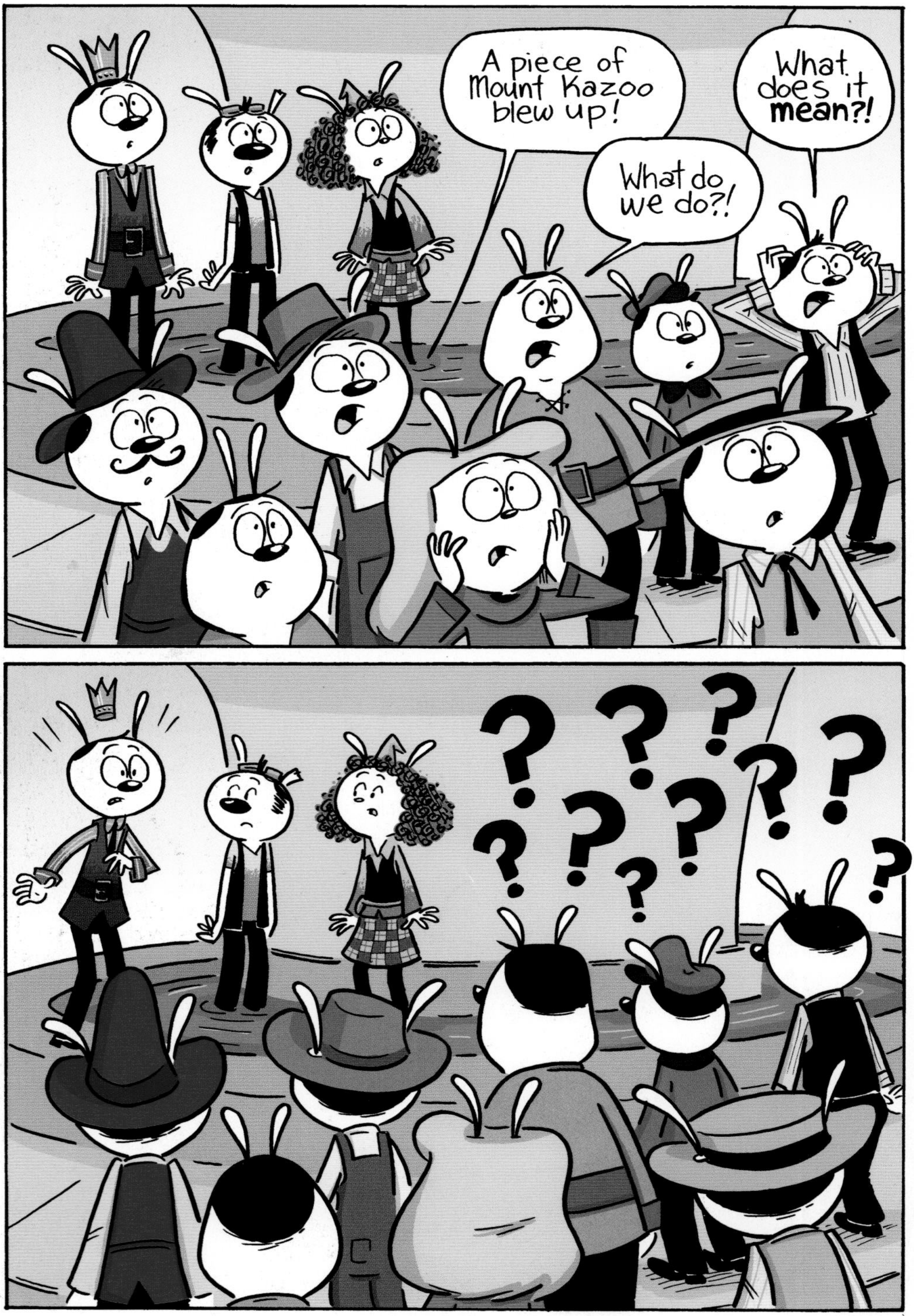
A piece of Mount Kazoo blew up!
What do we do?!
What does it **mean?!**
? ? ? ? ? ? ? ? ? ?

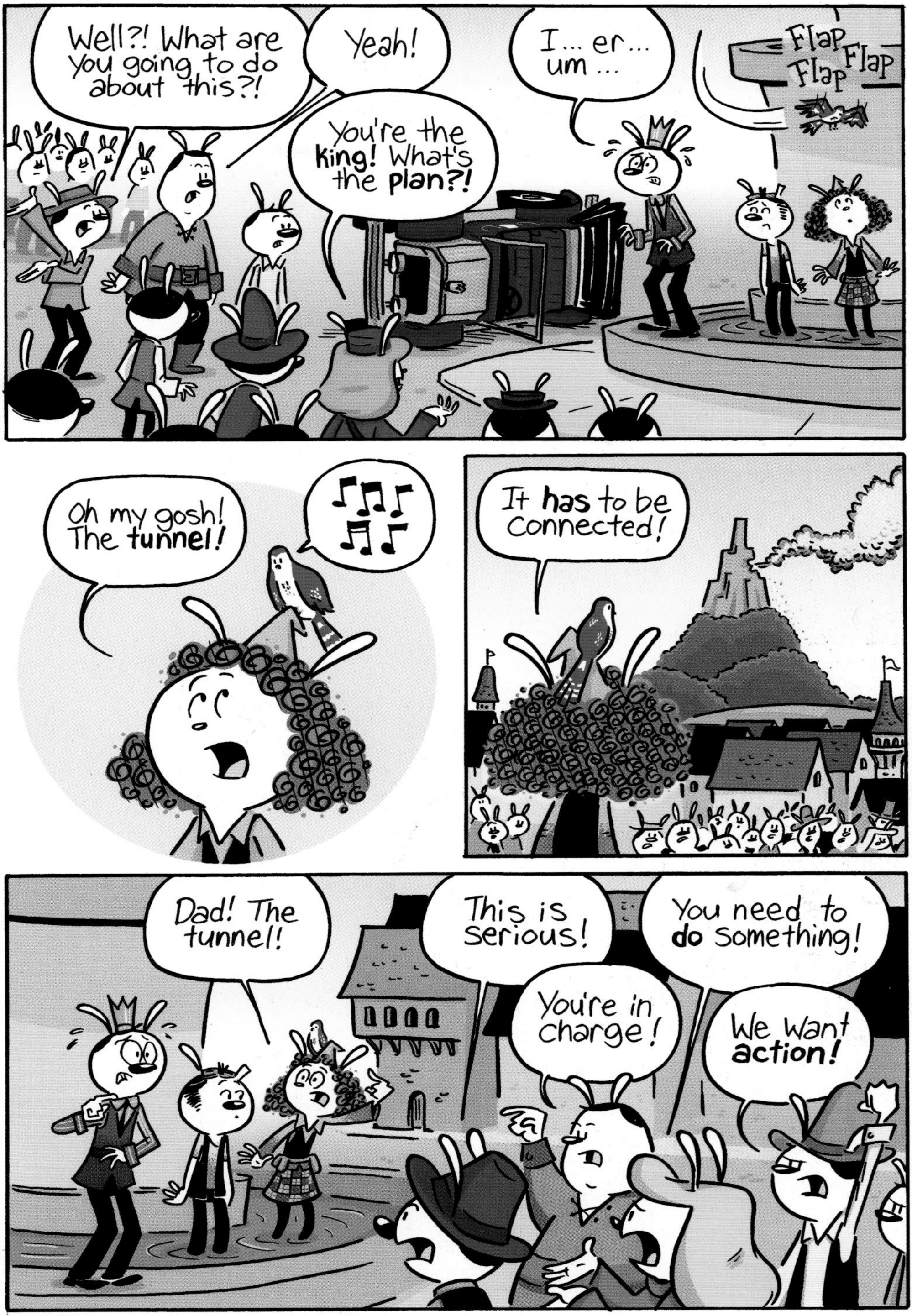
Well?! What are you going to do about this?!
Yeah!
You're the **king!** What's the **plan?!**
I... er... um...
Flap Flap Flap
Oh my gosh! The **tunnel!**
It **has** to be connected!
Dad! The tunnel!
This is serious!
You need to **do** something!
You're in charge!
We want **action!**

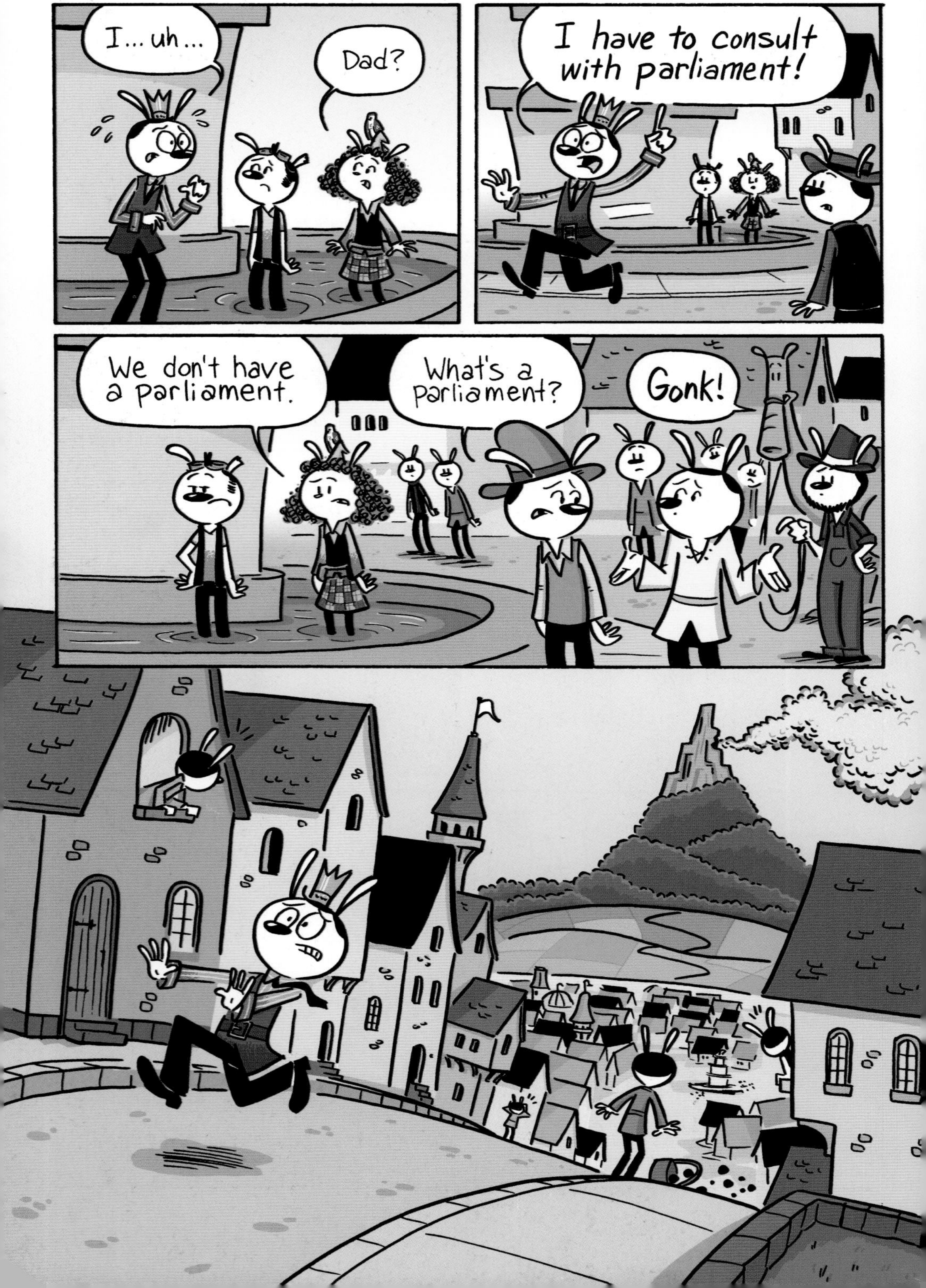
I... uh...
Dad?
I have to consult with parliament!
We don't have a parliament.
What's a parliament?
Gonk!

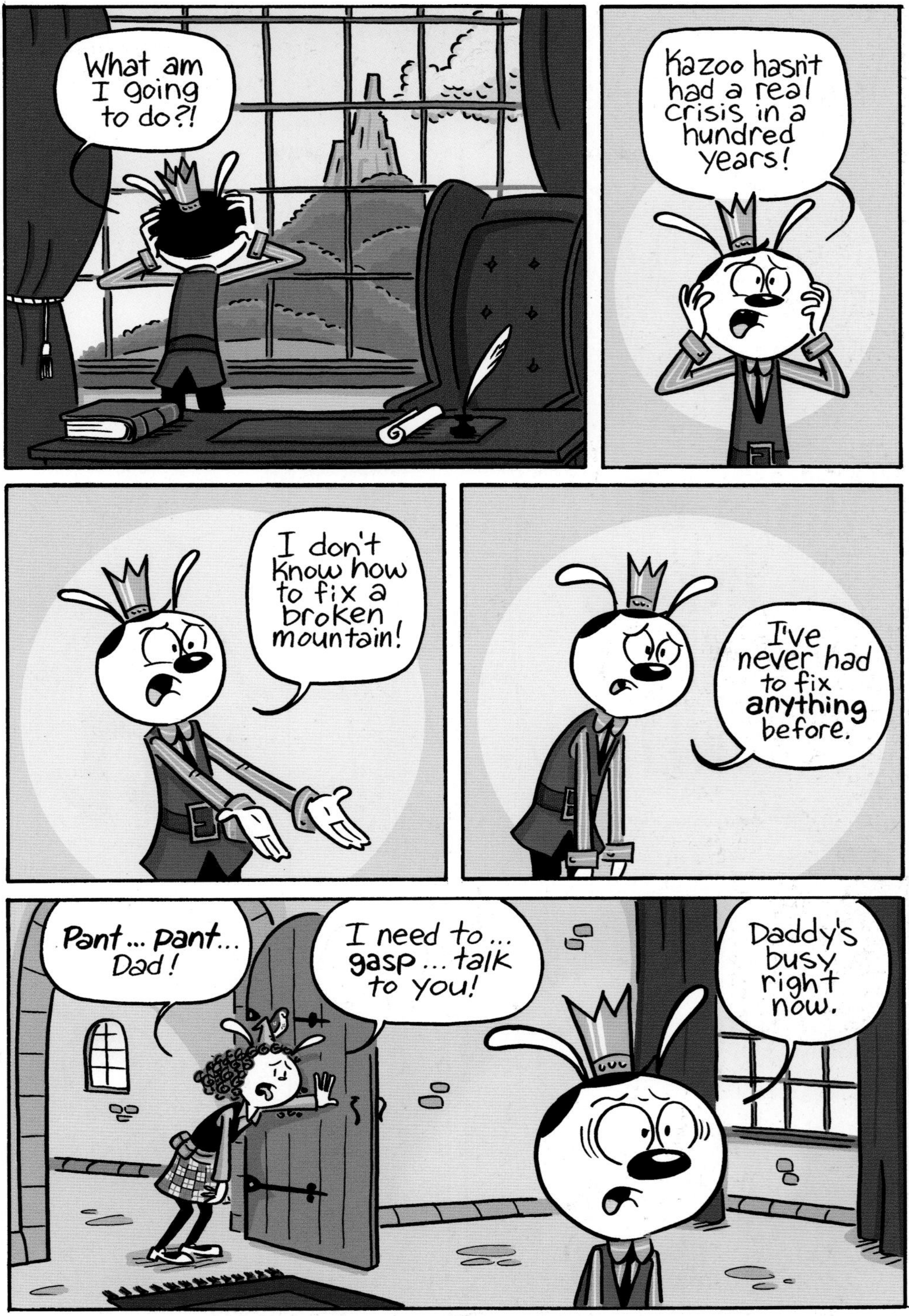
What am I going to do?!
Kazoo hasn't had a real crisis in a hundred years!
I don't know how to fix a broken mountain!
I've never had to fix **anything** before.
Pant ... **pant** ... Dad!
I need to ... **gasp** ... talk to you!
Daddy's busy right now.

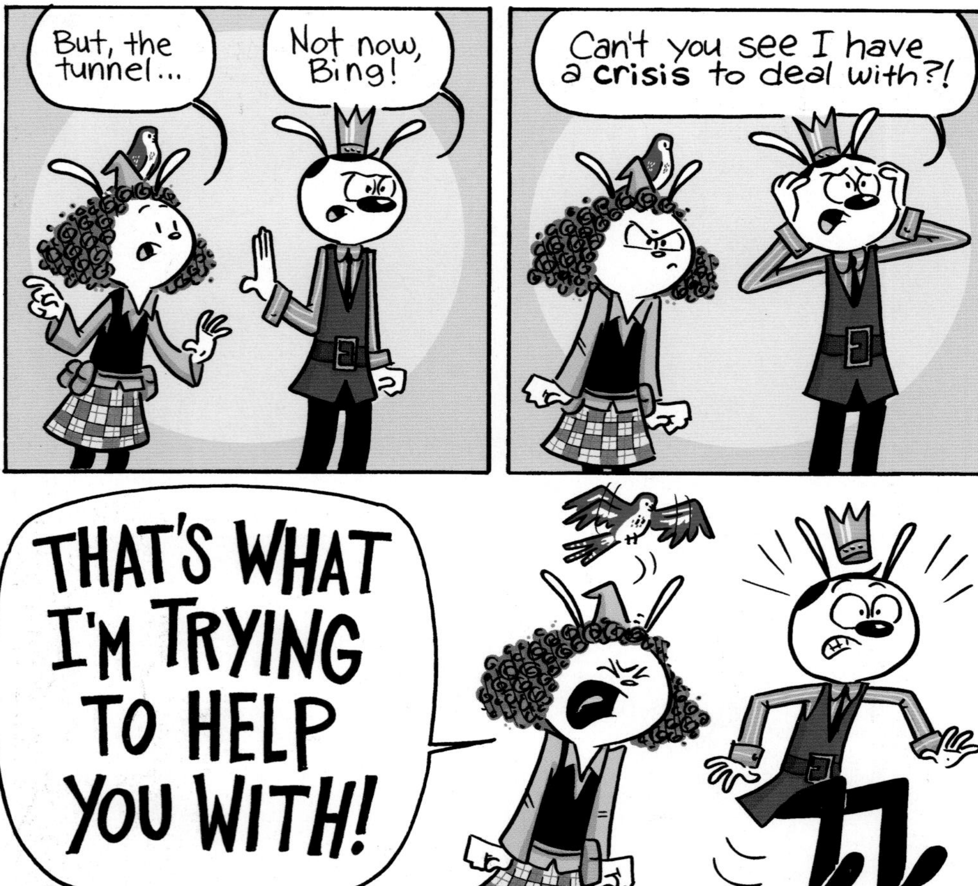
But, the tunnel...
Not now, Bing!
Can't you see I have a **crisis** to deal with?!
THAT'S WHAT I'M TRYING TO HELP YOU WITH!
Sorry.
You have my attention. Make it quick.
Finally.

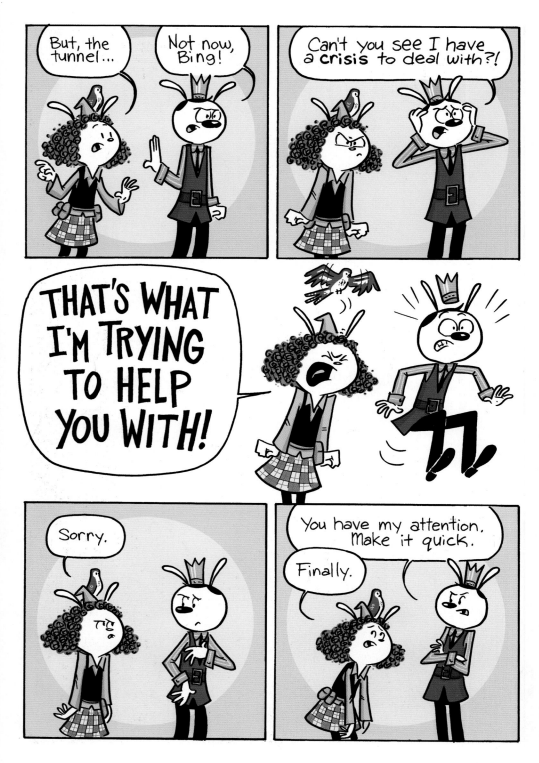

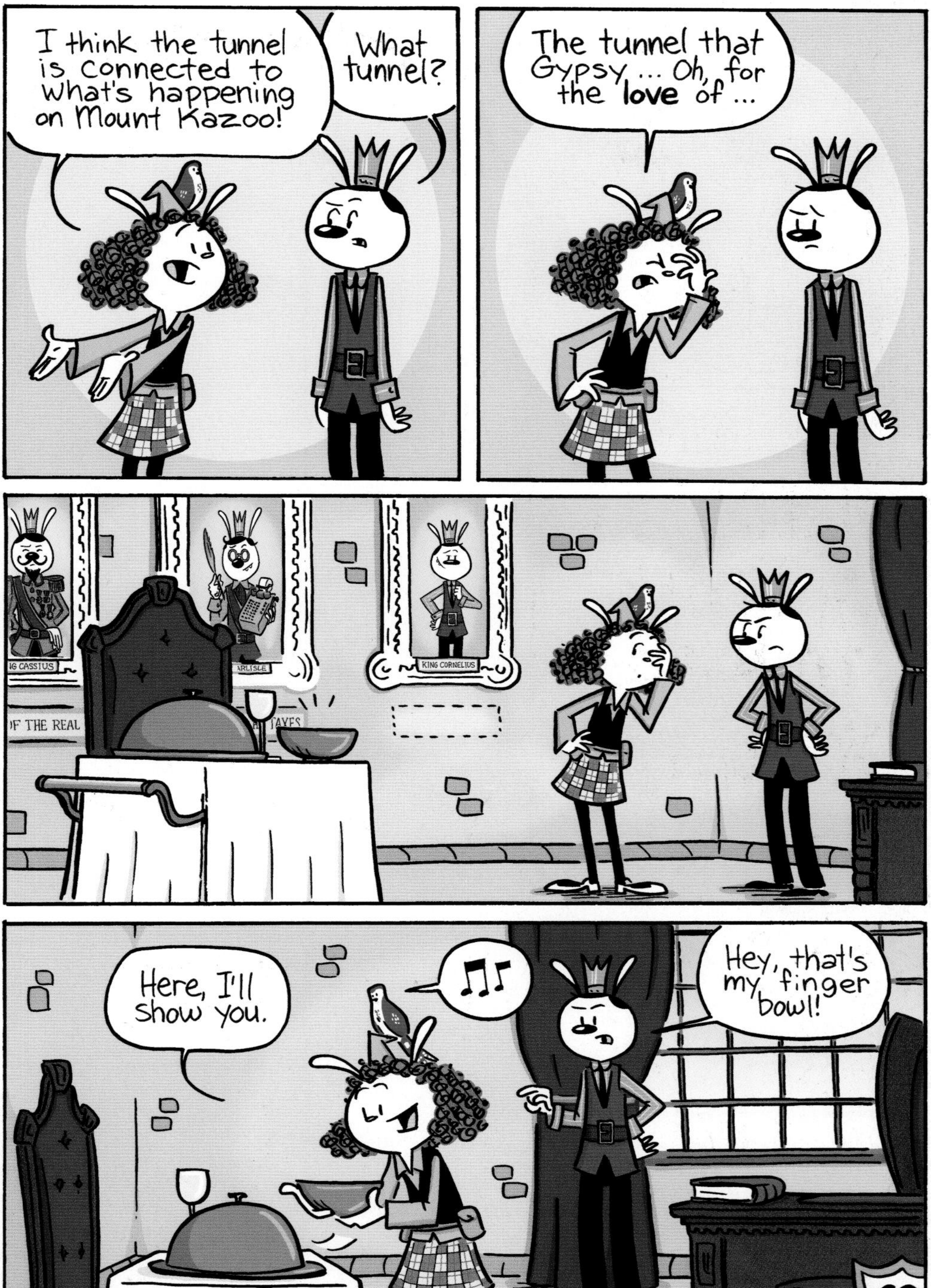
I think the tunnel is connected to what's happening on Mount Kazoo!
What tunnel?
The tunnel that Gypsy ... Oh, for the **love** of ...
KING CORNELIUS
Here, I'll show you.
Hey, that's my finger bowl!

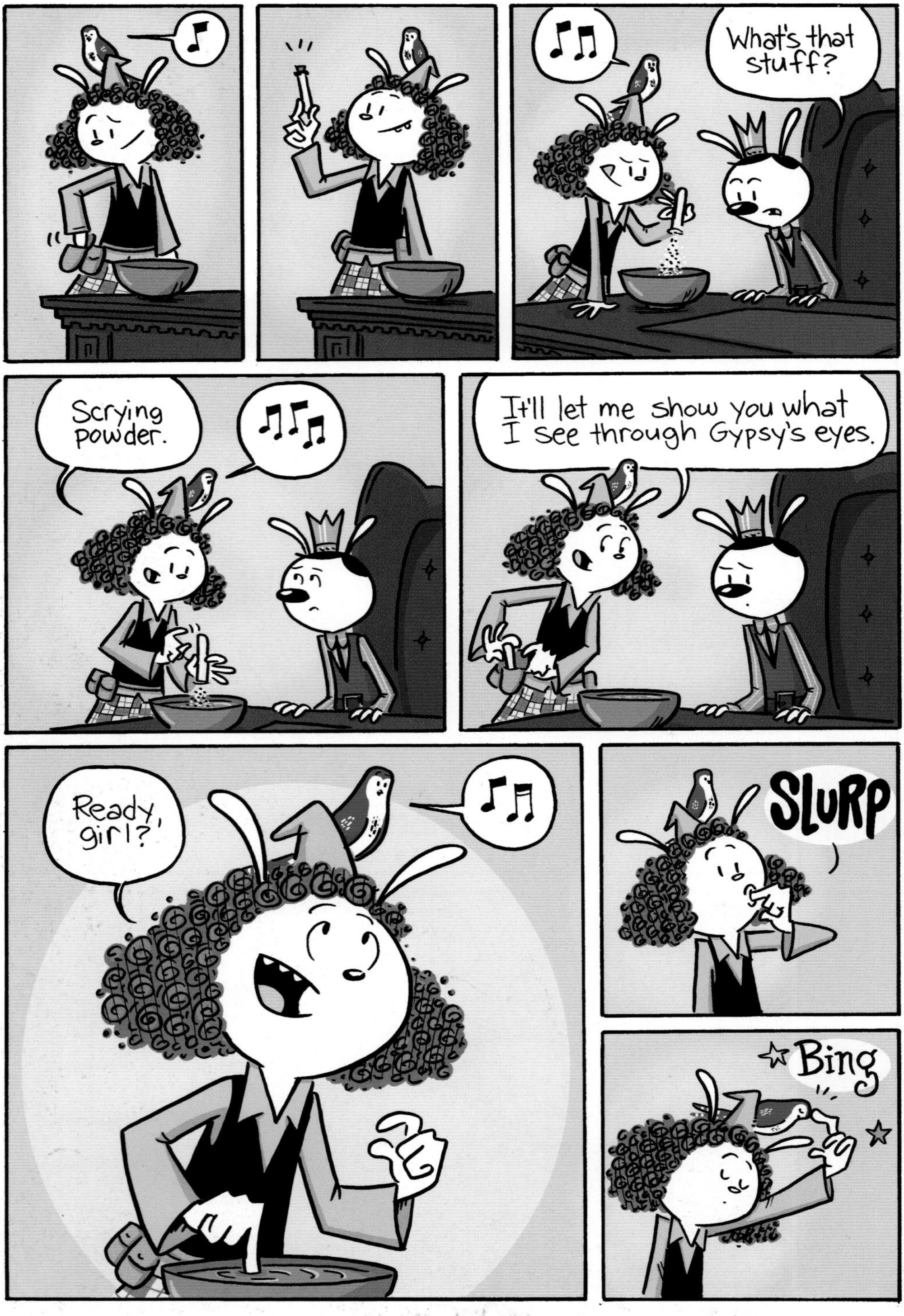
What's that stuff?
Scrying powder.
It'll let me show you what I see through Gypsy's eyes.
Ready, girl?
SLURP
Bing

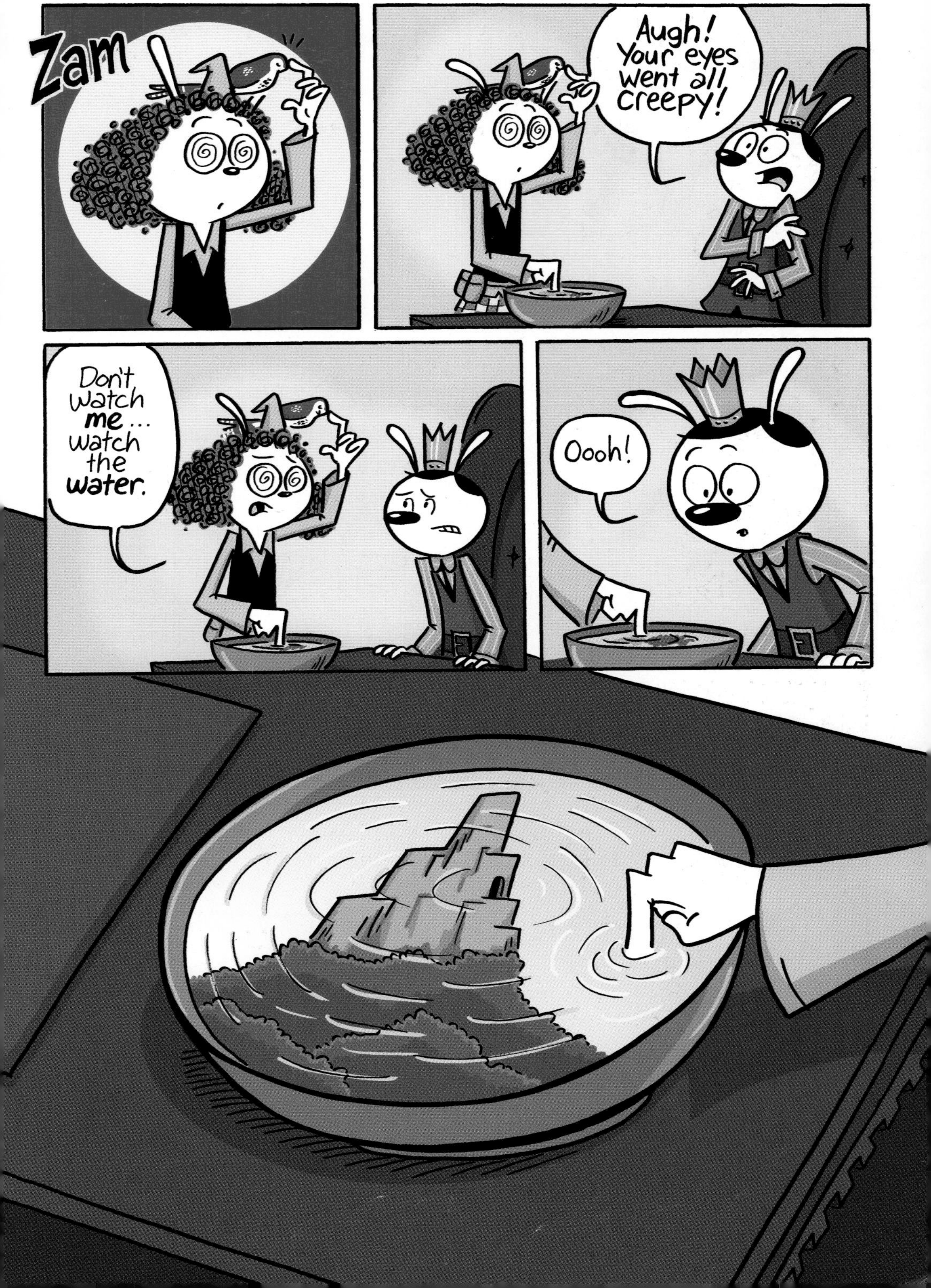
Zam
Augh! Your eyes went all creepy!
Don't watch **me**... watch the **water**.
Oooh!

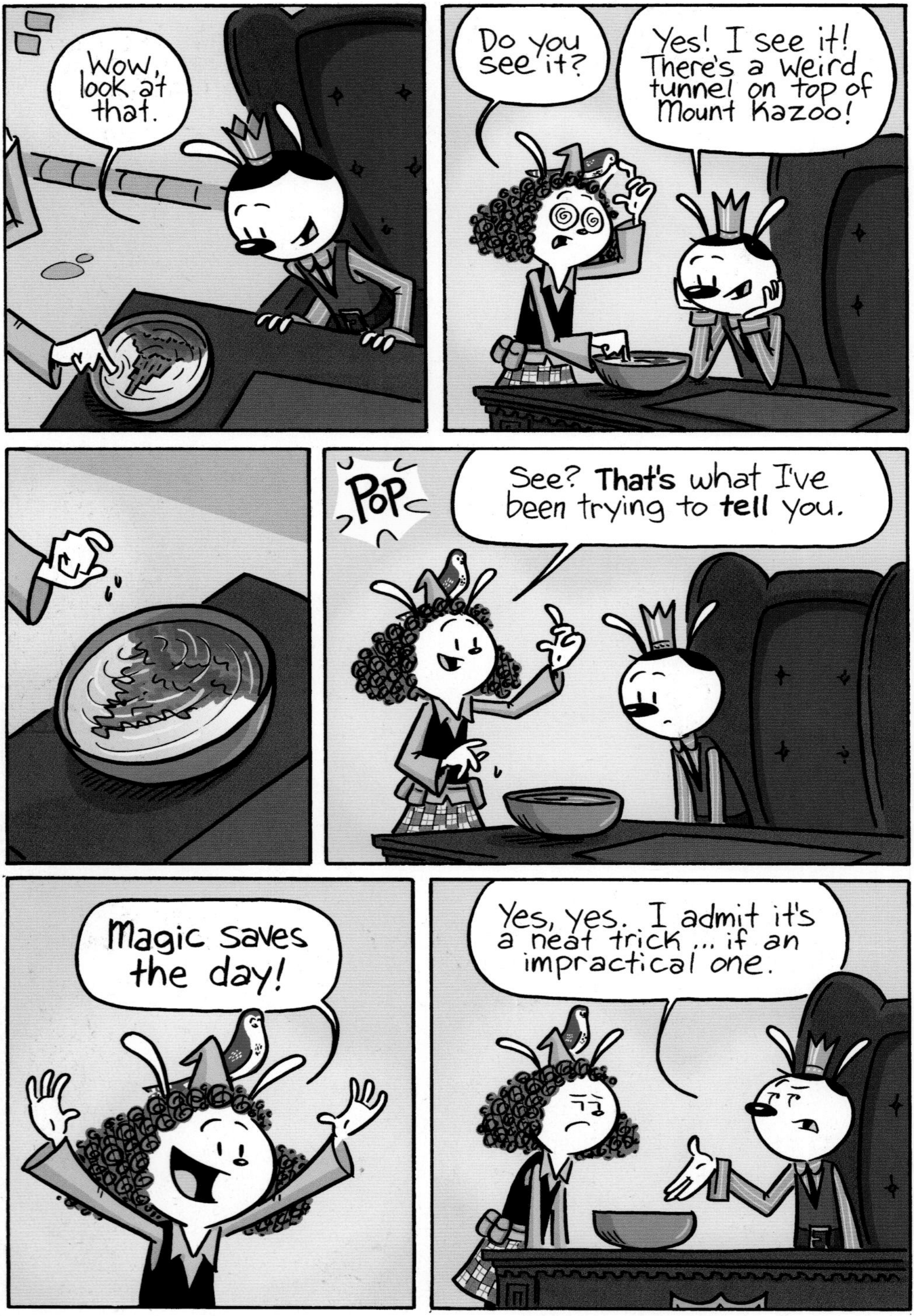
Wow, look at that.
Do you see it?
Yes! I see it! There's a weird tunnel on top of Mount Kazoo!
POP
See? That's what I've been trying to tell you.
Magic saves the day!
Yes, yes. I admit it's a neat trick ... if an impractical one.

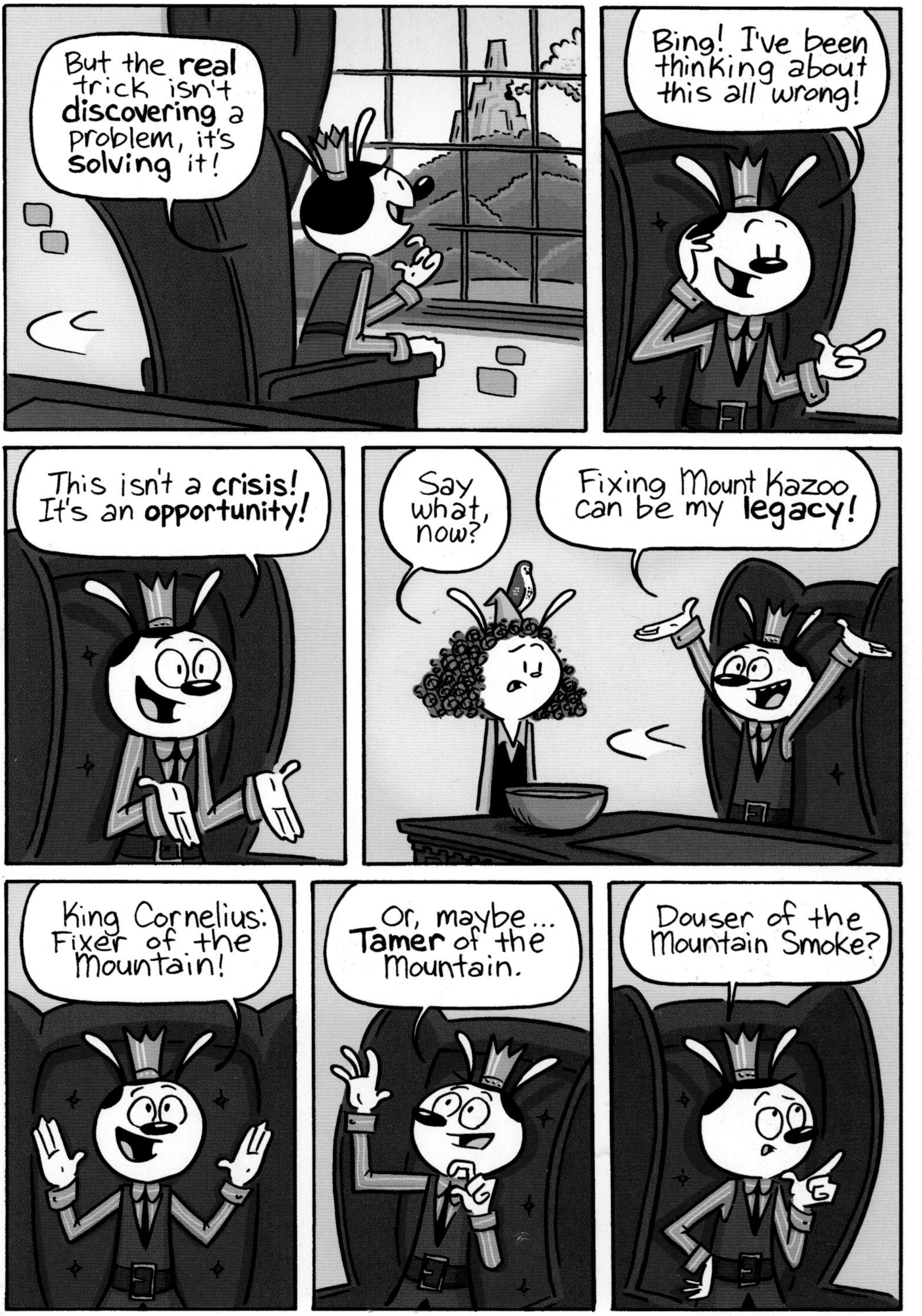
But the **real** trick isn't **discovering** a problem, it's **solving** it!
Bing! I've been thinking about this all wrong!
This isn't a **crisis**! It's an **opportunity**!
Say what, now?
Fixing Mount Kazoo can be my **legacy**!
King Cornelius: Fixer of the Mountain!
Or, maybe... **Tamer** of the Mountain.
Douser of the Mountain Smoke?

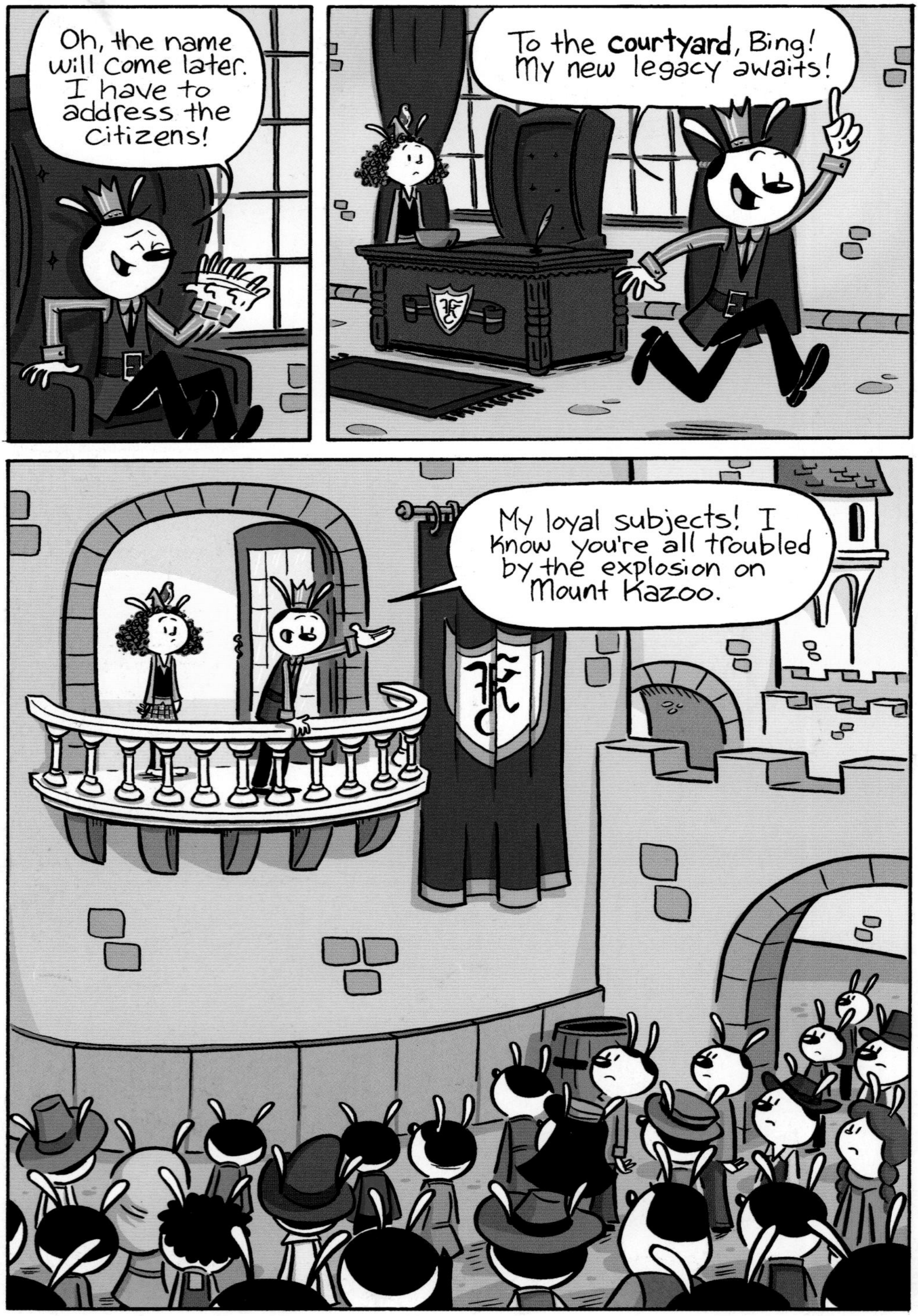
Oh, the name will come later. I have to address the citizens!
To the **courtyard**, Bing! My new legacy awaits!
My loyal subjects! I know you're all troubled by the explosion on Mount Kazoo.

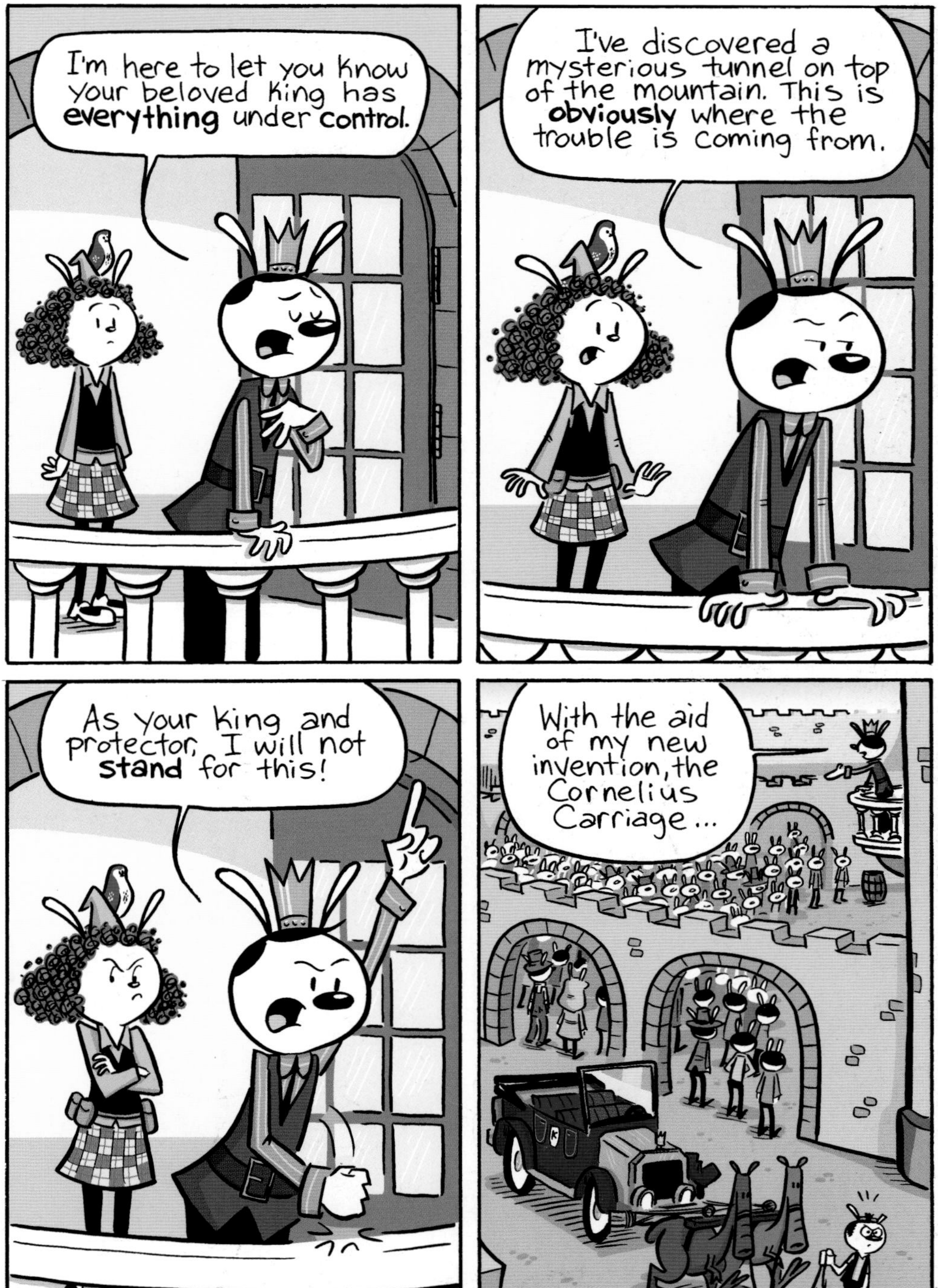
I'm here to let you know your beloved King has **everything** under **control**.
I've discovered a mysterious tunnel on top of the mountain. This is **obviously** where the trouble is coming from.
As your King and protector, I will not **stand** for this!
With the aid of my new invention, the Cornelius Carriage...

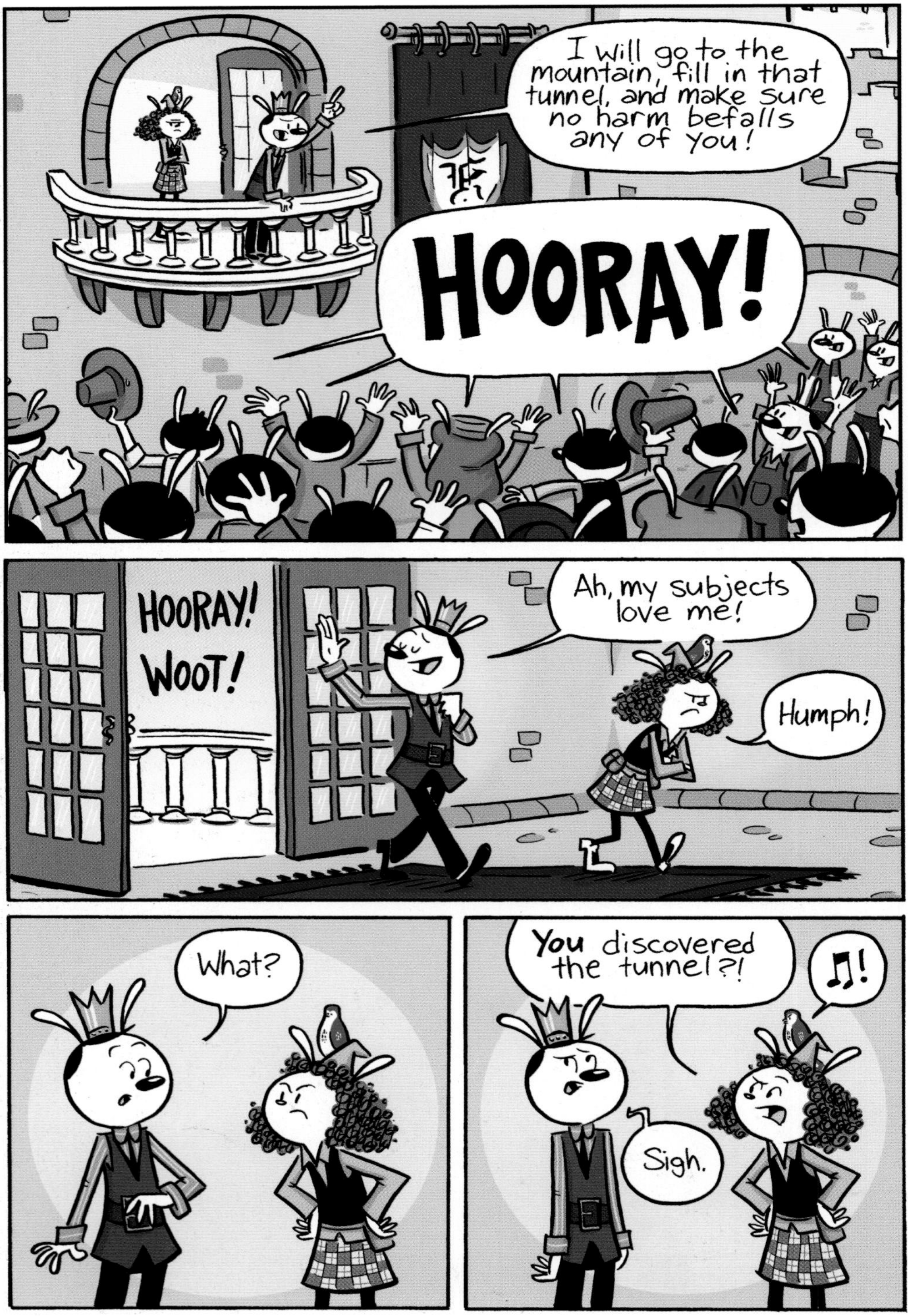
I will go to the mountain, fill in that tunnel, and make sure no harm befalls any of you!
HOORAY!
HOORAY!
WOOT!
Ah, my subjects love me!
Humph!
What?
You discovered the tunnel?!
♫!
Sigh.

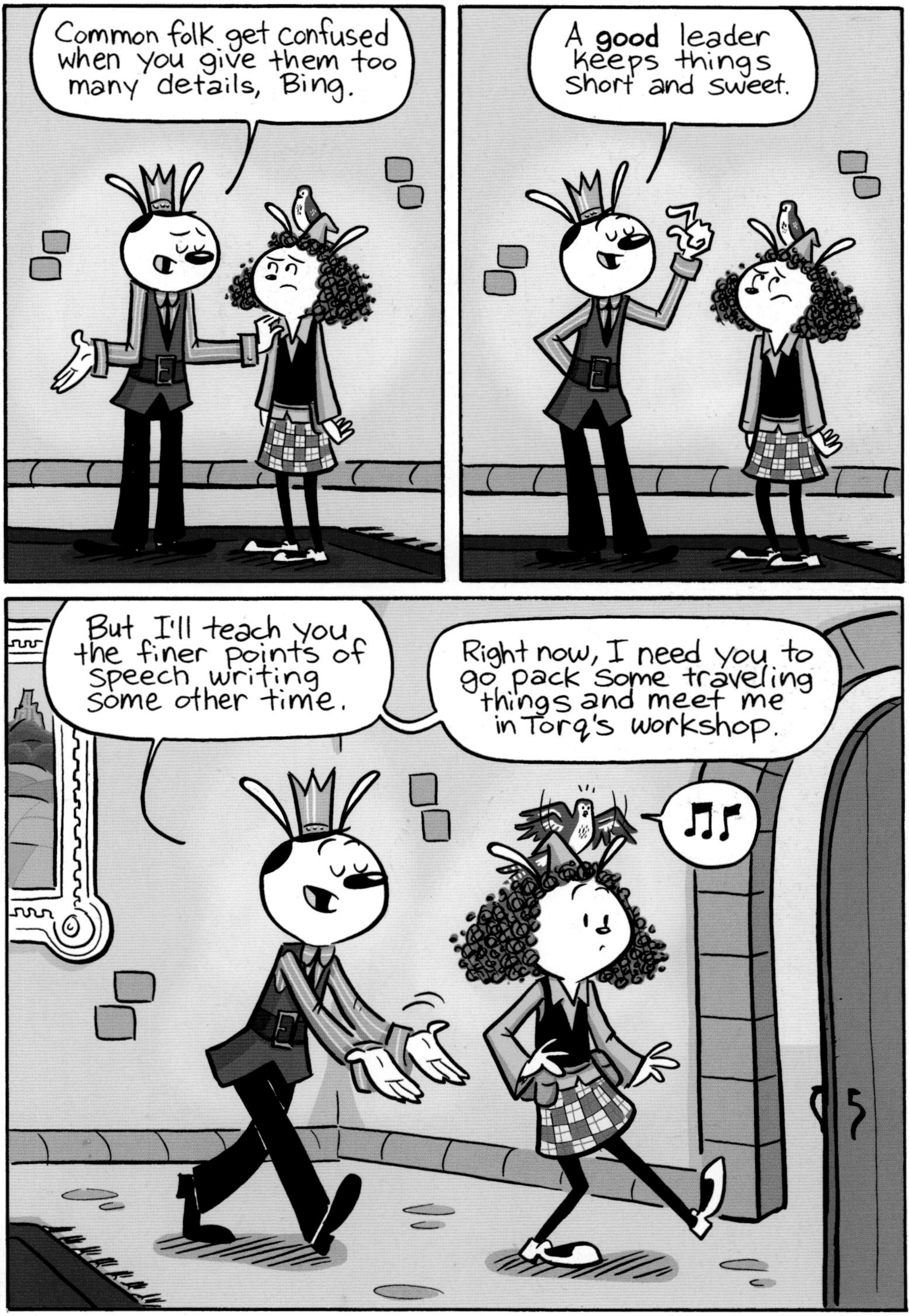
Common folk get confused when you give them too many details, Bing.
A good leader keeps things short and sweet.
But I'll teach you the finer points of speech writing some other time.
Right now, I need you to go pack some traveling things and meet me in Torq's workshop.
♫♪

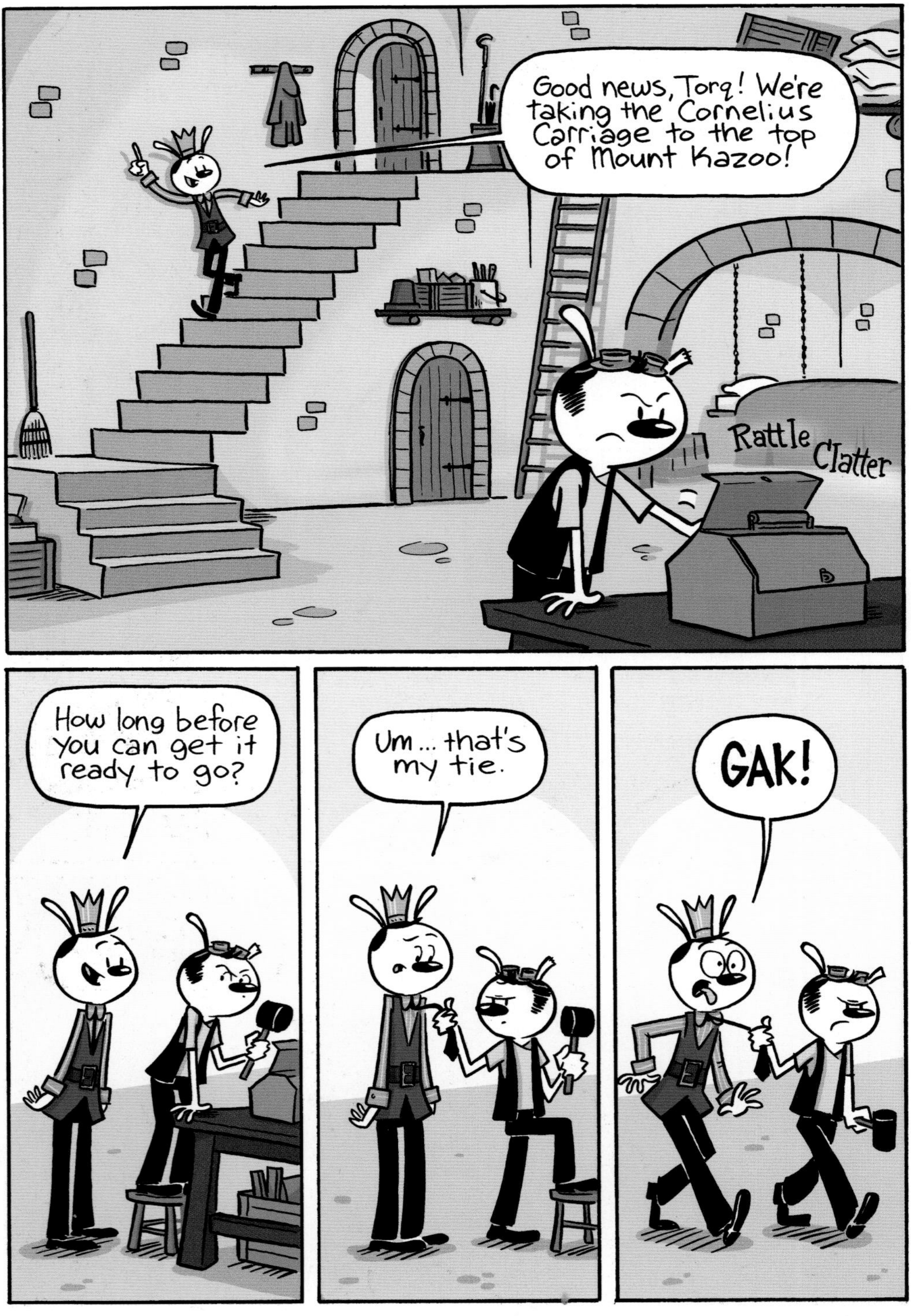
Good news, Torq! We're taking the Cornelius Carriage to the top of Mount Kazoo!
Rattle
Clatter
How long before you can get it ready to go?
Um... that's my tie.
GAK!

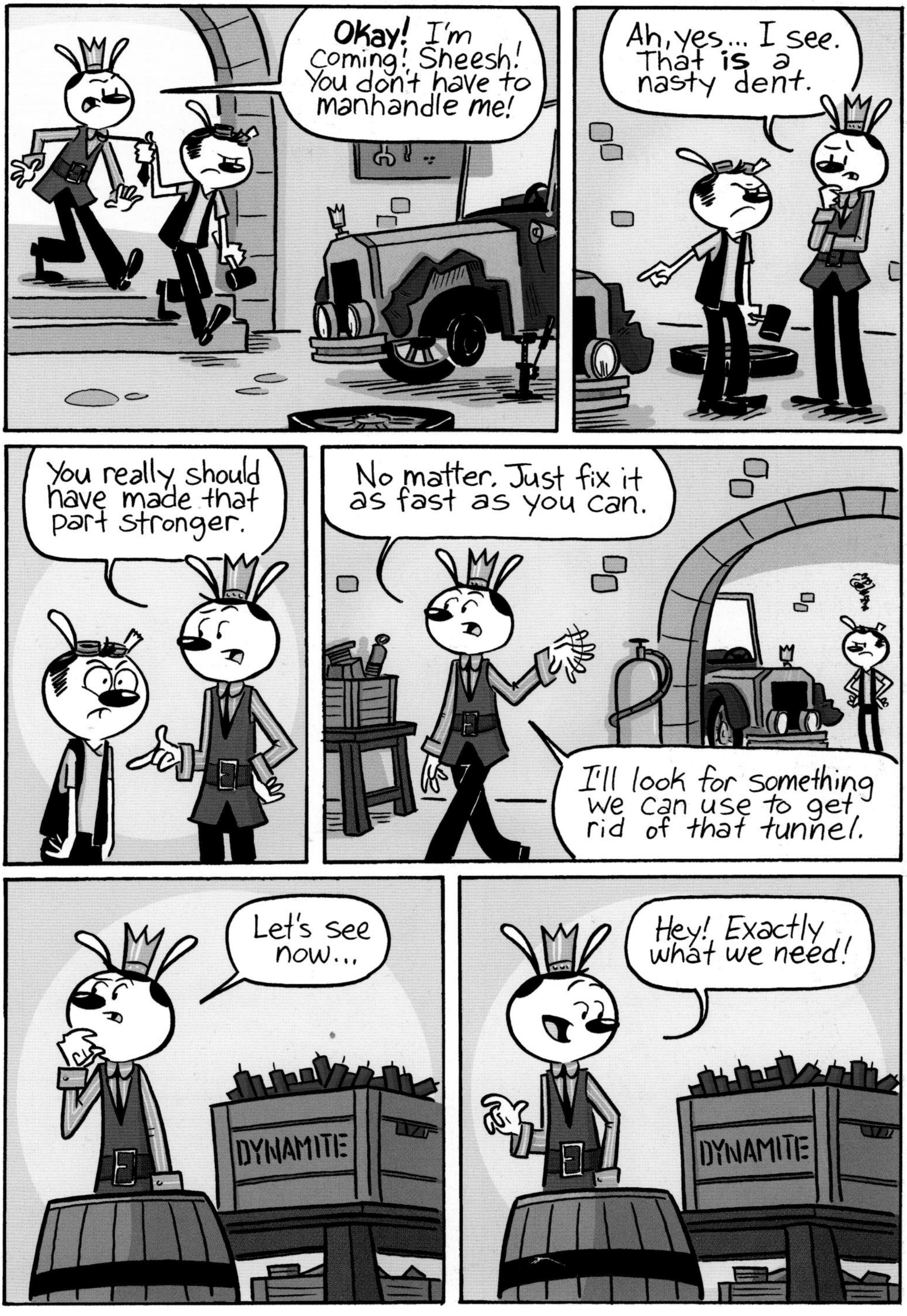
Okay! I'm coming! Sheesh! You don't have to manhandle me!
Ah, yes... I see. That is a nasty dent.
You really should have made that part stronger.
No matter. Just fix it as fast as you can.
I'll look for something we can use to get rid of that tunnel.
Let's see now...
DYNAMITE
Hey! Exactly what we need!
DYNAMITE

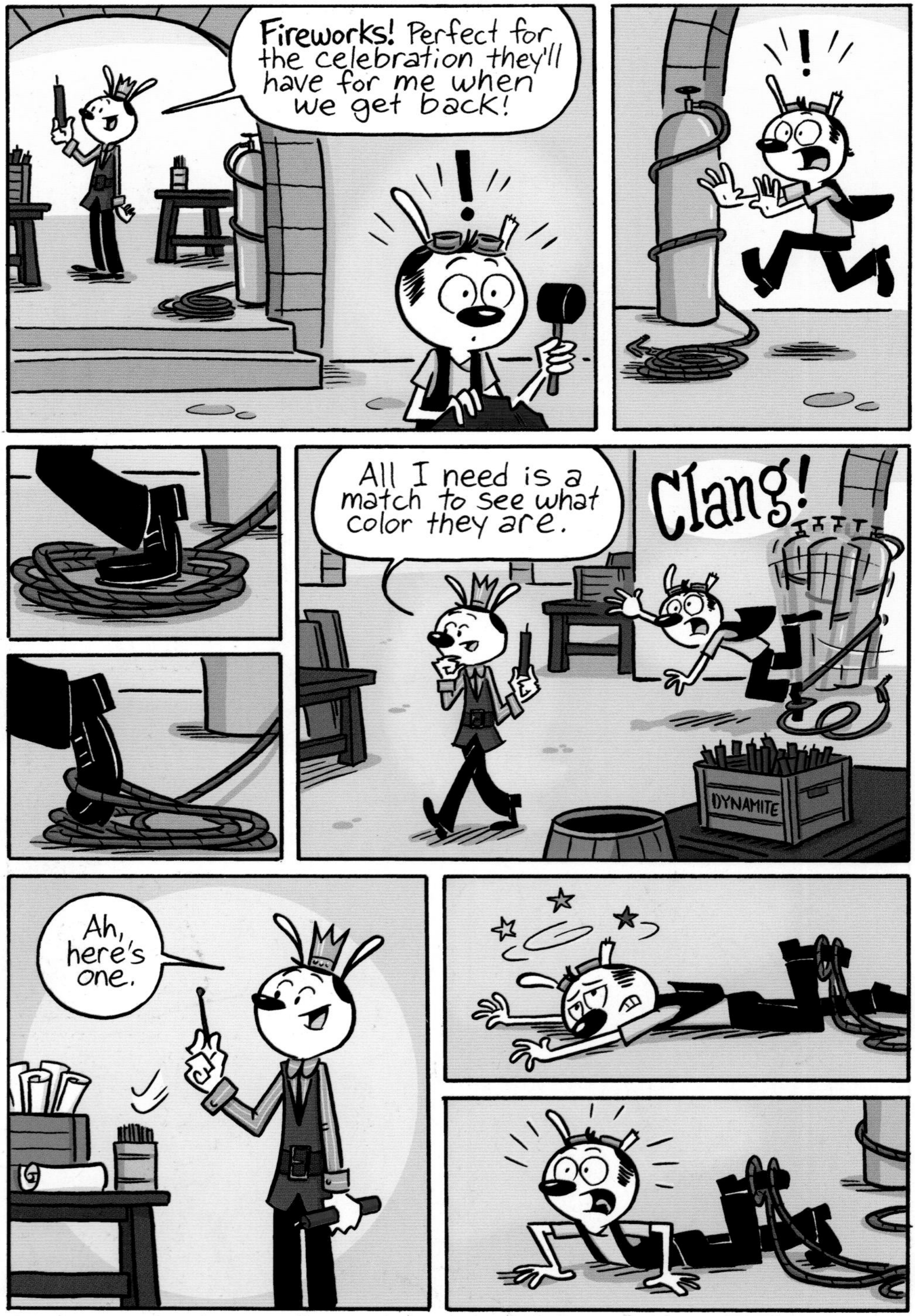

Fireworks! Perfect for the celebration they'll have for me when we get back!
!
!
All I need is a match to see what color they are.
Clang!
DYNAMITE
Ah, here's one.

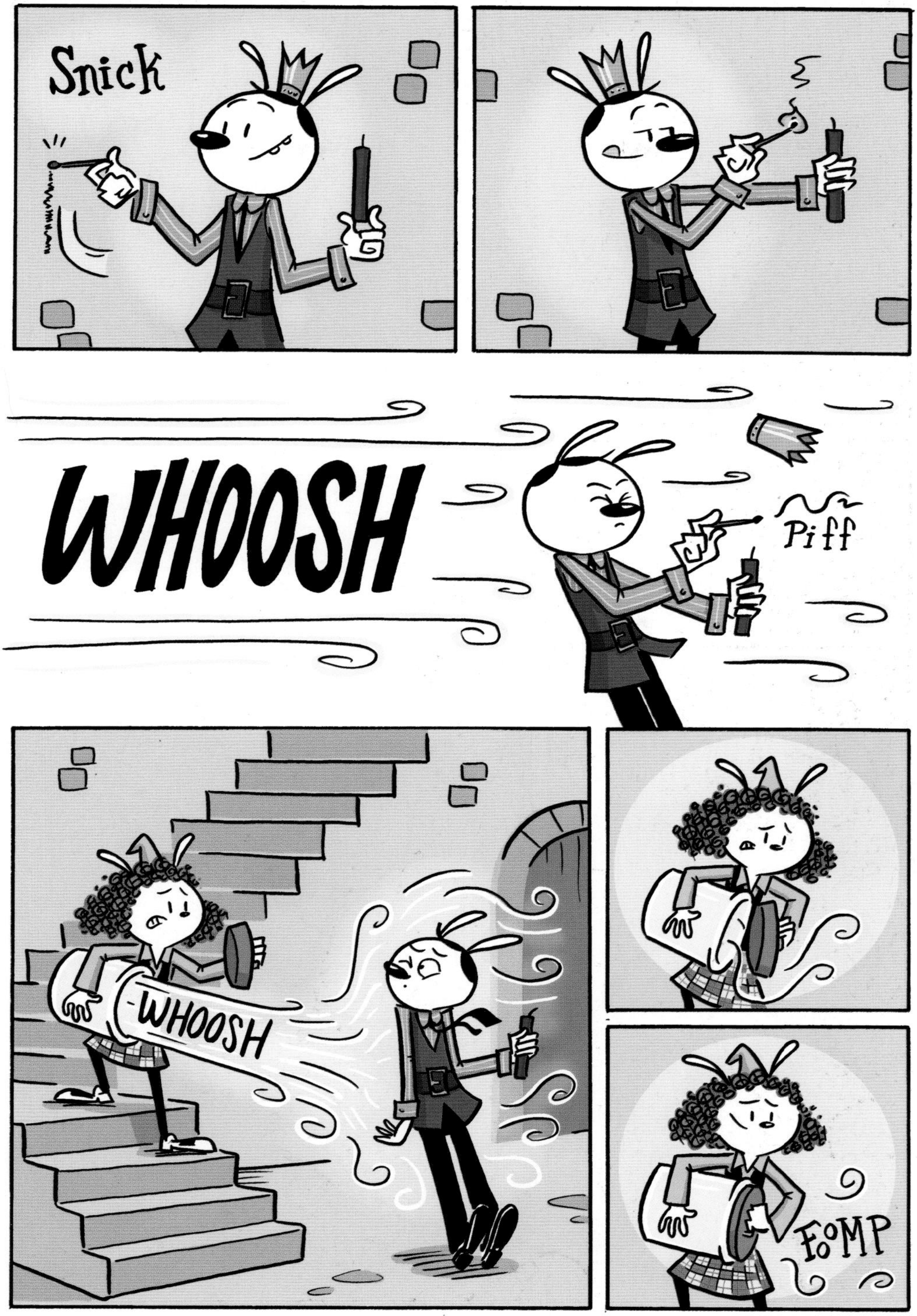
Snick
WHOOSH
Piff
WHOOSH
FOOMP

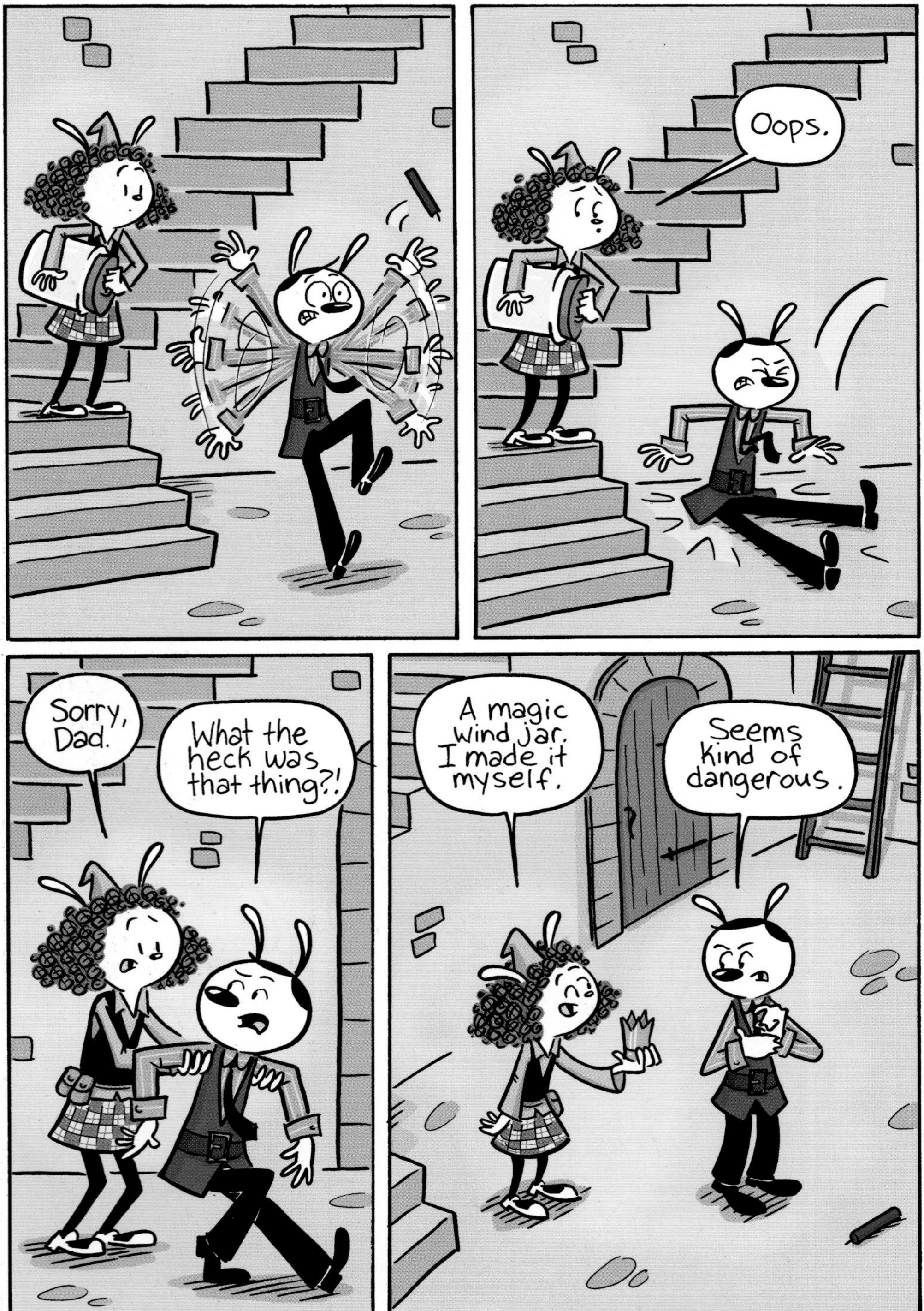
Oops.
Sorry, Dad.
What the heck was that thing?!
A magic wind jar. I made it myself.
Seems kind of dangerous.

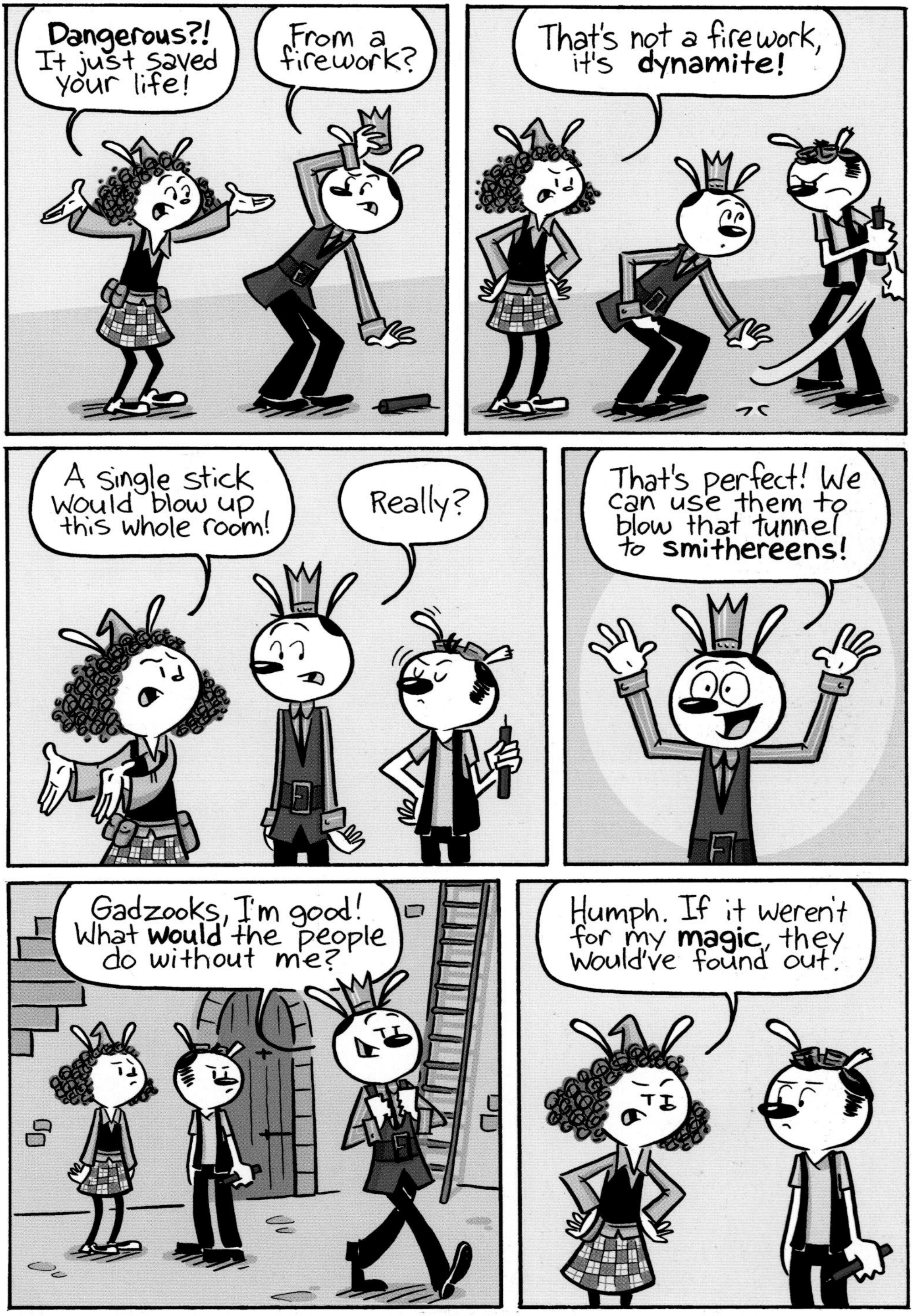

Dangerous?! It just saved your life!
From a firework?
That's not a firework, it's **dynamite!**
A single stick would blow up this whole room!
Really?
That's perfect! We can use them to blow that tunnel to **smithereens!**
Gadzooks, I'm good! What **would** the people do without me?
Humph. If it weren't for my **magic**, they would've found out.

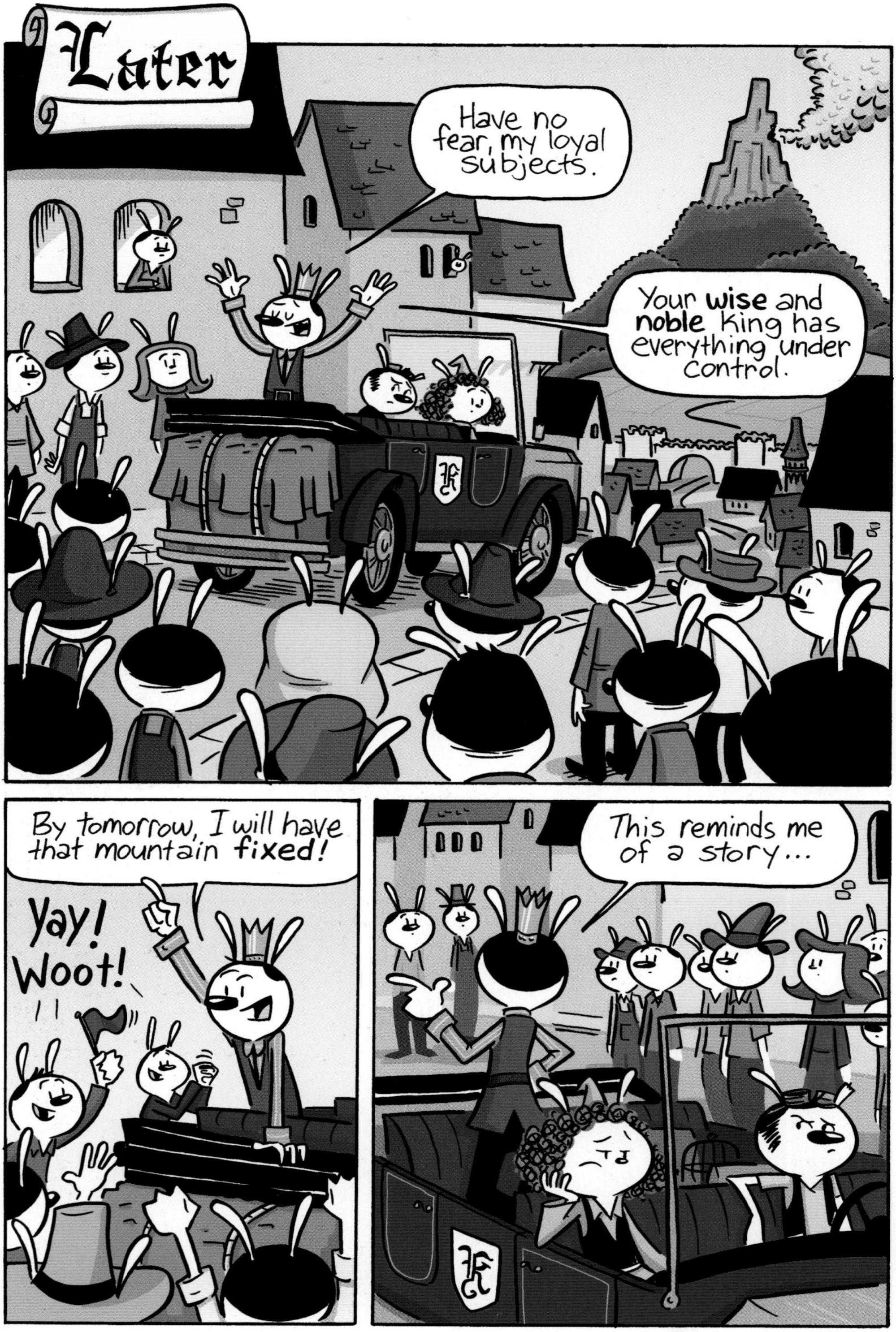
Later
Have no fear, my loyal subjects.
Your wise and noble King has everything under control.
By tomorrow, I will have that mountain fixed!
Yay!
Woot!
This reminds me of a story...

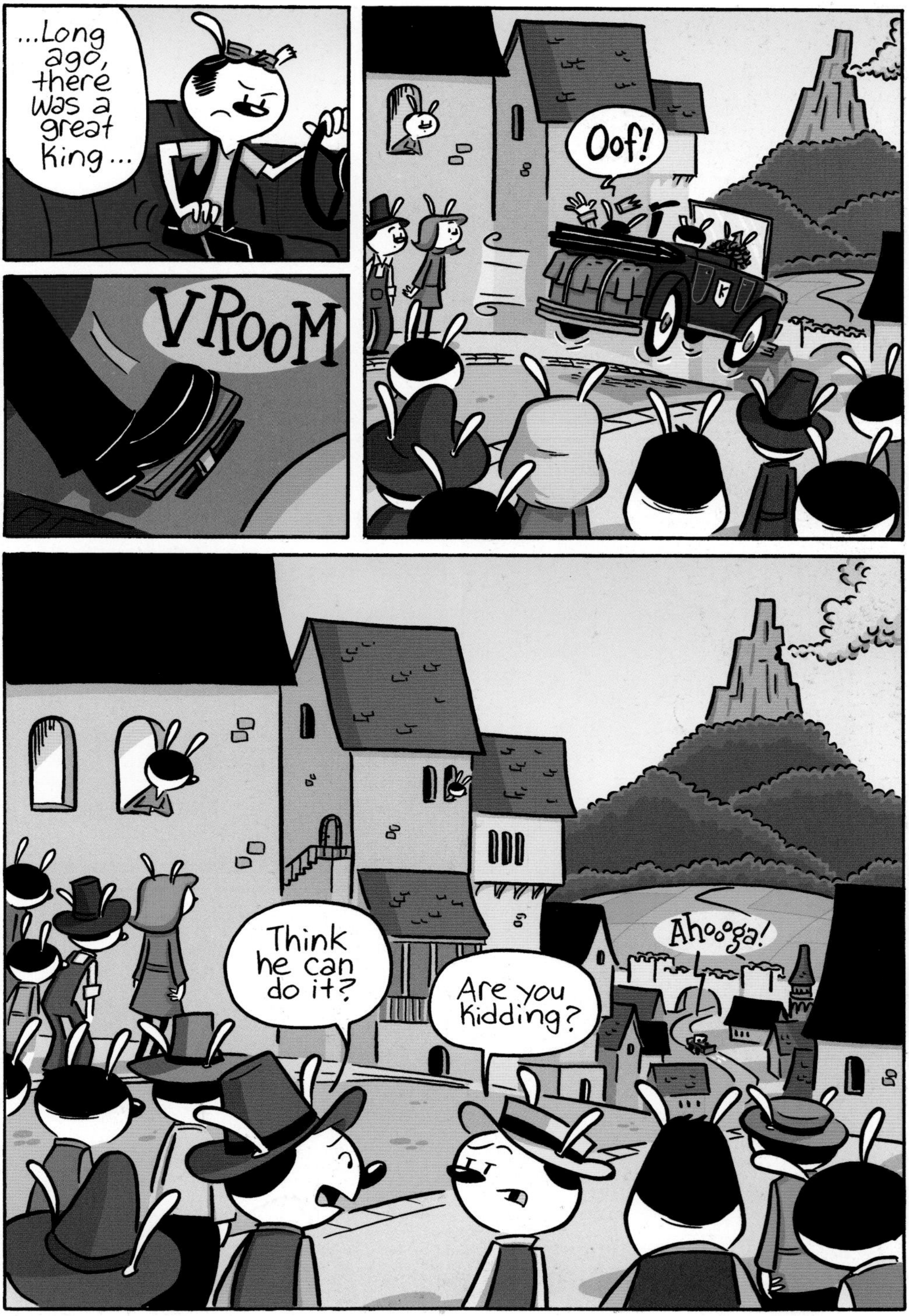
...Long ago, there was a great king...
VROOM
Oof!
Think he can do it?
Are you kidding?
Ahooga!

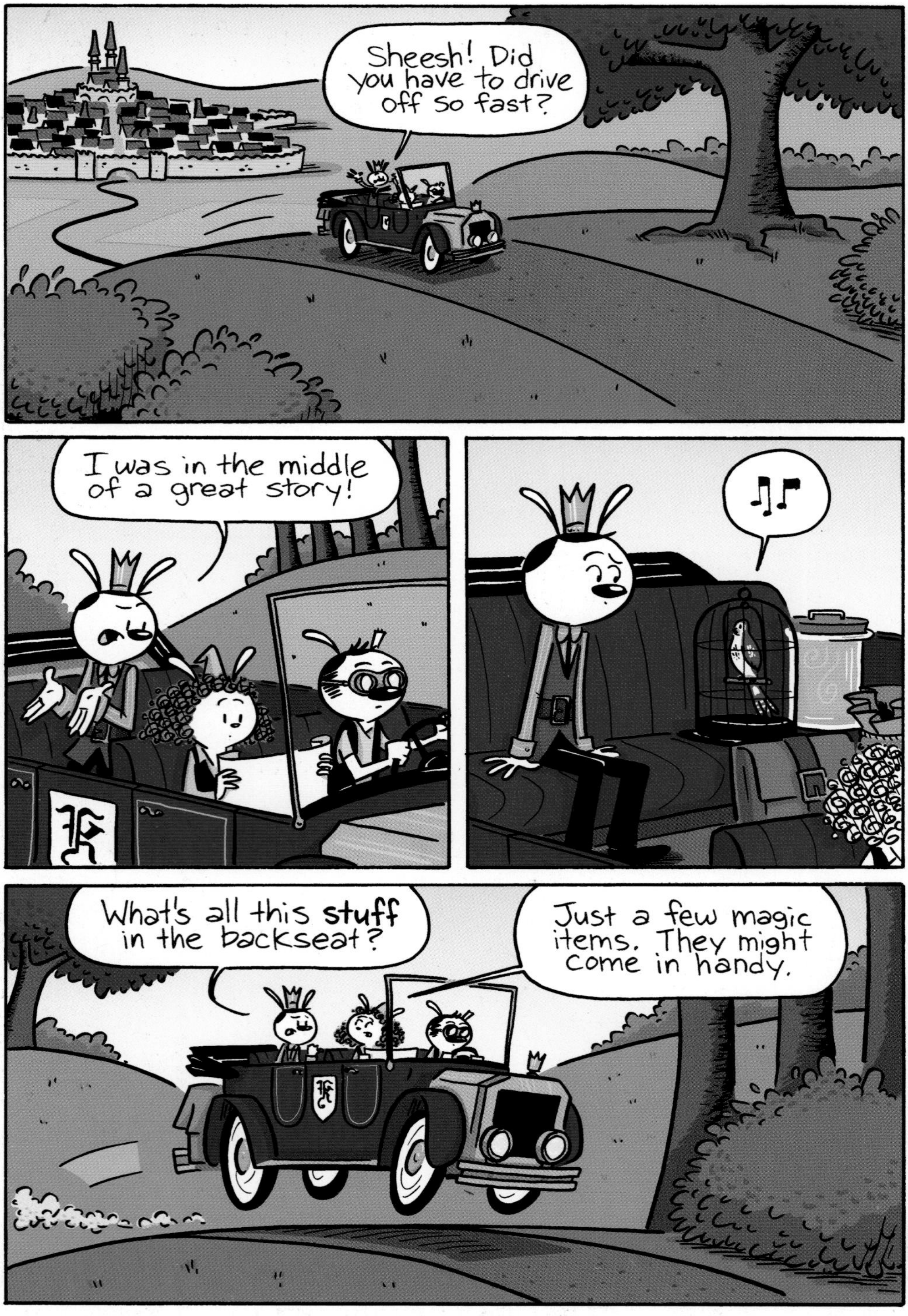
Sheesh! Did you have to drive off so fast?
I was in the middle of a great story!
What's all this **stuff** in the backseat?
Just a few magic items. They might come in handy.

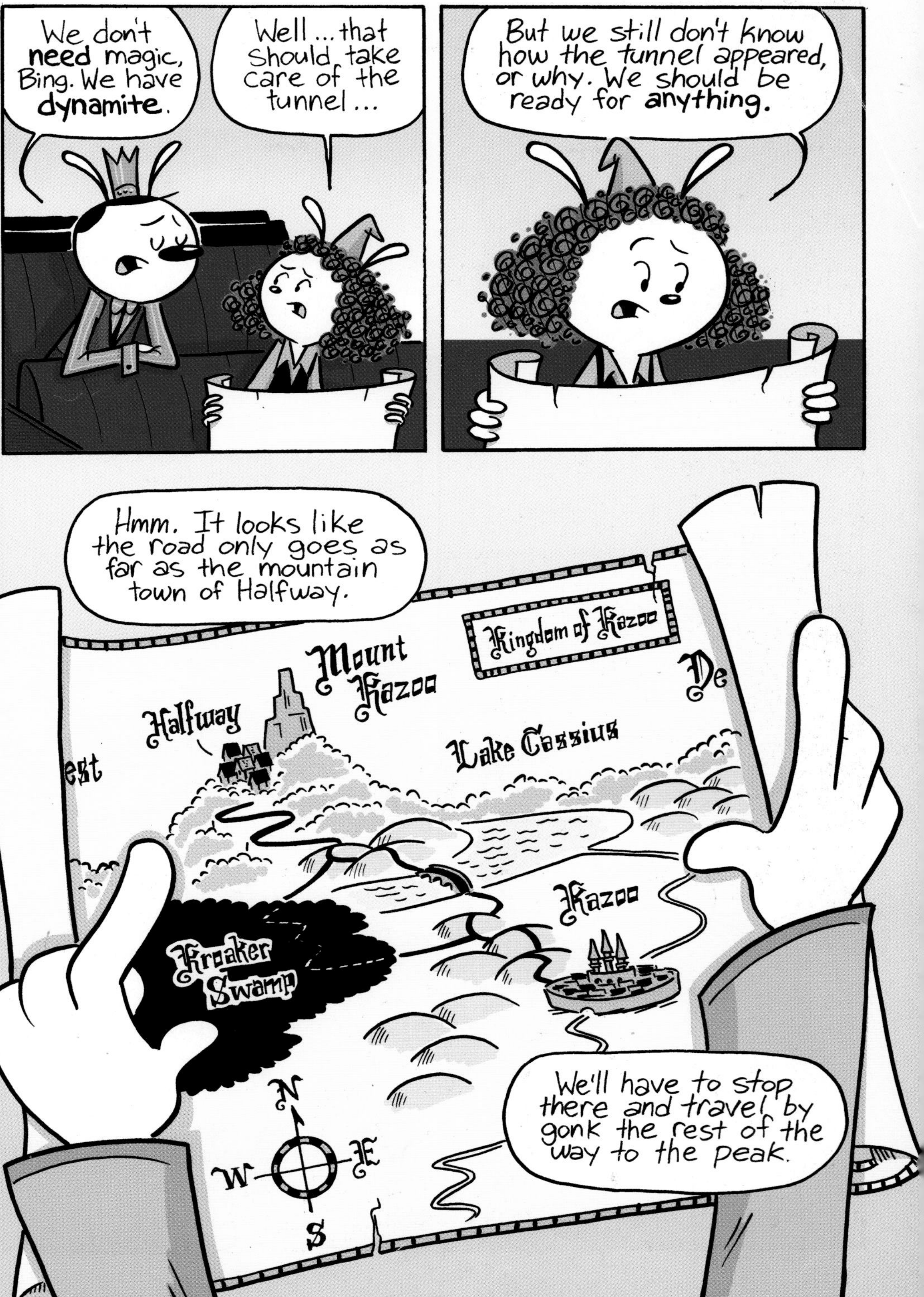
We don't **need** magic, Bing. We have **dynamite**.
Well ... that should take care of the tunnel ...
But we still don't know how the tunnel appeared, or why. We should be ready for **anything**.
Hmm. It looks like the road only goes as far as the mountain town of Halfway.
Kingdom of Kazoo
Mount Kazoo
Halfway
Lake Cassius
Kazoo
Kroaker Swamp
N
W
E
S
We'll have to stop there and travel by gonk the rest of the way to the peak.

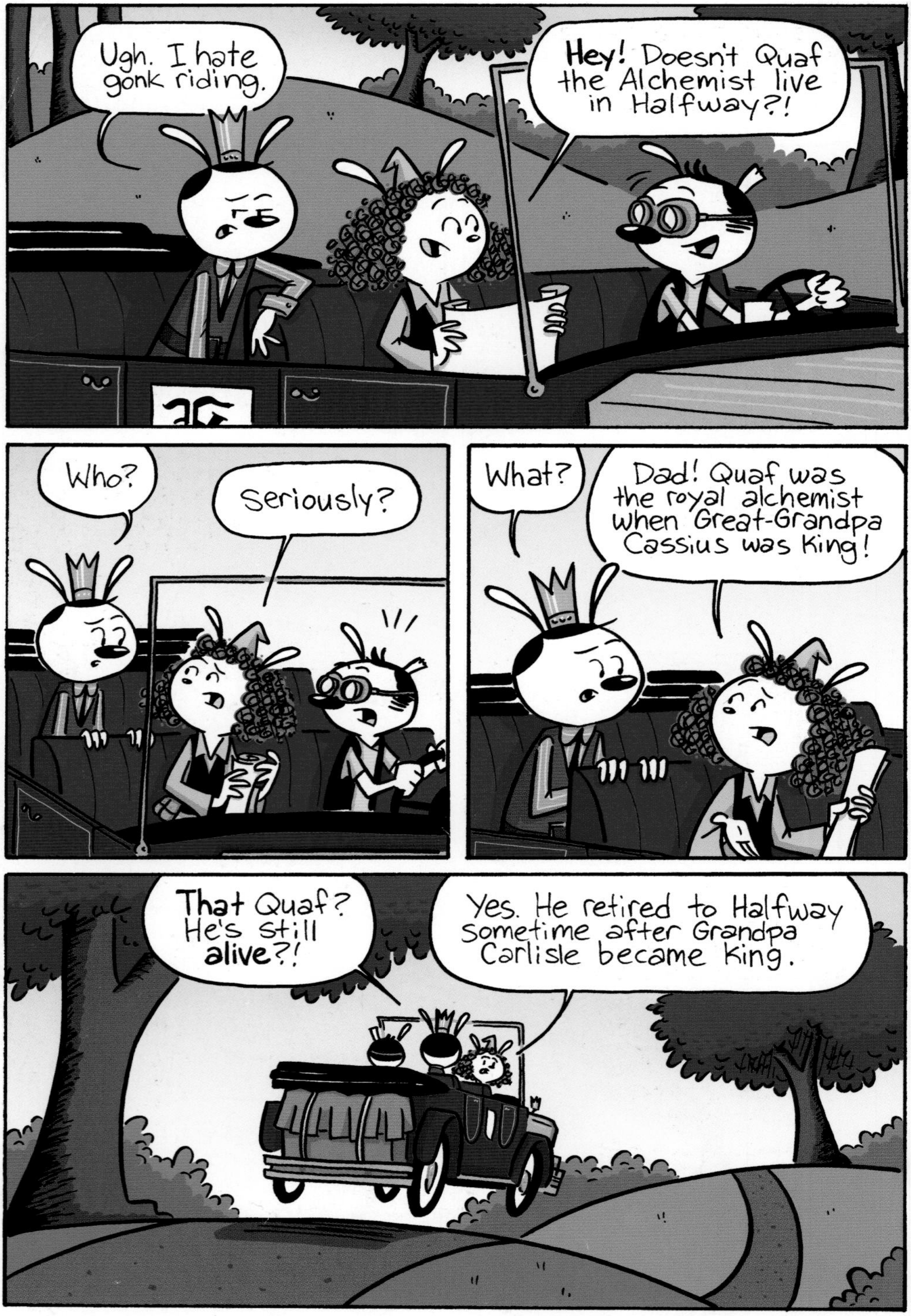
Ugh. I hate gonk riding.
Hey! Doesn't Quaf the Alchemist live in Halfway?!
Who?
Seriously?
What?
Dad! Quaf was the royal alchemist when Great-Grandpa Cassius was King!
That Quaf? He's still alive?!
Yes. He retired to Halfway sometime after Grandpa Carlisle became King.

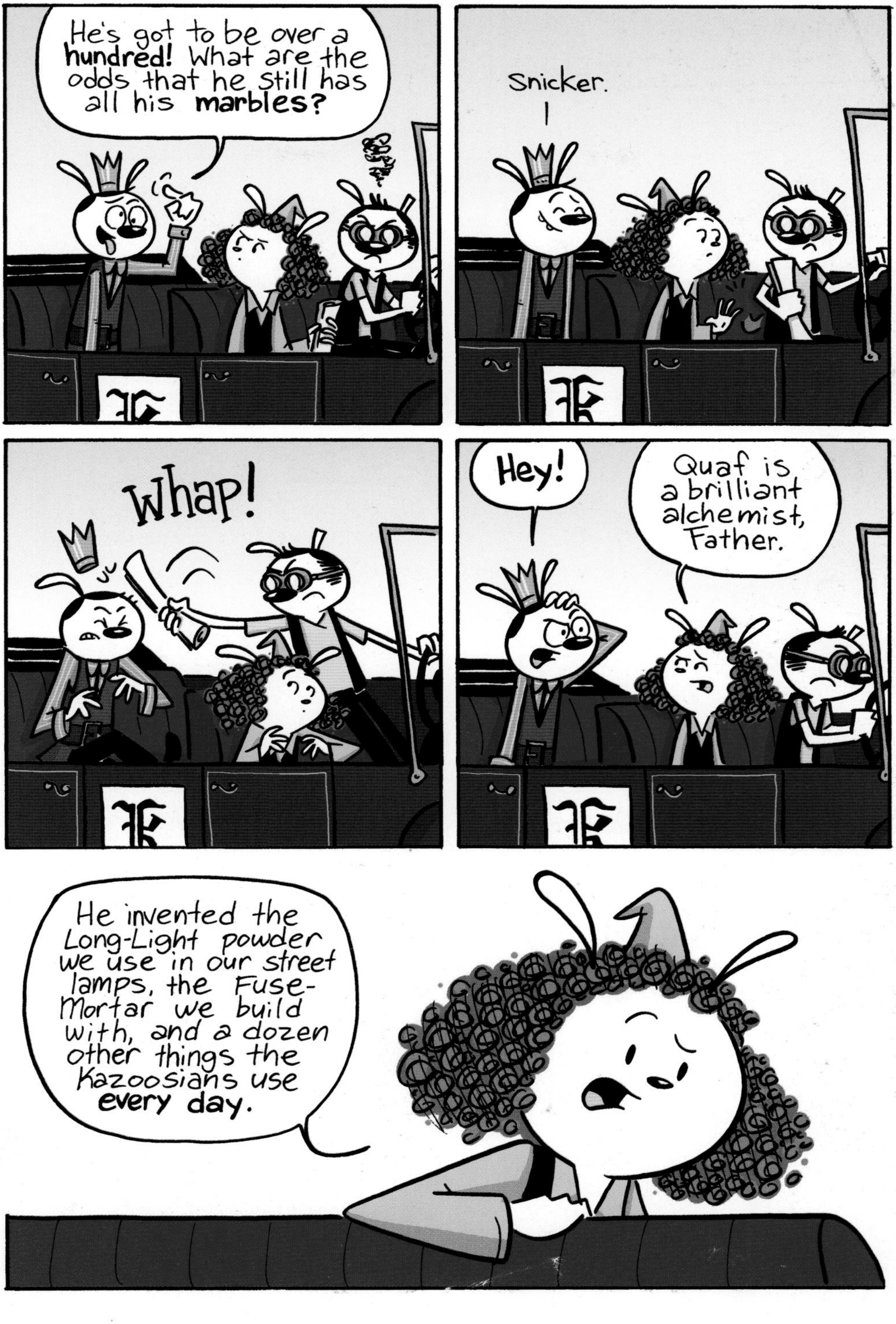
He's got to be over a **hundred!** What are the odds that he still has all his **marbles?**
Snicker.
Whap!
Hey!
Quaf is a brilliant alchemist, Father.
He invented the Long-Light powder we use in our street lamps, the Fuse-Mortar we build with, and a dozen other things the Kazoosians use **every day**.

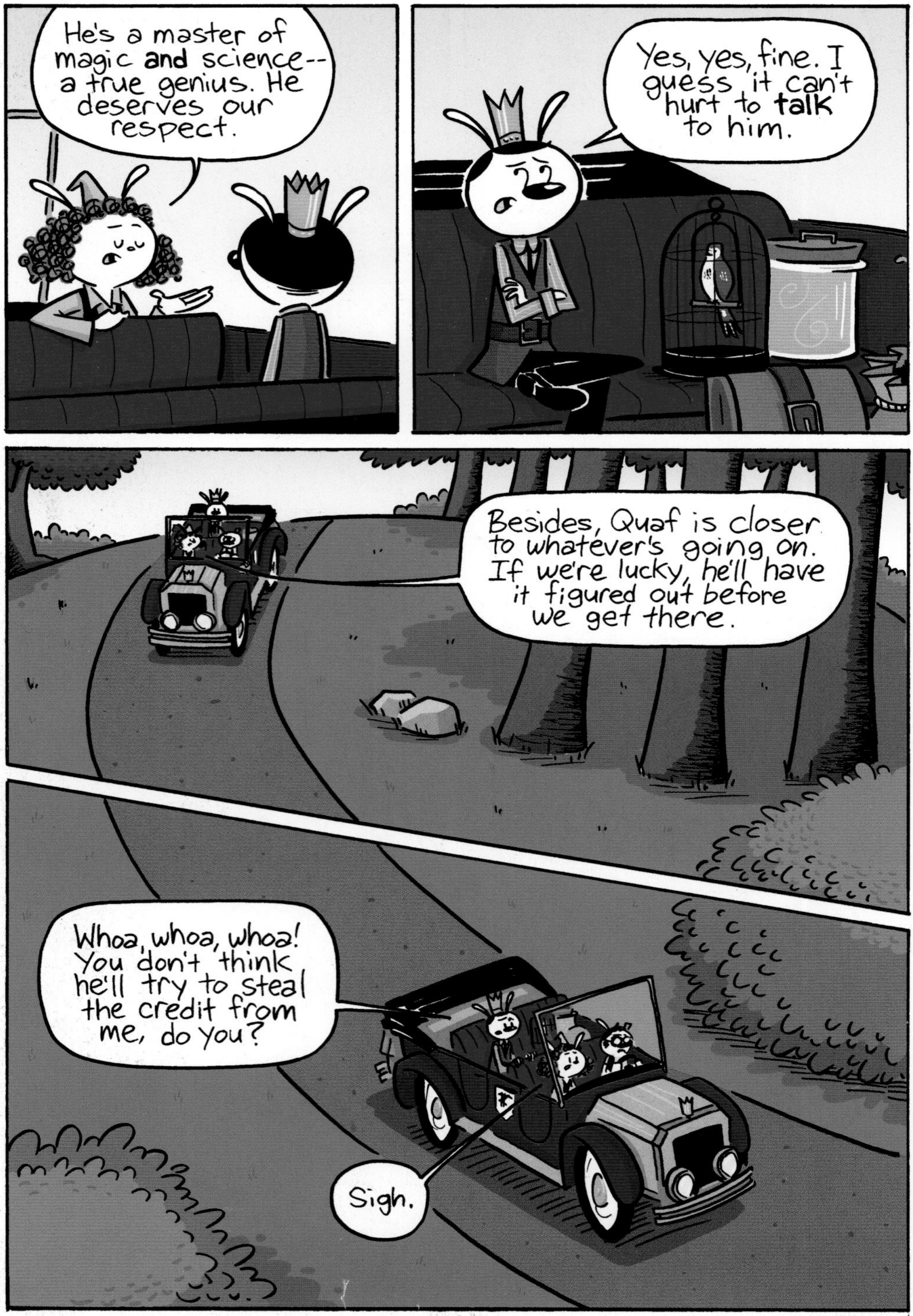
He's a master of magic **and** science--a true genius. He deserves our respect.
Yes, yes, fine. I guess it can't hurt to **talk** to him.
Besides, Quaf is closer to whatever's going on. If we're lucky, he'll have it figured out before we get there.
Whoa, whoa, whoa! You don't think he'll try to steal the credit from me, do you?
Sigh.

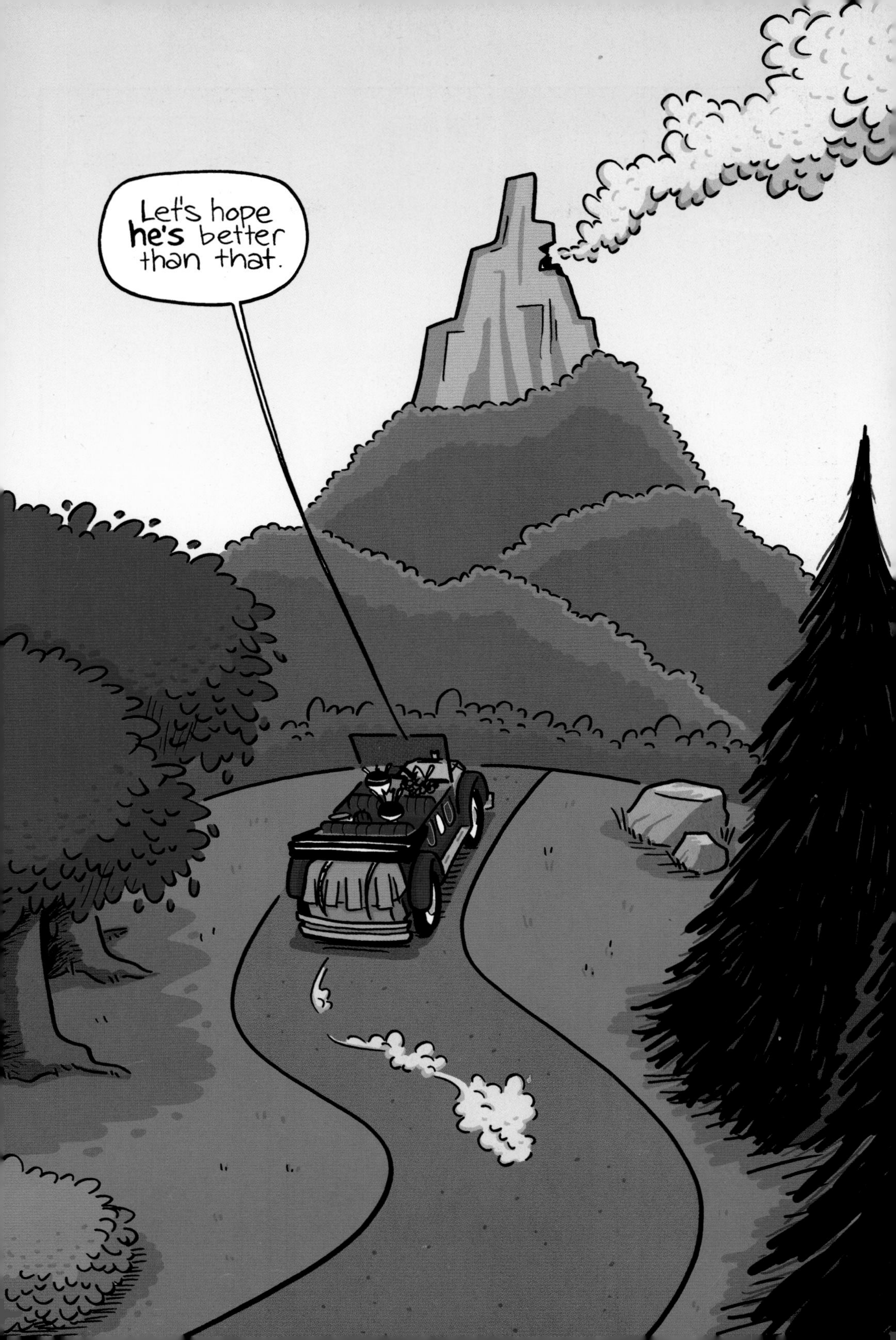
Let's hope **he's** better than that.

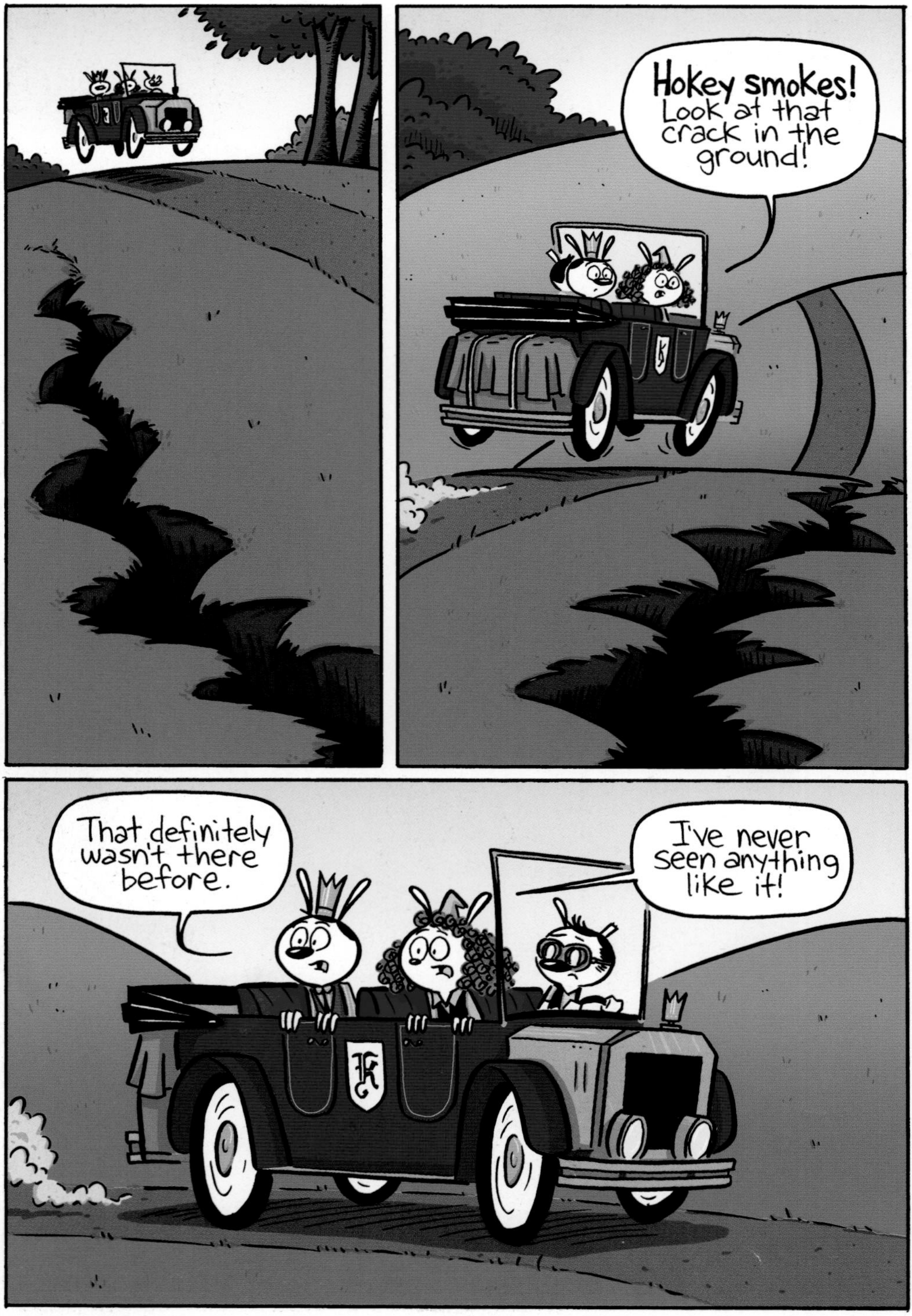
Hokey smokes! Look at that crack in the ground!
That definitely wasn't there before.
I've never seen anything like it!

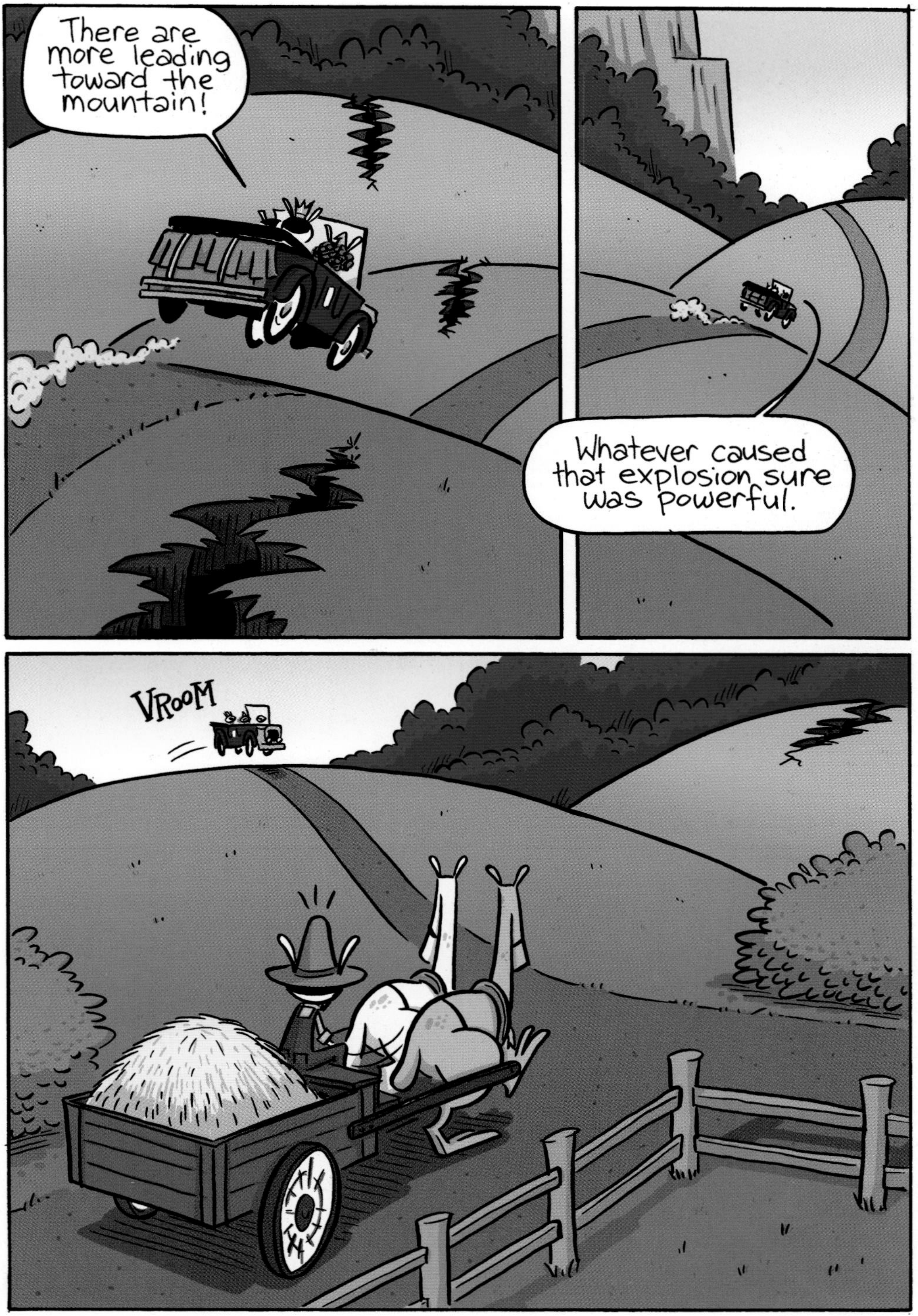
There are more leading toward the mountain!
Whatever caused that explosion sure was powerful.
VROOM

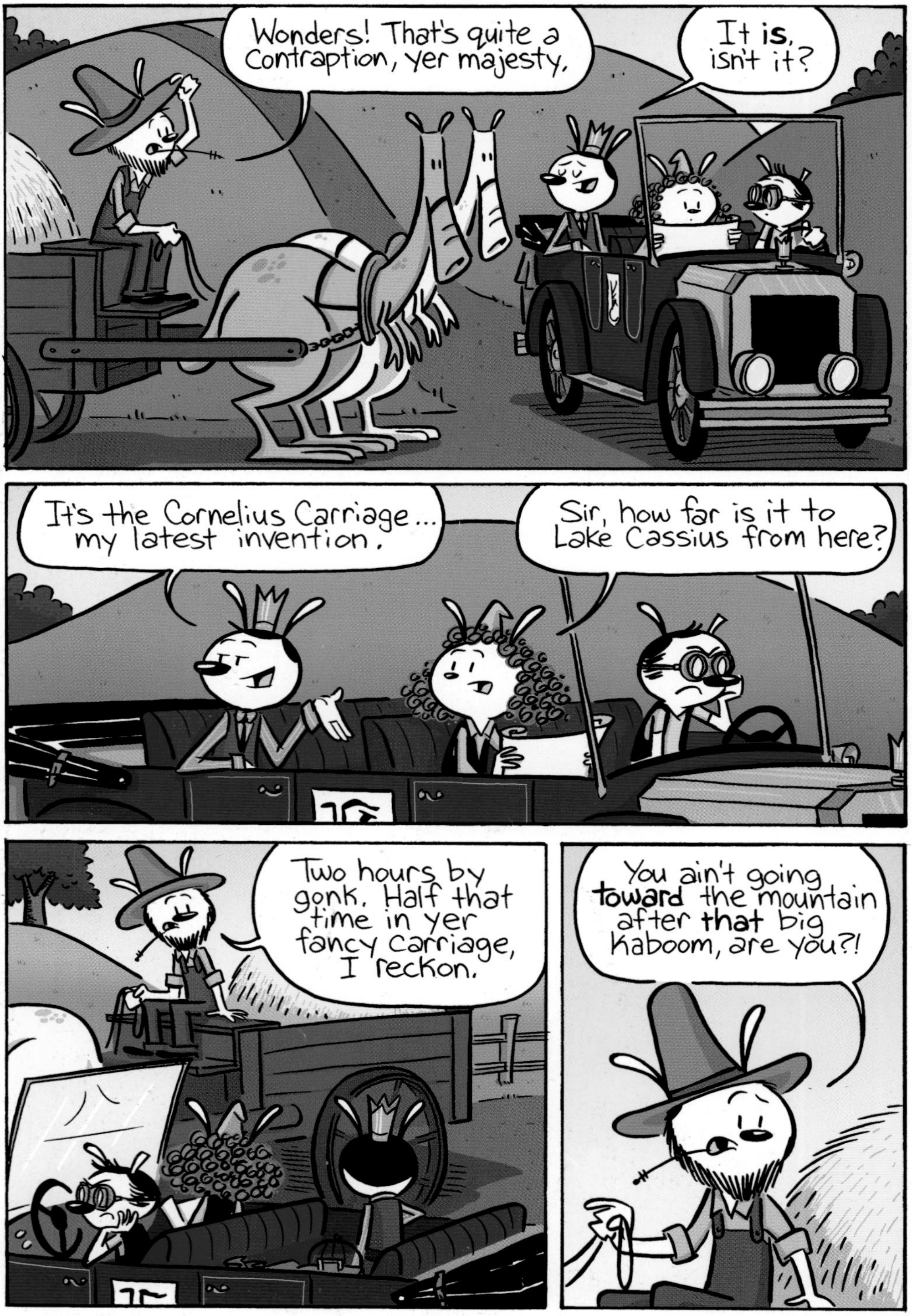
Wonders! That's quite a Contraption, yer majesty.
It **is**, isn't it?
It's the Cornelius Carriage... my latest invention.
Sir, how far is it to Lake Cassius from here?
Two hours by gonk. Half that time in yer fancy carriage, I reckon.
You ain't going **toward** the mountain after **that** big Kaboom, are you?!

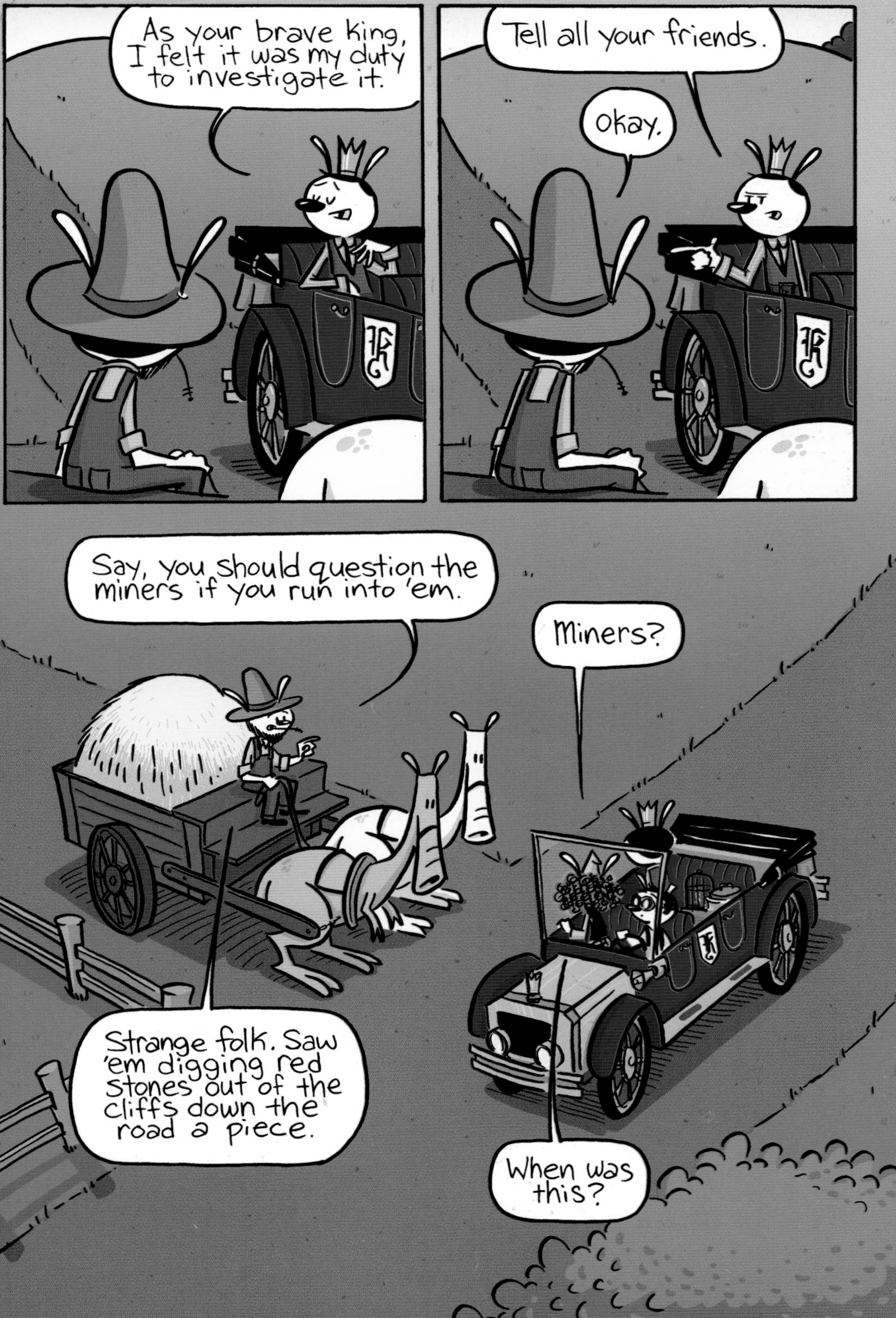
As your brave king, I felt it was my duty to investigate it.
Tell all your friends.
Okay.
Say, you should question the miners if you run into 'em.
Miners?
Strange folk. Saw 'em digging red stones out of the cliffs down the road a piece.
When was this?

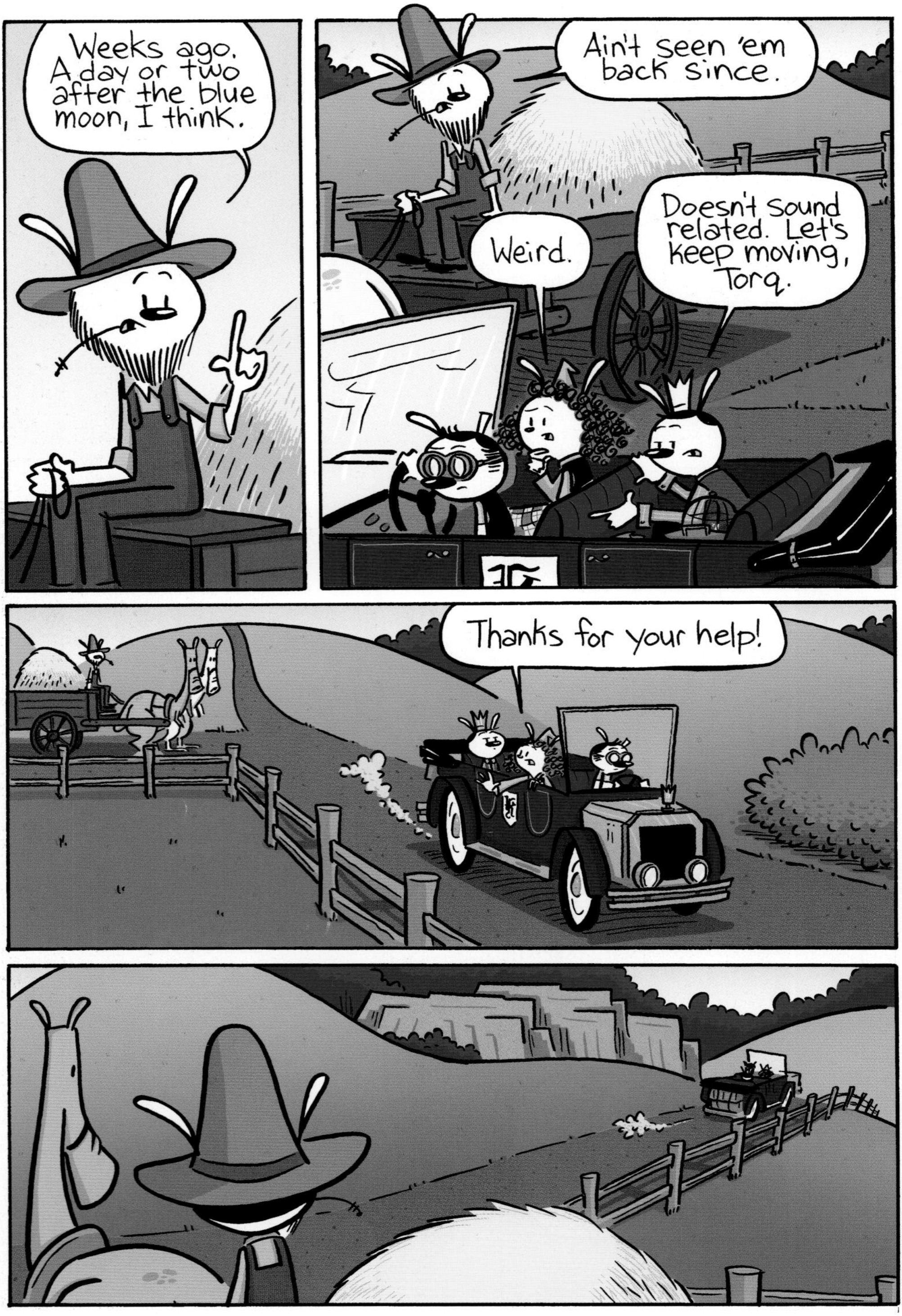
Weeks ago. A day or two after the blue moon, I think.
Ain't seen 'em back since.
Weird.
Doesn't sound related. Let's keep moving, Torq.
Thanks for your help!

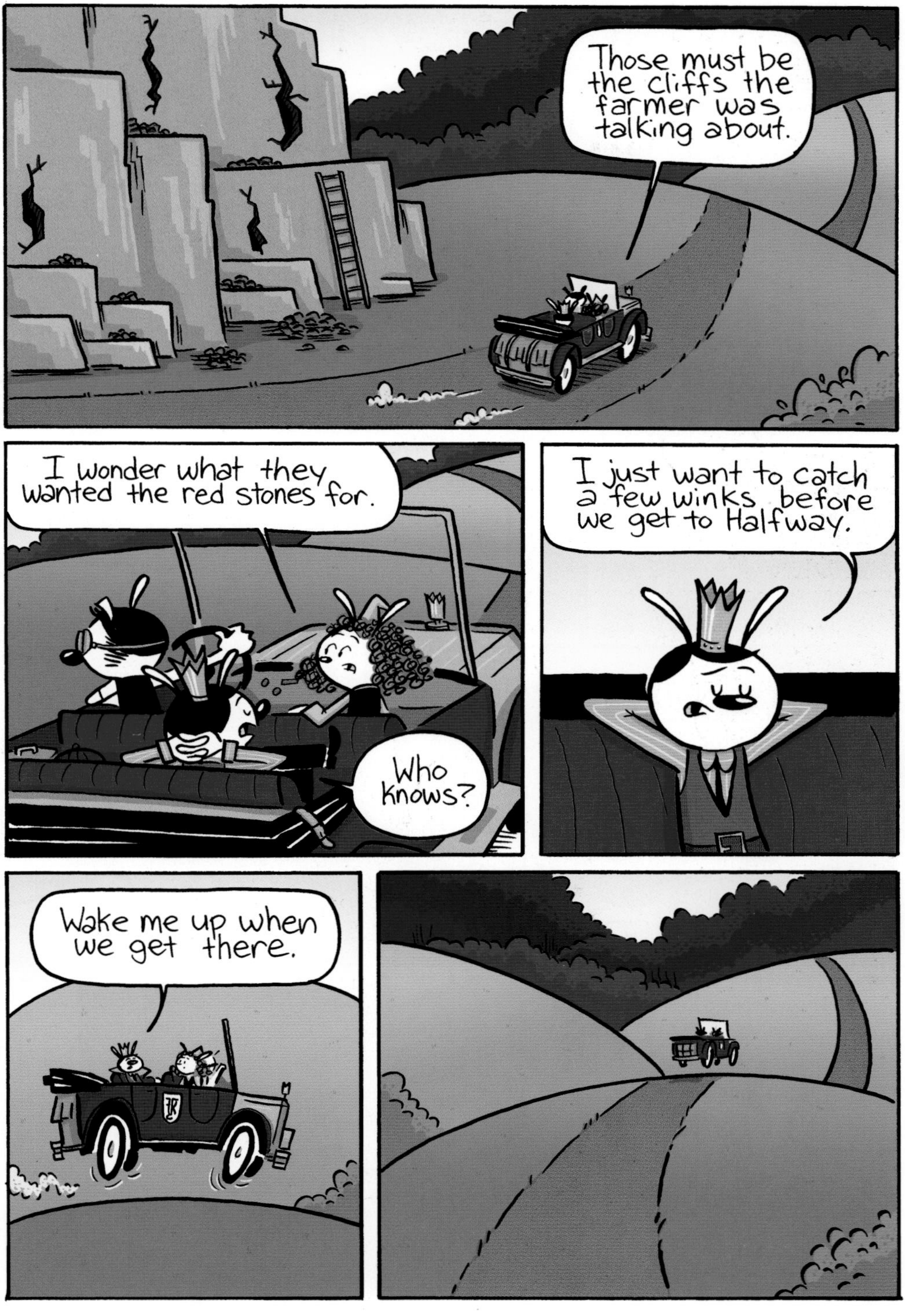
Those must be the cliffs the farmer was talking about.
I wonder what they wanted the red stones for.
Who knows?
I just want to catch a few winks before we get to Halfway.
Wake me up when we get there.

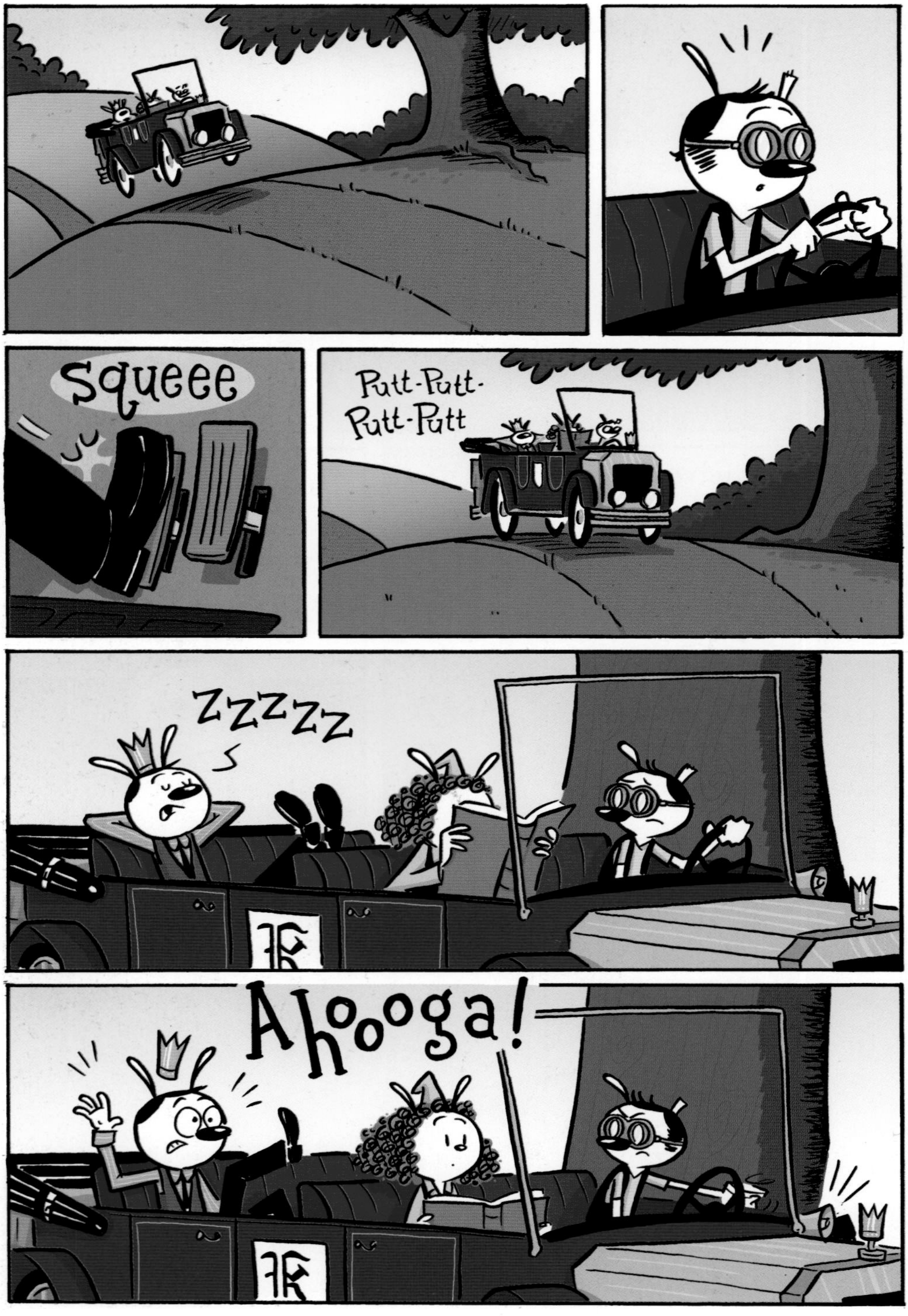
squeee
Putt-Putt-
Putt-Putt
ZZZZZ
Ahoooga!

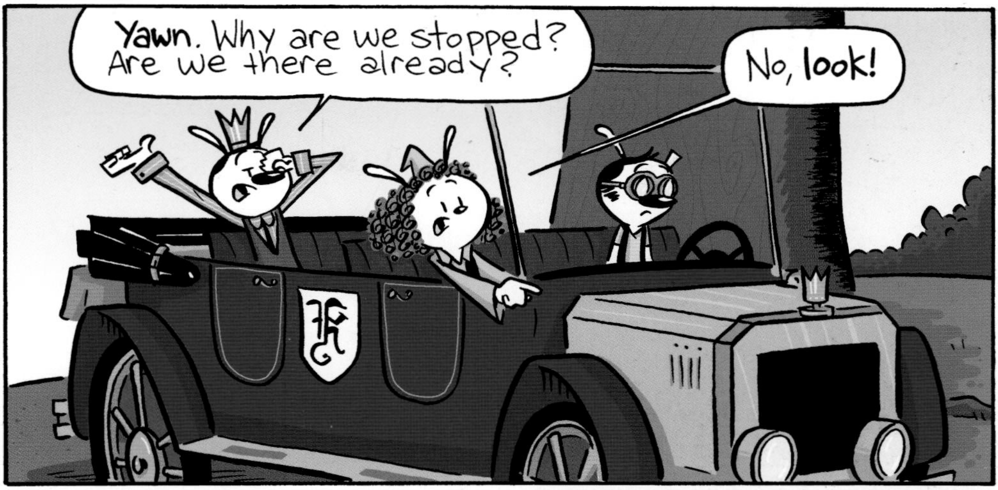
Yawn. Why are we stopped? Are we there already?
No, look!

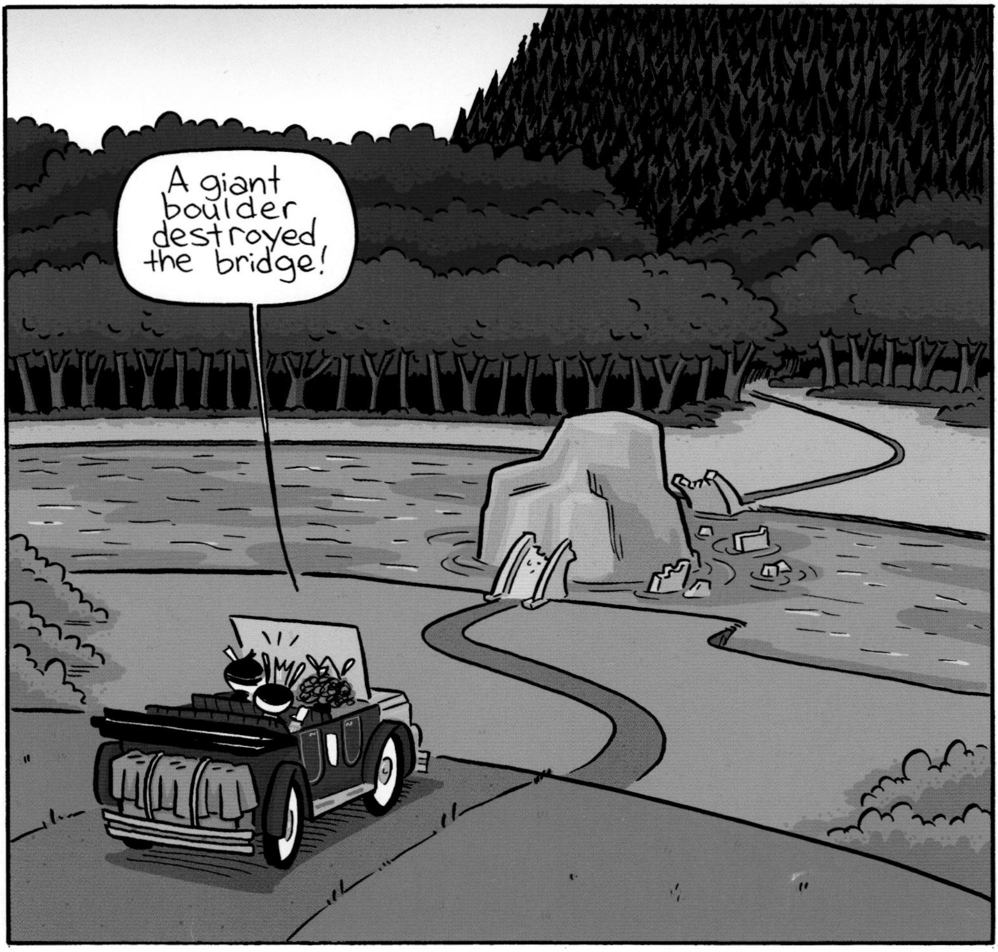
A giant boulder destroyed the bridge!

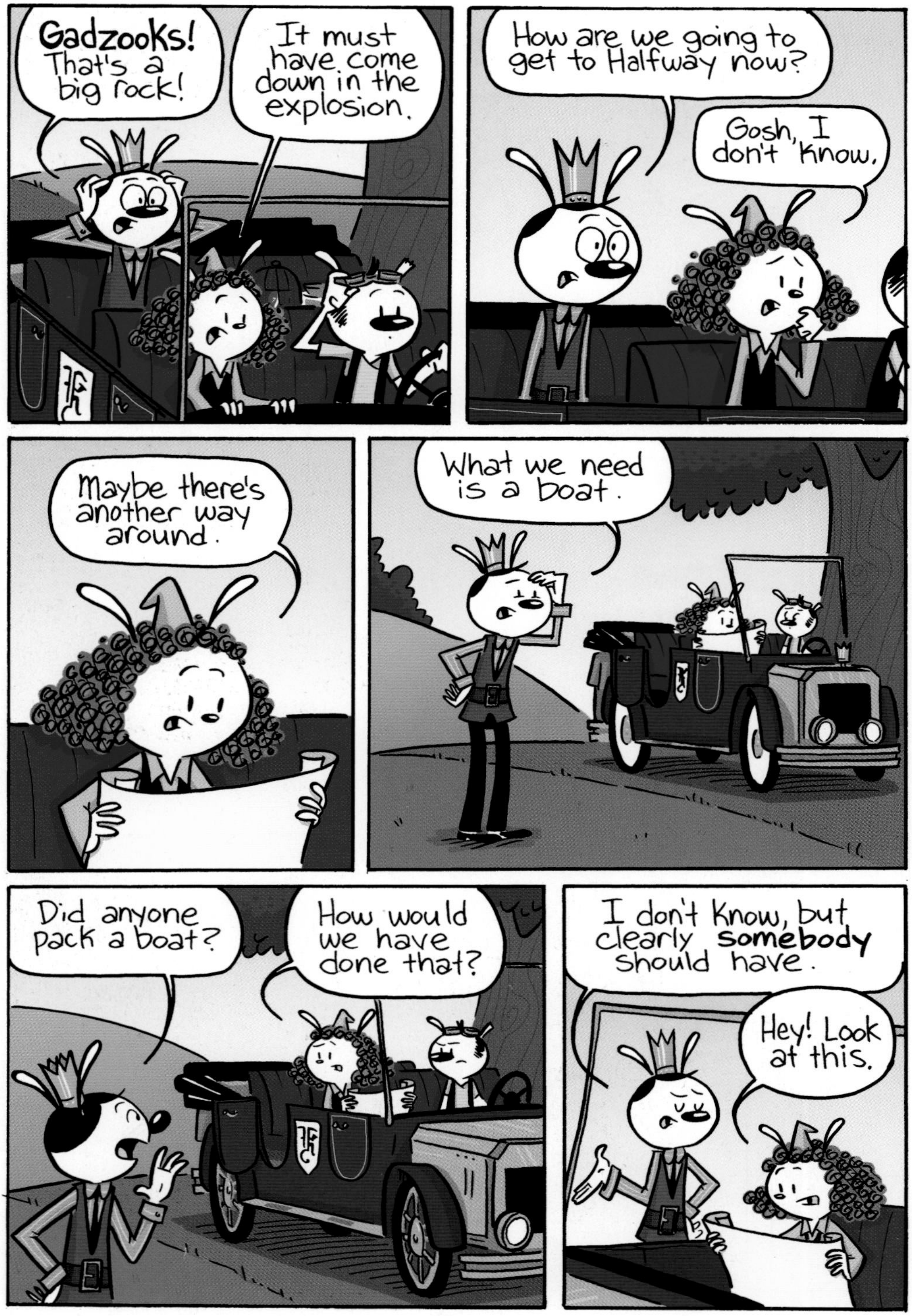
Gadzooks! That's a big rock!
It must have come down in the explosion.
How are we going to get to Halfway now?
Gosh, I don't know.
Maybe there's another way around.
What we need is a boat.
Did anyone pack a boat?
How would we have done that?
I don't know, but clearly **somebody** should have.
Hey! Look at this.

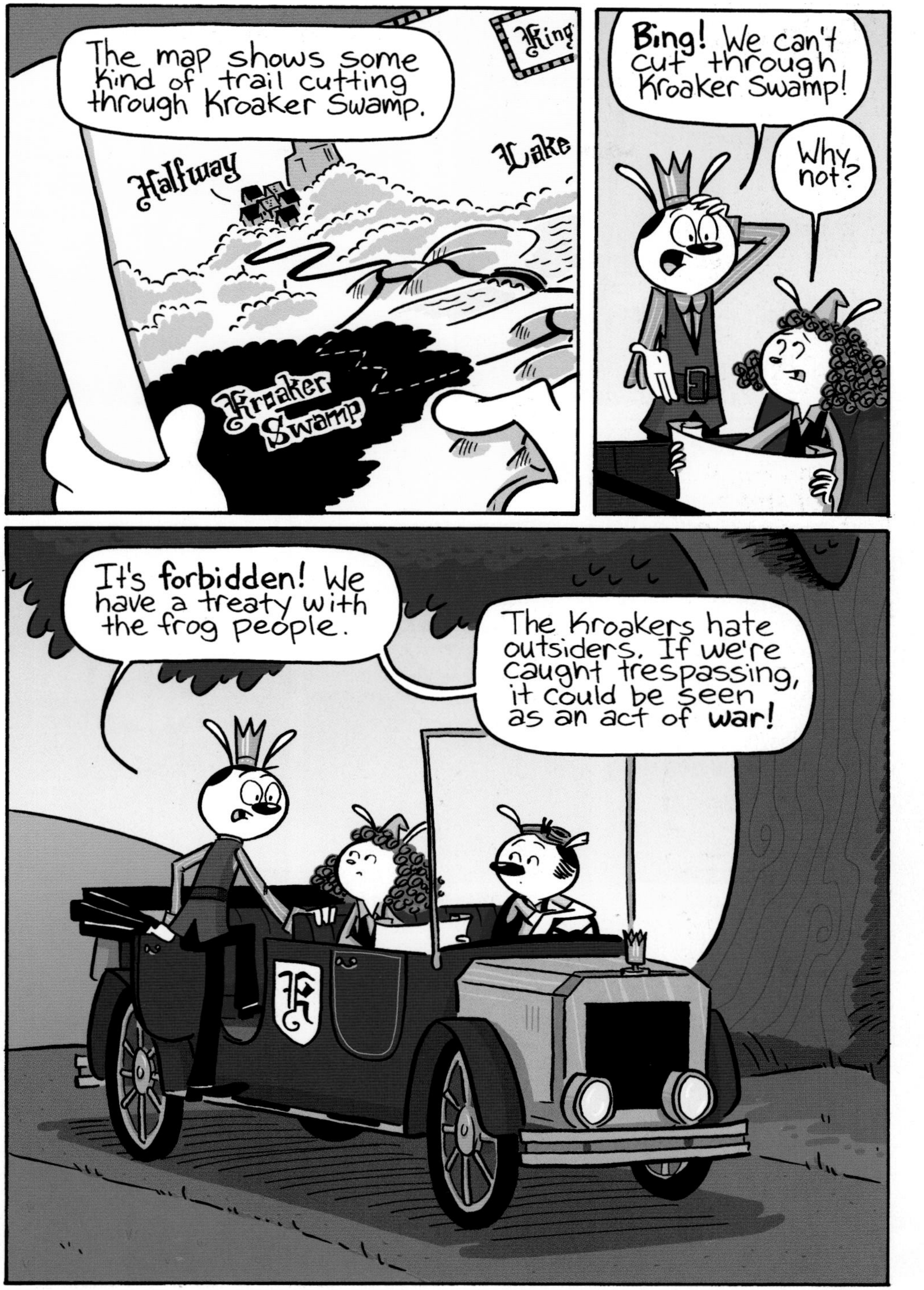
The map shows some kind of trail cutting through Kroaker Swamp.
King
Halfway
Lake
Kroaker Swamp
Bing! We can't cut through Kroaker Swamp!
Why not?
It's **forbidden**! We have a treaty with the frog people.
The Kroakers hate outsiders. If we're caught trespassing, it could be seen as an act of **war**!

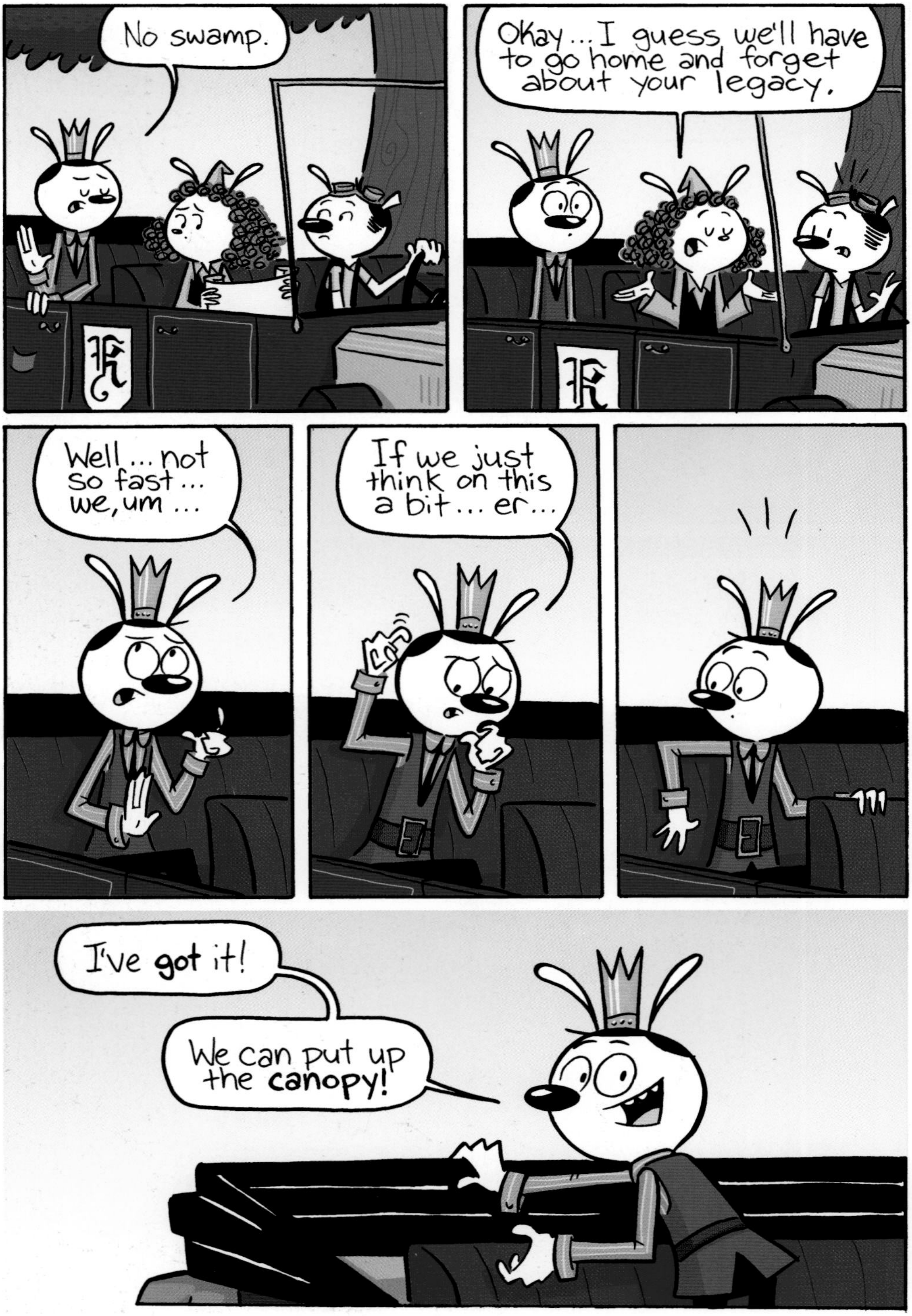
No swamp.
Okay... I guess we'll have to go home and forget about your legacy.
Well... not so fast... we, um...
If we just think on this a bit... er...
I've got it!
We can put up the canopy!

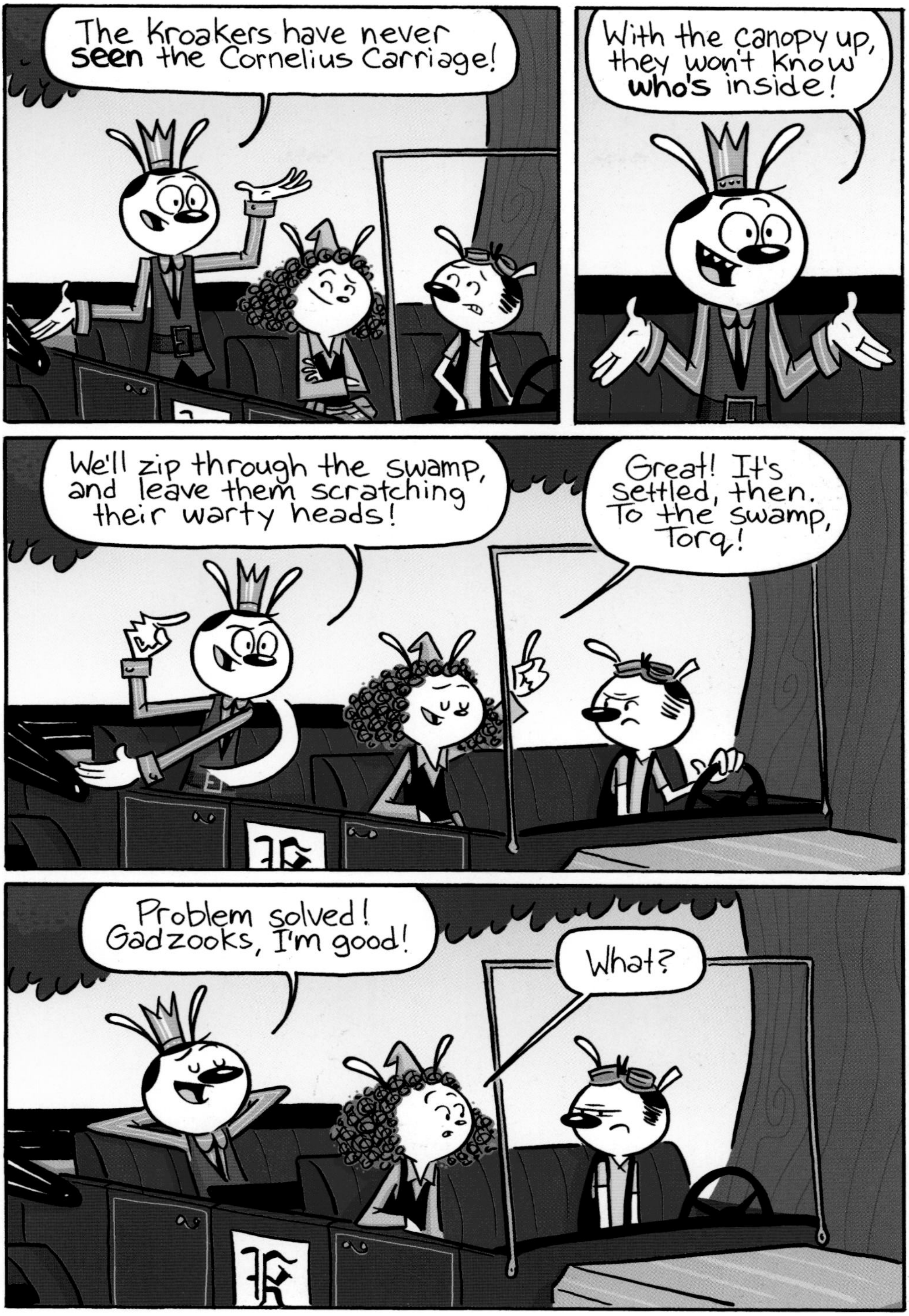
The Kroakers have never **seen** the Cornelius Carriage!
With the canopy up, they won't know **who's** inside!
We'll zip through the swamp, and leave them scratching their warty heads!
Great! It's settled, then. To the swamp, Torq!
Problem solved! Gadzooks, I'm good!
What?

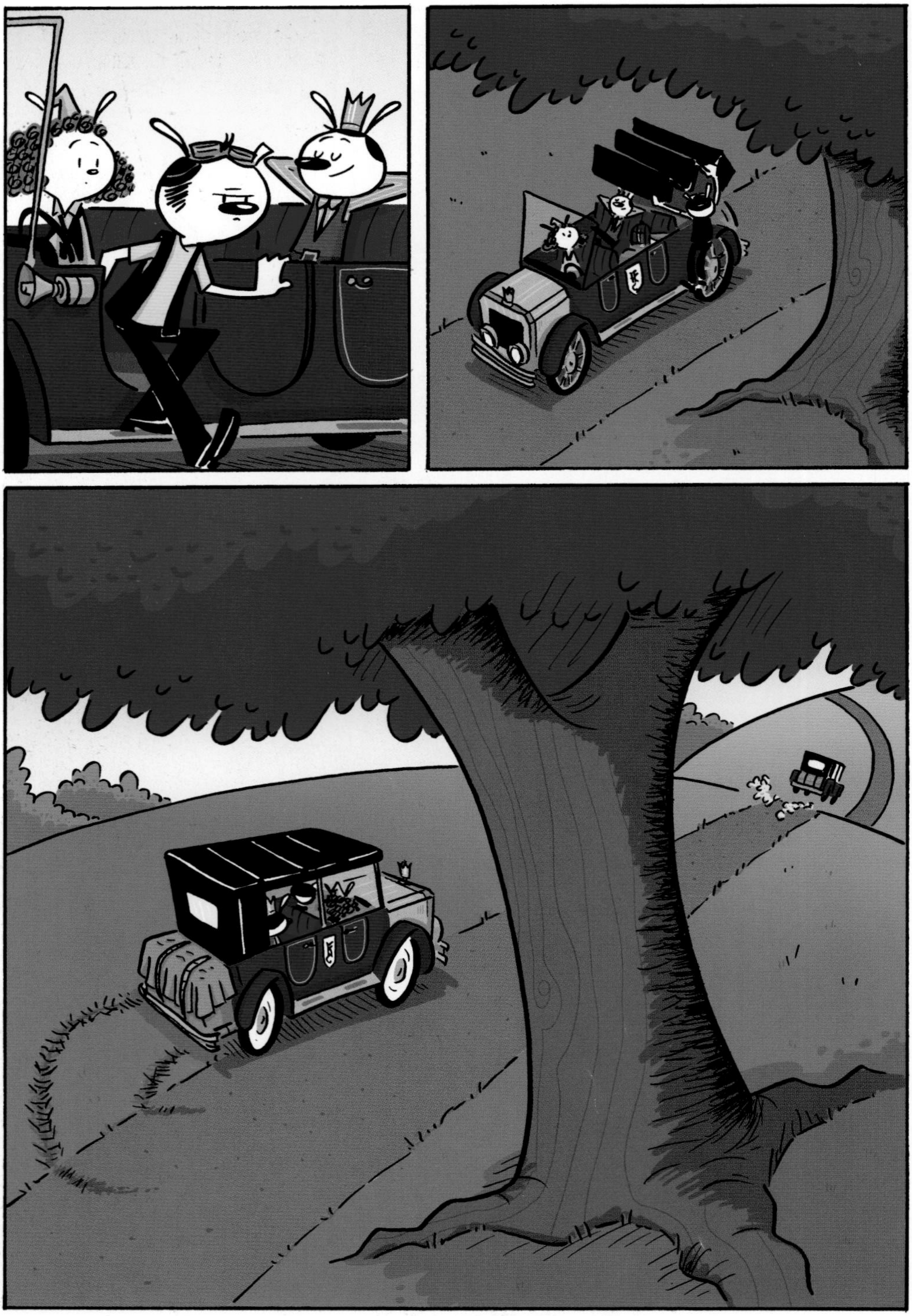

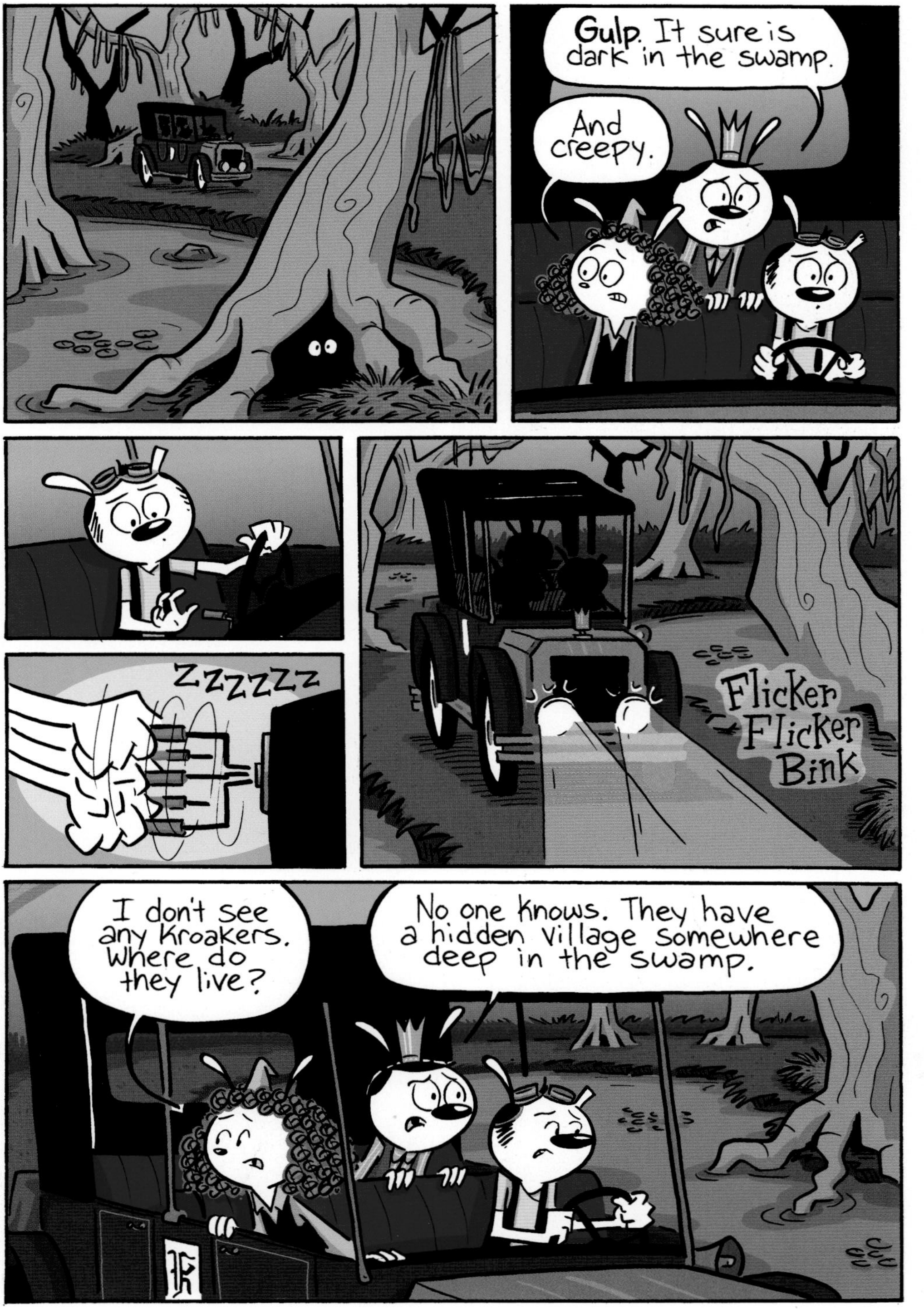
Gulp. It sure is dark in the swamp.
And creepy.
ZZZZZZ
Flicker Flicker Bink
I don't see any Kroakers. Where do they live?
No one knows. They have a hidden village somewhere deep in the swamp.

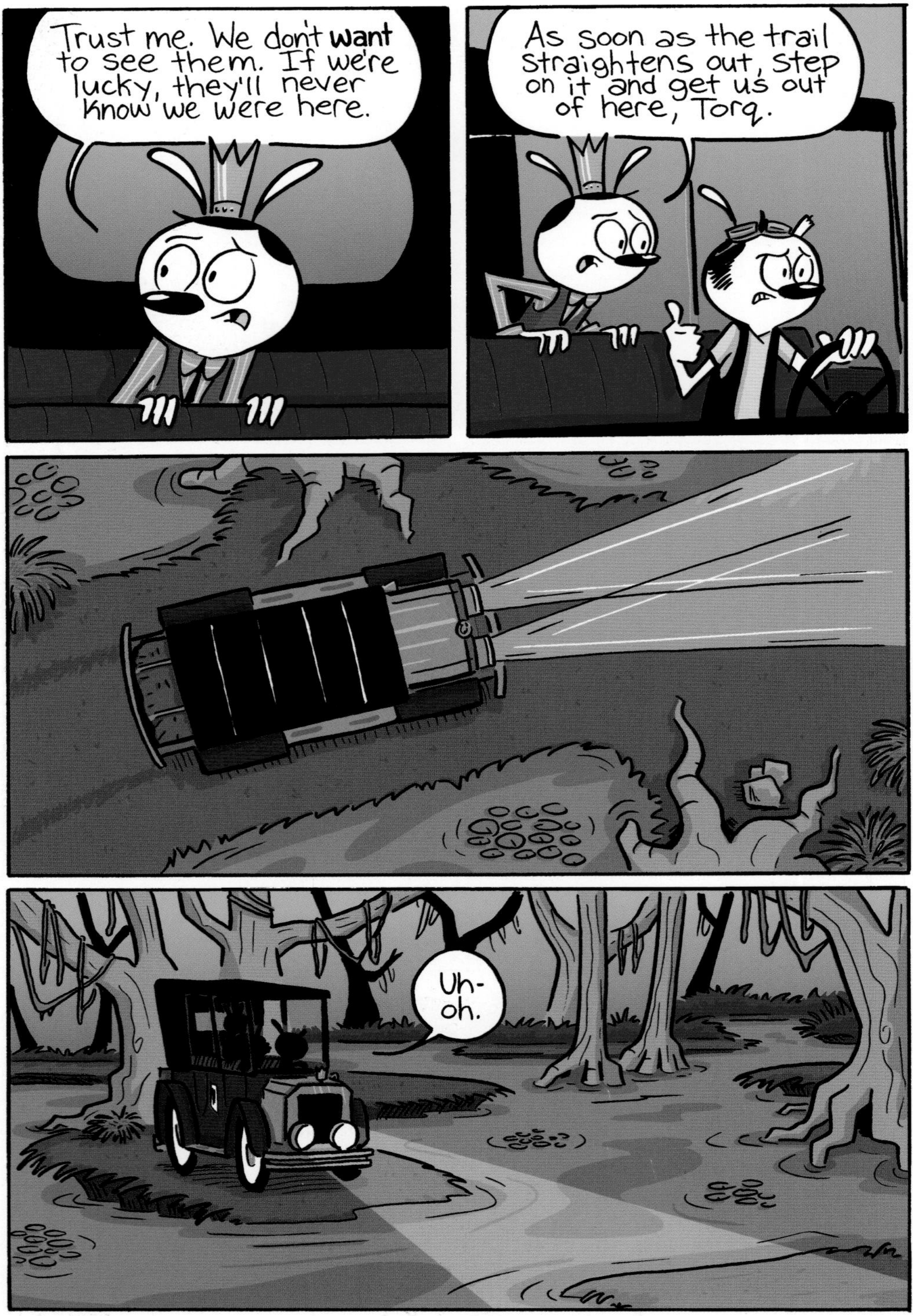
Trust me. We don't **want** to see them. If we're lucky, they'll never know we were here.
As soon as the trail straightens out, step on it and get us out of here, Torq.
Uh-oh.

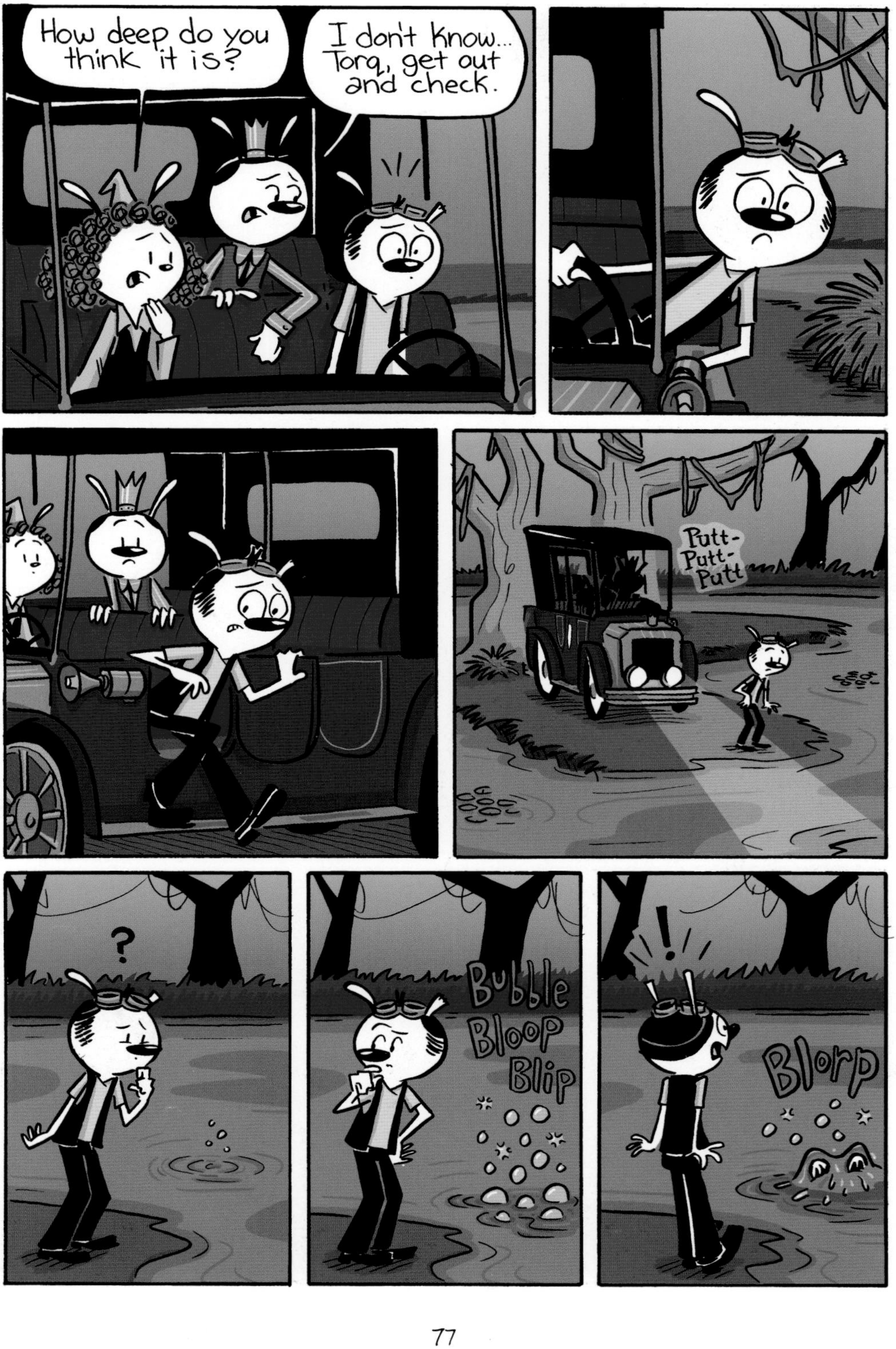
How deep do you think it is?
I don't know... Torq, get out and check.
Putt-Putt-Putt
?
Bubble Bloop Blip
!
Blorp

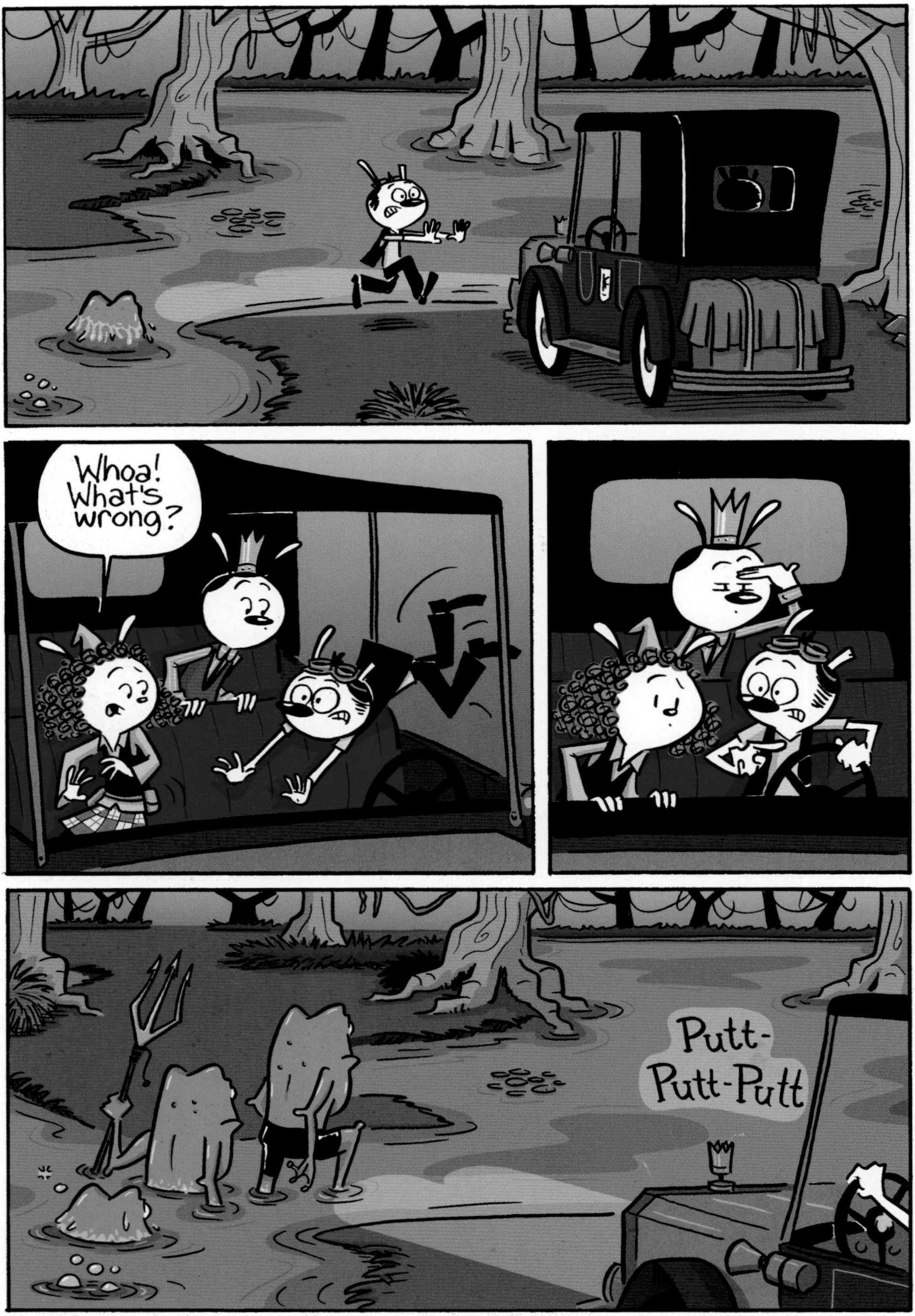
Whoa! What's wrong?
Putt-Putt-Putt

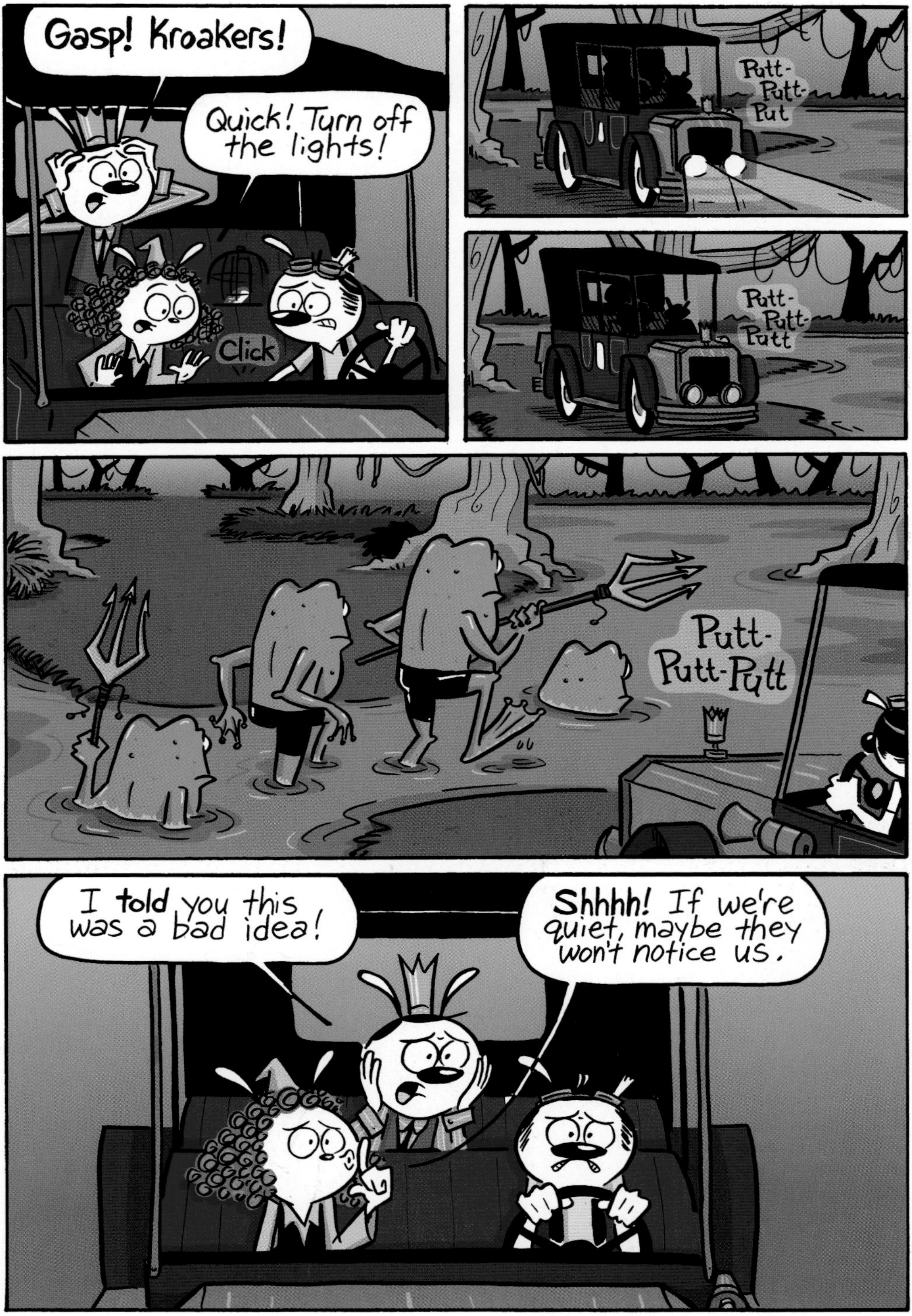

Gasp! Kroakers!
Quick! Turn off the lights!
Click
Putt-Putt-Put
Putt-Putt-Putt
Putt-Putt-Putt
I told you this was a bad idea!
Shhhh! If we're quiet, maybe they won't notice us.

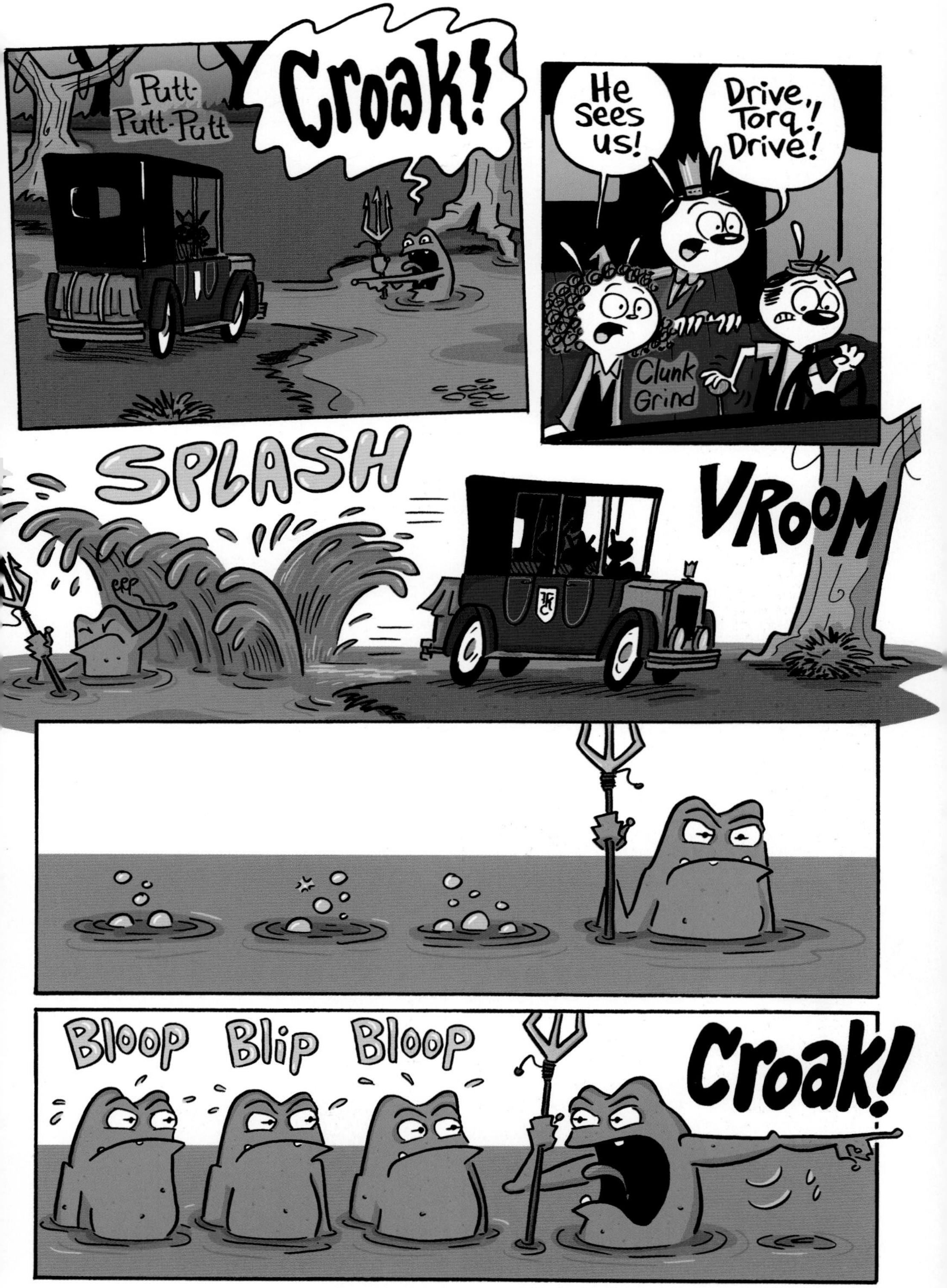
Putt-Putt-Putt
Croak!
He sees us!
Drive, Torq! Drive!
Clunk Grind
SPLASH
VROOM
Bloop Blip Bloop
Croak!

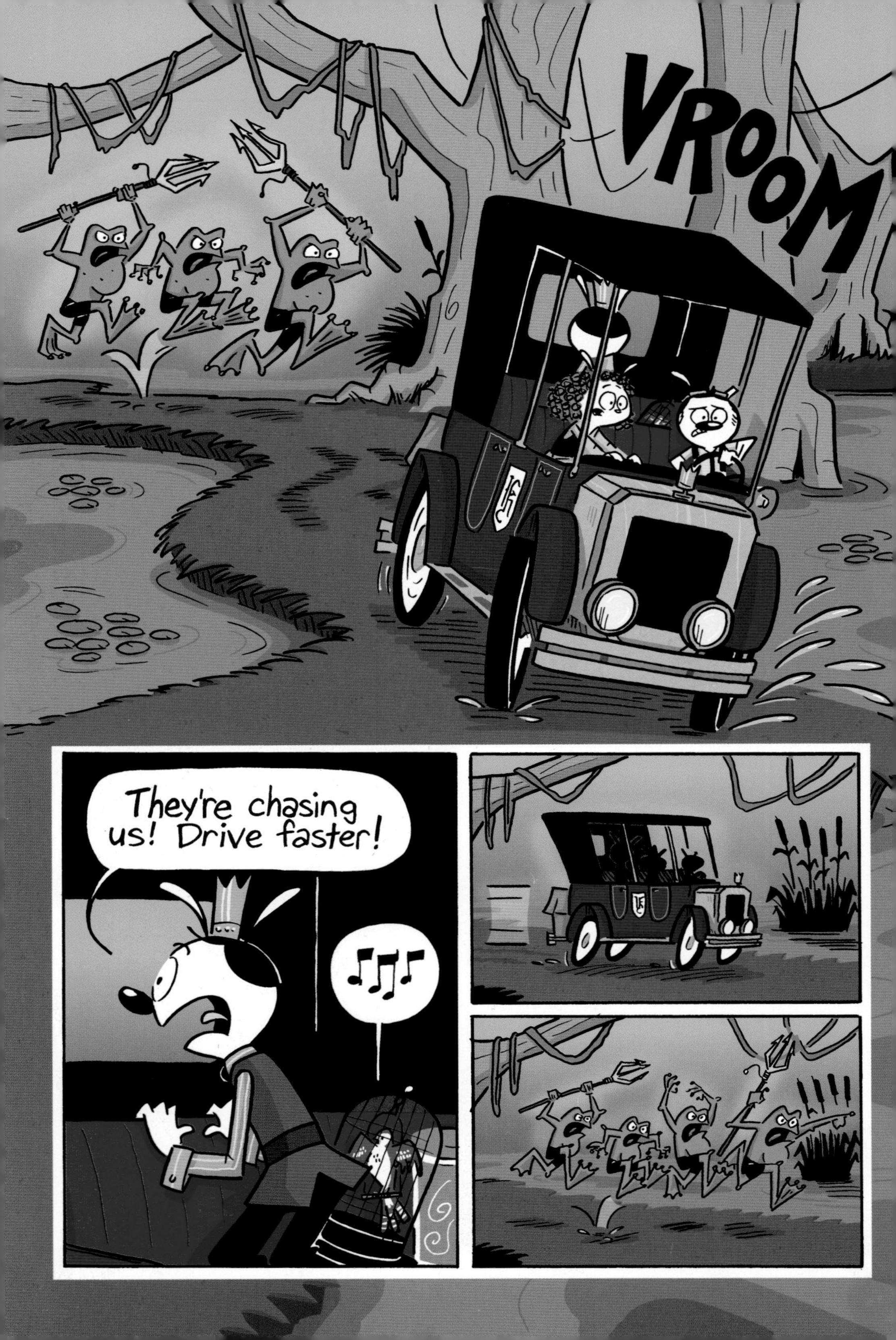
VROOM
They're chasing us! Drive faster!

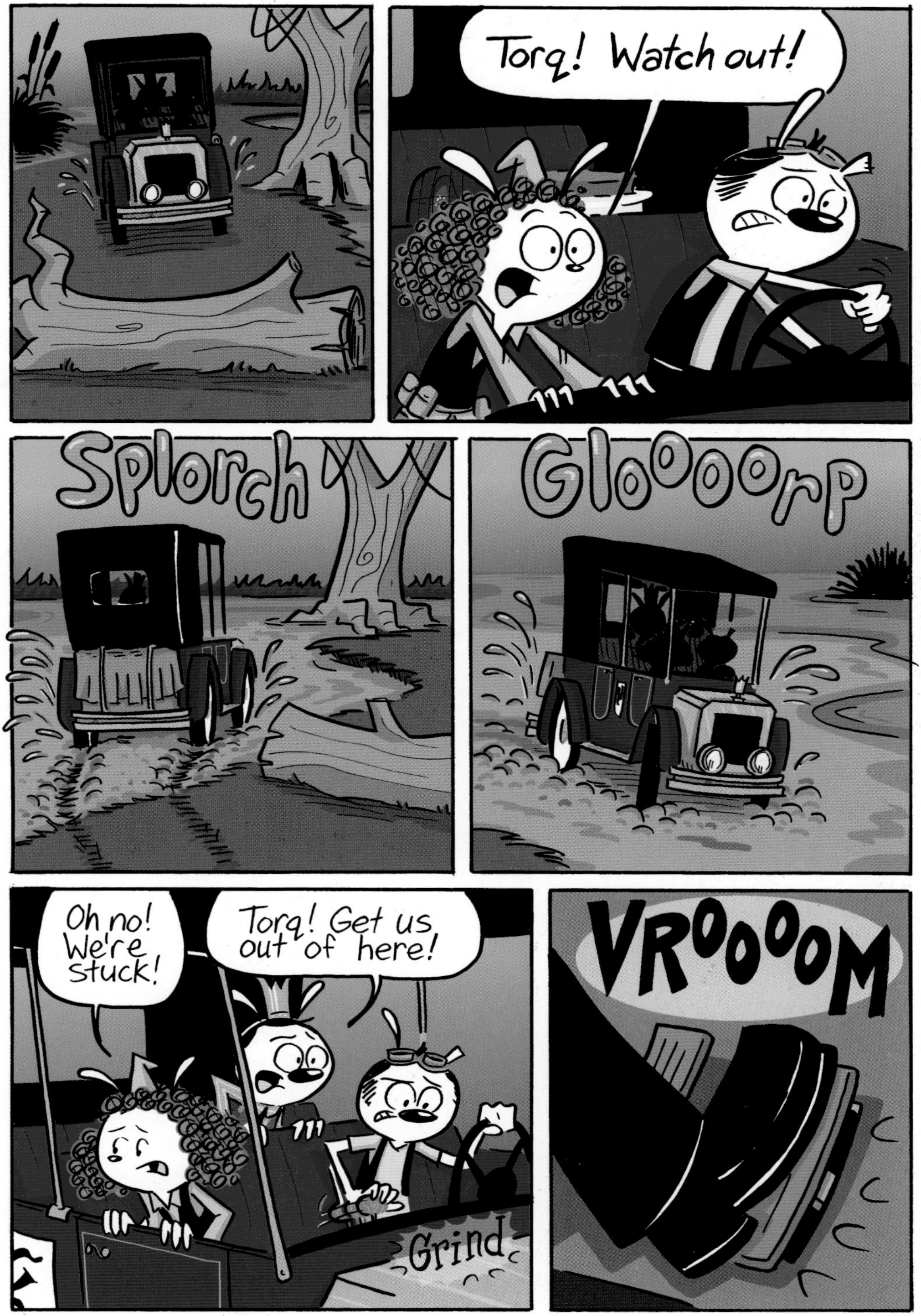

Torq! Watch out!
Splorch
Gloooorp
Oh no! We're stuck!
Torq! Get us out of here!
Grind
VROOOOM

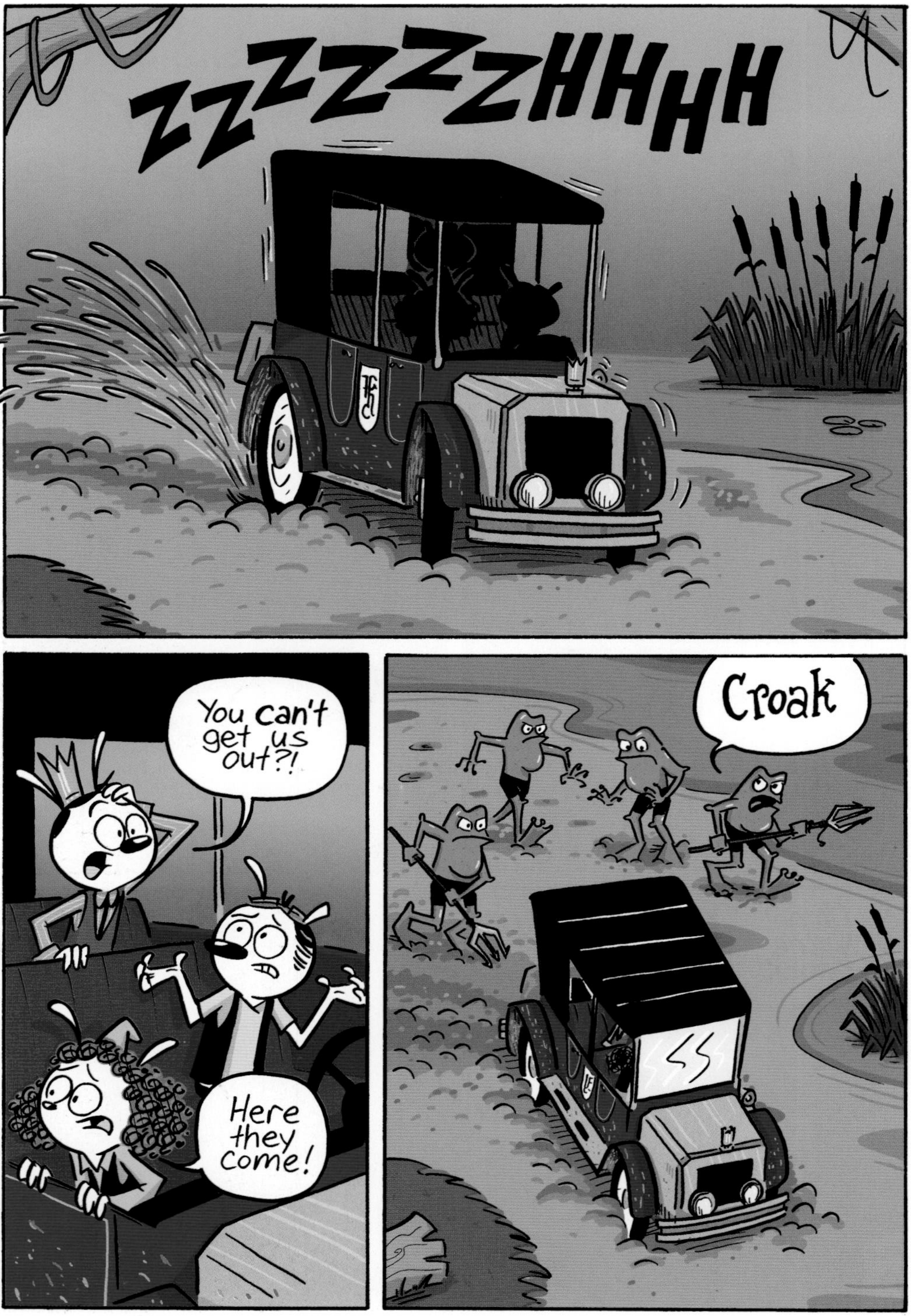
ZZZZZZZHHHHH
You can't get us out?!
Here they come!
Croak

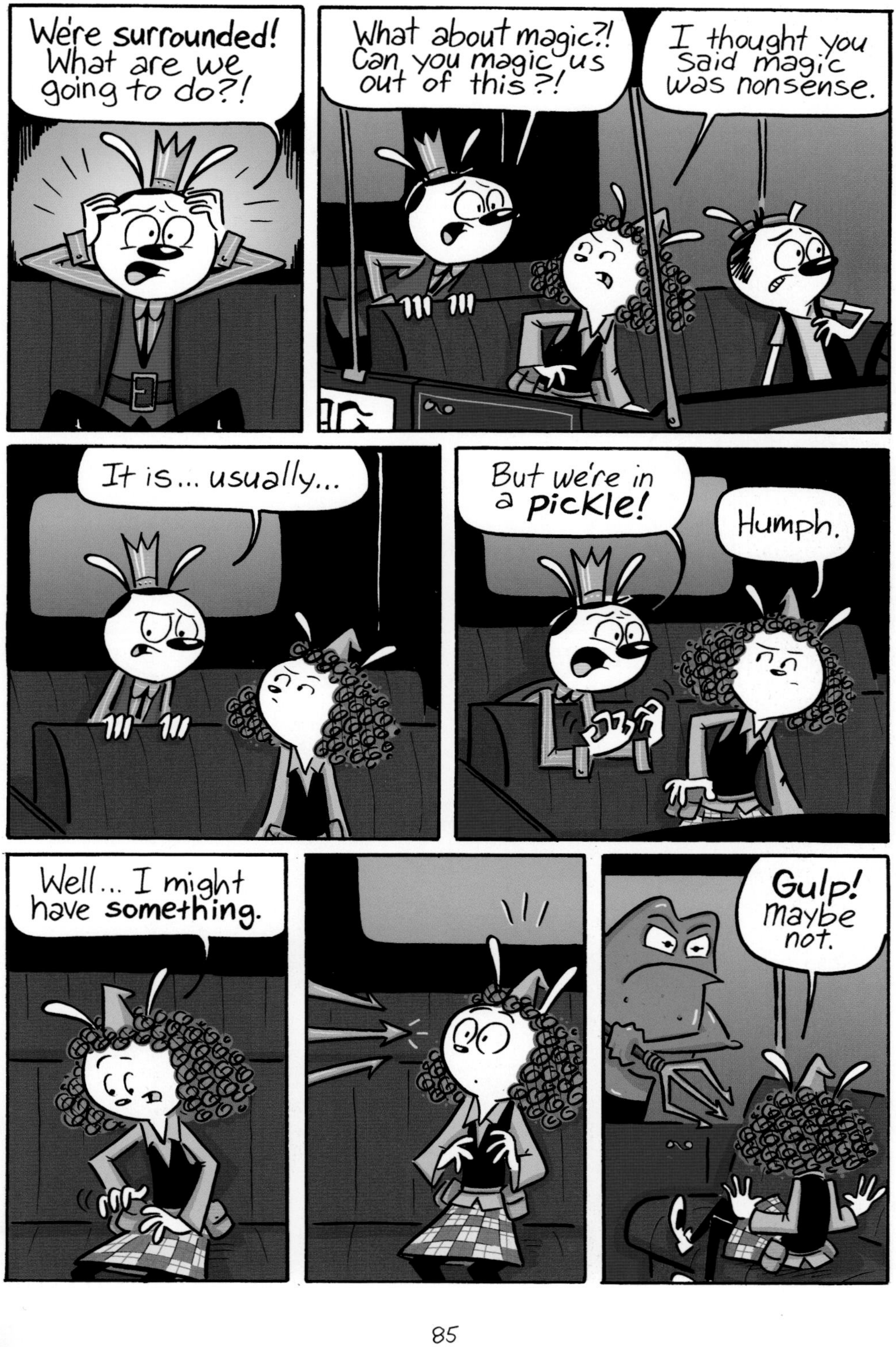
We're surrounded! What are we going to do?!
What about magic?! Can you magic us out of this?!
I thought you said magic was nonsense.
It is... usually...
But we're in a pickle!
Humph.
Well... I might have something.
Gulp! Maybe not.

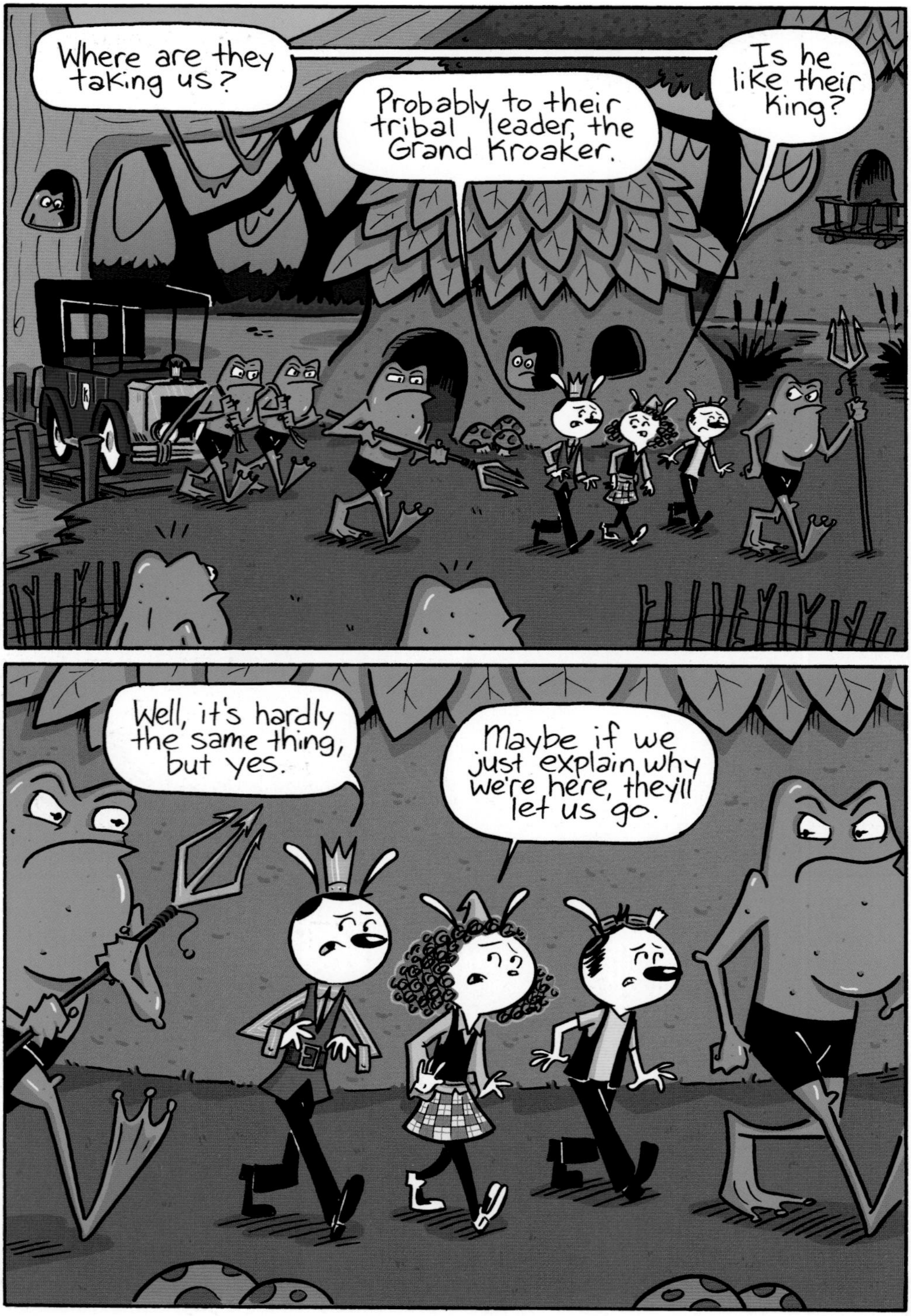
Where are they taking us?
Probably to their tribal leader, the Grand Kroaker.
Is he like their King?
Well, it's hardly the same thing, but yes.
Maybe if we just explain why we're here, they'll let us go.

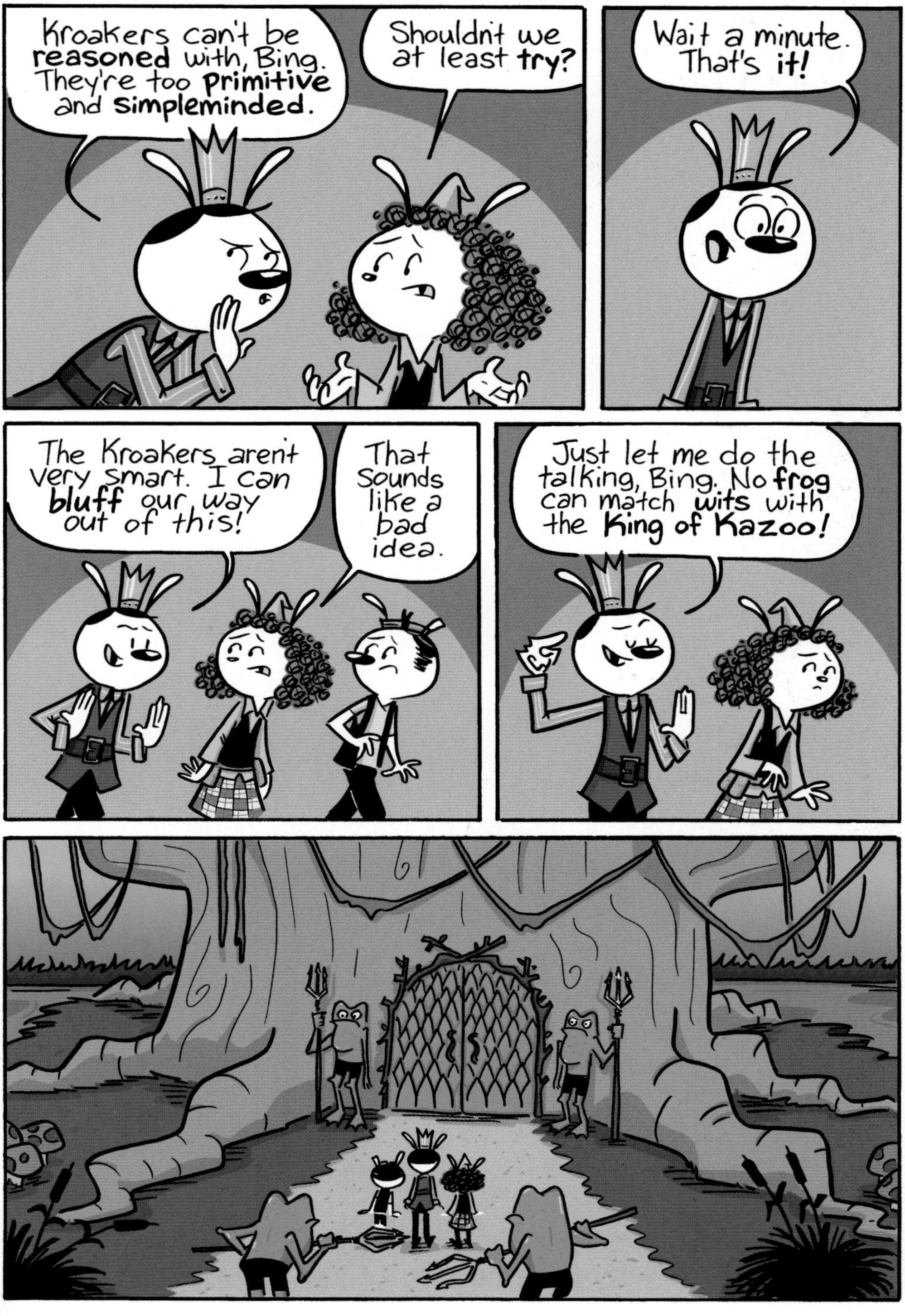
Kroakers can't be **reasoned** with, Bing. They're too **primitive** and **simpleminded**.
Shouldn't we at least **try?**
Wait a minute. That's **it!**
The Kroakers aren't very smart. I can **bluff** our way out of this!
That sounds like a bad idea.
Just let me do the talking, Bing. No **frog** can match **wits** with the **King of Kazoo!**

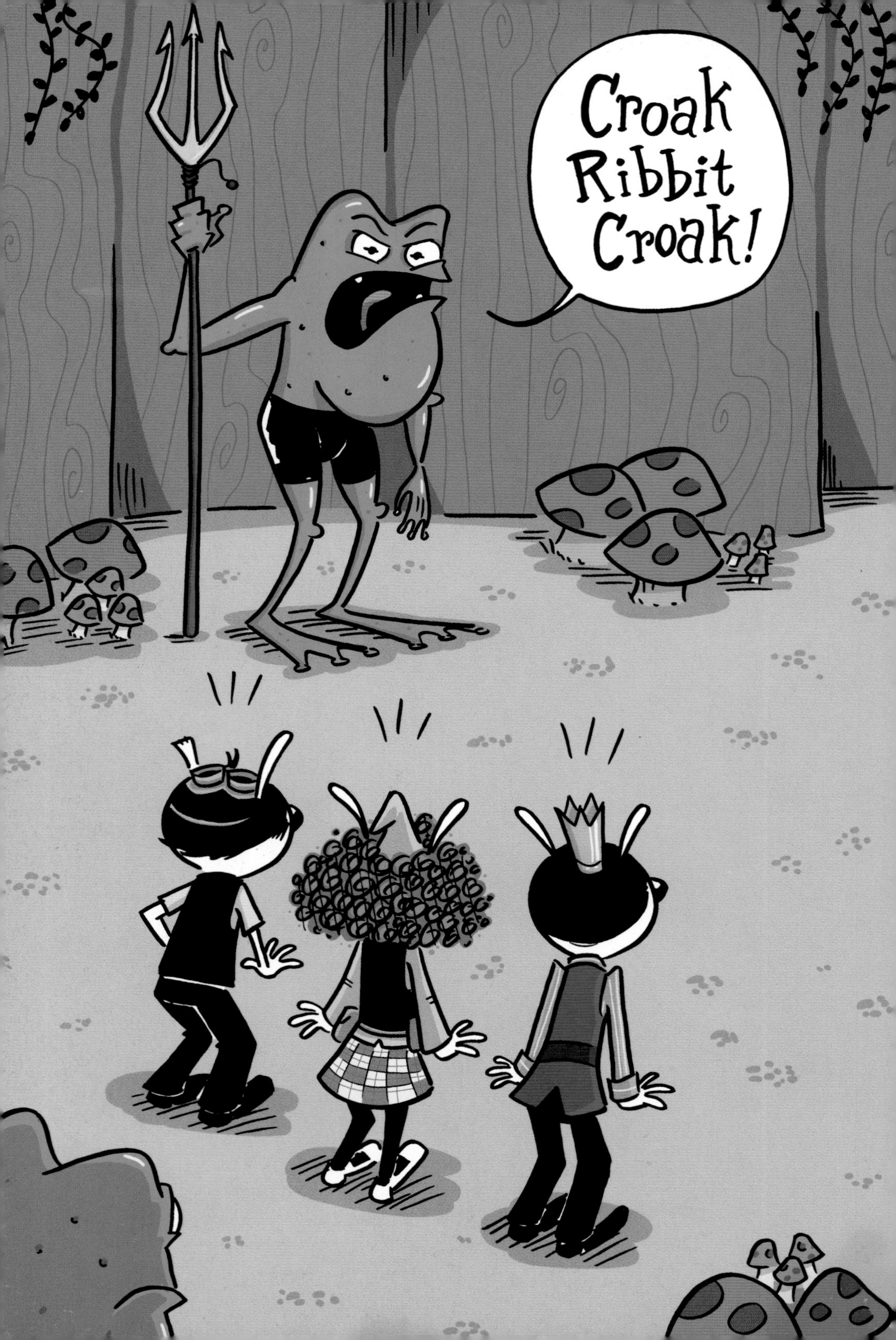
Croak Ribbit Croak!

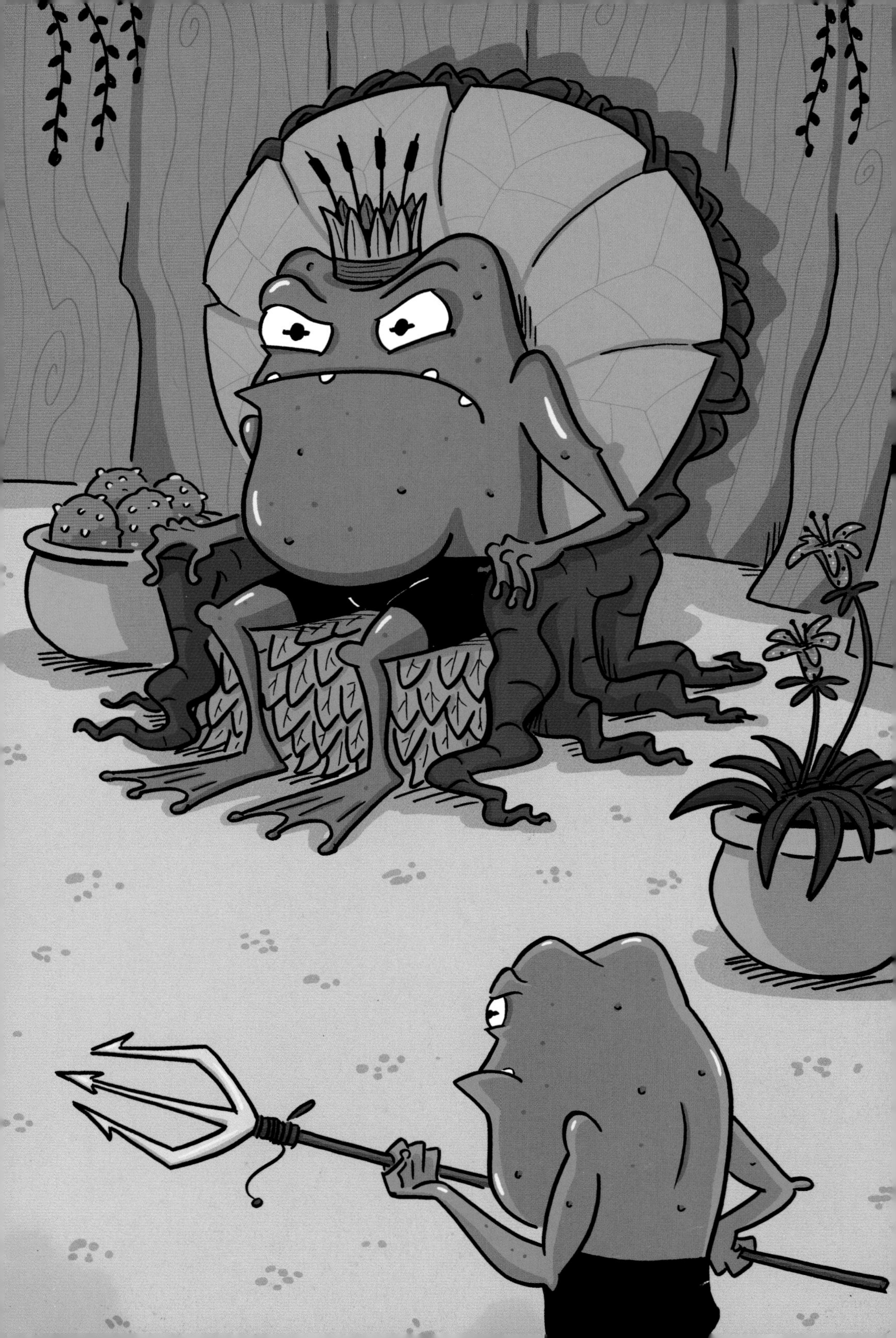

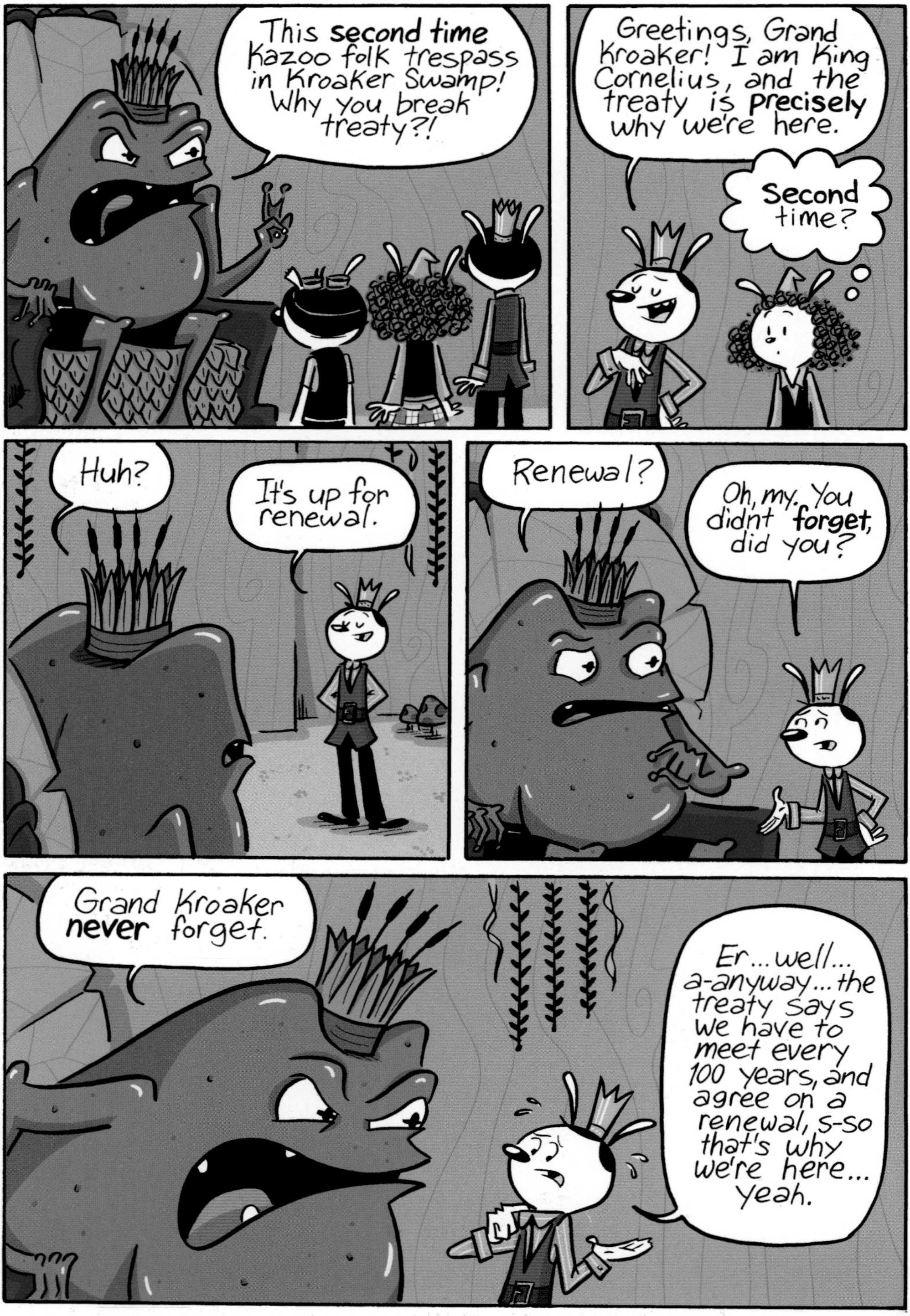

This **second time** Kazoo folk trespass in Kroaker Swamp! Why you break treaty?!
Greetings, Grand Kroaker! I am King Cornelius, and the treaty is **precisely** why we're here.
Second time?
Huh?
It's up for renewal.
Renewal?
Oh, my. You didn't **forget**, did you?
Grand Kroaker **never** forget.
Er... well... a-anyway... the treaty says we have to meet every 100 years, and agree on a renewal, s-so that's why we're here... yeah.

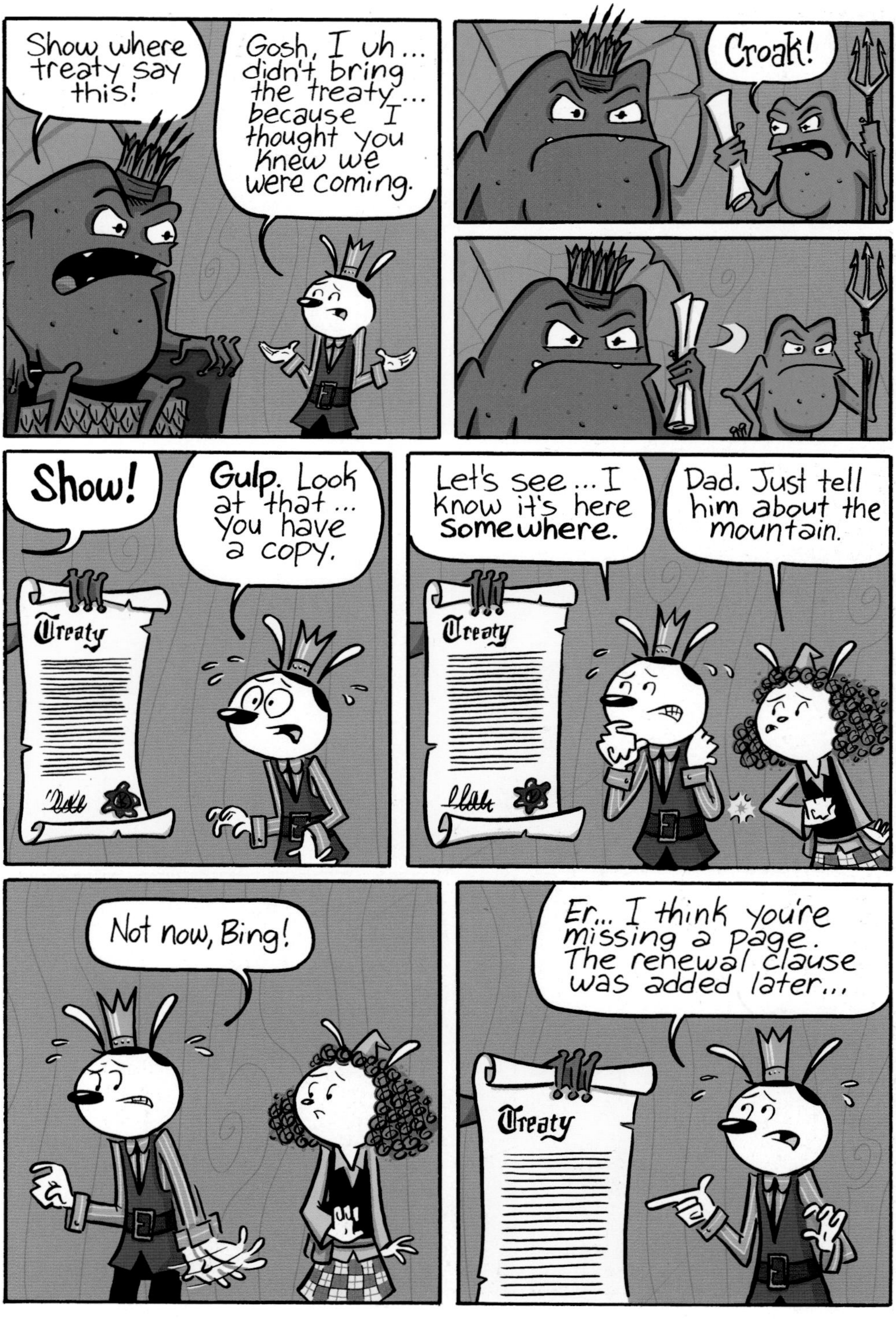

Show where treaty say this!
Gosh, I uh... didn't bring the treaty... because I thought you knew we were coming.
Croak!
Show!
Gulp. Look at that... you have a copy.
Treaty
Let's see... I know it's here somewhere.
Dad. Just tell him about the mountain.
Treaty
Not now, Bing!
Er... I think you're missing a page. The renewal clause was added later...
Treaty

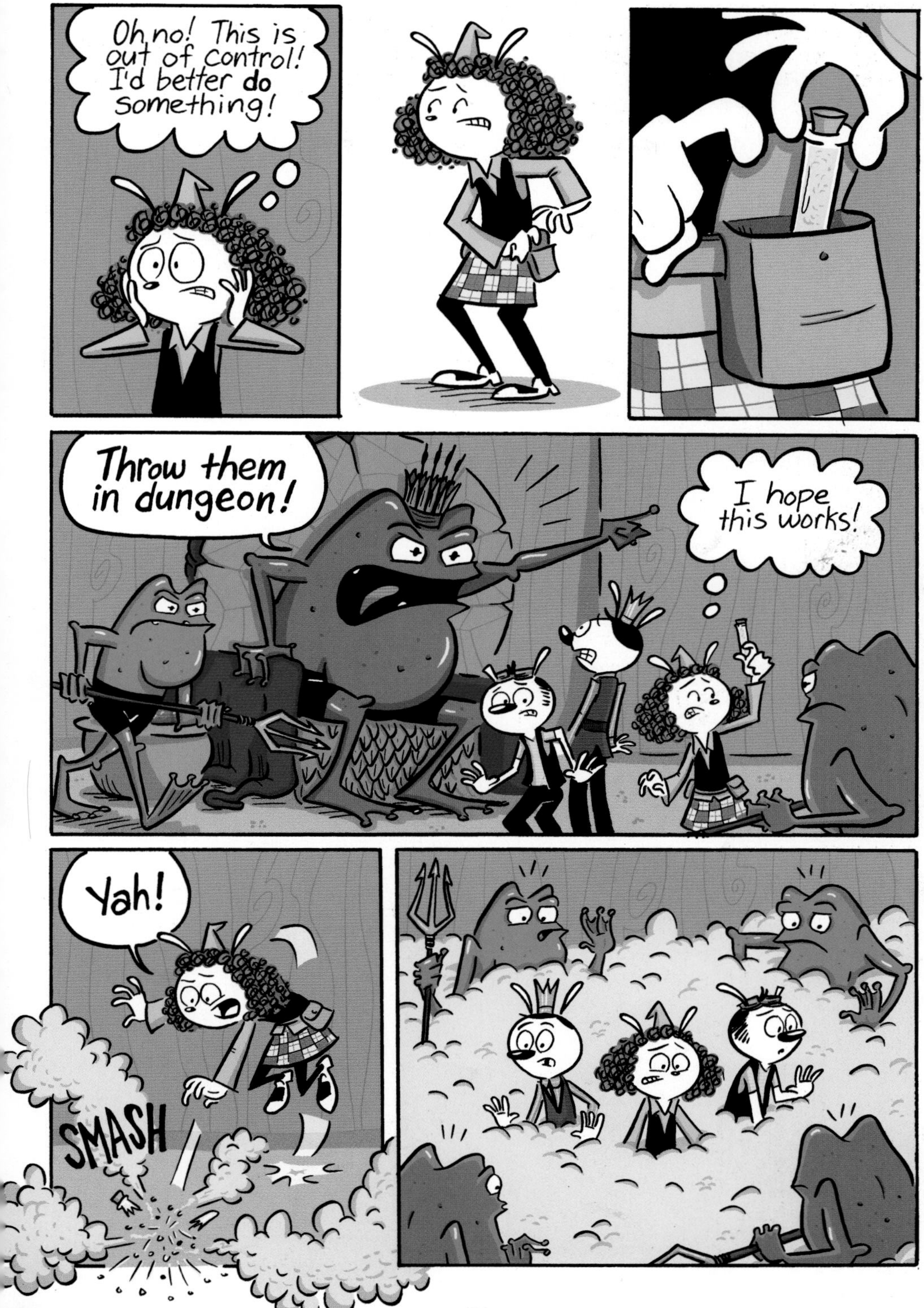
Oh, no! This is out of control! I'd better **do** something!
Throw them in dungeon!
I hope this works!
Yah!
SMASH

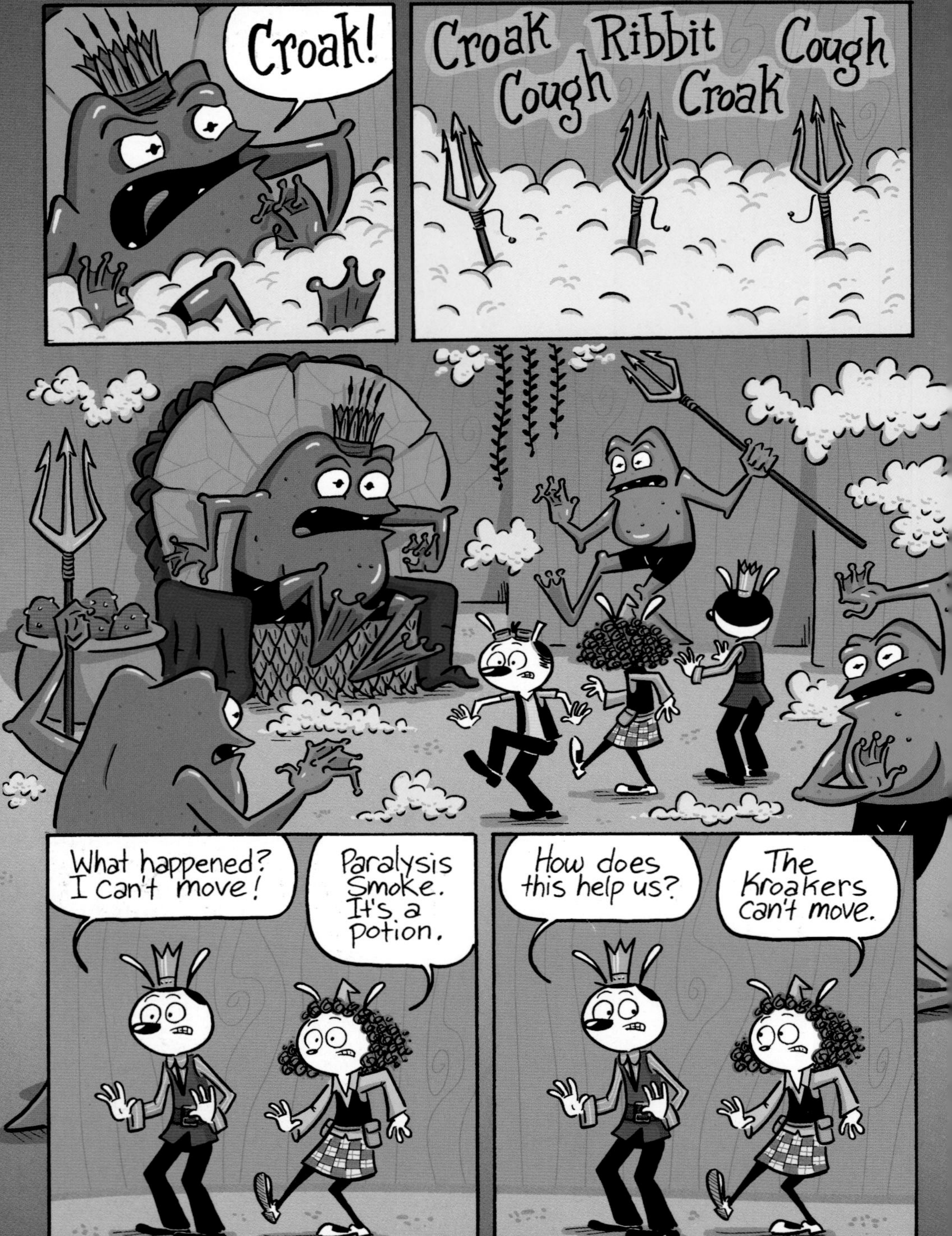
Croak!
Croak
Cough
Ribbit
Croak
Cough
What happened? I can't move!
Paralysis Smoke. It's a potion.
How does this help us?
The Kroakers can't move.

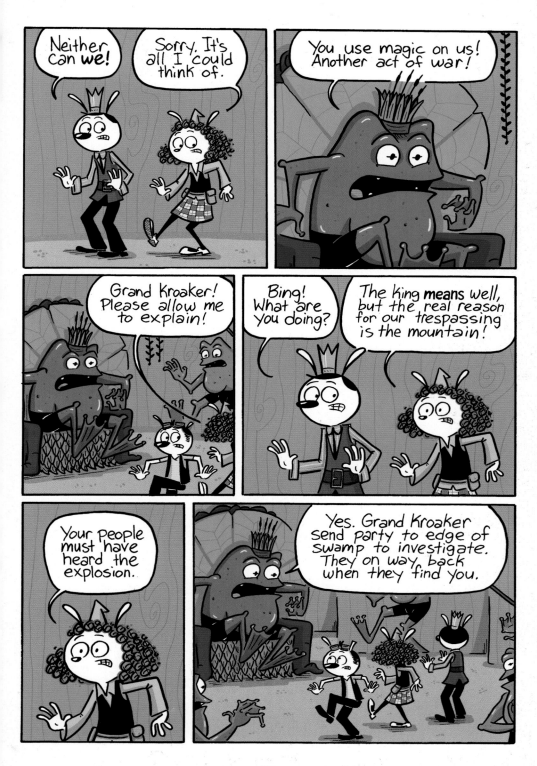

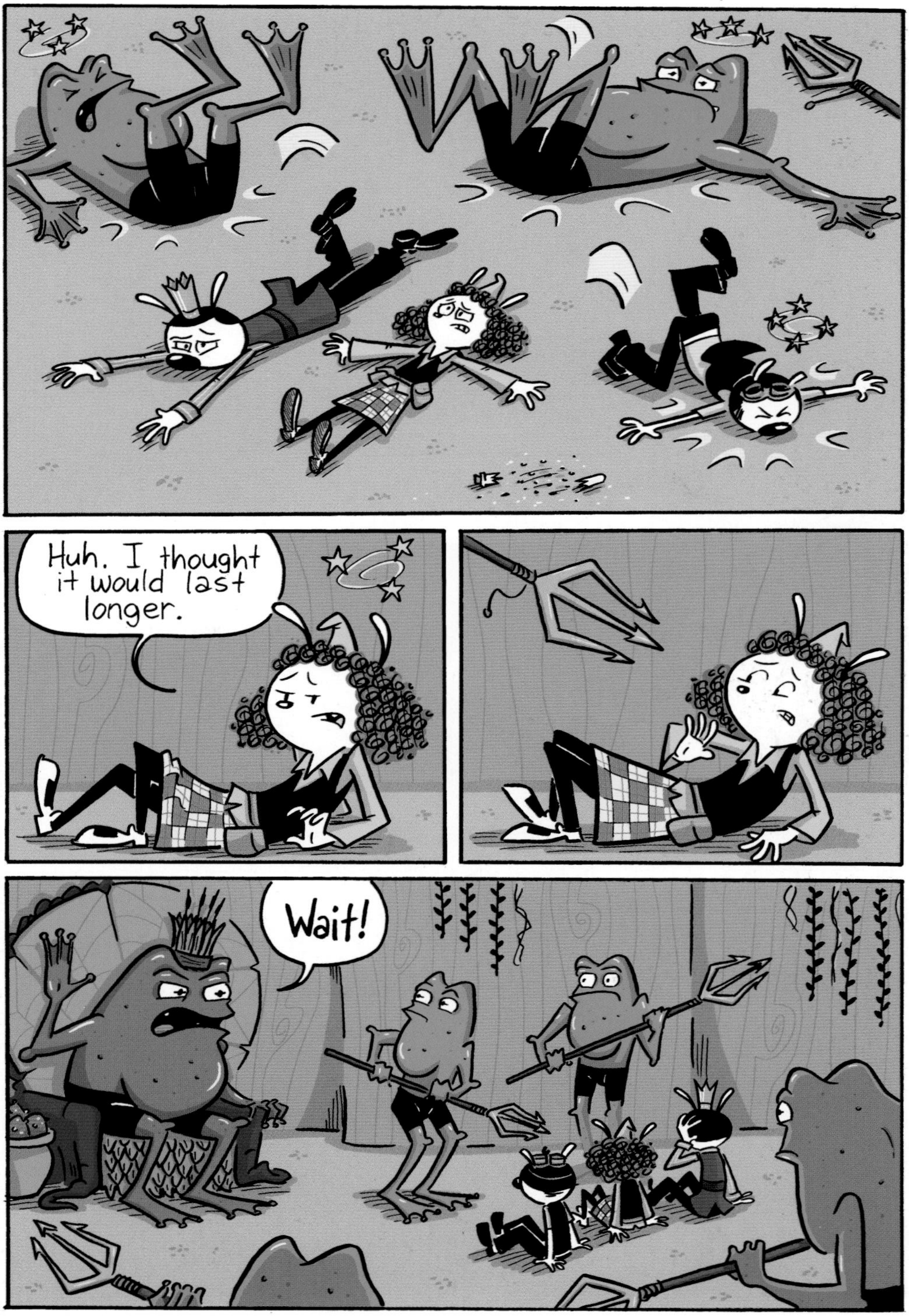
Huh. I thought it would last longer.
Wait!

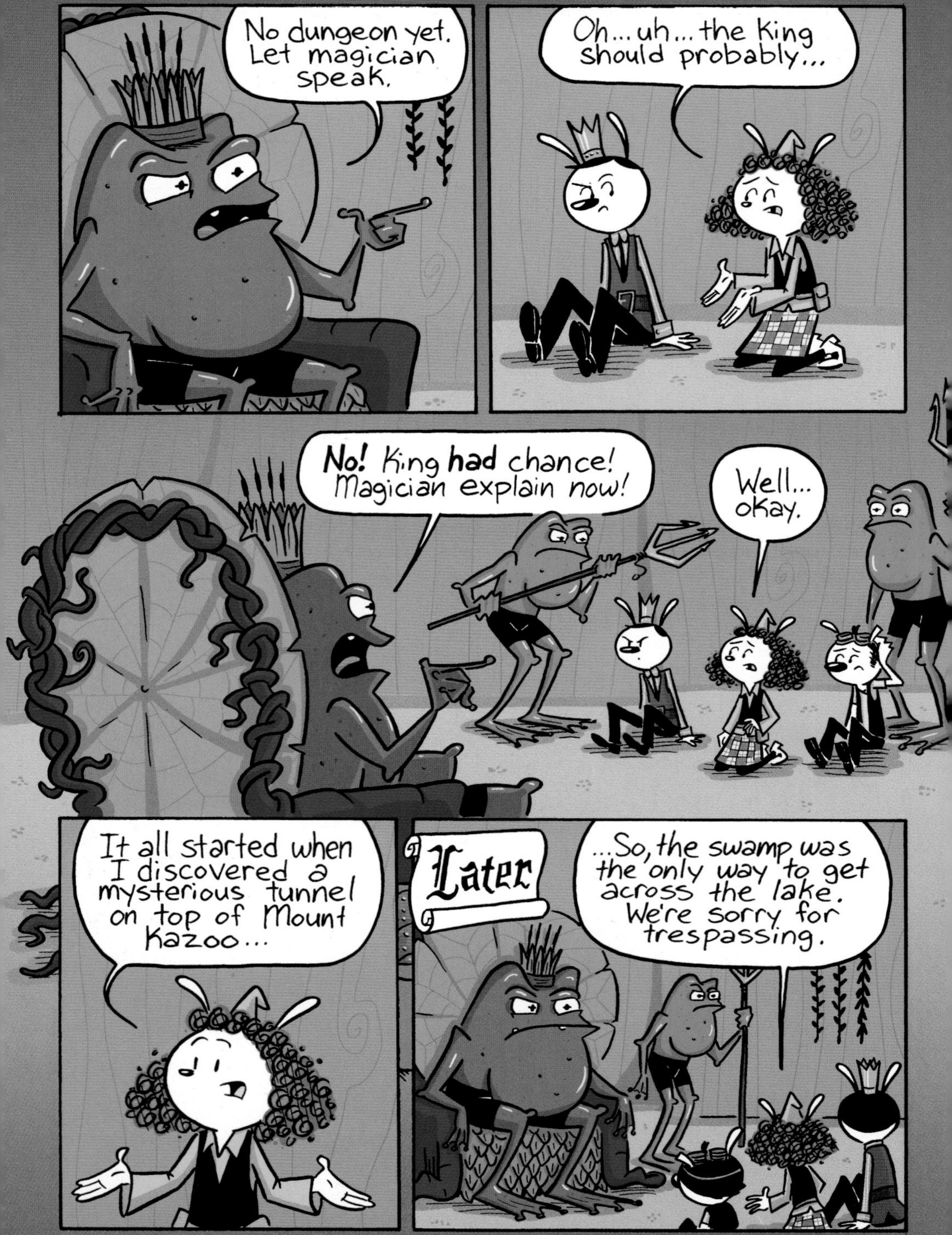
No dungeon yet. Let magician speak.
Oh... uh... the King should probably...
No! King **had** chance! Magician explain now!
Well... okay.
It all started when I discovered a mysterious tunnel on top of Mount Kazoo...
Later
...So, the swamp was the only way to get across the lake. We're sorry for trespassing.

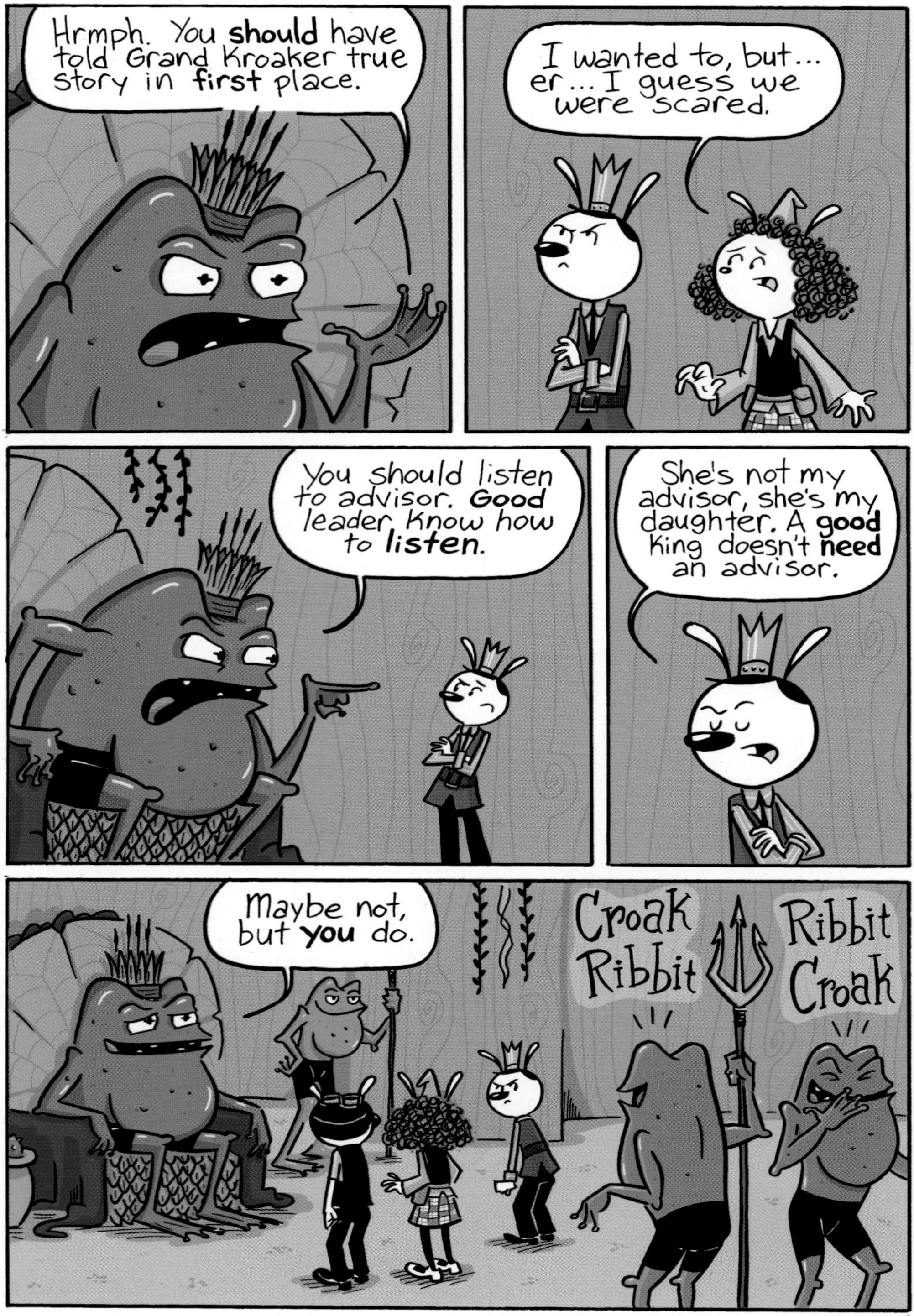
Hrmph. You **should** have told Grand Kroaker true story in **first** place.
I wanted to, but... er... I guess we were scared.
You should listen to advisor. **Good** leader know how to **listen**.
She's not my advisor, she's my daughter. A **good** king doesn't **need** an advisor.
Maybe not, but **you** do.
Croak Ribbit
Ribbit Croak

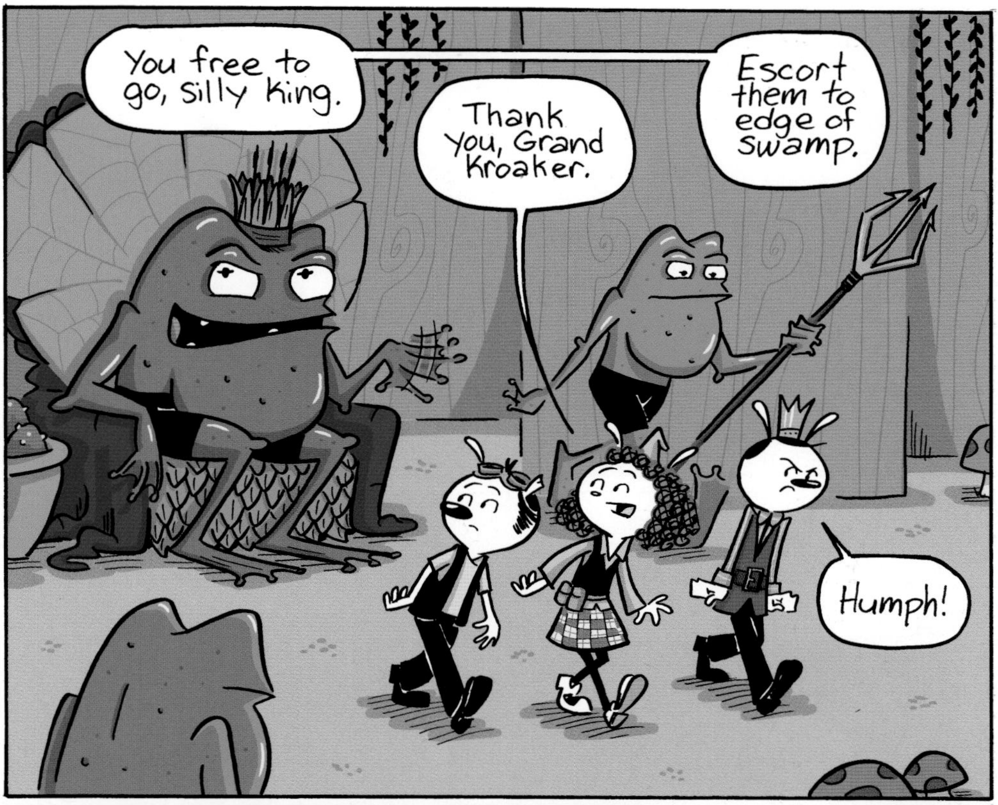
You free to go, Silly King.
Thank You, Grand Kroaker.
Escort them to edge of swamp.
Humph!

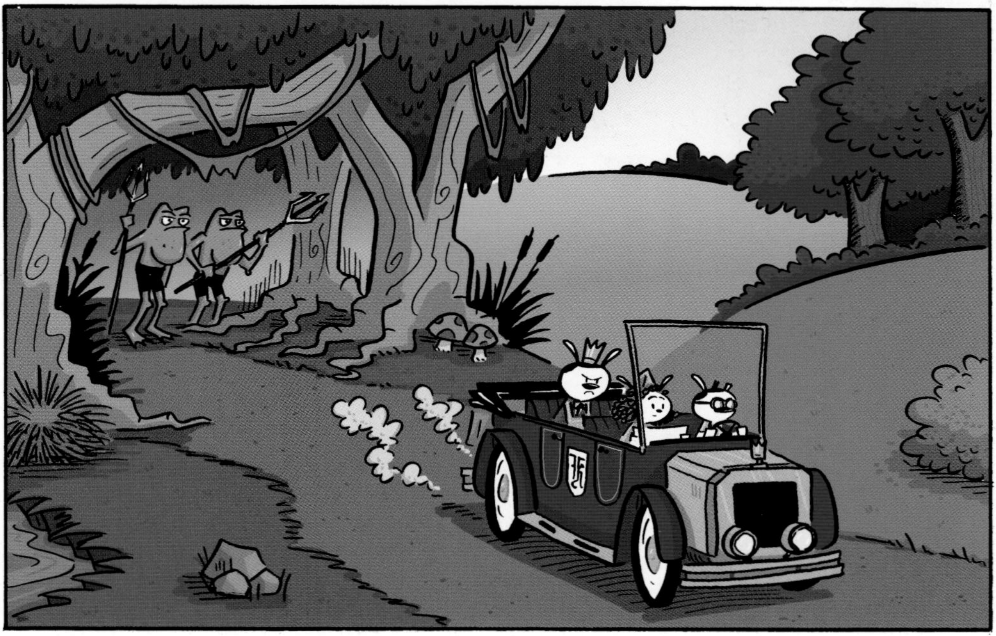

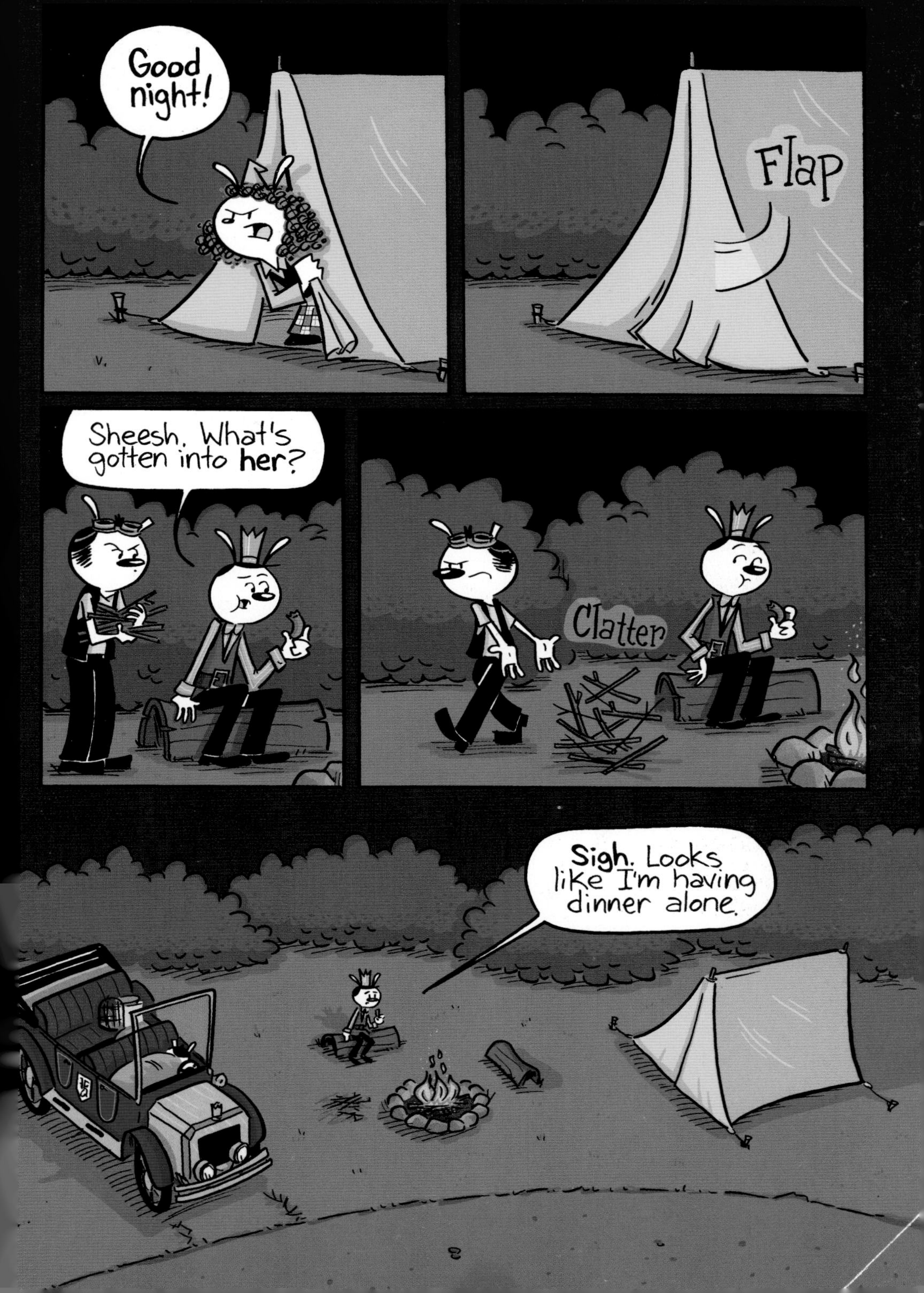
Good night!
Flap
Sheesh. What's gotten into her?
Clatter
Sigh. Looks like I'm having dinner alone.

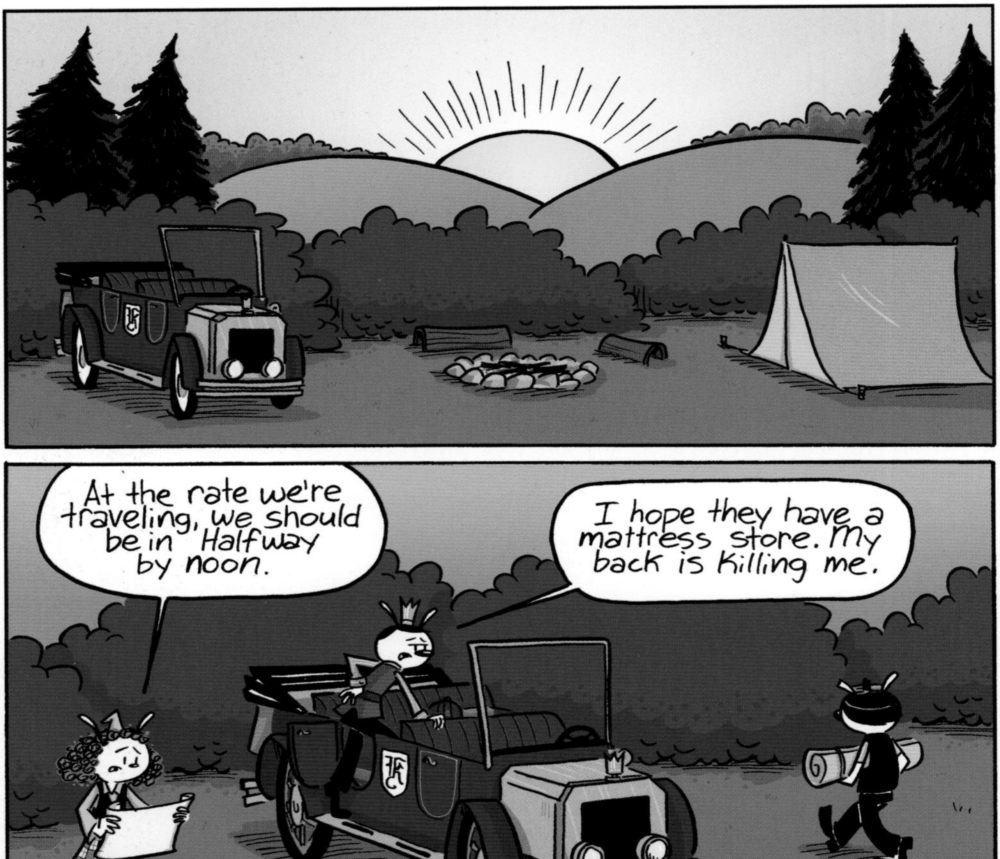
At the rate we're traveling, we should be in Halfway by noon.
I hope they have a mattress store. My back is Killing me.

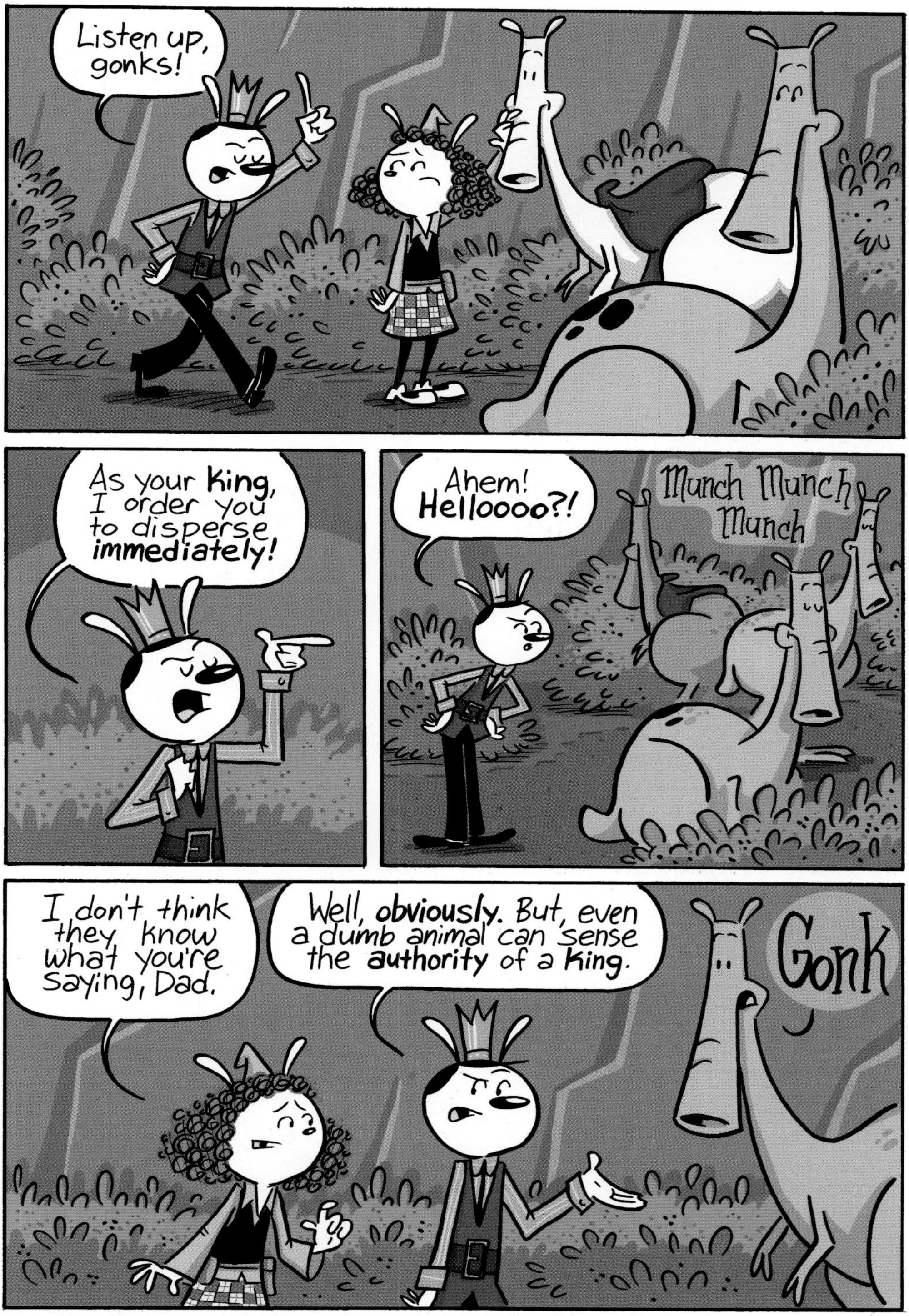
Listen up, gonks!
As your **King**, I order you to disperse **immediately**!
Ahem! **Helloooo?!**
Munch Munch Munch
I don't think they know what you're saying, Dad.
Well, **obviously**. But, even a dumb animal can sense the **authority** of a **King**.
Gonk

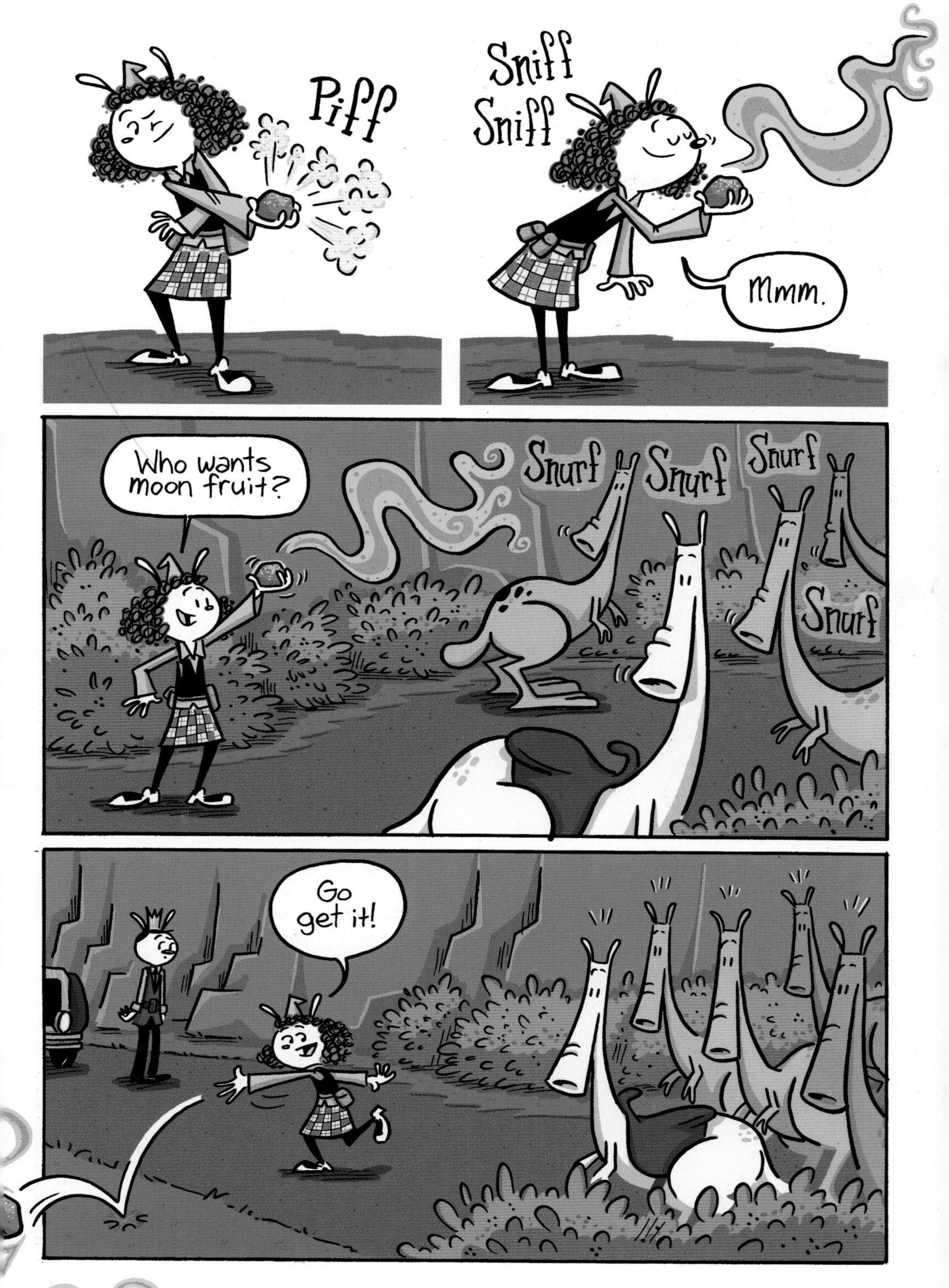
Piff
Sniff
Sniff
Mmm.
Who wants moon fruit?
Snurf
Snurf
Snurf
Snurf
Go get it!

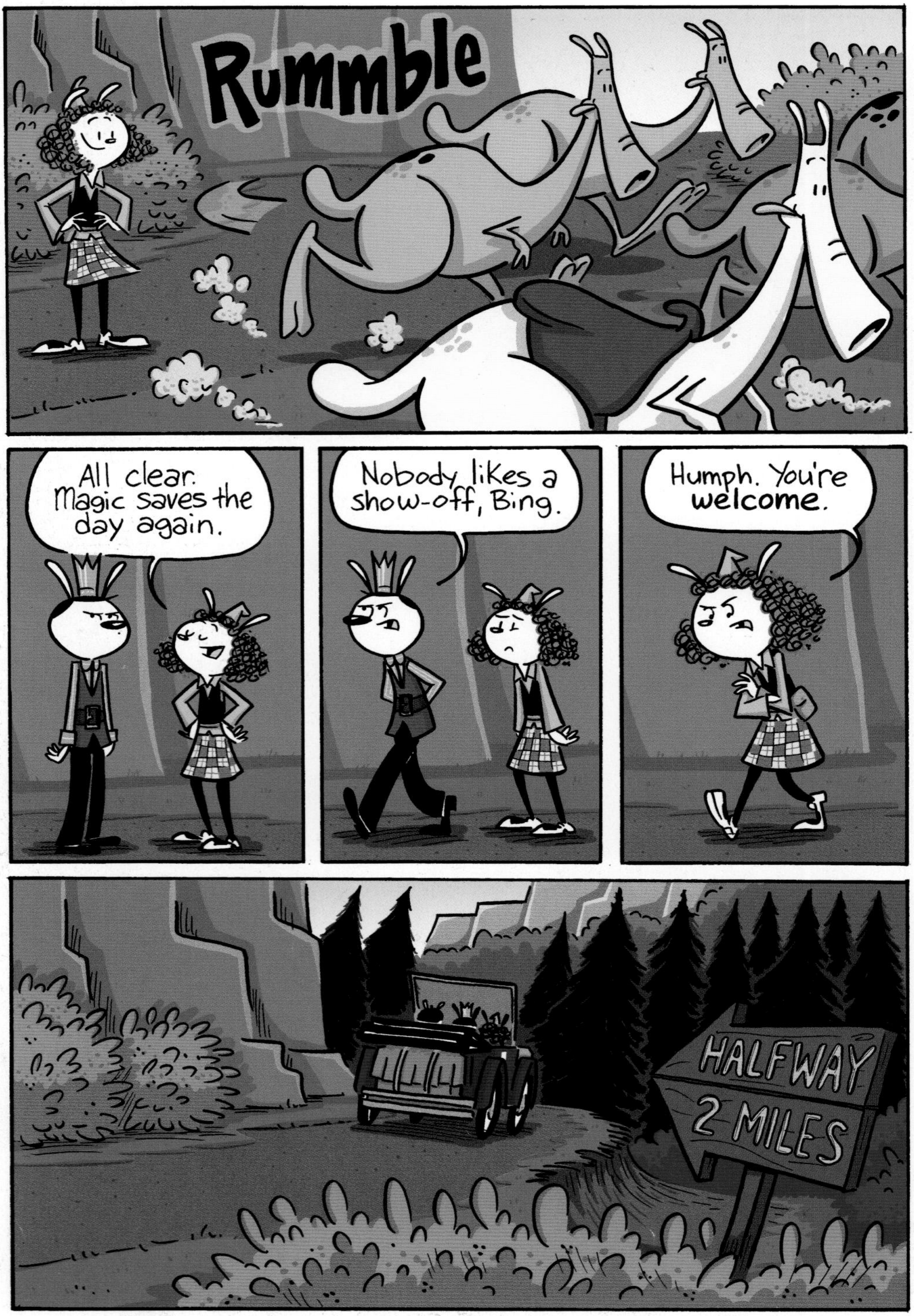

Rummble
All clear. Magic saves the day again.
Nobody likes a show-off, Bing.
Humph. You're **welcome**.
HALFWAY 2 MILES

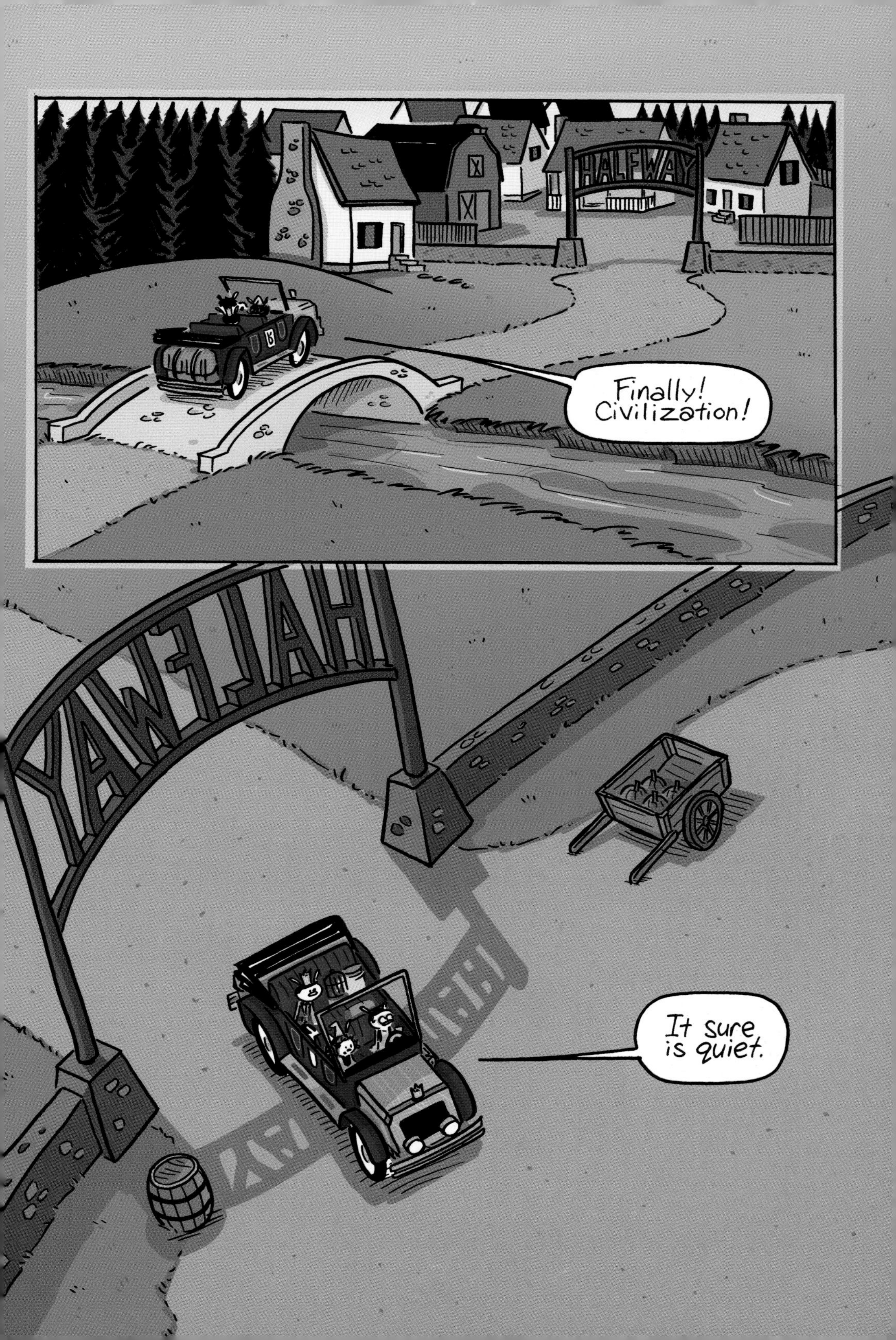
HALFWAY
Finally! Civilization!
It sure is quiet.

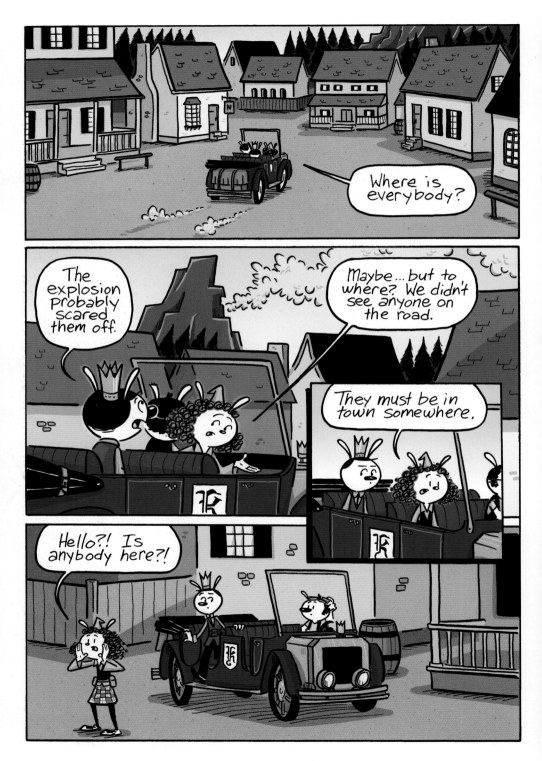

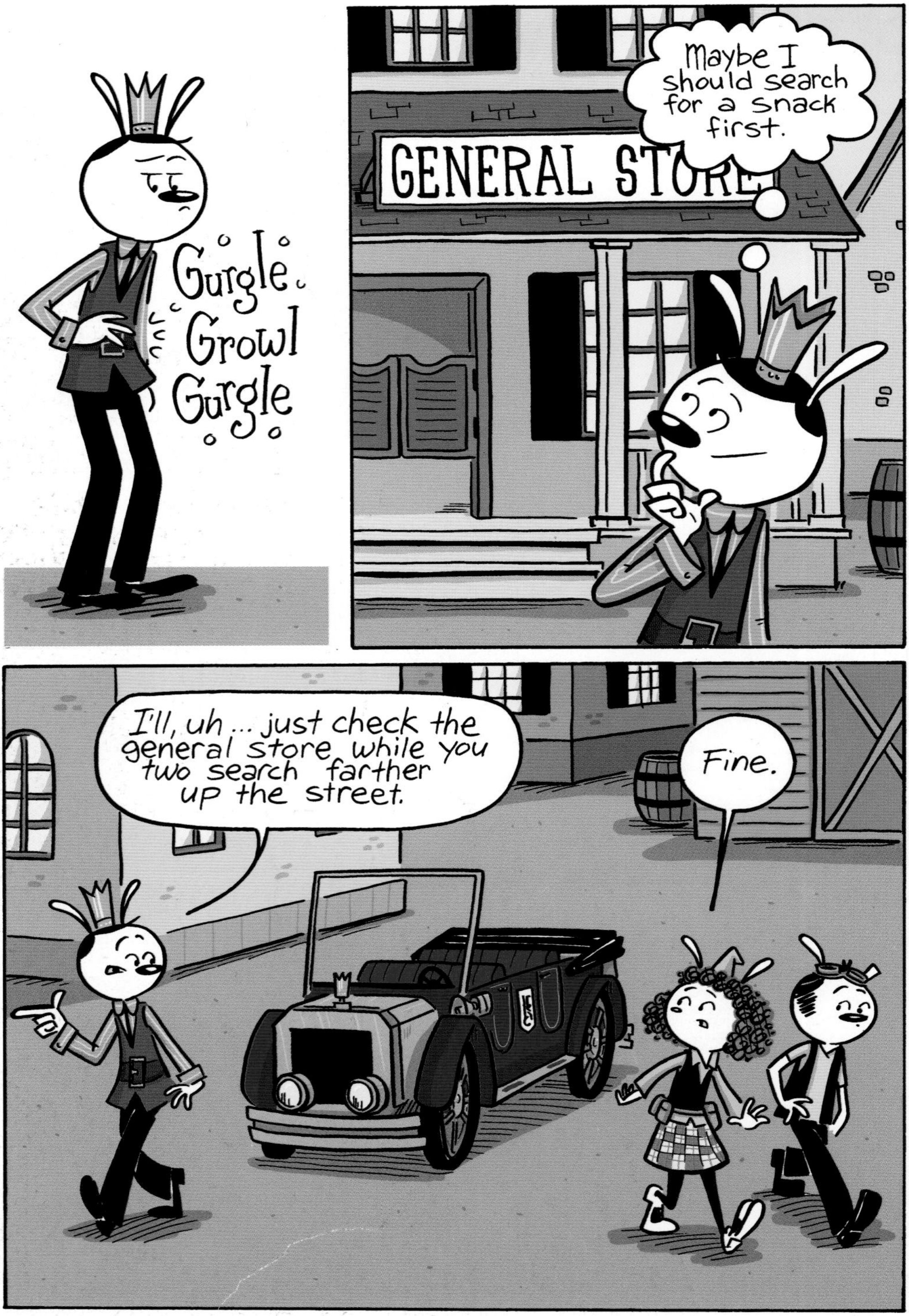
Gurgle
Growl
Gurgle
Maybe I should search for a snack first.
GENERAL STORE
I'll, uh... just check the general store while you two search farther up the street.
Fine.

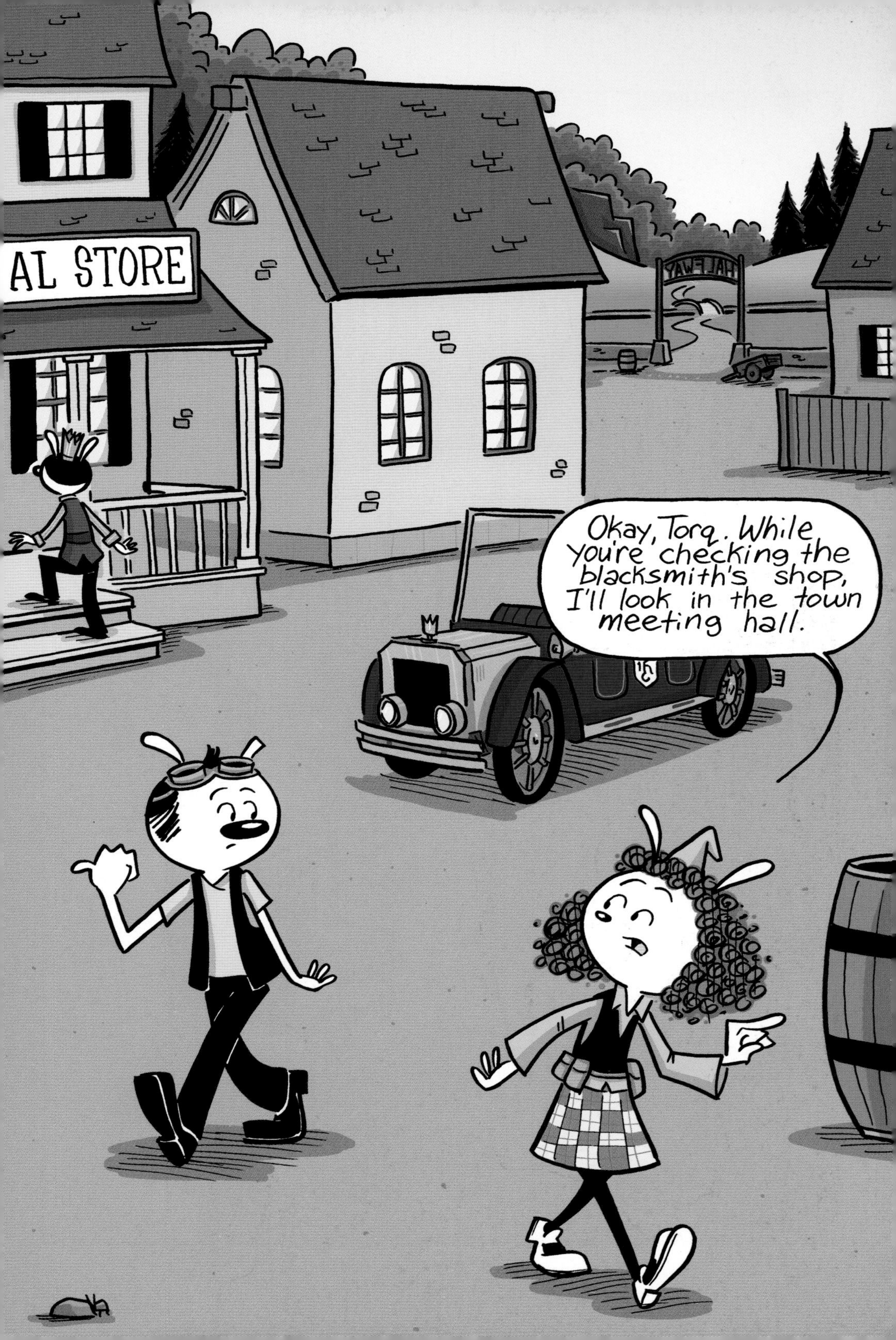
AL STORE
HALFWAY
Okay, Torq. While you're checking the blacksmith's shop, I'll look in the town meeting hall.

116

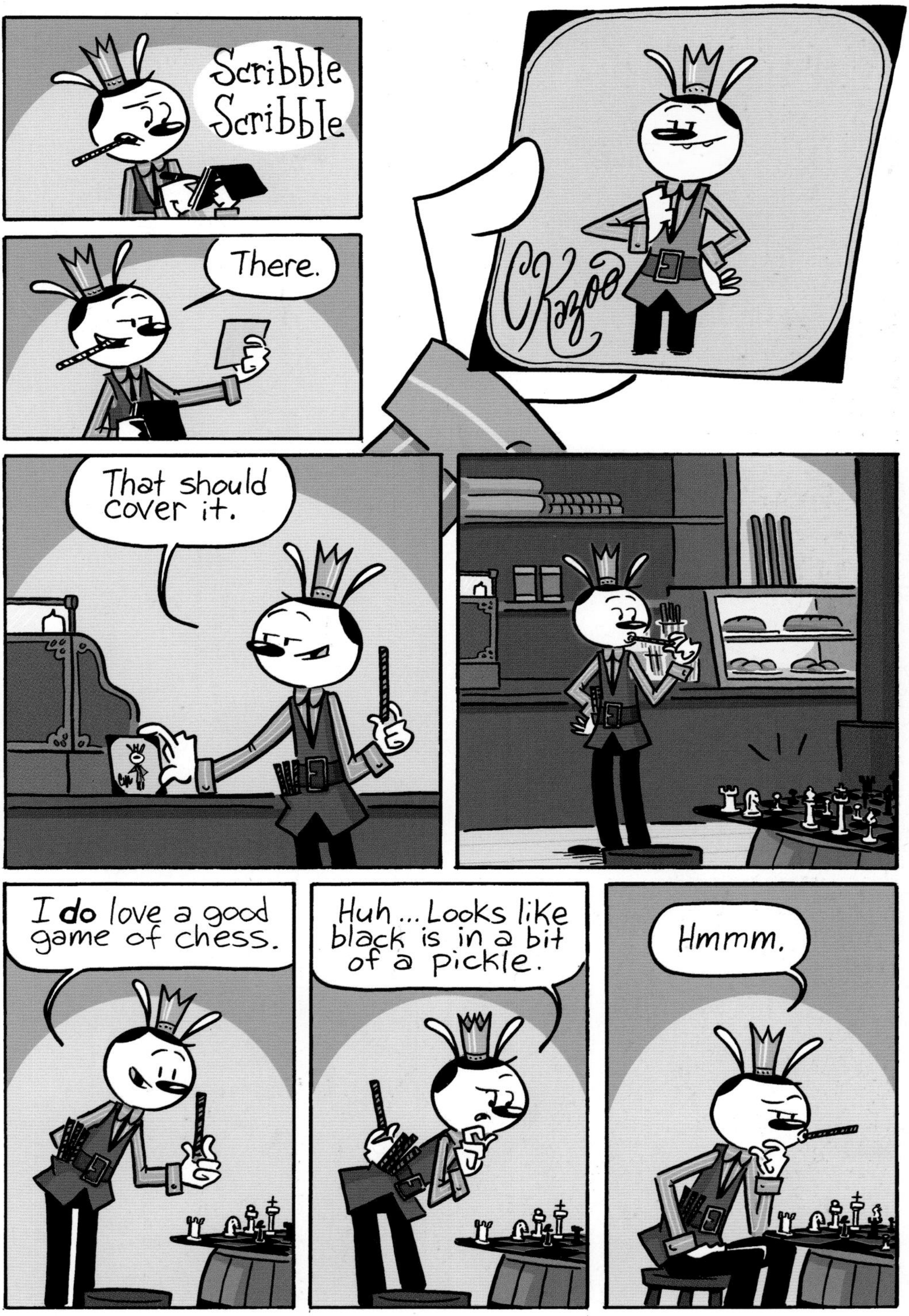
Scribble
Scribble
Kazoo
There.
That should cover it.
I do love a good game of chess.
Huh ... Looks like black is in a bit of a pickle.
Hmmm.

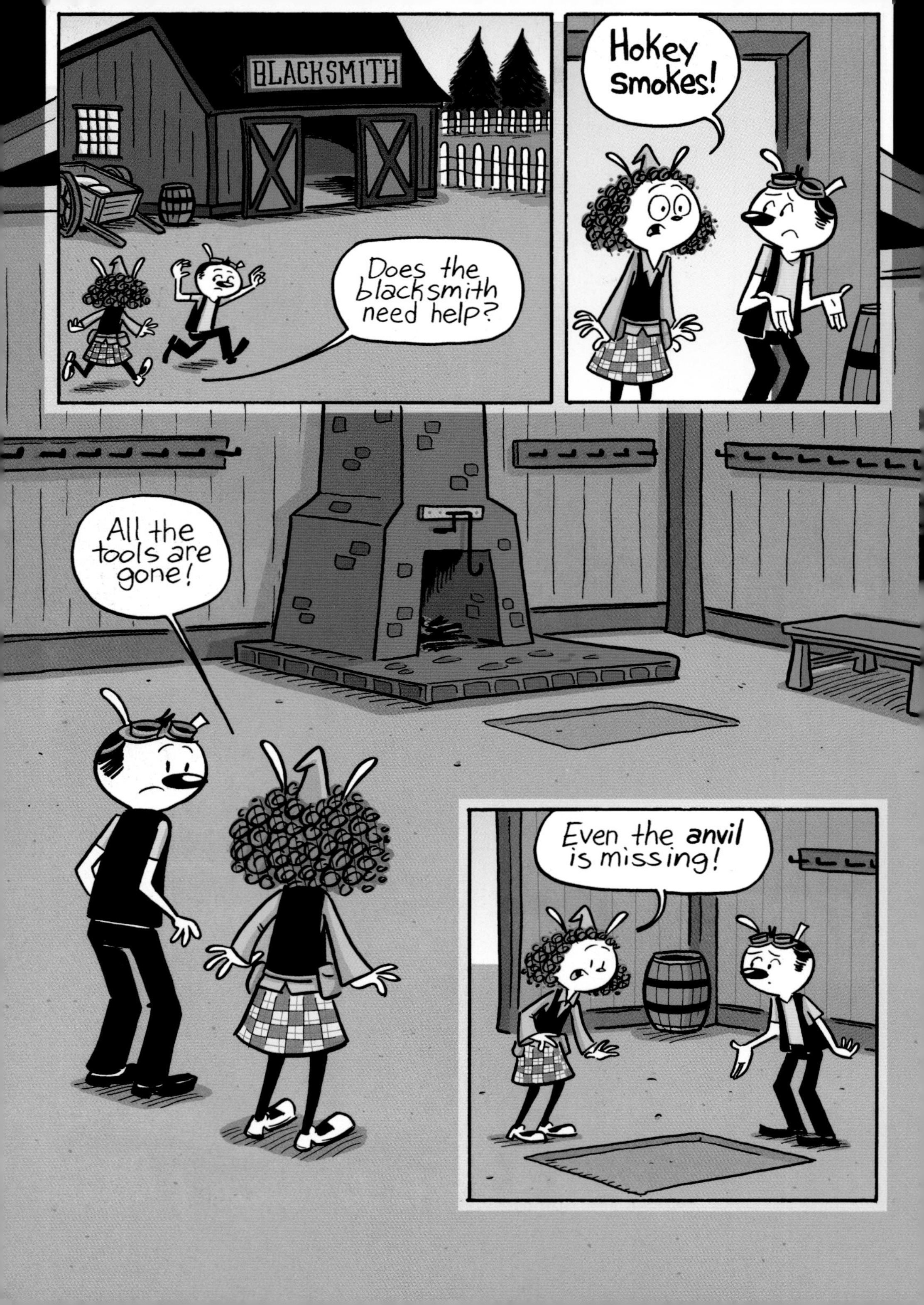
BLACKSMITH
Does the blacksmith need help?
Hokey smokes!
All the tools are gone!
Even the anvil is missing!

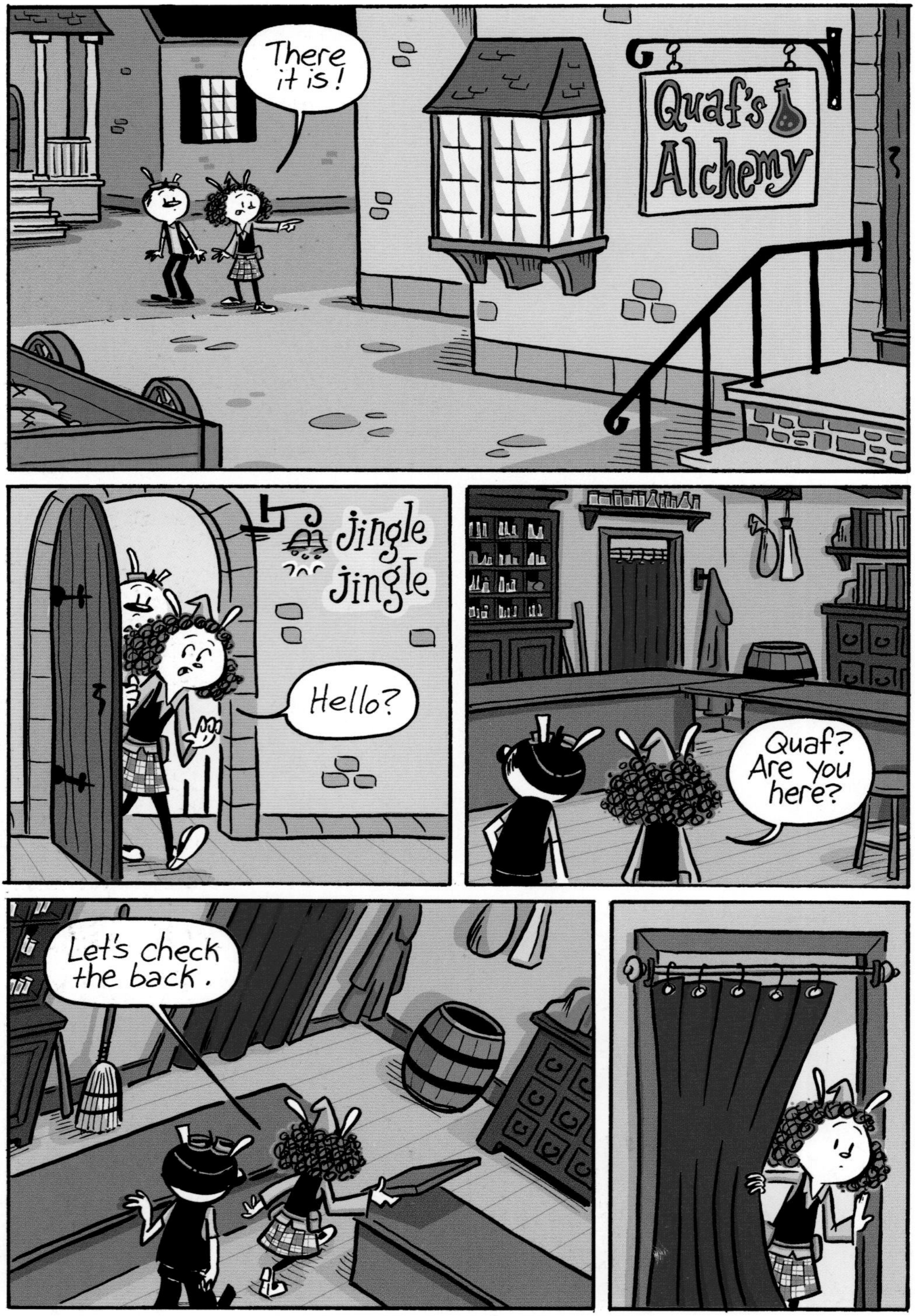
There it is!
Quaf's Alchemy
Jingle jingle
Hello?
Quaf? Are you here?
Let's check the back.

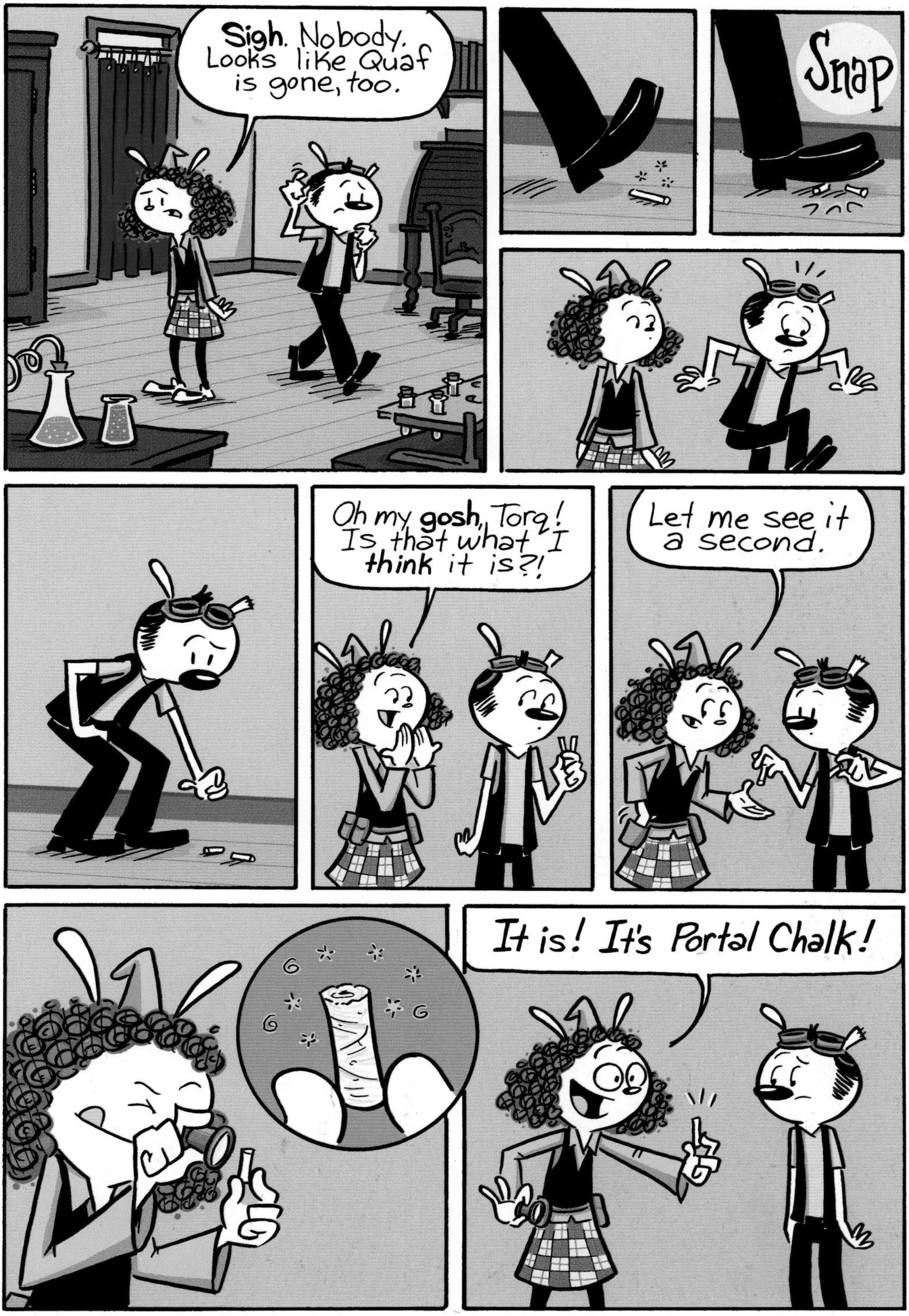
Sigh. Nobody. Looks like Quaf is gone, too.
Snap
Oh my gosh, Torq! Is that what I think it is?!
Let me see it a second.
It is! It's Portal Chalk!

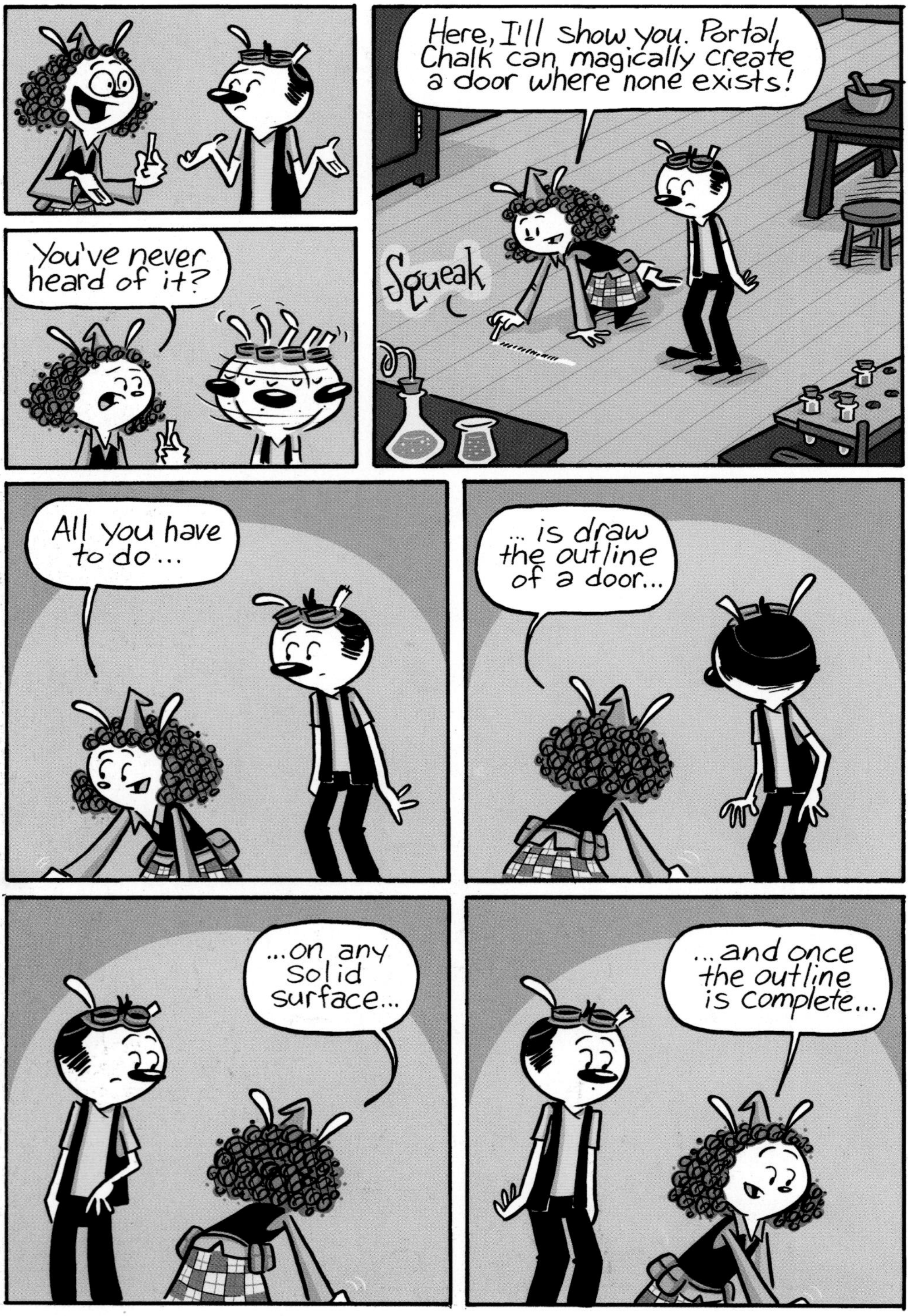
You've never heard of it?
Here, I'll show you. Portal Chalk can magically create a door where none exists!
Squeak
All you have to do...
... is draw the outline of a door...
...on any solid surface...
...and once the outline is complete...

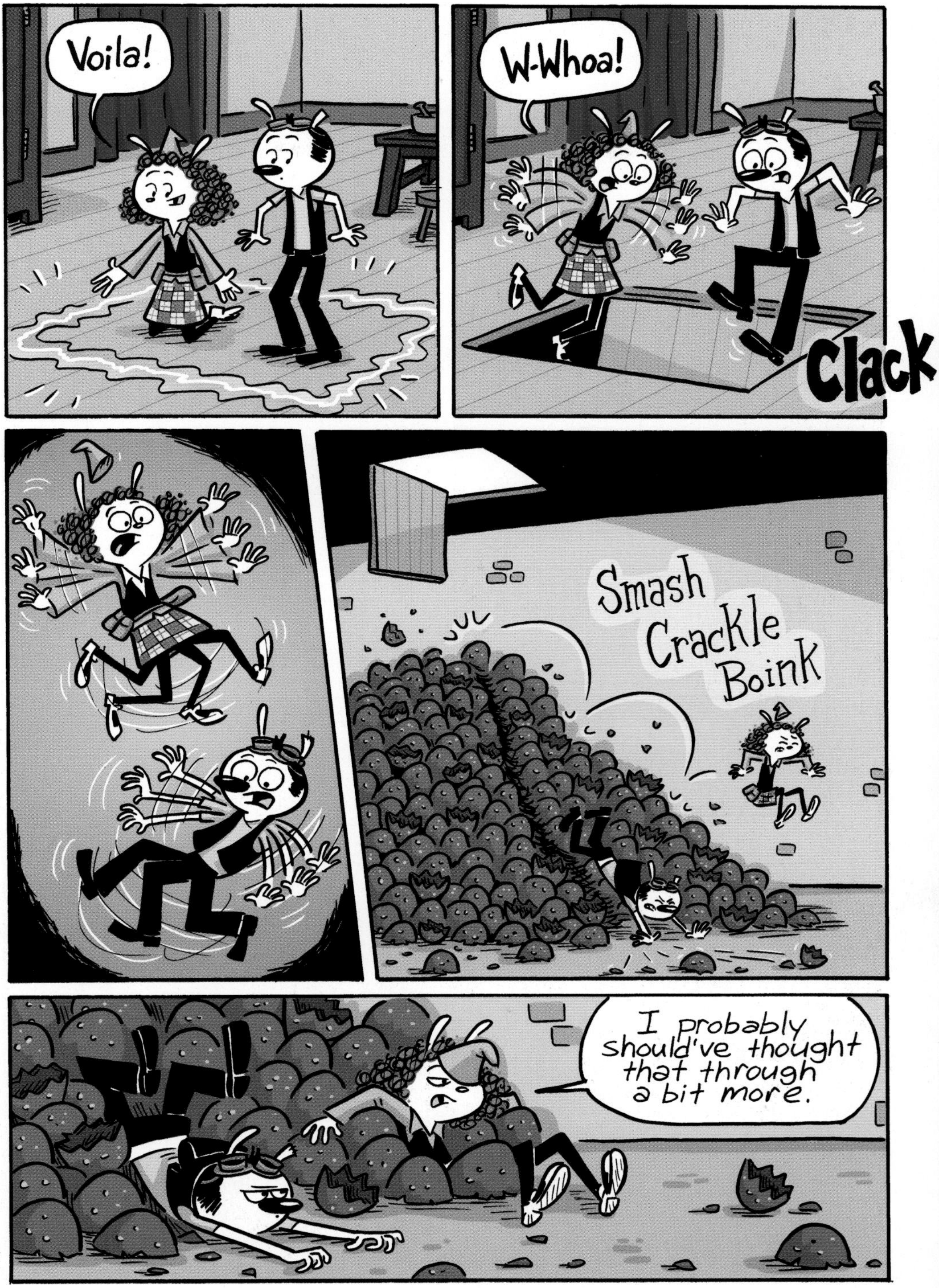
Voila!
W-Whoa!
Clack
Smash
Crackle
Boink
I probably should've thought that through a bit more.

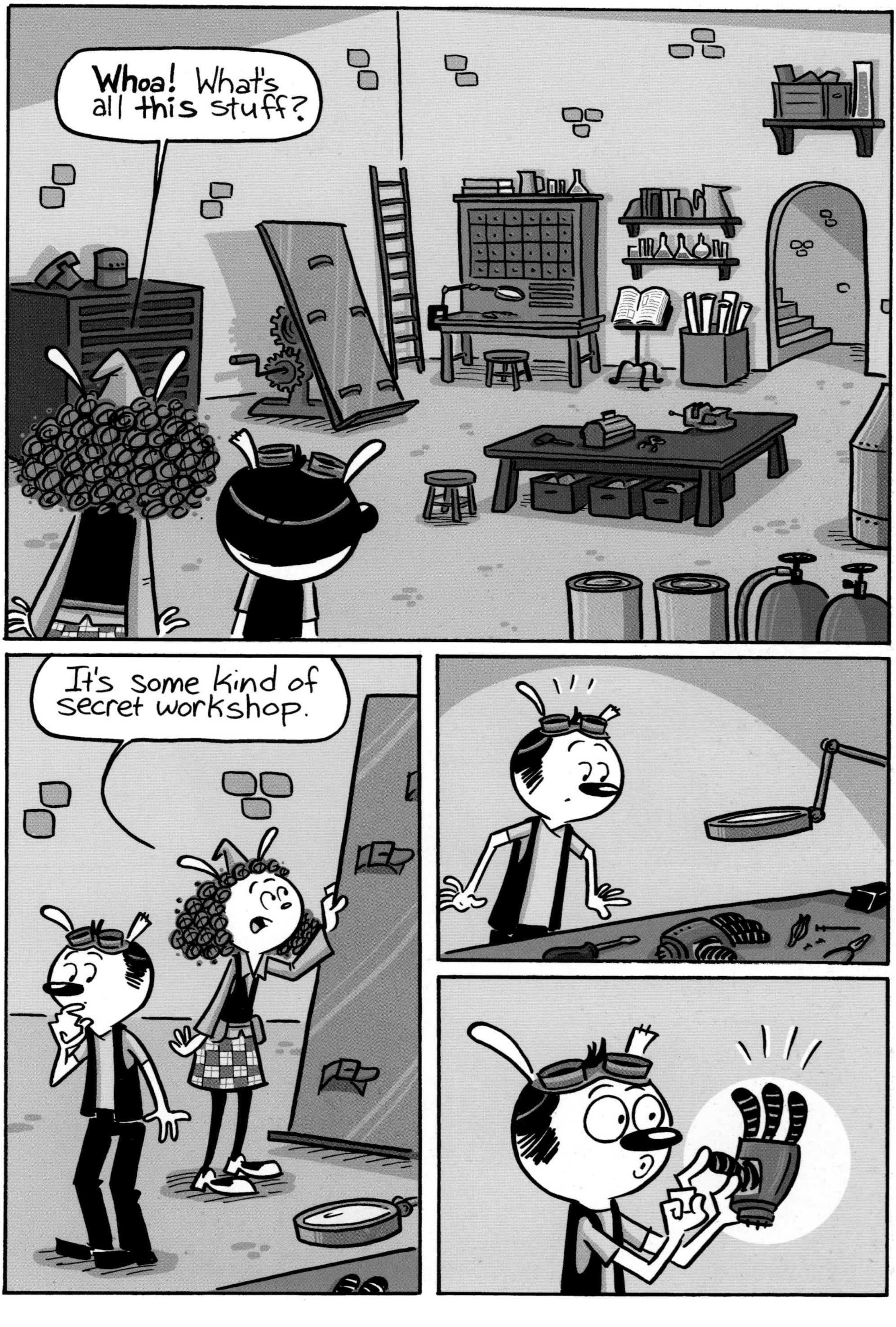
Whoa! What's all this stuff?
It's some kind of secret workshop.

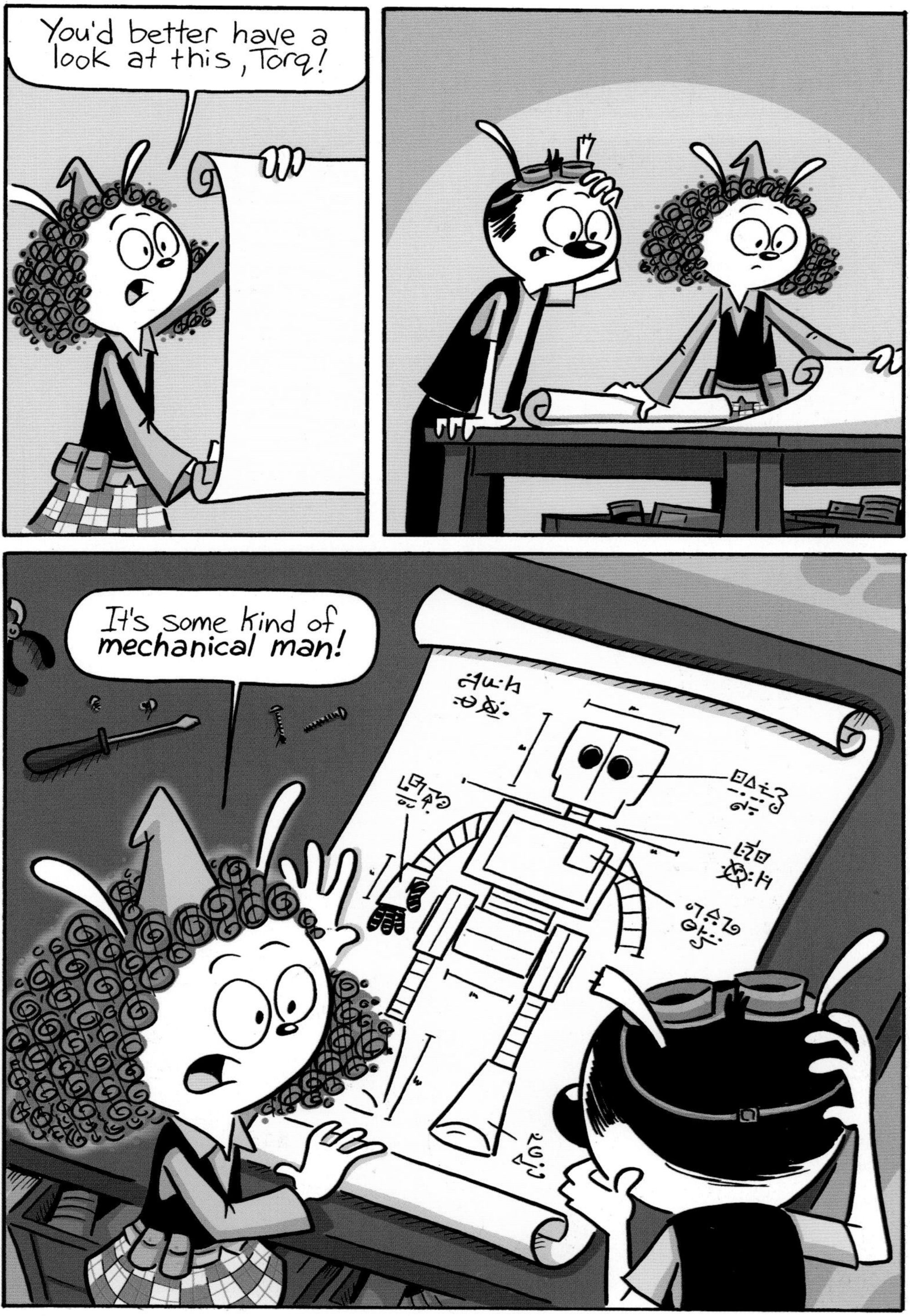
You'd better have a look at this, Torq!
It's some kind of mechanical man!

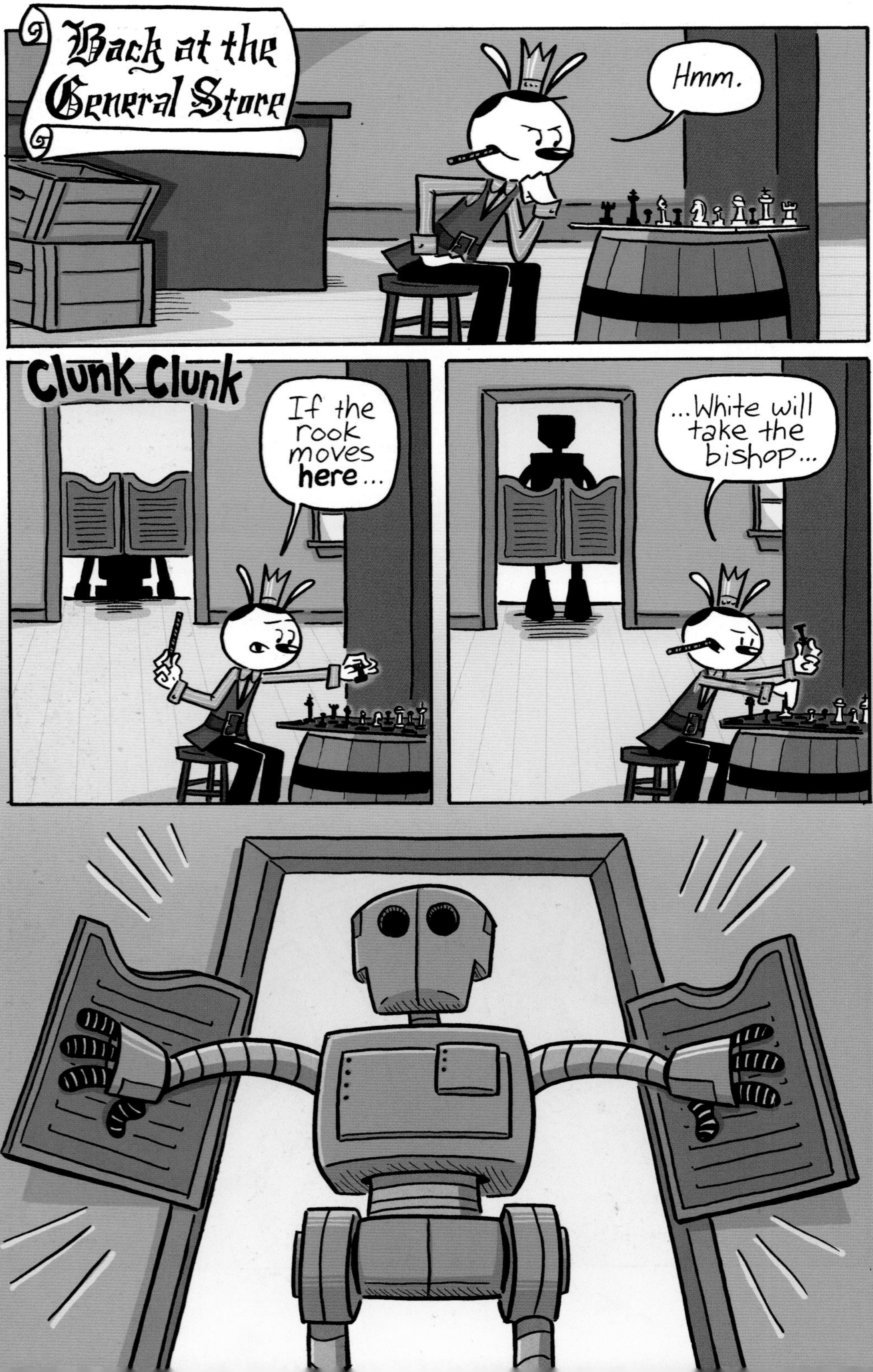
Back at the General Store
Hmm.
Clunk Clunk
If the rook moves **here**...
...White will take the bishop...

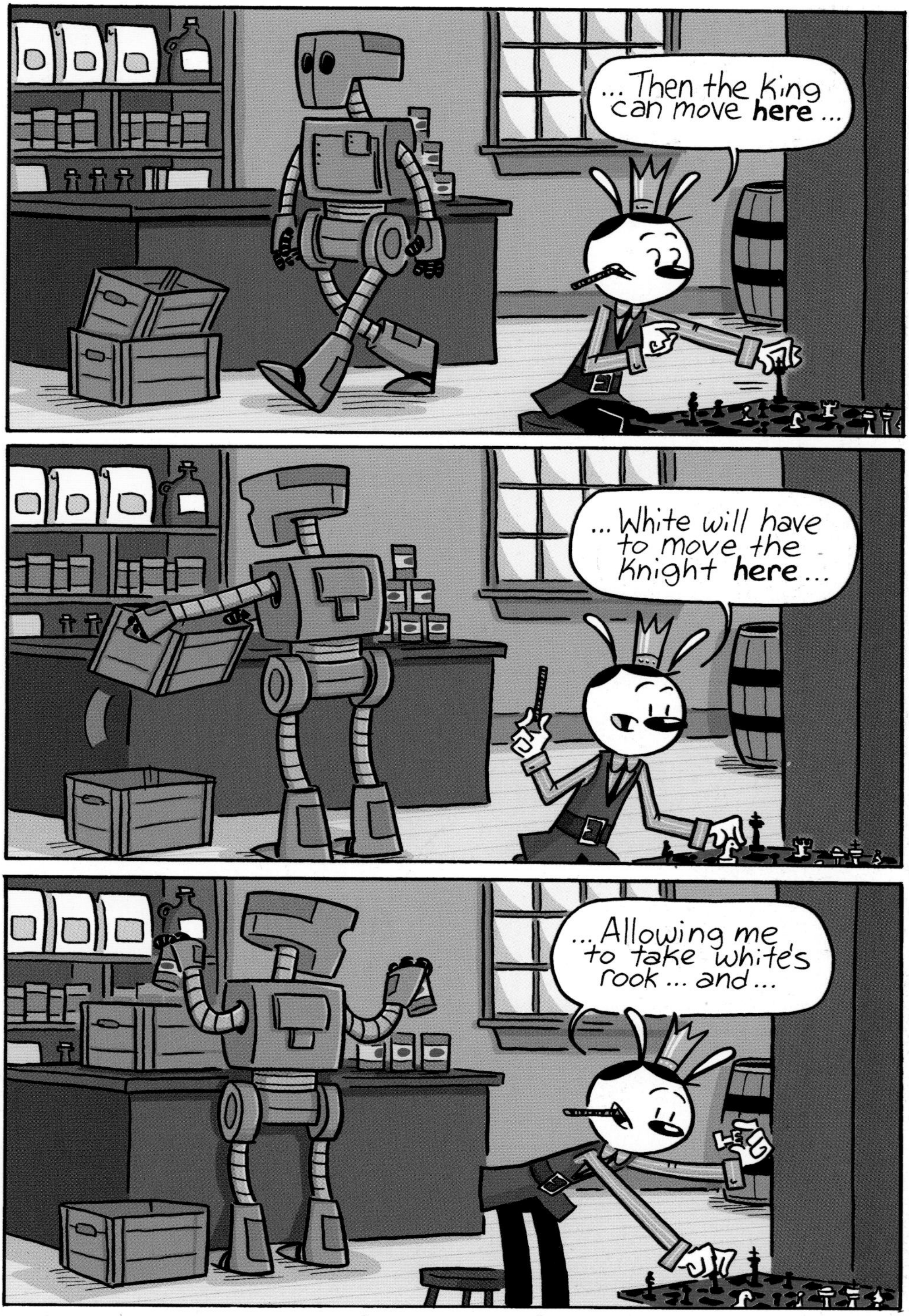

...Then the King can move **here**...
...White will have to move the Knight **here**...
...Allowing me to take white's rook... and...

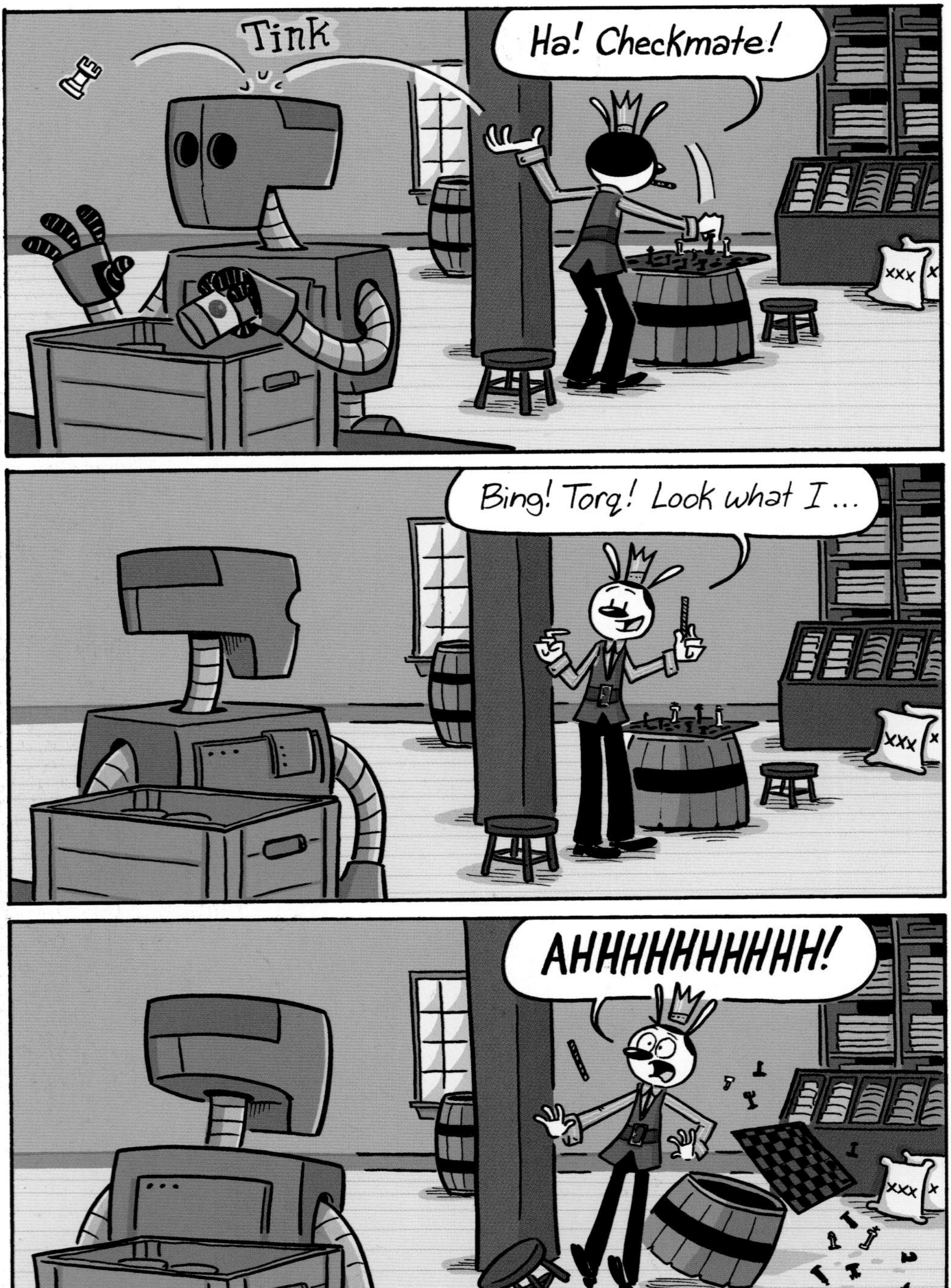
Tink
Ha! Checkmate!
Bing! Torq! Look what I...
AHHHHHHHHHH!

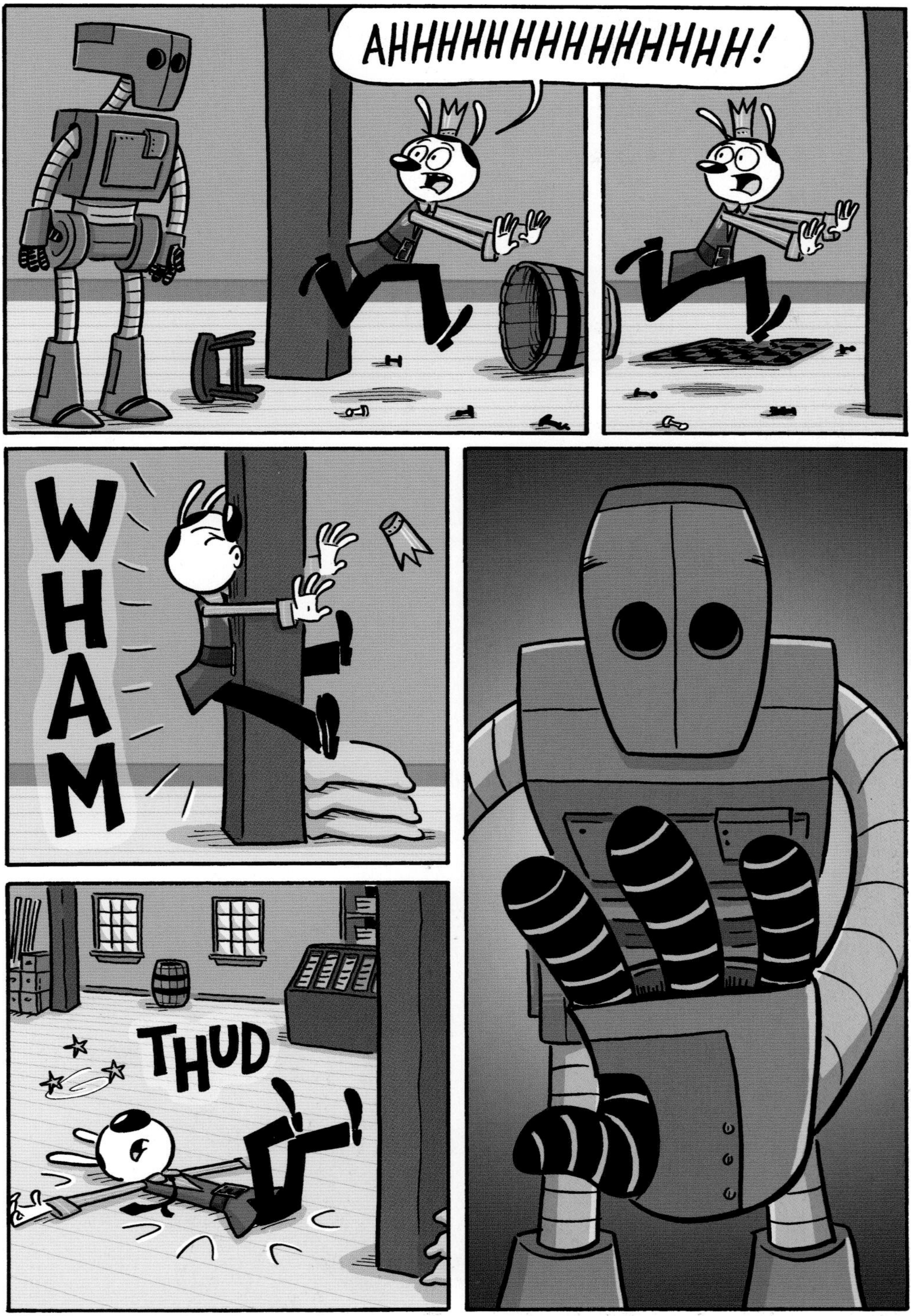
AHHHHHHHHHHHHHHH!
WHAM
THUD

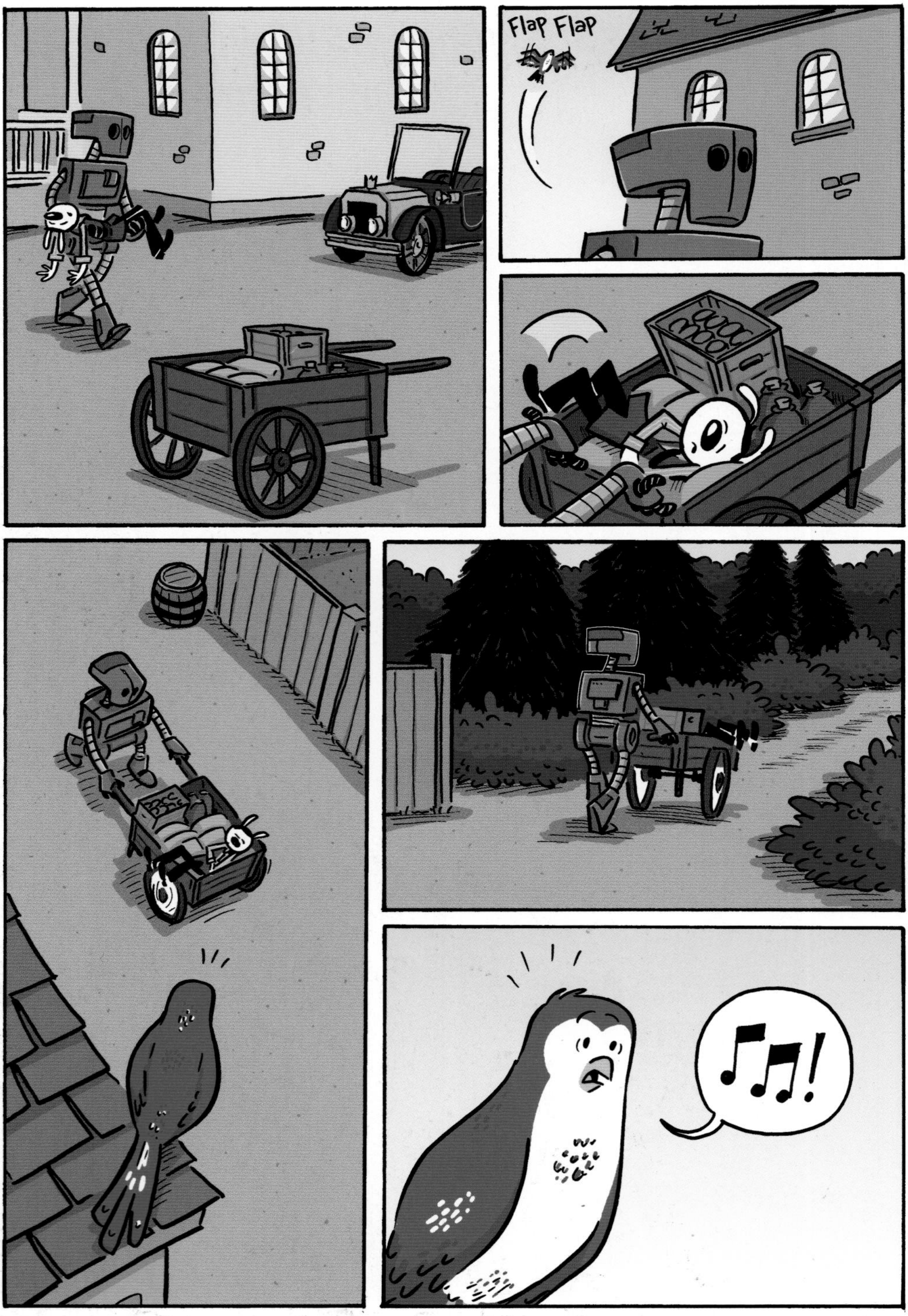
Flap Flap
♪♫!

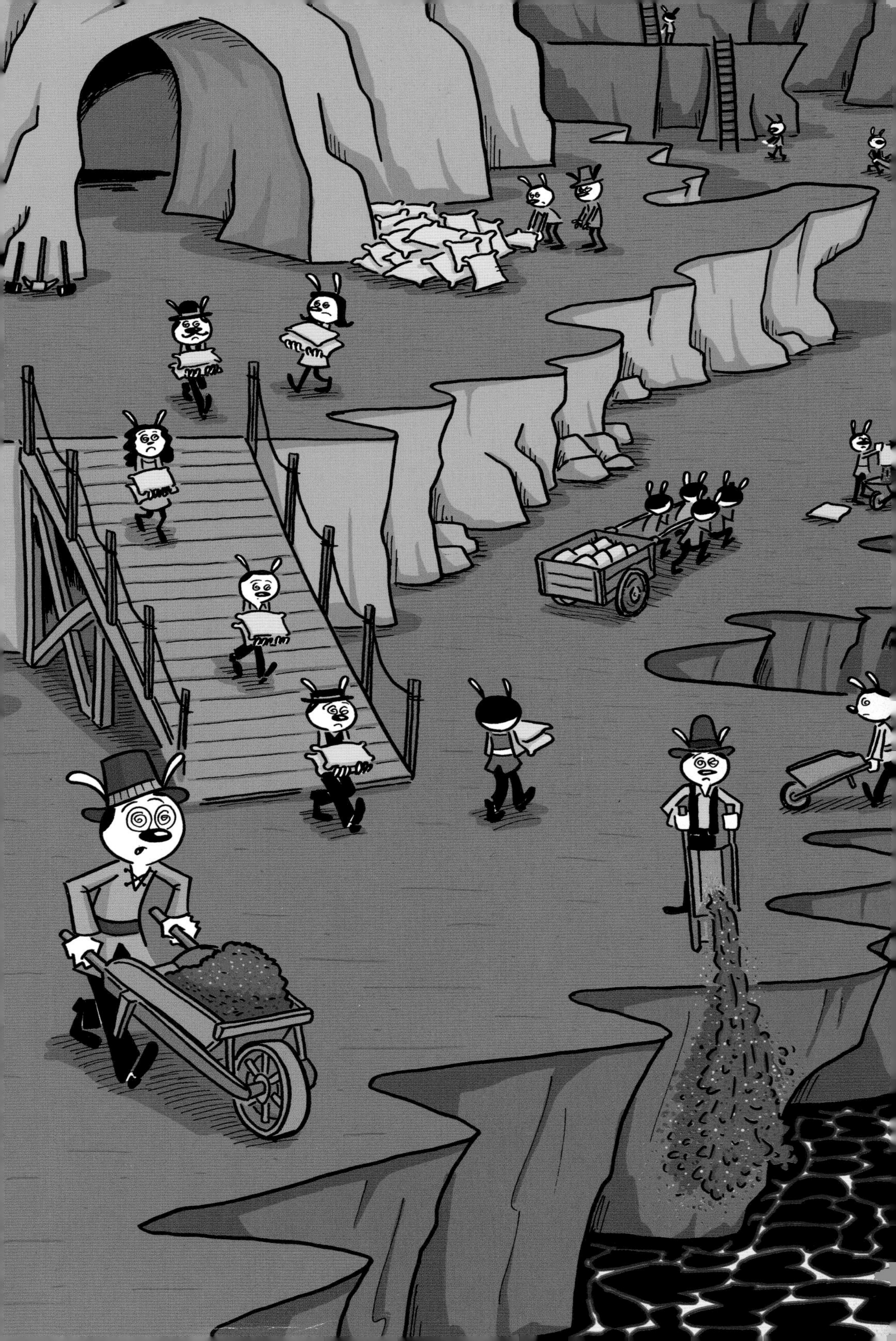

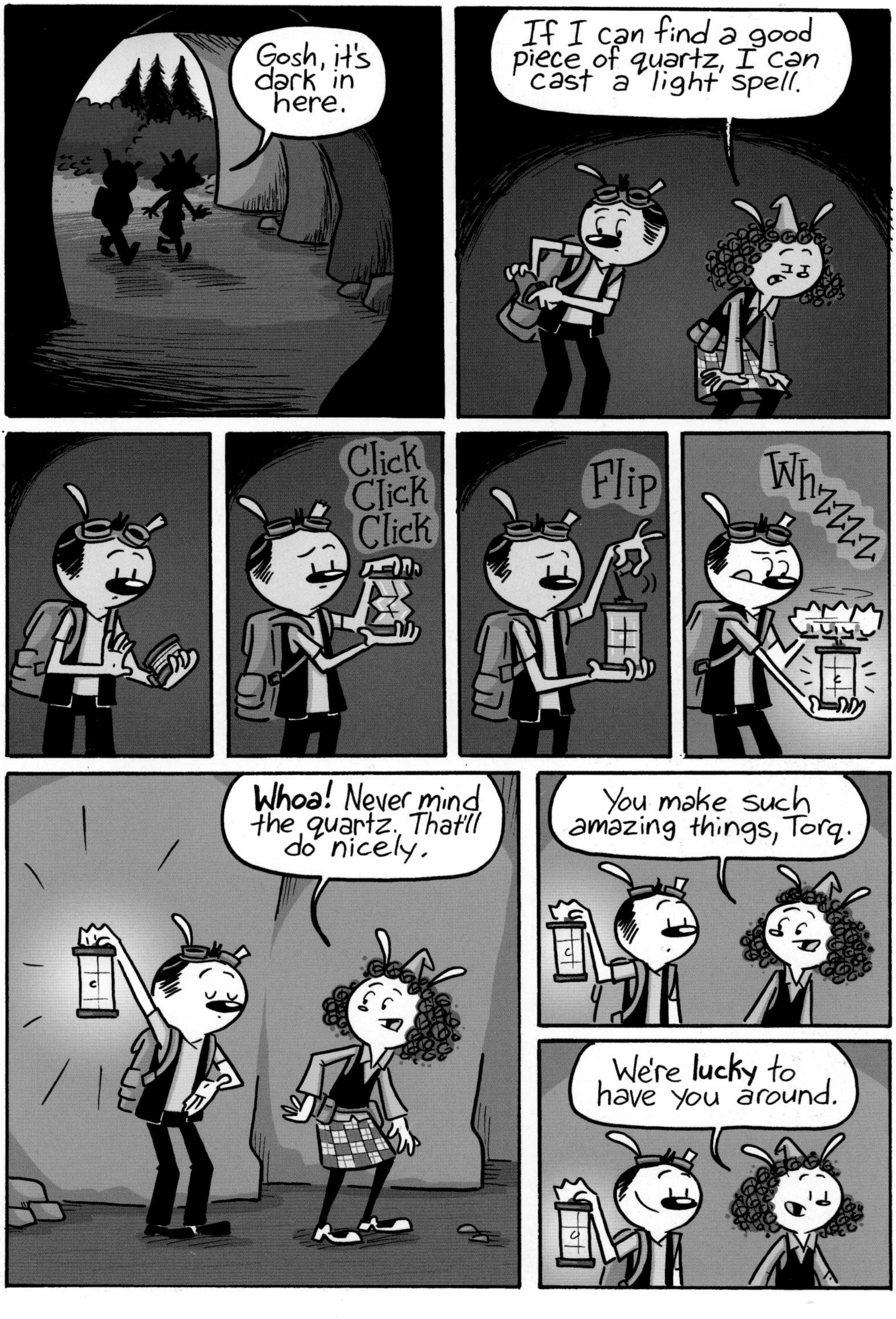
Gosh, it's dark in here.
If I can find a good piece of quartz, I can cast a light spell.
Click Click Click
Flip
Whzzzz
Whoa! Never mind the quartz. That'll do nicely.
You make such amazing things, Torq.
We're **lucky** to have you around.

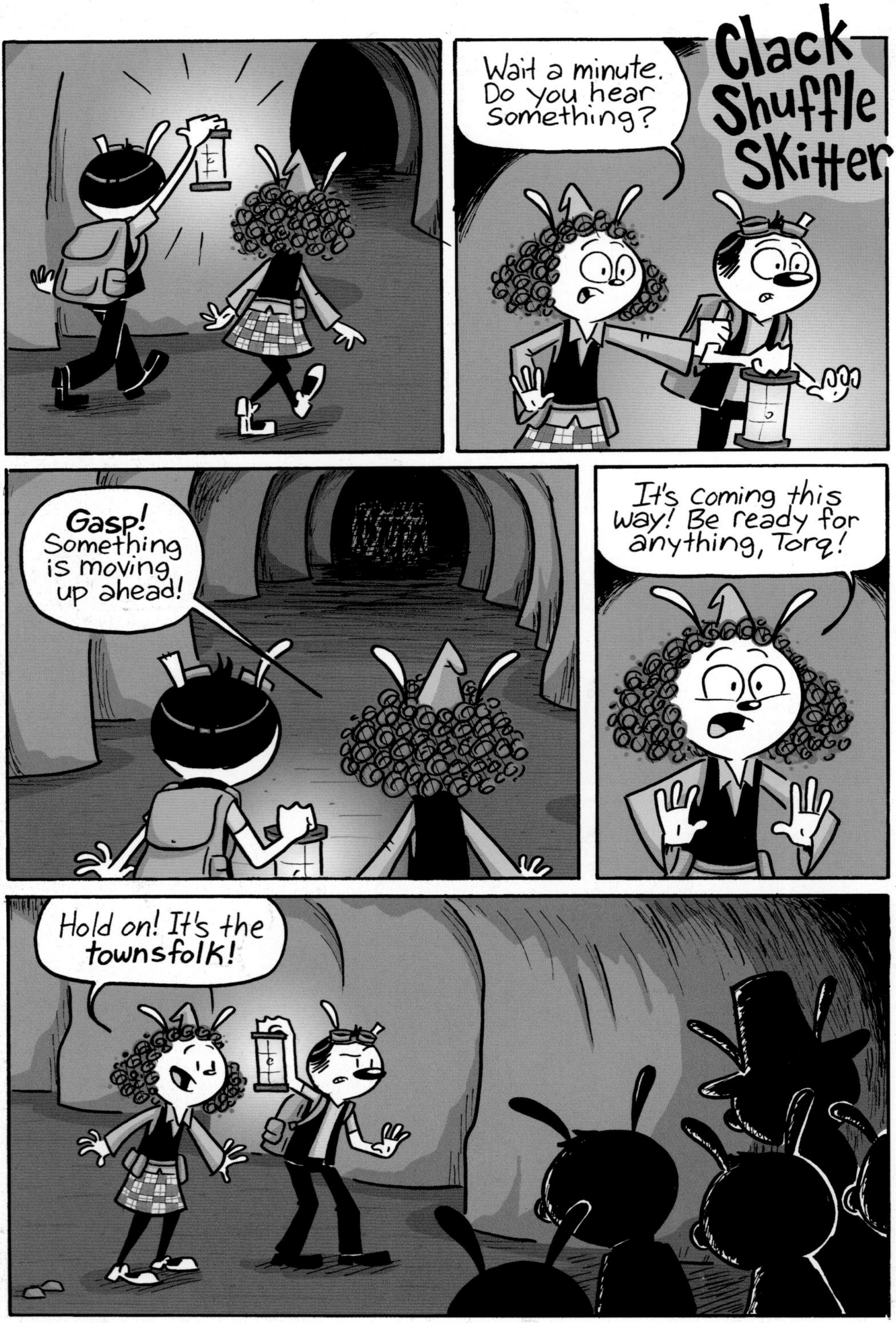

Wait a minute. Do you hear Something?
Clack
Shuffle
Skitter
Gasp! Something is moving up ahead!
It's coming this way! Be ready for anything, Torq!
Hold on! It's the townsfolk!

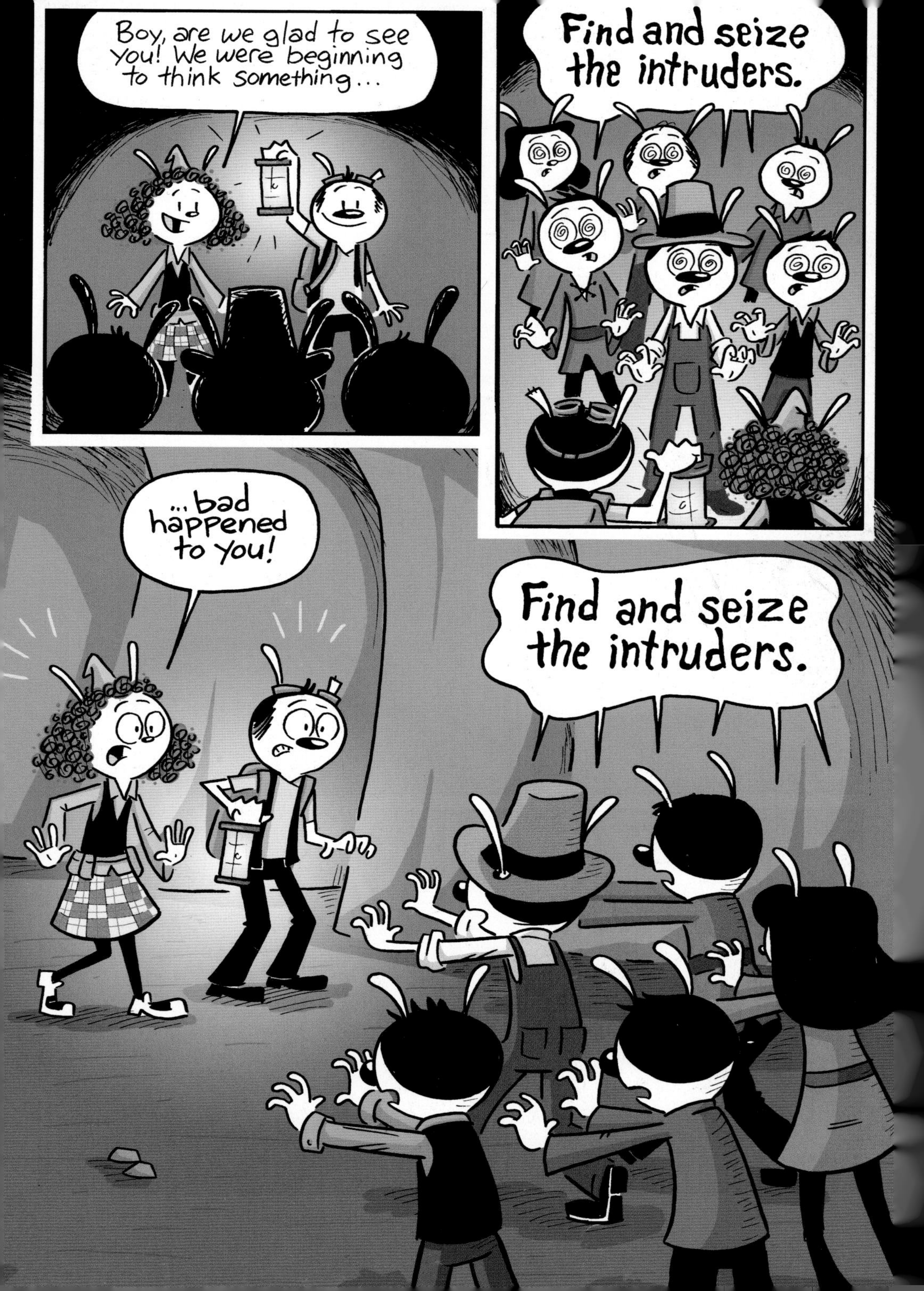
Boy, are we glad to see you! We were beginning to think something...
Find and seize the intruders.
...bad happened to you!
Find and seize the intruders.

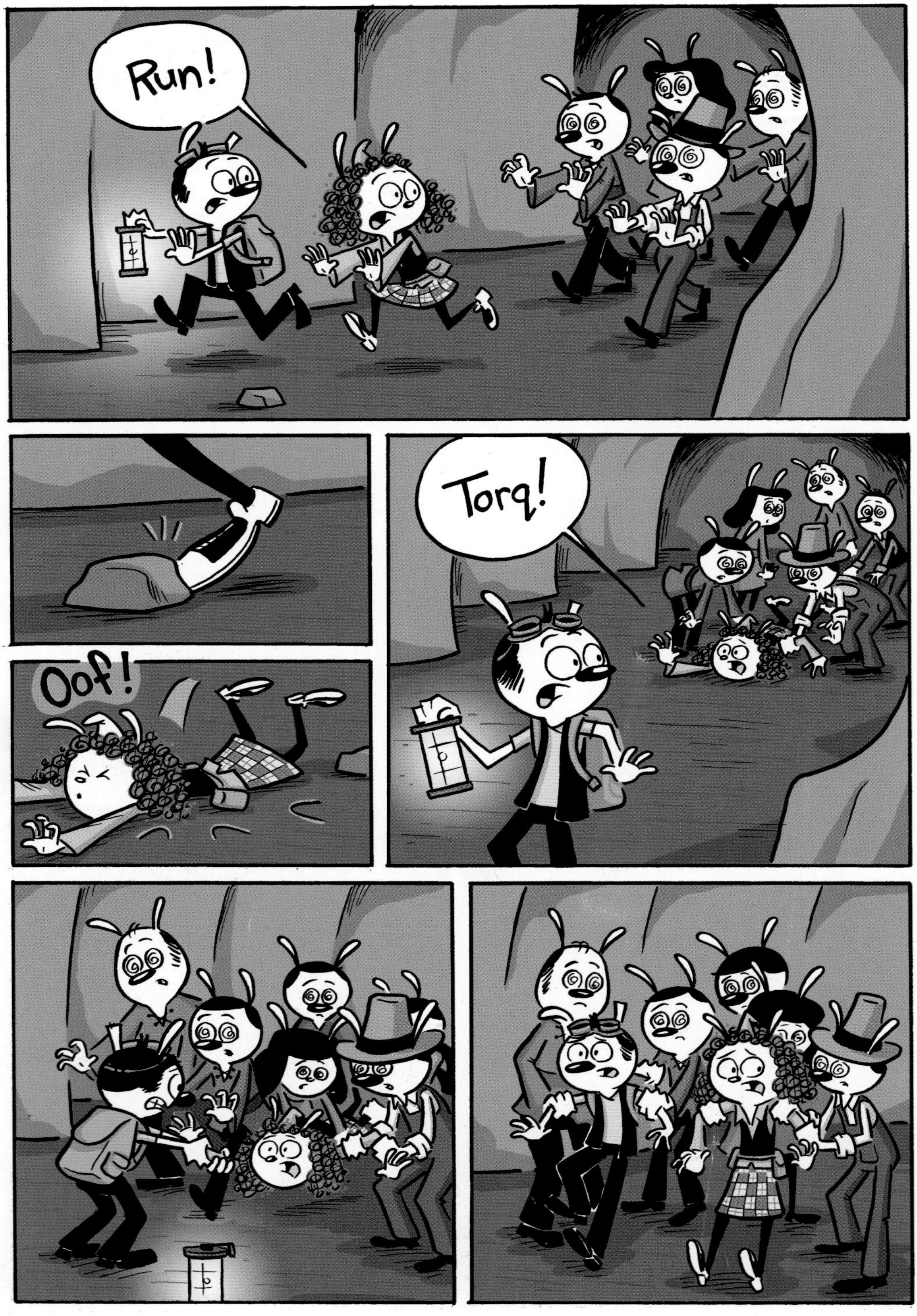
Run!
Oof!
Torq!

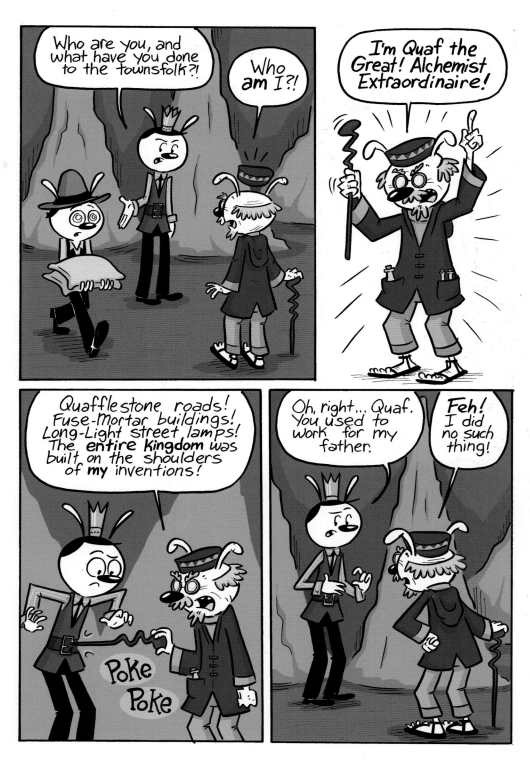

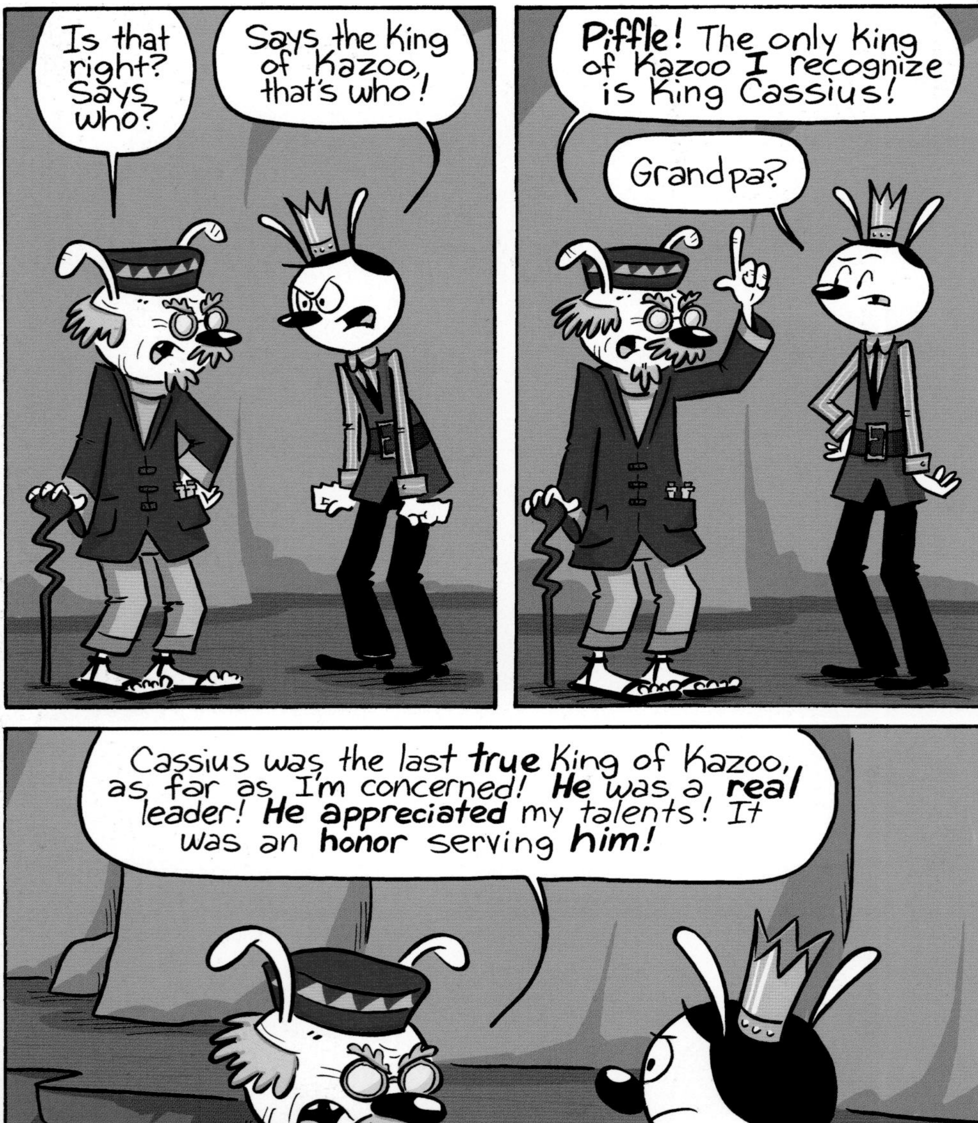
Is that right? Says who?
Says the King of Kazoo, that's who!
Piffle! The only King of Kazoo I recognize is King Cassius!
Grandpa?
Cassius was the last true King of Kazoo, as far as I'm concerned! He was a real leader! He appreciated my talents! It was an honor serving him!

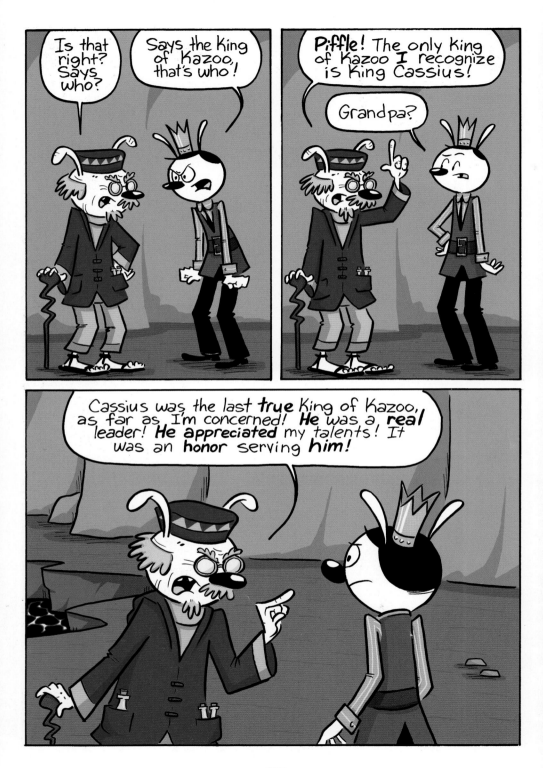

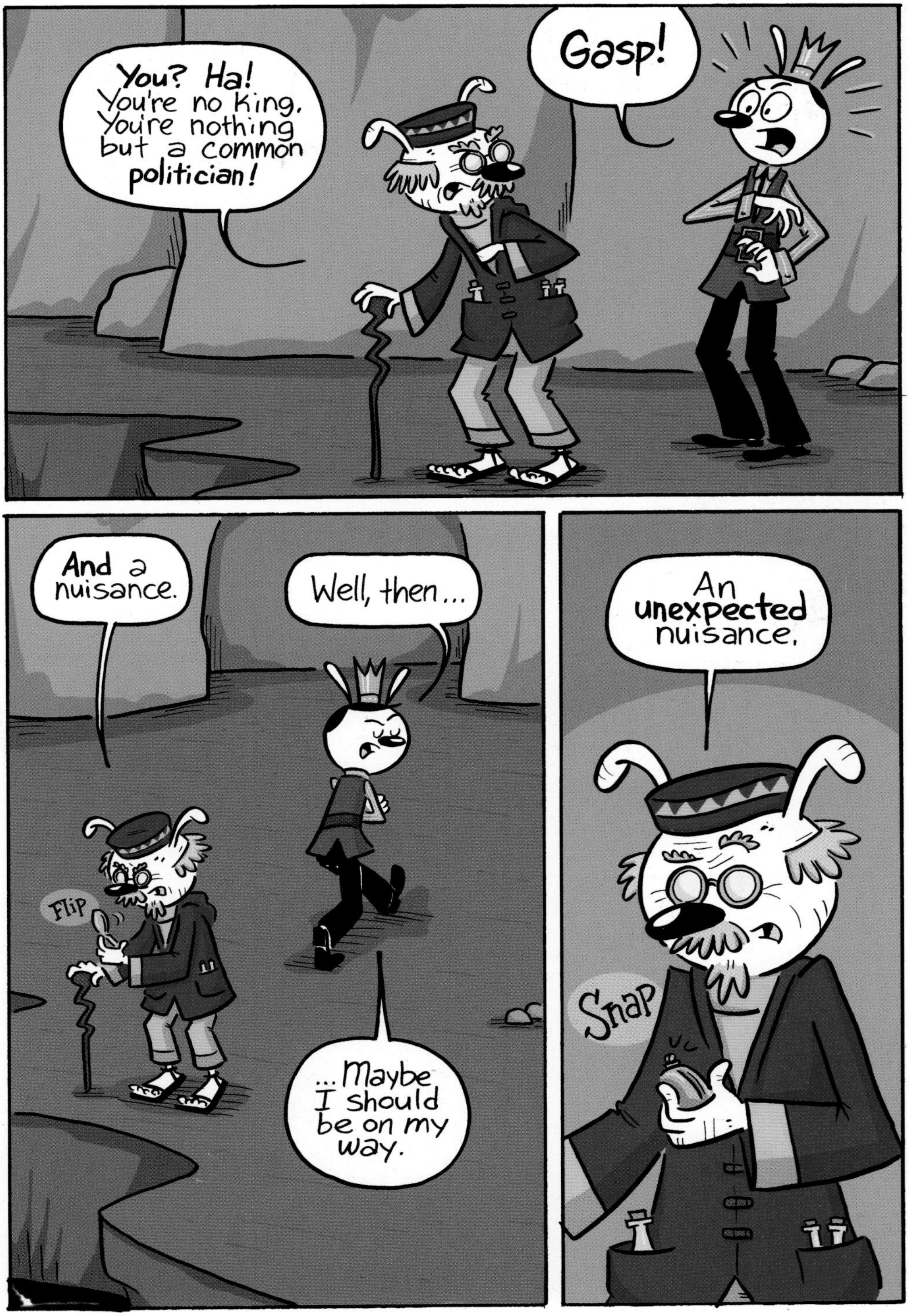
You? Ha! You're no king. You're nothing but a common politician!
Gasp!
And a nuisance.
Well, then...
Flip
...Maybe I should be on my way.
An unexpected nuisance.
Snap

153

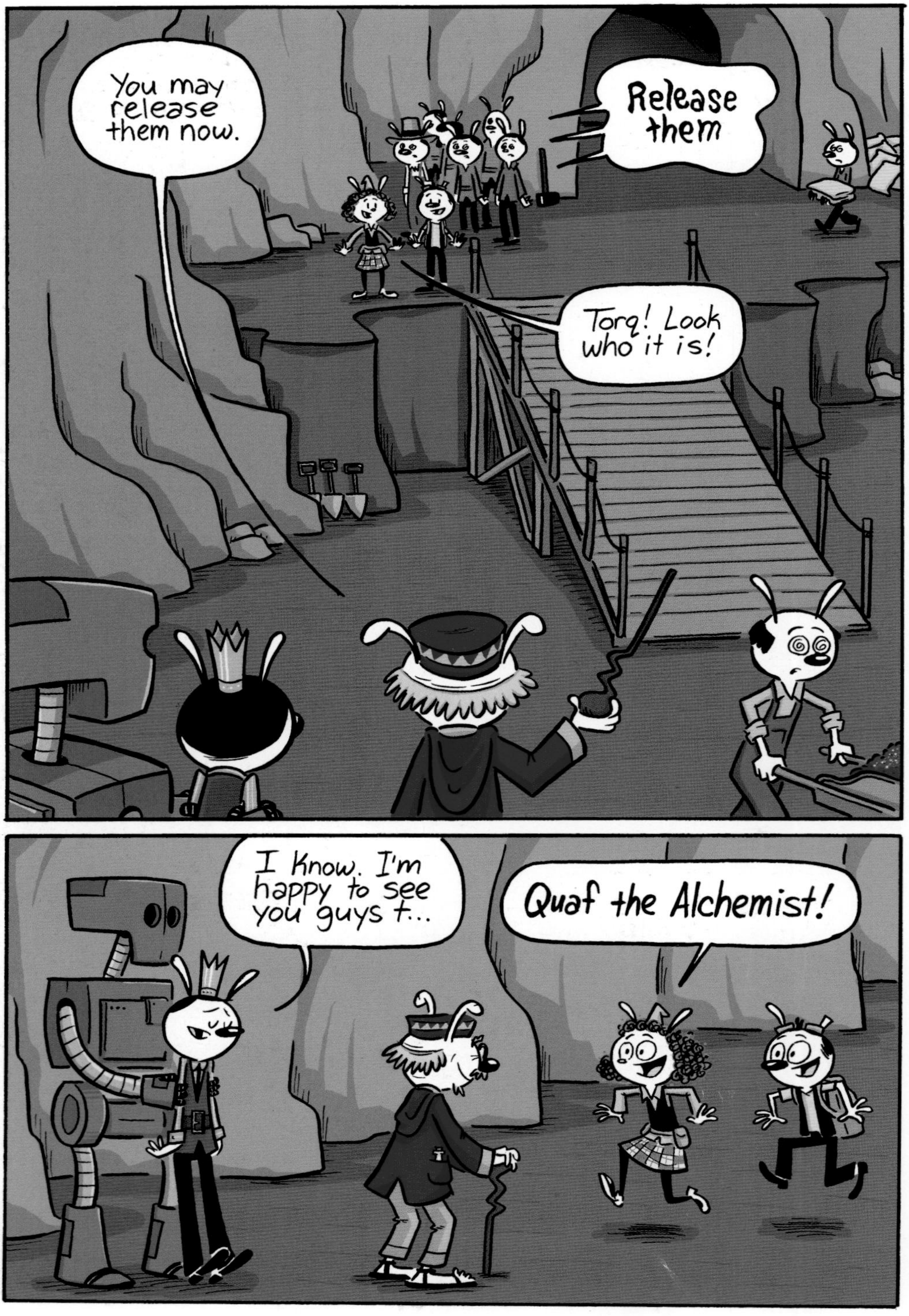
You may release them now.
Release them
Torq! Look who it is!
I know. I'm happy to see you guys t...
Quaf the Alchemist!

156

161

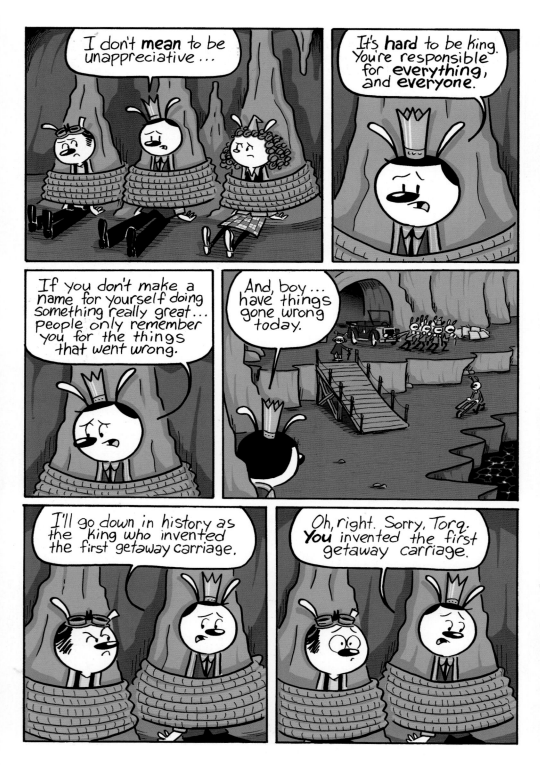

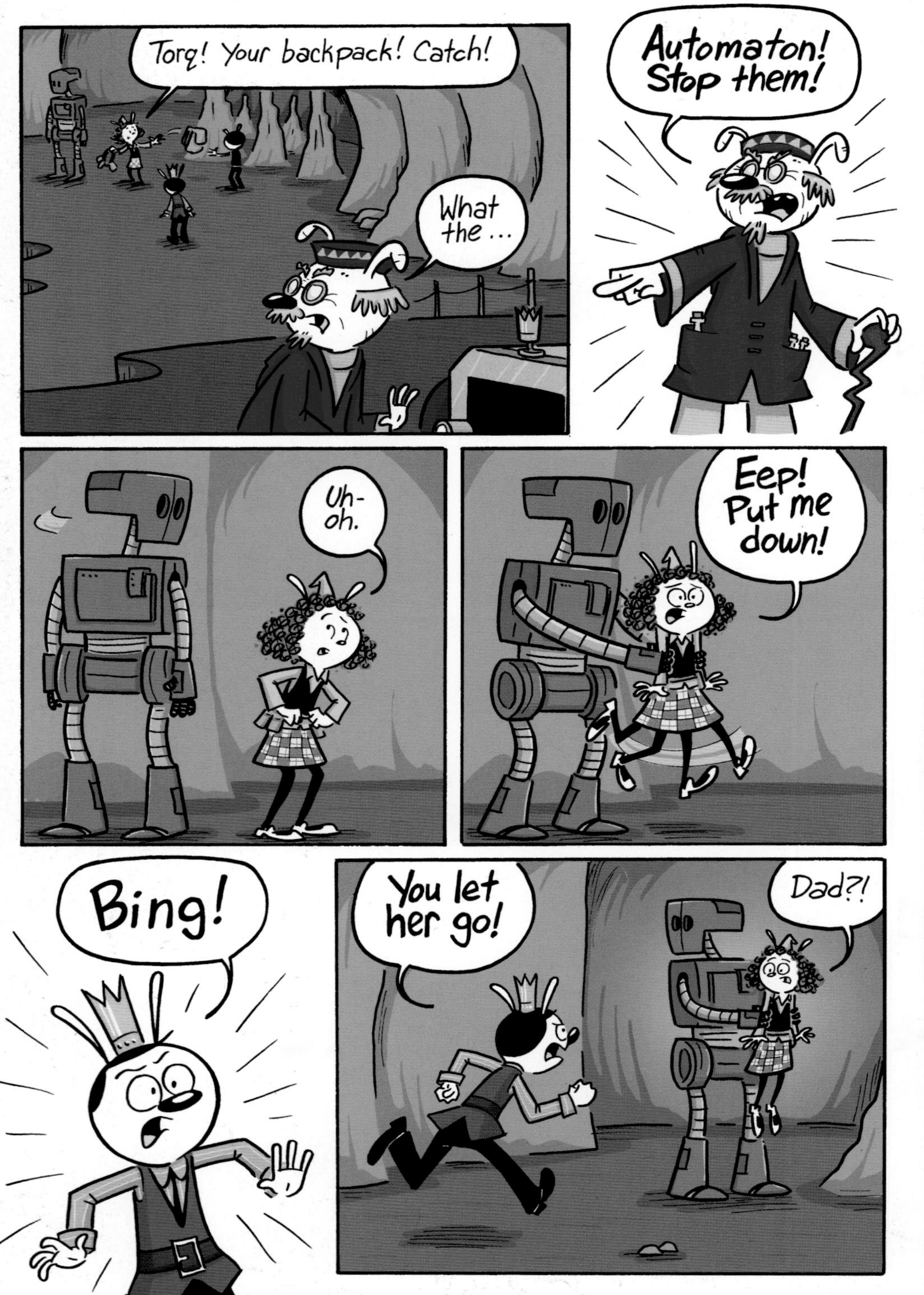
Torq! Your backpack! Catch!
What the ...
Automaton! Stop them!
Uh-oh.
Eep! Put me down!
Bing!
You let her go!
Dad?!

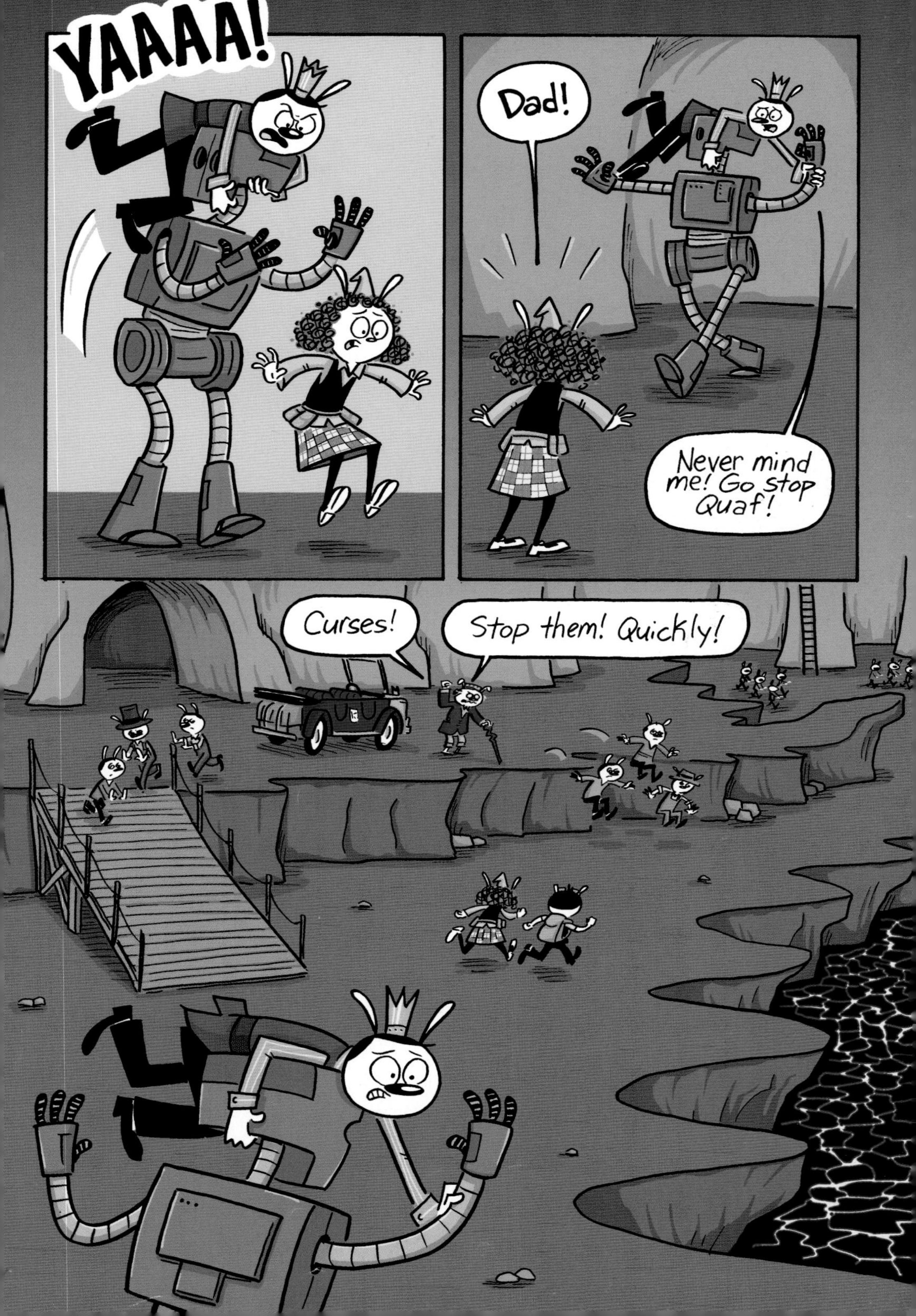
YAAAA!
Dad!
Never mind me! Go stop Quaf!
Curses!
Stop them! Quickly!

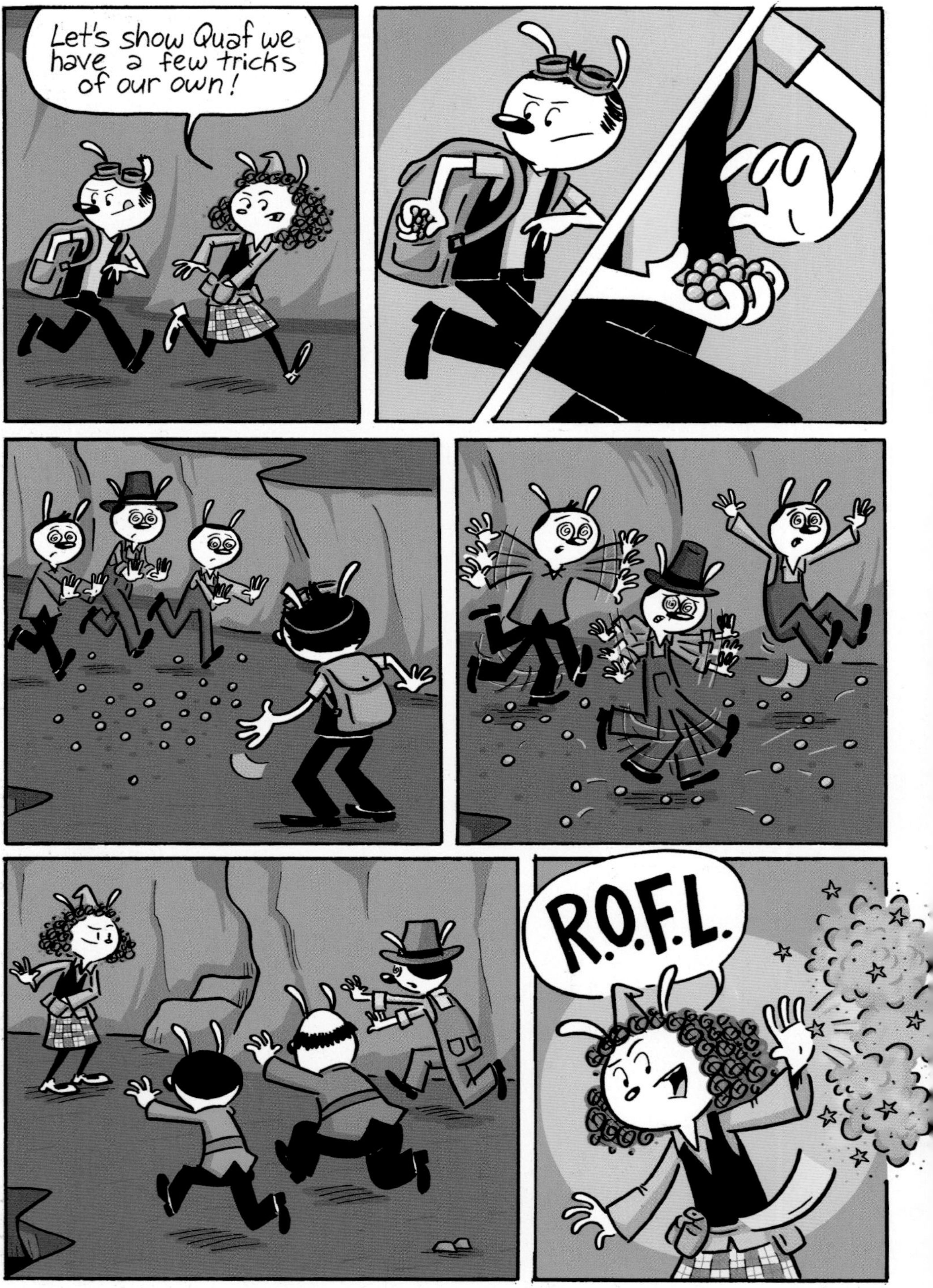
Let's show Quaf we have a few tricks of our own!
R.O.F.L.

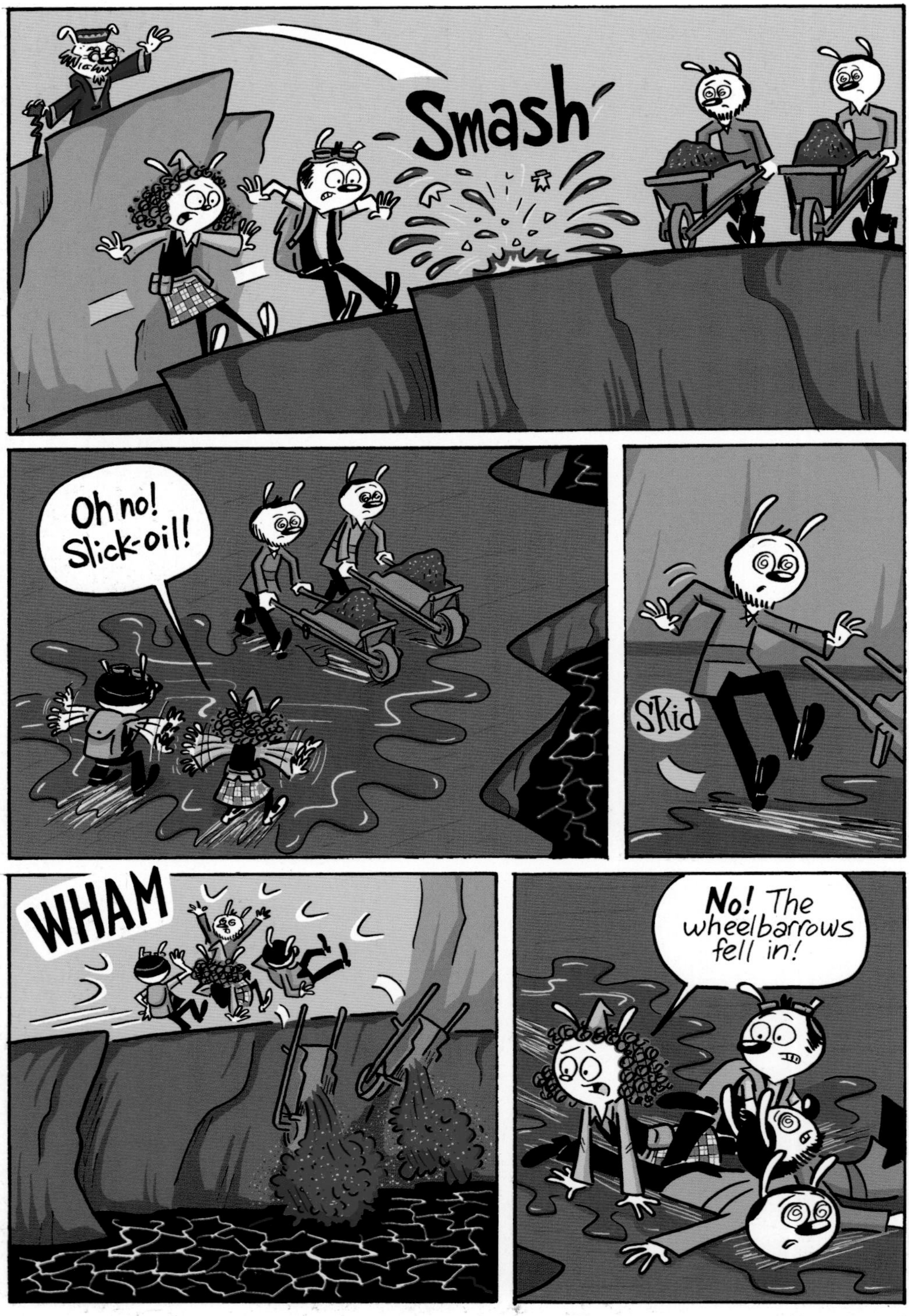
Smash
Oh no! Slick-oil!
SKid
WHAM
No! The wheelbarrows fell in!

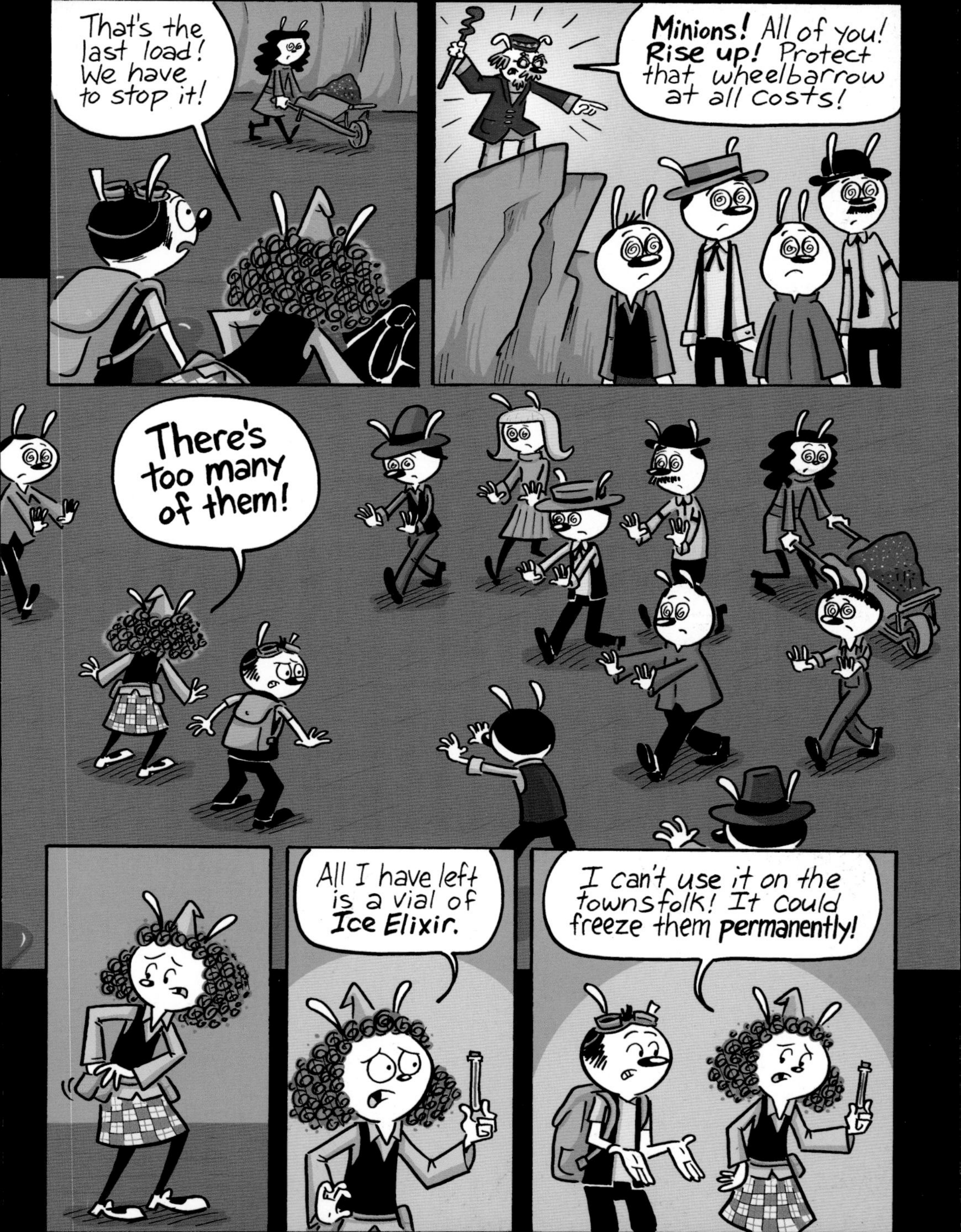
That's the last load! We have to stop it!
Minions! All of you! Rise up! Protect that wheelbarrow at all costs!
There's too many of them!
All I have left is a vial of Ice Elixir.
I can't use it on the townsfolk! It could freeze them permanently!

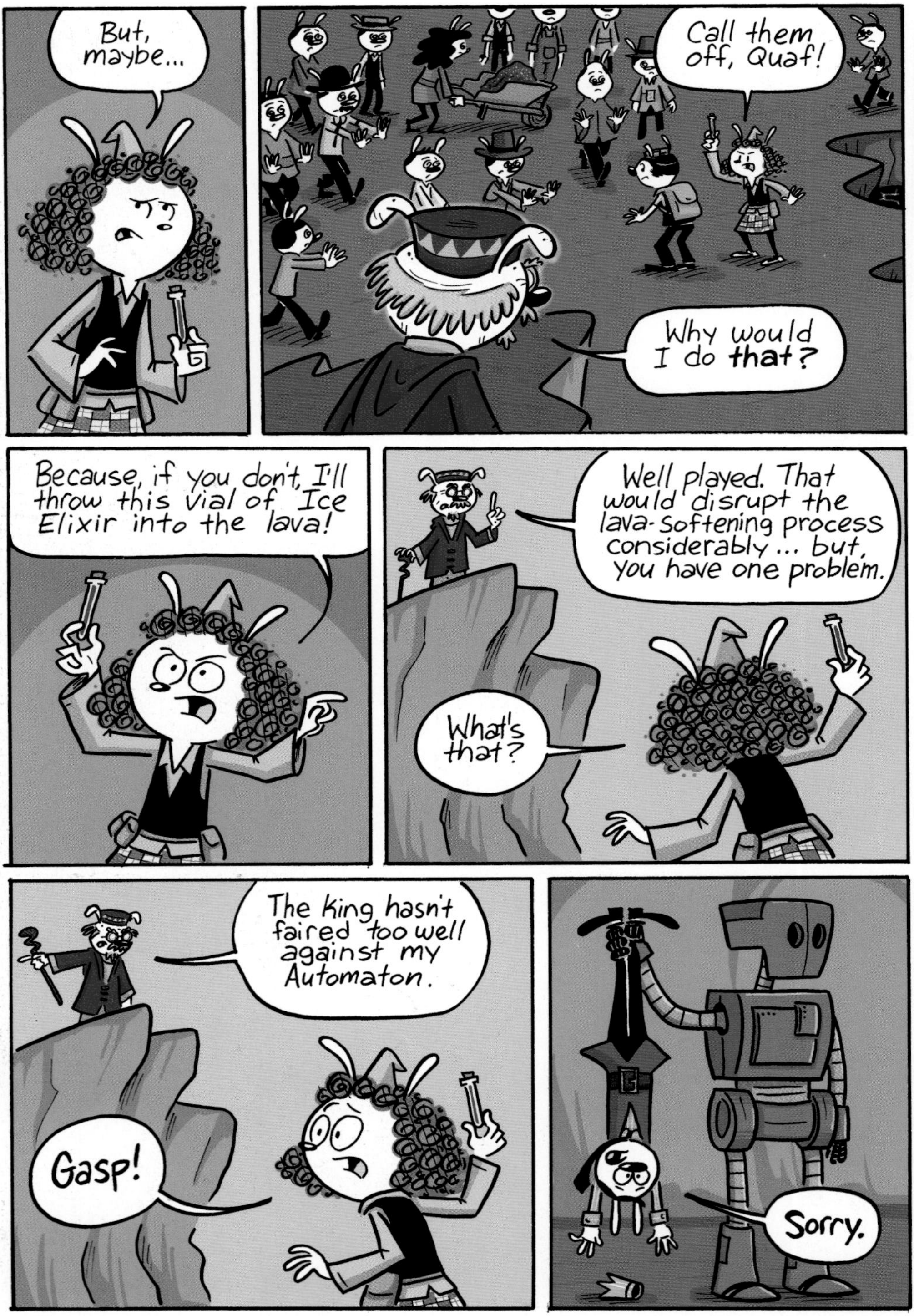
But, maybe...
Call them off, Quaf!
Why would I do **that**?
Because, if you don't, I'll throw this vial of Ice Elixir into the lava!
Well played. That would disrupt the lava-softening process considerably ... but, you have one problem.
What's that?
The king hasn't faired too well against my Automaton.
Gasp!
Sorry.

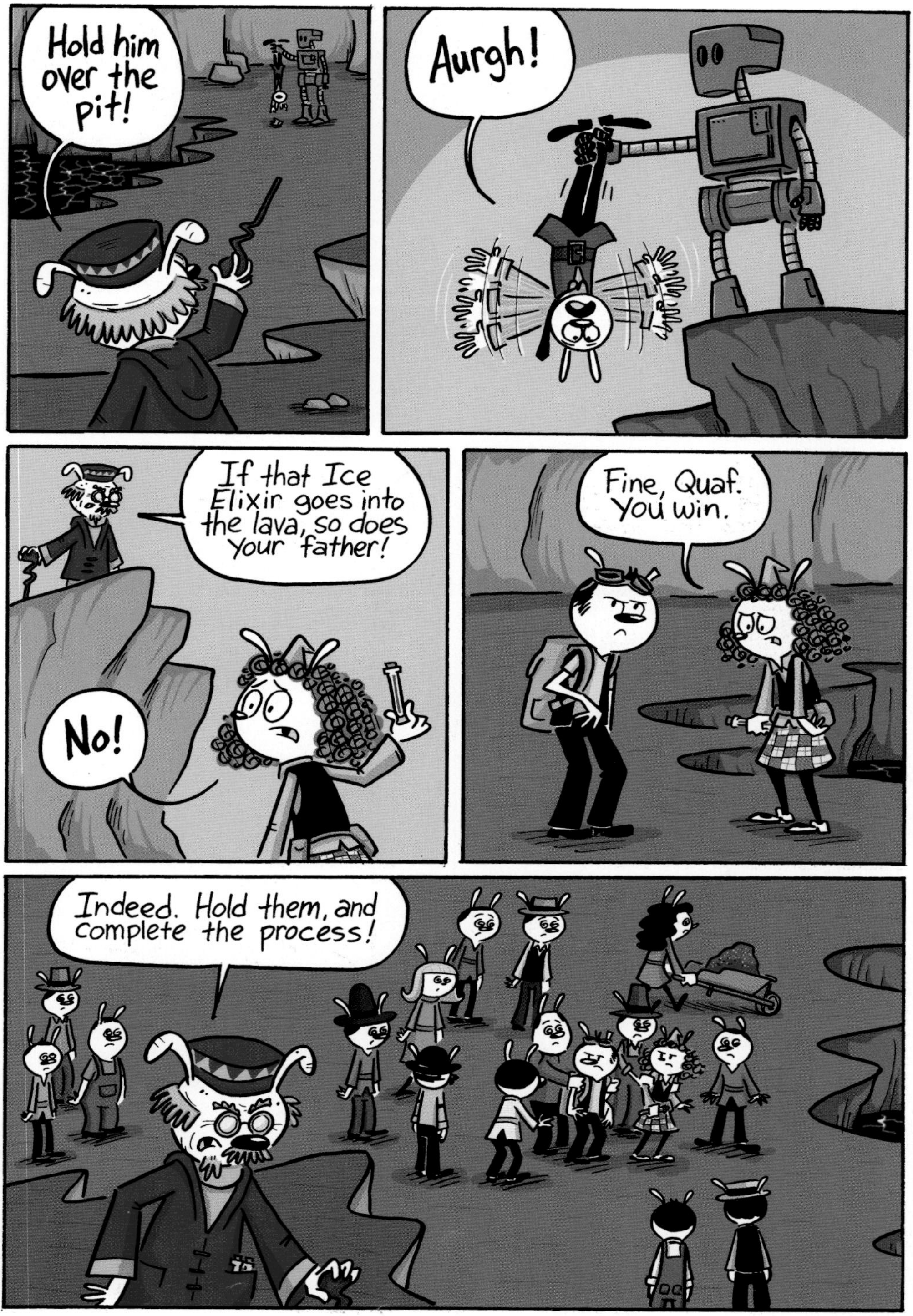
Hold him over the pit!
Aurgh!
If that Ice Elixir goes into the lava, so does your father!
No!
Fine, Quaf. You win.
Indeed. Hold them, and complete the process!

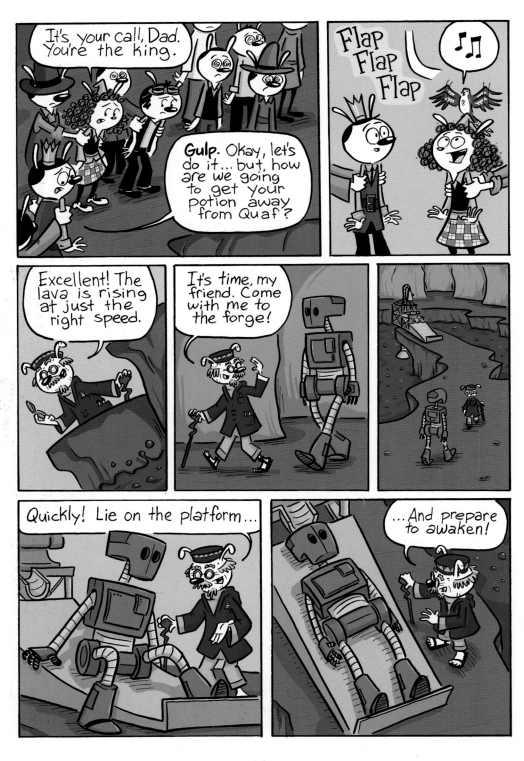

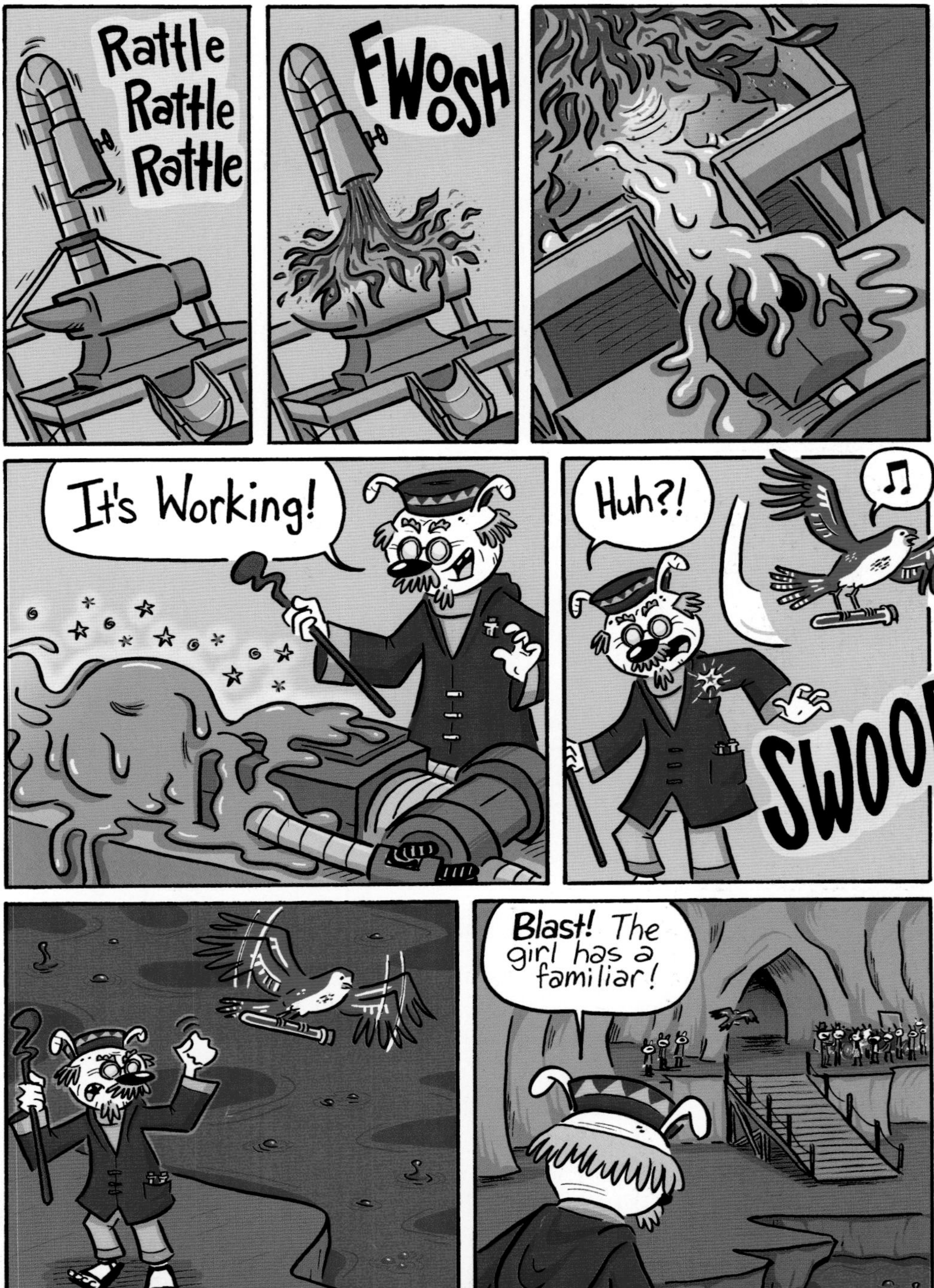
Rattle
Rattle
Rattle
FWOOSH
It's Working!
Huh?!
♫
SWOOP
Blast! The girl has a familiar!

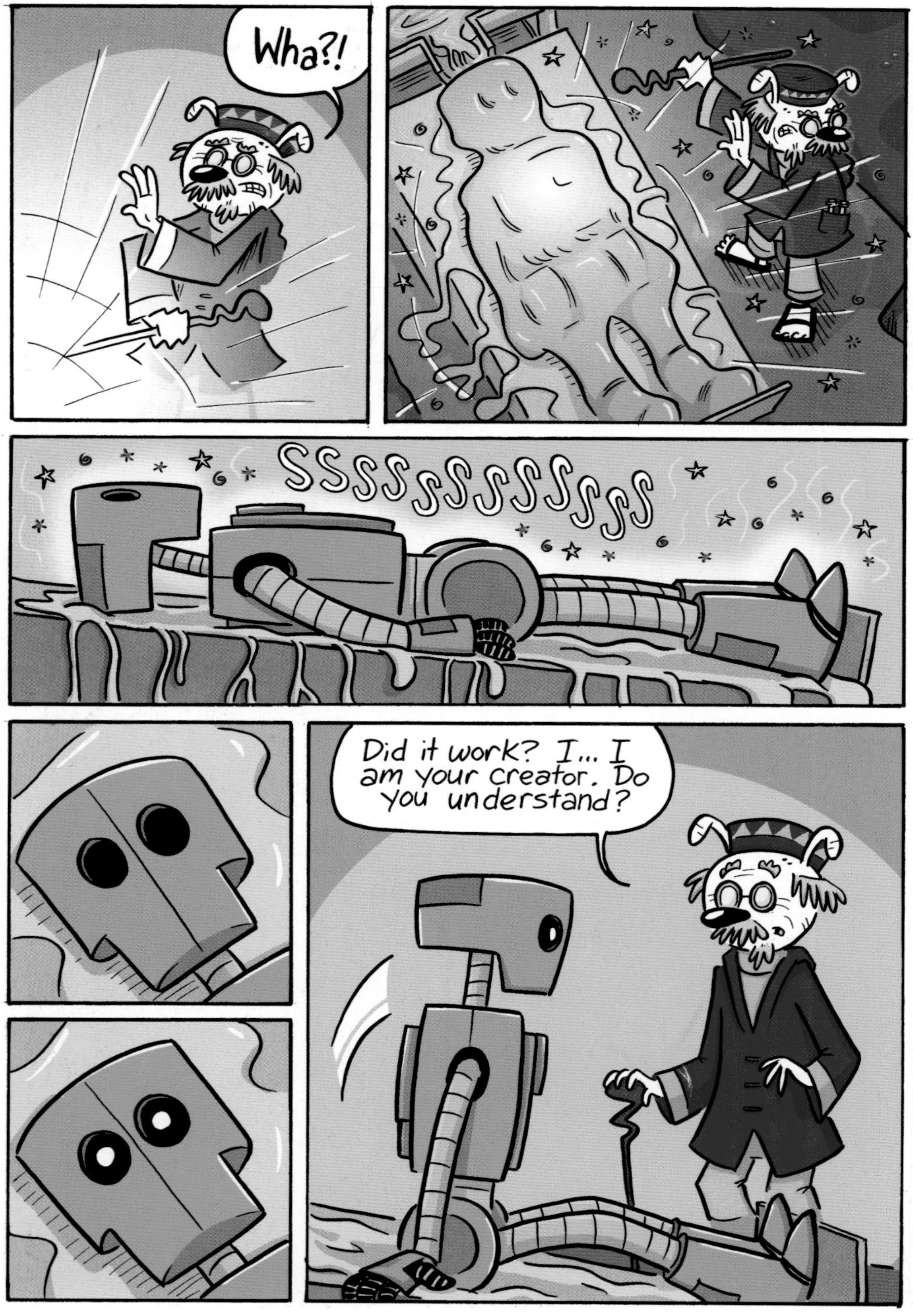
Wha?!
SSSSSSSSSSSSS
Did it work? I... I am your creator. Do you understand?

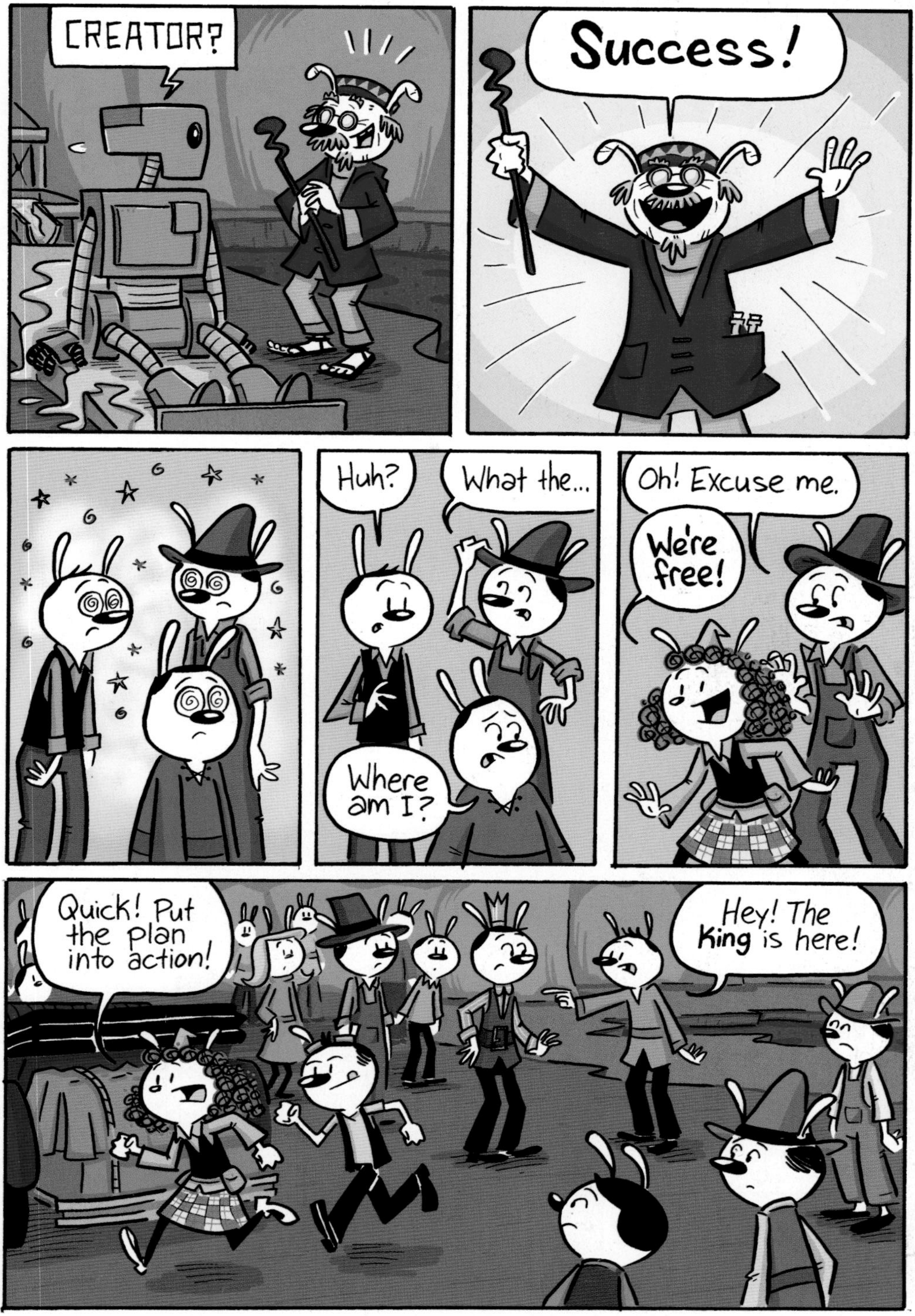
CREATOR?
Success!
Huh?
What the...
Where am I?
Oh! Excuse me.
We're free!
Quick! Put the plan into action!
Hey! The **King** is here!

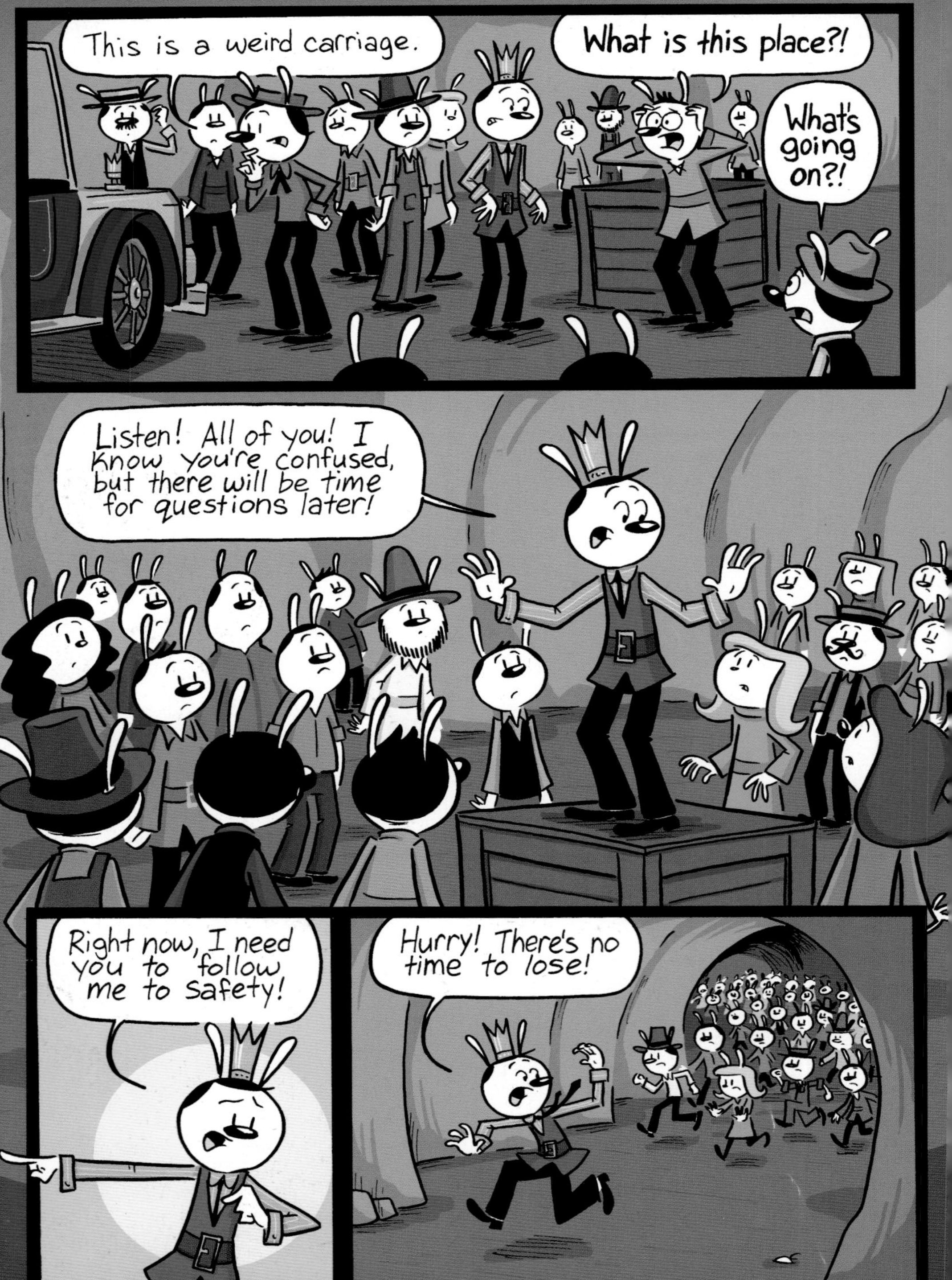
This is a weird carriage.
What is this place?!
What's going on?!
Listen! All of you! I know you're confused, but there will be time for questions later!
Right now, I need you to follow me to safety!
Hurry! There's no time to lose!

187

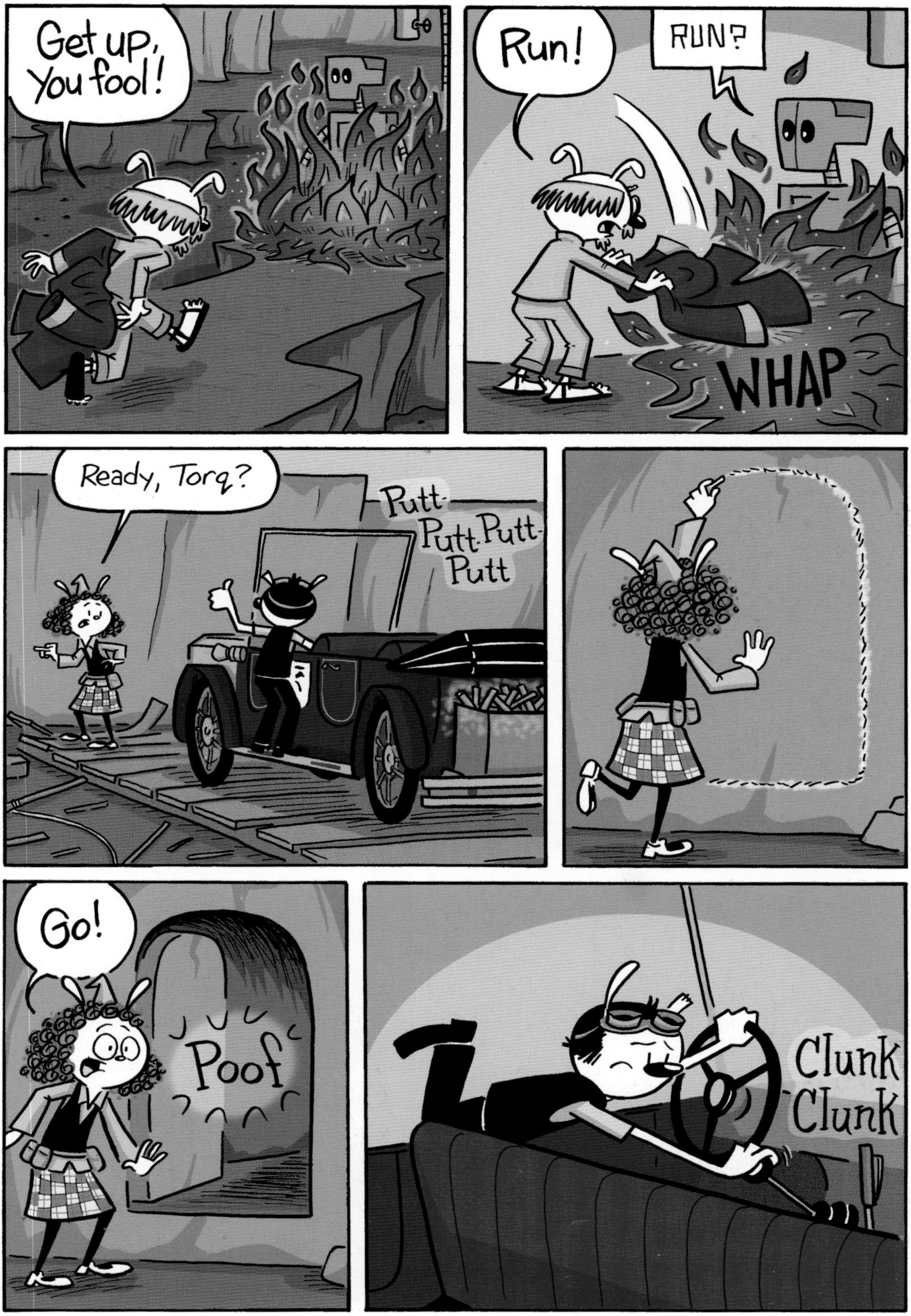
Get up, You fool!
Run!
RUN?
WHAP
Ready, Torq?
Putt-Putt-Putt-Putt
Go!
Poof
Clunk Clunk

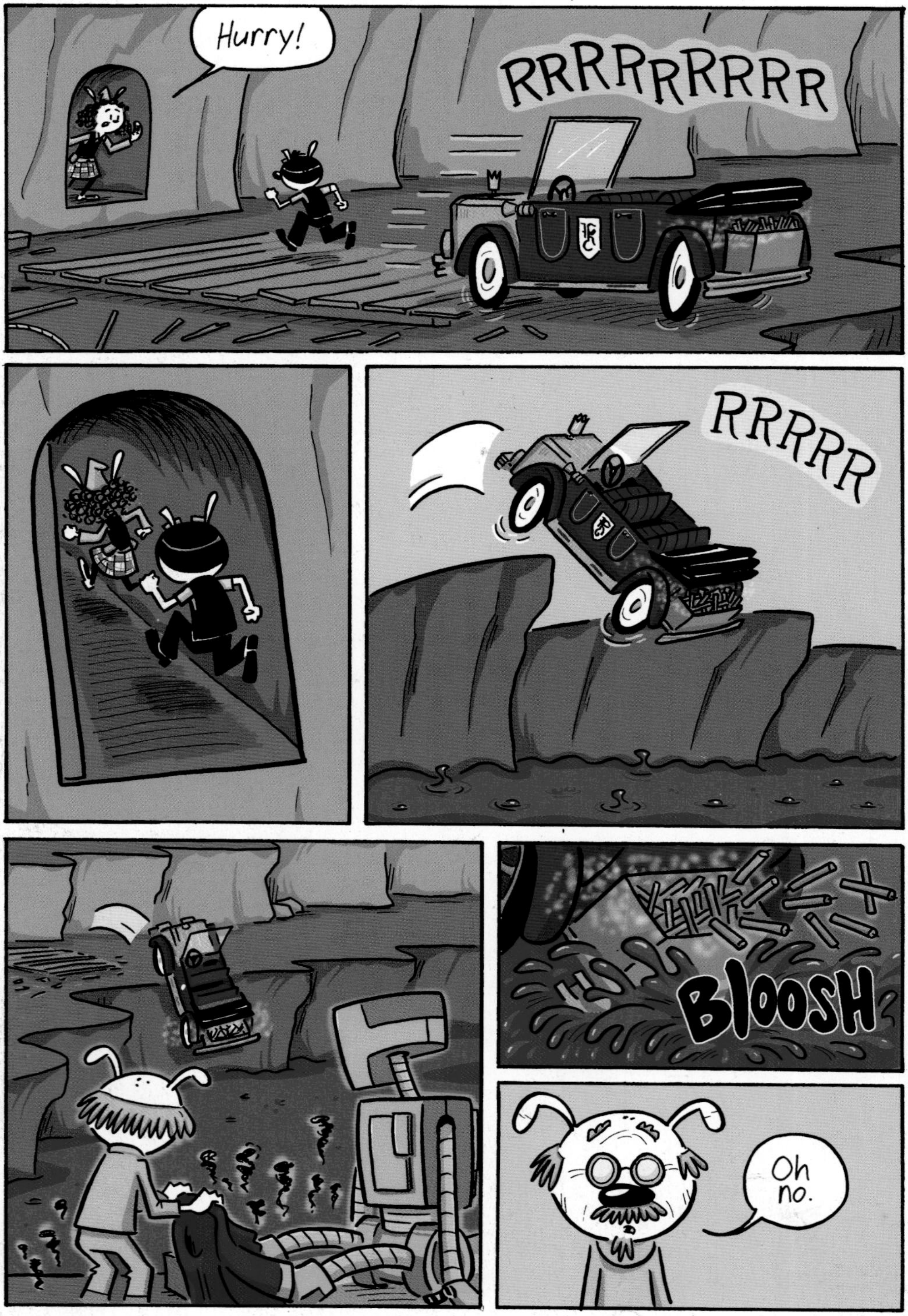
Hurry!
RRRRRRRRRR
RRRRR
BLOOSH
Oh no.

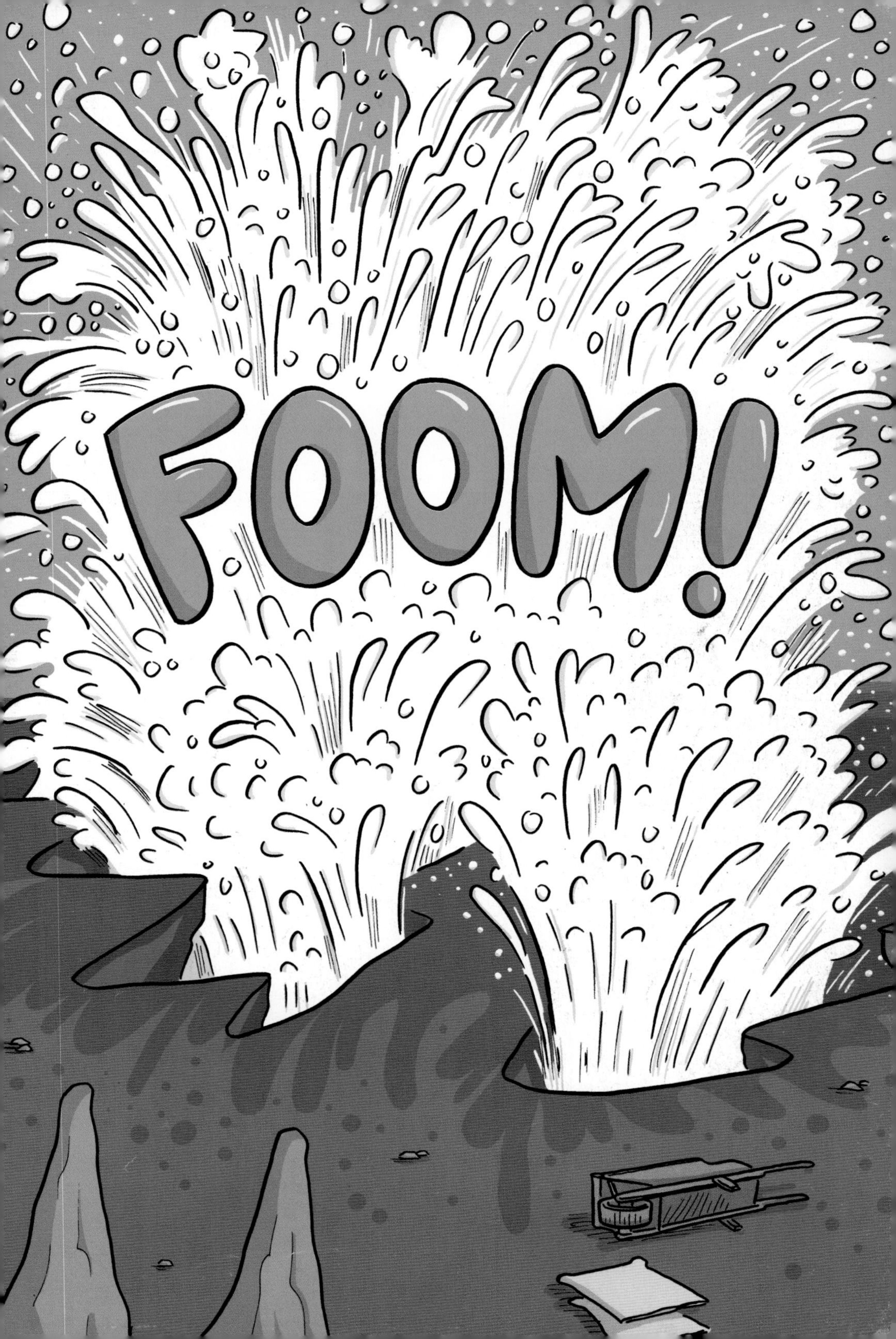
FOOM!

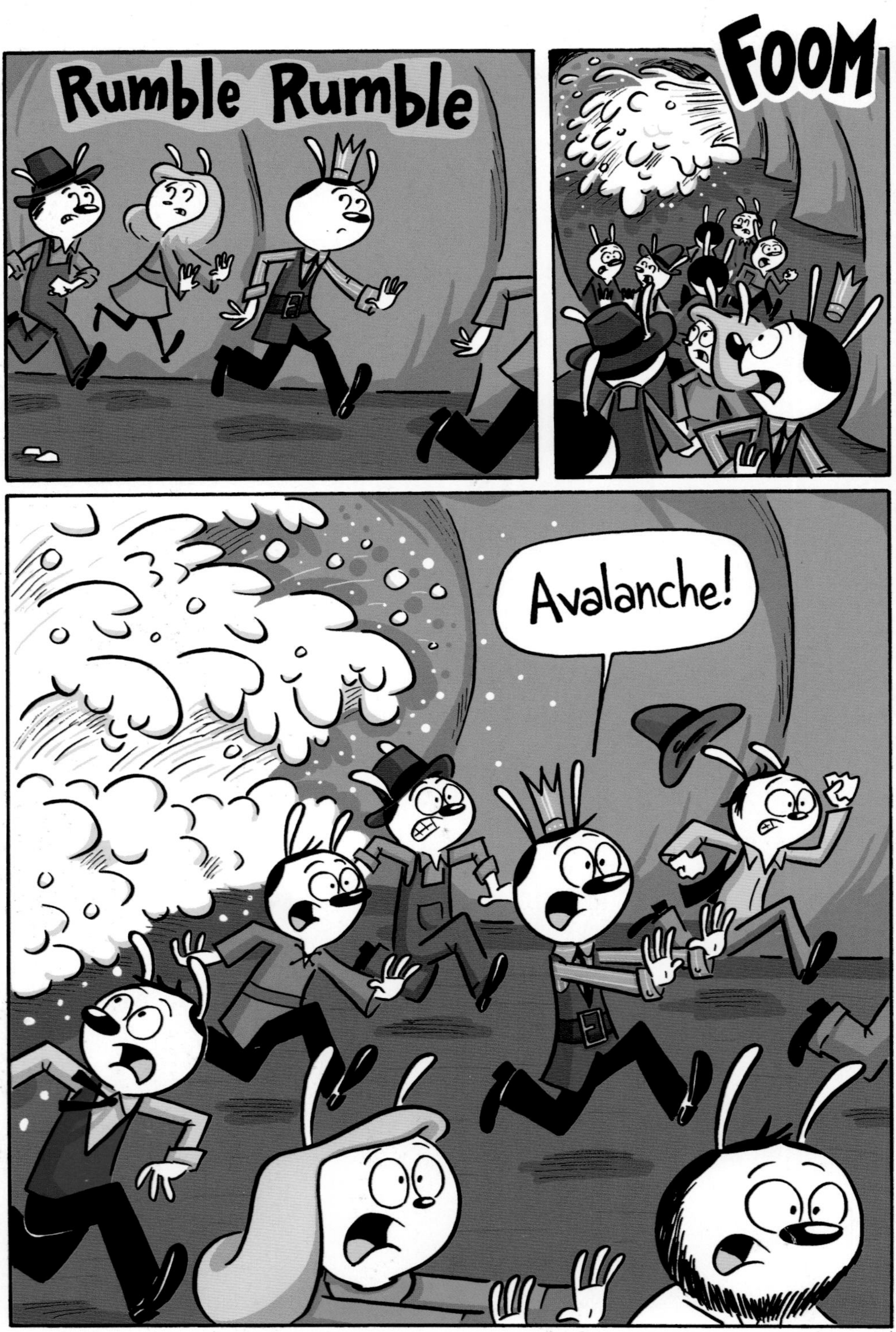
Rumble Rumble
FOOM
Avalanche!

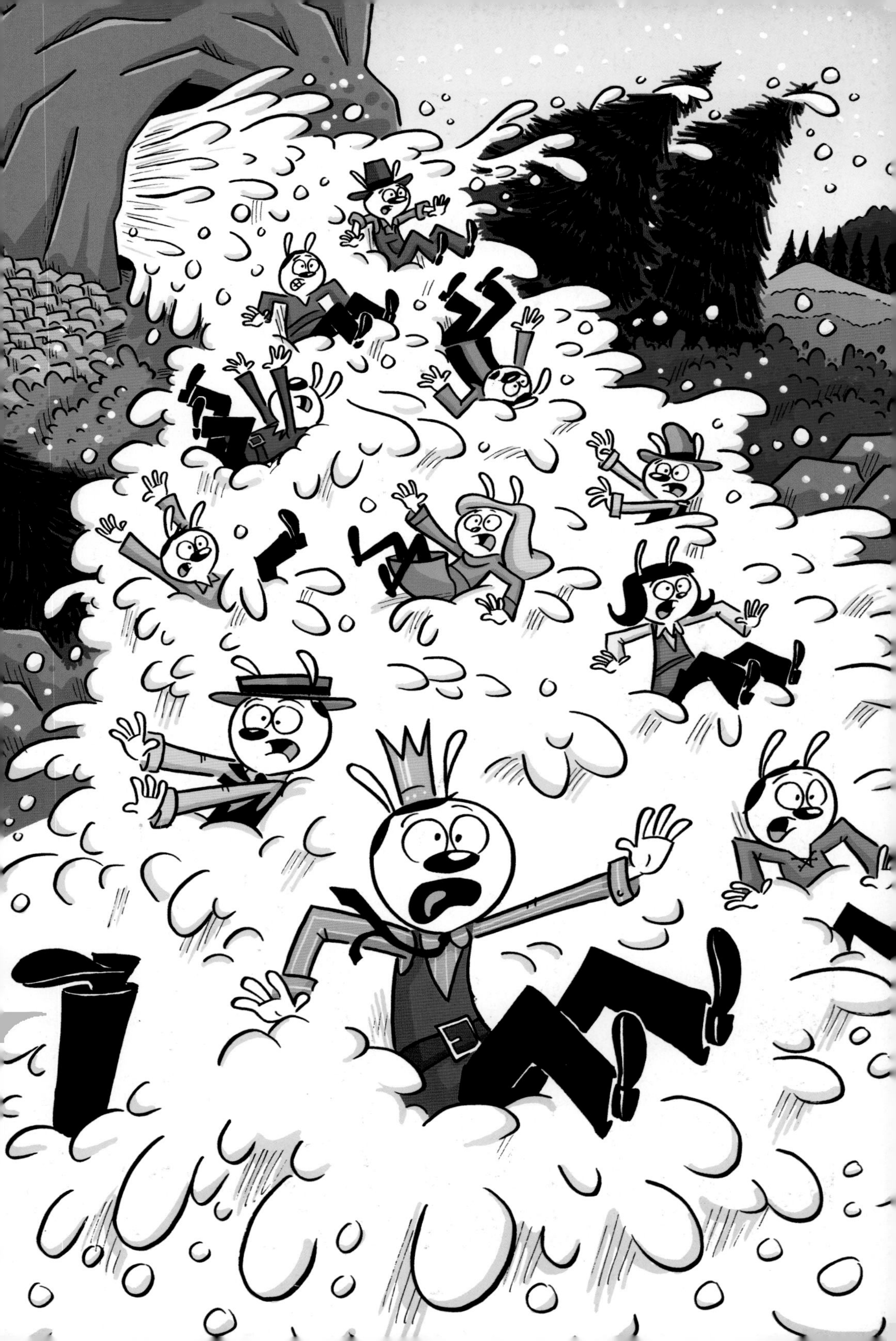

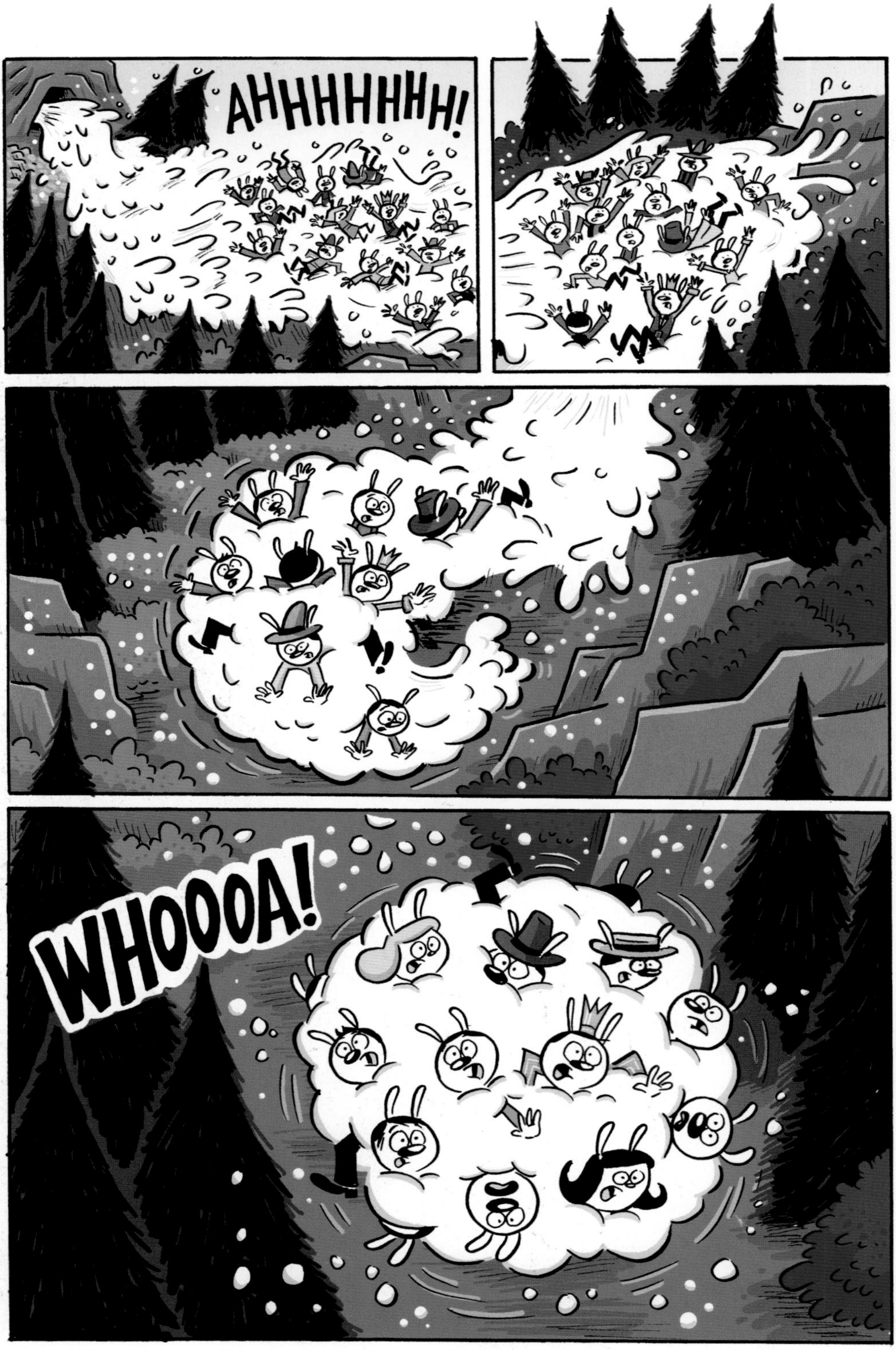
AHHHHHHH!
WHOOOA!

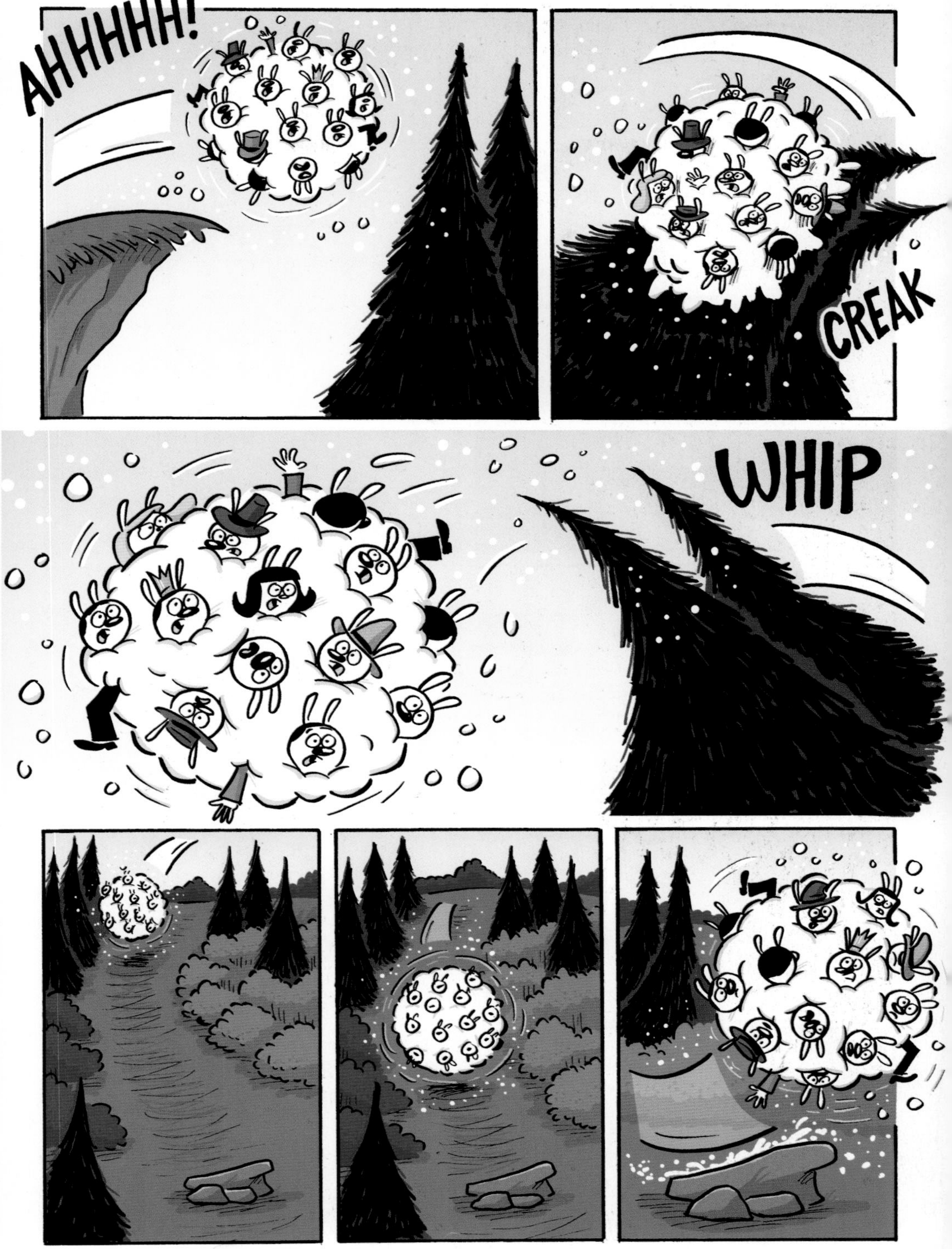
AHHHHH!
CREAK
WHIP

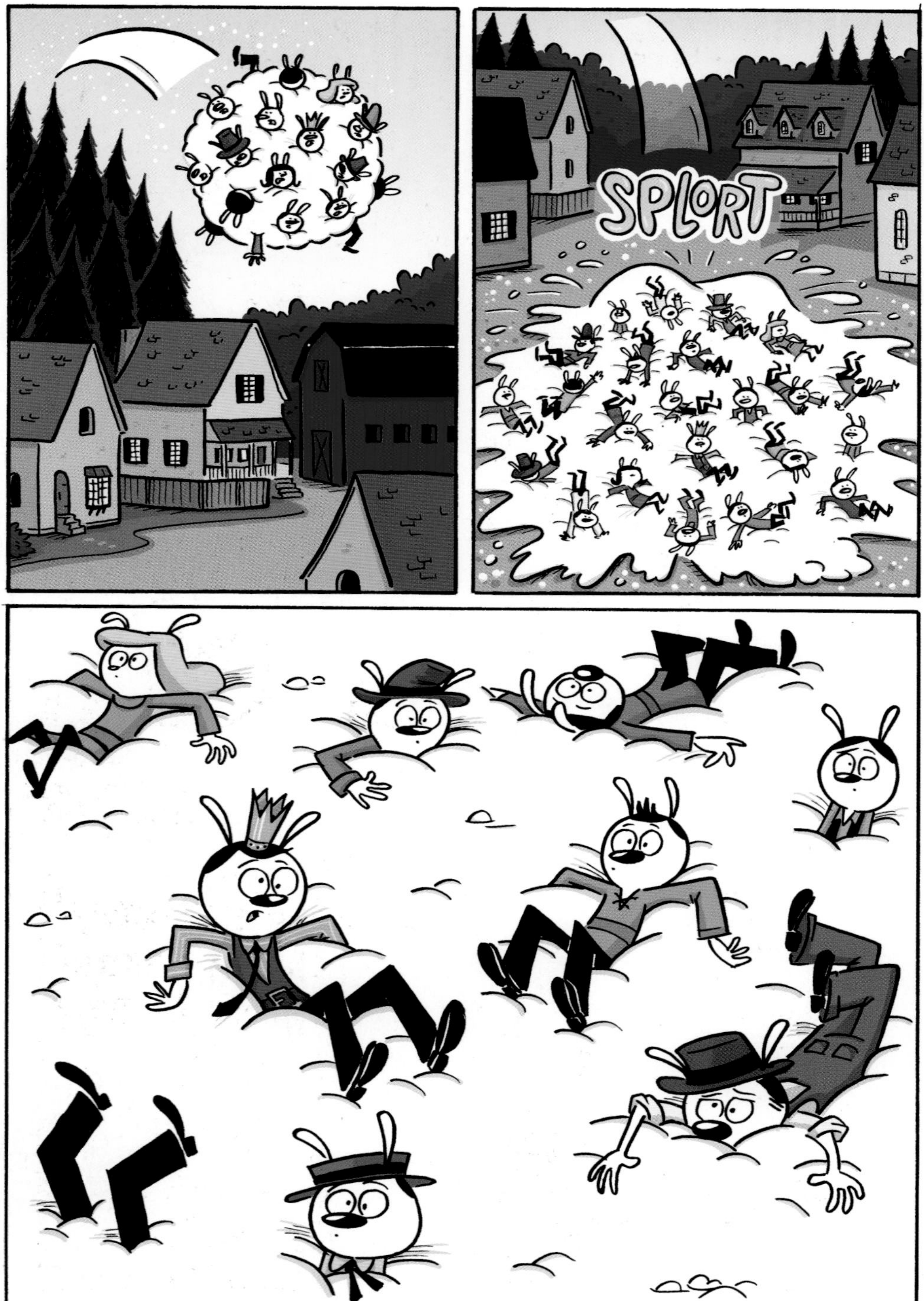
SPLORT

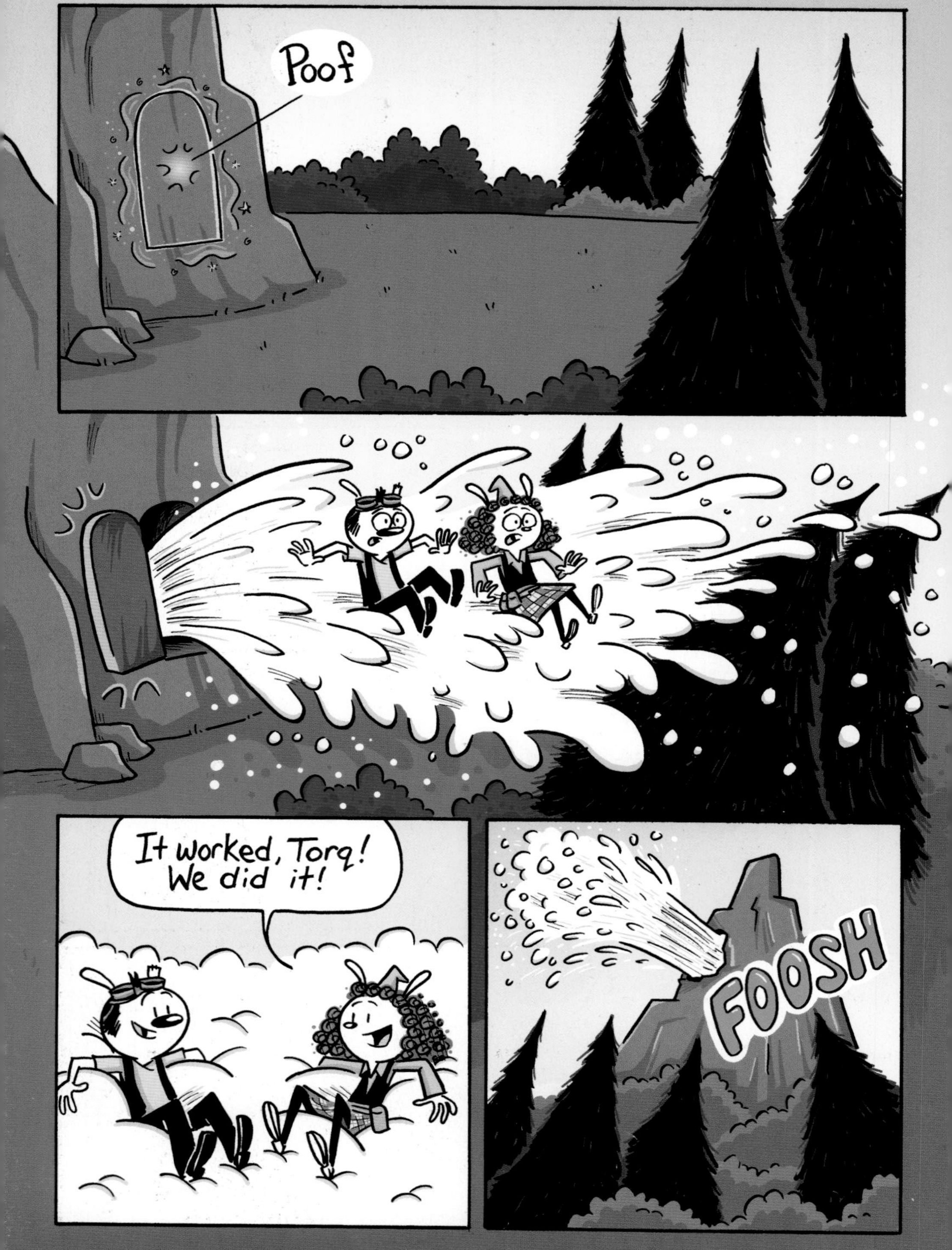
Poof
It worked, Torq! We did it!
FOOSH

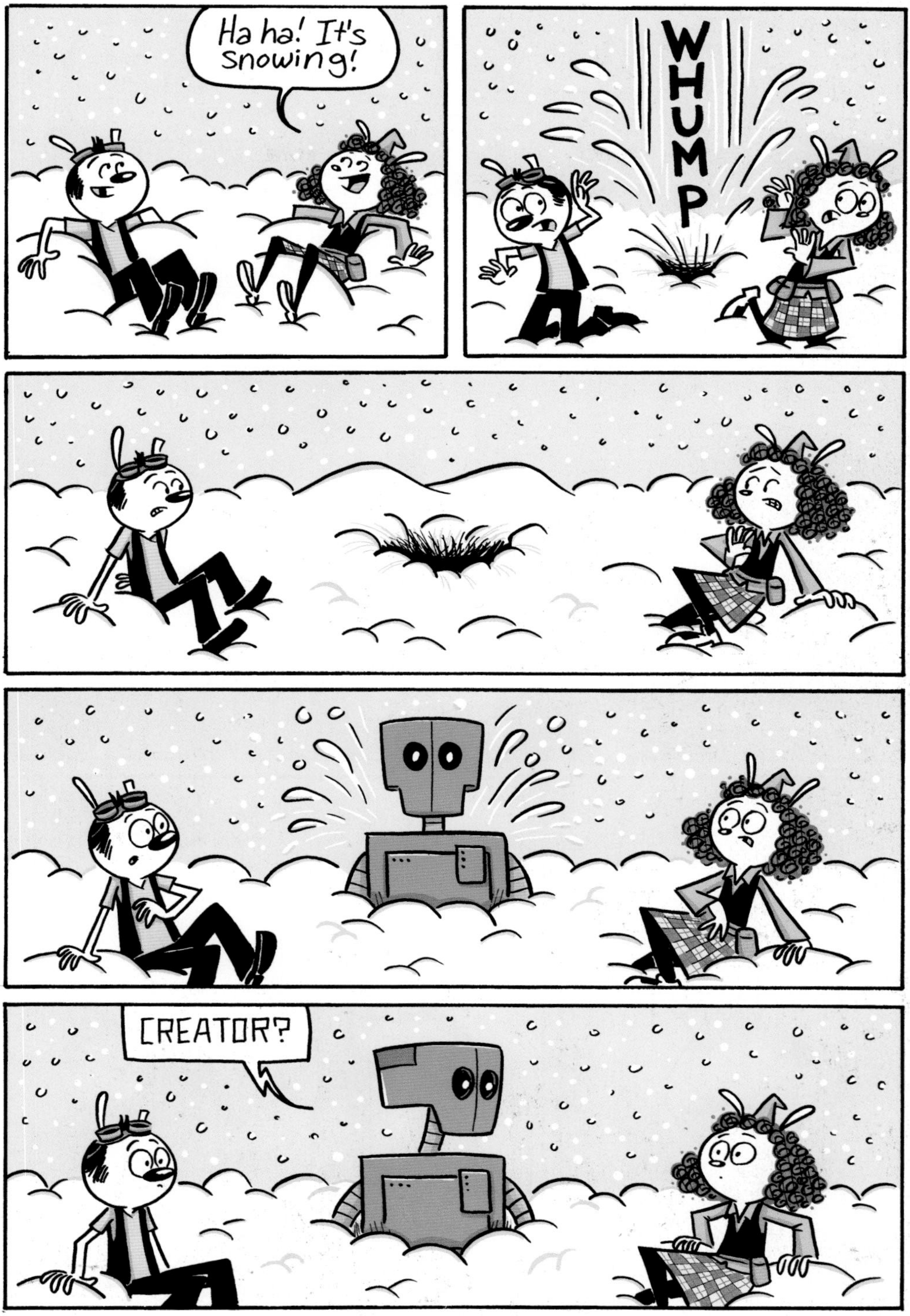
Ha ha! It's snowing!
WHUMP
CREATOR?

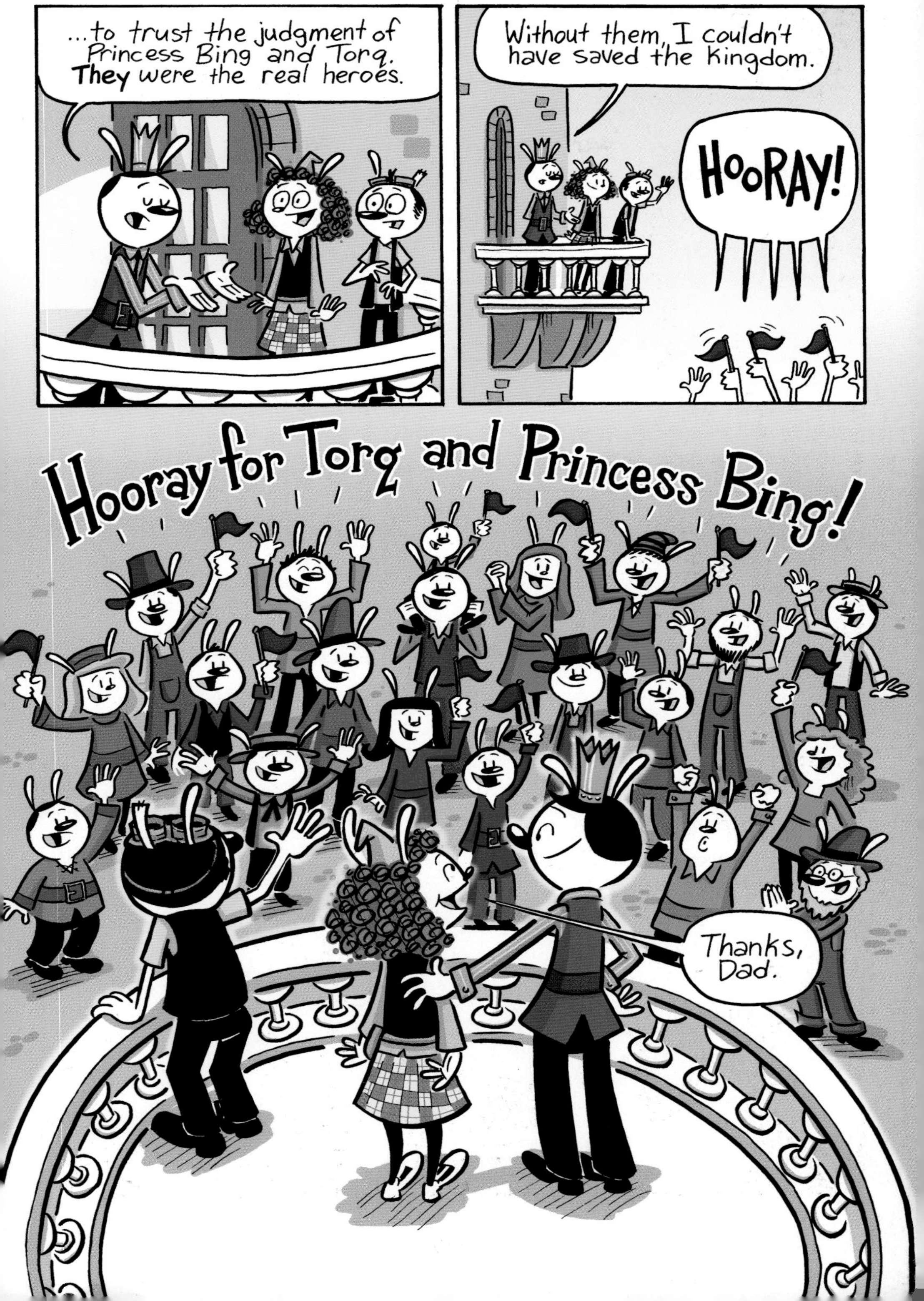
...to trust the judgment of Princess Bing and Torq. **They** were the real heroes.
Without them, I couldn't have saved the kingdom.
HOORAY!
Hooray for Torq and Princess Bing!
Thanks, Dad.

203

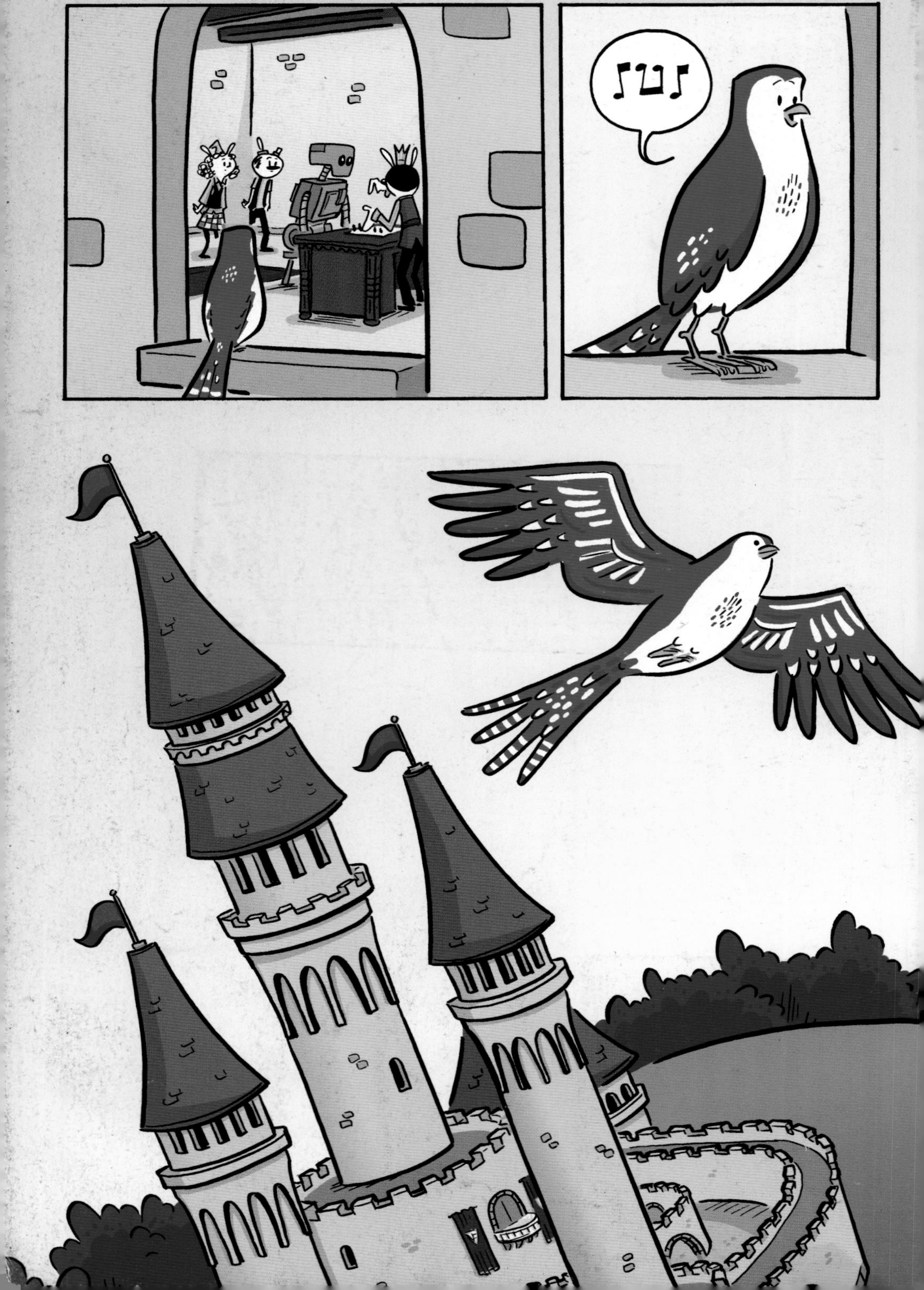